Would you continue to sea
change you and your world—
Lana Christian's engagin
journey of discovery with the ...agi. Through intrigue, danger, and the quest for truth, Akilah and his fellow Wise Men risk everything to prove a star and a Savior are real. With the blending of biblical narrative and true historical events, Christian crafts a compelling story.

> — Barbara M. Britton, Author of the *Tribes of Israel* series and *Daughters of Zelophehad* series

As a reader who's generally cynical about any Christian fiction, I was pleasantly surprised that I loved reading this book. Lana Christian writes with clarity about a pivotal point in historical events. Her ability to show how Magi culture motivated the book's characters helps create believable characters whom you care about. Ms. Christian takes you beyond what you think you know to what you need to know about the Magi's story. As a pastor who has been immersed in Christian ministry for 45 years and is passionate about remaining true to biblical truths, I can assure you that I have learned a great deal from her book while enjoying a good story.

> — Woody Roland, Missionary to South America for 30 years, recently retired pastor

Accolades to Lana Christian for the hours of research she undertook to write *New Star*. The book is an intelligent look at who the Wise Men may have been yet was creative and entertaining at the same time. I enjoyed every word of it, from the Magi society in Persia to the suspense of their enemies within, to the lovely, vivid descriptions of a land and people lost to us. One chapter was so beautiful that I cried (and I don't like crying when I read books)

— Ora Smith, Author of heritage fiction, including *The Pulse of His Soul* and *White Oak River*

With vivid detail and meticulous research, Lana Christian's *New Star* transports readers to the ancient Persian world, where three Magi discover a new star. As they tread a fine line between science and religion, they must report their findings to the Lower Council, which controls their research—and their resources. Akilah, head of the Wise Men's quest, realizes their study hinges on one sighting, a few sentences from the Hebrews' Books of Moses, and his skills of persuasion. In the past, those would have been enough. So why is the Council now blocking them at each step? Despite the risks and perils, Akilah is driven to pursue his goal and learn everything he can about the new star and what it portends. Readers will be swept along by Ms. Christian's portrayal of ancient astronomers, political intrigues, and the dangers faced along the journey that follows.

— Dana McNeely, Christy and Carol Award double-finalist, Author of *Whispers in the Wind* series

Much of what we "know" about the Magi rests more on tradition than fact. Let yourself be drawn into Lana Christian's telling of the Magi and the powerful society they represented. Ms. Christian brings to life a well-crafted and researched biblical fiction novel rich within the culture and history of Persia and the Parthian Empire at the time of the birth of Jesus. Experience its sights, smells, and intrigue. Prepare to be drawn in as a fellow traveler in the Magi's quest for truth, with all its implications for then and now.

For some characters, their passion for discovering the mystery contained in ancient Hebrew scrolls will drive them to risk everything, while others will protect Persia's religion at all costs. May this book stir your imagination and soul as it did mine.

— Karl Bunch, Bible study leader, Biblical Studies and Ancient History enthusiast

BOOK ONE OF THE MAGI'S ENCOUNTERS

LANA CHRISTIAN

Quench your thirst for story.
www.ScriveningsPress.com

Copyright © 2024 by Lana Christian

Published by Scrivenings Press LLC

15 Lucky Lane
Morrilton, Arkansas 72110
https://ScriveningsPress.com

Printed in the United States of America

All rights reserved. No part of this publication may be reproduced, stored in a retrieval system, or transmitted in any form or by any means—for example, electronic, photocopy, or recording—without the prior written permission of the publisher. The only exception is brief quotations in printed reviews.

Paperback ISBN 978-1-64917-397-3
eBook ISBN 978-1-64917-398-0

Editors: Suzie Waltner and Linda Fulkerson

Cover by Linda Fulkerson, www.bookmarketinggraphics.com

Original artwork (map and ornamental break images) by Bree Cook, Illustrator and Graphic Designer

All characters are fictional, and any resemblance to real people, either factual or historical, is purely coincidental.

Scripture quotations marked ESV are taken from the ESV® Bible (The Holy Bible, English Standard Version®), copyright © 2001 by Crossway, a publishing ministry of Good News Publishers. Used by permission. All rights reserved.

Scripture quotations marked NASB are taken from the NASB® (New American Standard Bible®), copyright © 1960, 1971, 1977, 1995, 2020 by The Lockman Foundation. Used by permission. All rights reserved.

NO AI TRAINING: Without in any way limiting the author's [and publisher's] exclusive rights under copyright, any use of this publication to "train" generative artificial intelligence (AI) technologies to generate text is expressly prohibited. The author reserves all rights to license uses of this work for generative AI training and development of machine learning language models.

*To everyone at Shadow Mountain Community Church
who made its 2017 live Nativity possible*

For to us a child is born, to us a son is given ...
and his name shall be called
Wonderful Counselor,
Mighty God,
Everlasting Father,
Prince of Peace.
Of the increase of his government and of peace there will be no end ...
to establish it and to uphold it with justice and with righteousness from
this time forth and forevermore.
Isaiah 9:6-7 (ESV)

*You know the Wise Men's part in the Christmas story.
But do you know the Wise Men's story?*

Note from the Author

Writing biblical fiction is a privilege as well as a responsibility. First and foremost, the story must remain true to the biblical account. Where those details end, extensive research draws upon historical records to help create a plausible, compelling story.

Incomplete accounts, calendar differences, and other variables divide scholars on the dates of some events. This book reflects realistic time frames based on best available evidence for key dates.

New Star respectfully depicts cultures, governments, religions, inventions, people, and events that, in many cases, have all but been lost to history. I pray those moments of discovery will deepen your immersive experience with this book.

With gratitude and thanks for your patronage,
Lana

Introduction

As the world pivots on a point that forever divides time as B.C. or A.D., the Roman and Parthian empires dominate as world superpowers. Rome's centralized rule is iron-fisted, while Parthia's decentralized rule grants more local freedoms. Rome worships a pantheon of gods but is intolerant of any religion that refuses to embrace Roman gods. Parthia maintains an official religion but tolerates the practice of many. Religion and politics fuel conquests for both empires.

For the past fifty years, Rome and Parthia have warred against each other. Herod the Great alternates his support of Rome and Parthia in a complex political dance. On the southeastern border of Herod's kingdom lies the next-largest neighboring empire, that of the mysterious Nabateans. It does not ally itself to anyone—although it occasionally fights for or against a country or people group if doing so suits their purposes.

Second only to royalty in influence and standing, Magi society flourishes in Persia, the heart of the Parthian Empire. Magi society's priest-scholar division, the Lower Council, produces great thinkers and inventors. The Lower Council also

Introduction

upholds the religious fabric of the empire. Magi society's elite governmental division, the Upper Council, wields great executive influence, including selecting Parthia's king.

Near the end of Herod's reign, a few Magi from the Lower Council note a star like no other. They risk their reputations, careers, and even their lives, to follow their convictions. Life will never be the same for them—or for the world.

Roman and Parthian Empires
at the time of Christ

Parthian Empire

Boundaries of key countries

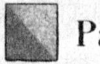

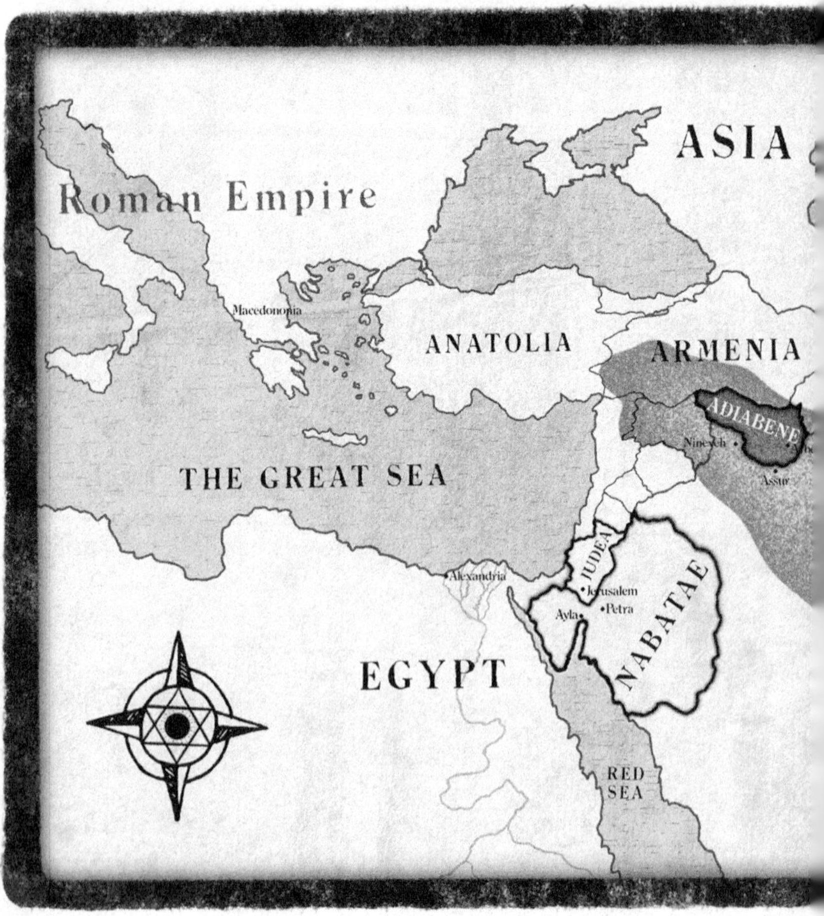

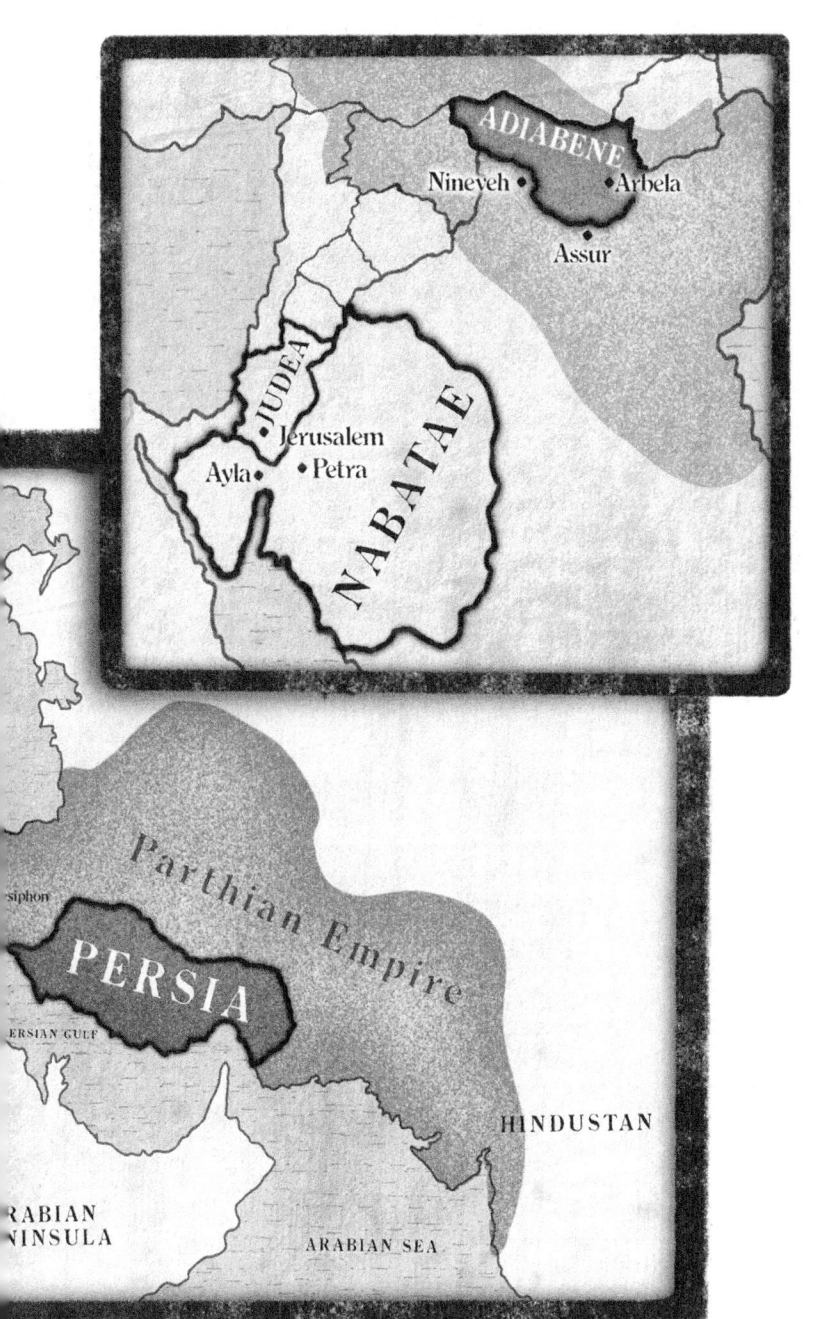

Chapter 1

This Could Change Everything

Persia, the second week of March, 4 BC

Akilah pored over the last scroll in his stack. Again, nothing. At the opposite end of his reading table, his younger colleague remained hunched over a codex. Akilah tapped the table. "Anything?"

"No." Rashidi shut the codex with a sigh.

Akilah rose and paced the length of the room. "Then we keep looking."

"Where?" Rashidi leapt from his seat and double-timed his steps to match Akilah's long-legged strides. "I think the head librarian suspects something."

"There's nothing suspect about doing research."

"He suspects we haven't found anything." Rashidi plucked Akilah's sleeve. "He questioned me on how all the volumes we've pulled on history, world cultures, and religion pertained to an astronomy project. Somehow he knows I went to Nineveh's library for three weeks. And yesterday, the head of the Lower Council almost smirked when he asked me how our research was progressing."

"That's Sassanak's way. He was baiting you. Only the lead researcher of any study can report its results." Akilah dismissed Rashidi's concern with a hand wave, but his brow furrowed. What Akilah's superior knew—or thought he knew—about this study could influence the Council at large.

Rashidi stepped in front of Akilah so abruptly that the two collided, Rashidi's nose getting the brunt of Akilah's chest.

"Your progress report to the Council is due in a week. We have no progress to report." Rashidi's voice rose like water coming to a boil. "How can that not concern you?" Eyebrows raised, he stabbed a finger toward the tumble of scrolls on the floor next to Akilah's reading table.

Lack of progress concerned Akilah greatly, but he wouldn't admit it. Everyone esteemed him as a wise man, yet his current study defied logic. Neither his thirty years of service to Magi society nor his previous astronomical discoveries would be enough to secure the Council's continuing support to pursue an elusive star he had seen—once.

"Sassanak is the head of the Lower Council. He is bound by duty to evaluate all Magi's scholarly studies impartially," Akilah said. He reassuringly clapped his hand on Rashidi's shoulder, but it stiffened.

Akilah's gut lurched. If he were head of the Lower Council, would he continue to fund his work? His entire study hinged on a single sighting, a few sentences from the Hebrews' Books of Moses, and his skills of persuasion. The Lower Council would need more substantiation than that.

Akilah had rehearsed how he would counter the Council's arguments and persuade them to keep funding his study, but he still hoped Tallis, their third colleague in this endeavor, would return with irrefutable information that would win the Council's undisputed approval. Tallis had a knack for uncovering resources that initially seemed to have no apparent connection with the topic at hand but ultimately yielded invaluable particulars. Yet, after so many months of searching, he wasn't sure what that perfect piece of information might be.

While Rashidi had exhausted two libraries' holdings, Akilah had scoured every star chart and parapegmata at his disposal. Every arcane record of astronomical and meteorological events in the Magi's library. Even hemerologies and shadowy astrology volumes.

For the past year, Akilah had sat in the observatory through cold and heat, scanning the sky from dusk to dawn, hoping to catch another glimpse of the star. A star that didn't look or act like any other he had ever seen.

The late afternoon sun cast a glow on Akilah's spacious study, turning the gold threads in his wall tapestry into shimmering points of light against its red-orange-indigo motif of stars and orbs. The commissioned piece, his most cherished rug, embodied all he held dear and dominated a wall otherwise occupied by shelves of scrolls and memorabilia.

This was Akilah's sanctuary, his most sacred place to read and meditate. His carefully appointed collection of beauty and knowledge never failed to bring him order, peace, and solutions. Science and scholarship comforted him. Made him feel in control. What he didn't know, he could learn, if he persisted.

Except now.

Akilah motioned for Rashidi to join him on his matching reclining couches. Perhaps a softer seat would do them both good.

But Rashidi didn't seem concerned with comfort. He scooted to the edge of his couch. "What will you say about the star?"

"You're frustrated." Akilah sank deeper into his couch's plush, kilim-covered cushions.

"I—we've been at this so long. It's like searching through the city's trash heap for treasure."

"Research is mostly sifting. Heightens the excitement when we finally uncover something, yes?" Akilah's philosophica didn't erase the discontent etched into Rashidi's face. "You must admit, what we have brought to light is compelling. Unusually specific."

Akilah reached behind him to a shelf that contained his silver lockbox containing his field notes. Cradling it in his lap, he brushed his fingers across the lid's bas-relief stars. "Rashidi, the star didn't move."

"How could I forget? You woke me up and dragged me to the observatory to see it."

Akilah knit his eyebrows in feigned disapproval.

"And I am grateful you did," Rashidi added hastily.

"Curiosity moves us to find the undiscovered." Akilah traced the largest star on the silver lid. "Persistence moves us to understand what we discover." He gripped his lockbox to contain his excitement. "We're on the cusp of claiming discovery of a new star. Not just an unmapped star—but a new *kind* of star! One that doesn't behave like anything previously described. Until now."

Akilah poked Rashidi's chest. "And you, my friend, started us on this path."

Six seasons ago, while studying other cultures' religions, Rashidi had found an oracle of Balaam, a Babylonian precursor of the Magi. Those words from a Book of Moses foretold a star's appearance. And, strangely, linked the star to a king.

At first, the words had intrigued Akilah. Then they haunted him. *I see him, but not now; I behold him, but not near. A star shall come forth from Jacob. A scepter shall rise from Israel.*[1]

Akilah had considered those words an academic curiosity until twelve full moons ago when he saw a new star. A star

---

1. Numbers 24:17 (ESV)

hanging so low and bright in the predawn sky that it seemed to touch the earth.

How many times since then had he wrestled Balaam's oracle to wring all its meaning from it?

Studying a star was one thing. Studying one that heralded a scepter—a king—was quite another. Wouldn't that strengthen their proposal to the Council? One would hope. Yet the same glaring problem remained. He hadn't seen the star in a year.

"Akilah."

"Hmm?"

"What if we don't see the star again?"

If only he knew.

Persia's annals credited Akilah with a dozen significant astronomical findings. He had never failed to complete a study, and he certainly would not concede this one. "We—"

Tallis burst into the room, almost toppling an ornate, metal-and-marble three-legged stand and the *orbitus* on it. He lunged to steady the wobbling astronomy device while protectively clutching a trampled, mud-splattered object. "You won't believe what this is."

"A dirty pouch?"

"No. What's in it."

Amid dried mud and gravelly dust, golden shavings glinted. Electrum. A diplomat's chariot must have run over the pouch. As Tallis hastily wiped its flap, grit fluttered onto the cypress-patterned rug beneath his feet. Akilah pursed his lips. His colleague was usually more thoughtful than that.

"I've been looking for information to authenticate what we found in the Books of Moses. And I just received this." Carefully extracting a flattened, torn scroll that had suffered but somehow survived the travails of travel, Tallis gingerly turned the broken spool. The papyrus unrolled unevenly at Akilah's feet.

The middle third was all but unreadable. But the rest showed uncommonly precise penmanship.

Akilah squinted at the perfect letterforms. They were practically art. "And this is …?"

"A message from a Hebrew scribe who lives in Adiabene." Despite the cool evening, Tallis's brow beaded with sweat. "He's a direct descendent of a scribe who lived in Babylonian captivity six hundred years ago."

"How did you find someone like that?"

"Long story."

"We have time." Akilah settled deeper into his cushion. *This should be good.*

"I've been tracing my Mesopotamian roots."

Akilah shifted on his cushion. "Yes, well. But what about the scribe?"

"Hebrew scribes do more than copy holy texts. They memorize them. When the Hebrews were exiled in Babylonia, their scribes kept Israel's culture and religion alive, even though they were ordered to not write the words. I wanted to get as close to that source as possible. And here it is." He gently patted the edge of the crinkled, torn scroll.

Rashidi scowled. "Whatever you have there, how can you be sure it's valid? Six-hundred-year-old history—that's twenty-one generations ago."

"A scribe's work must be so precise that if one stroke or line of a holy text doesn't match the source they copy from, they destroy their work and start over.

"But here's what's most important." Tallis stabbed a finger at four lines near the bottom of the message. "Words from the Hebrew prophet Isaiah two hundred years before the captivity. Copied directly from a scroll my contact's ancestor salvaged and hid while captive. It says the king we're looking for is a child who will rule—"

Rashidi grunted. "Every king starts out as a child."

"Keep reading."

Akilah drew a sharp breath. This evidence was immeasurably

more than he could have hoped for. It more than supported their case. It catapulted their quest to a new level. "My friends, this could be the greatest purpose we have ever aspired to attain. We must find this child."

"*For to us a child is born, to us a son is given. And his name shall be called Wonderful Counselor, Mighty God, Everlasting Father, Prince of Peace.*" His voice shook as he read. "*Of the increase of his government and of peace there will be no end ... to establish it and to uphold it with justice and with righteousness from this time forth and forevermore.*"[2] His voice shook as he read.

Four radical lines.

A child and *everlasting* king?

This could change everything.

---

2. Isaiah 9:6-7 (ESV)

Chapter 2

The Circle

One week later

Akilah lingered with Tallis and Rashidi on the front steps of the Great Hall of Audiences as long as he dared. "It's time, my friends. Rules, you see. As our group's leader, 'one speaks for all' before the Council." He clapped his colleagues on their shoulders. "All will be fine."

Rashidi drew back, his brow knit in a frown. "We agreed we wouldn't say a thing about this eternal king business, yet it's spread throughout the entire Magi complex. Now everyone is wondering about our study. Some think we're fools. Others think we're insurrectionists. The rest don't know what to think."

Tallis nodded. "That's bad enough, but a meeting right before *Nowruz*? Unheard of."

Akilah shrugged. "The Head Magus has the authority to call a meeting whenever he wishes. Even on the eve of our most important holiday. If there's a problem, I'd rather face it openly than let whispers multiply behind my back."

Muffled talk wafted over the trio each time the two-story double doors opened.

"Quite the crowd gathering," Tallis said. "But you need not worry. I have faith in you."

More Magi, all in official robes of the Lower Council, brushed past the trio.

Rashidi craned his neck to peer inside. "Maybe Burhan leaked something about our latest findings and twisted it to make us look bad."

Akilah harrumphed. "Burhan is an Orderal, entrusted with cataloging and guarding the Magi's research. He would not misuse his position."

Rashidi's eyes darkened deeper than the gathering nightfall. "Don't be so sure."

Akilah sliced his hand through the air to dismiss his colleague's foreboding. "Burhan is not a Magus, so he's not allowed in the meeting. Besides, any breach of trust would cost Burhan his job. He can't afford that. He has no family or other means of support."

Had Akilah's words quelled his team's misgivings? He couldn't tell. He wished his words would unknot his stomach. Although Burhan didn't concern him, rumors had a way of growing out of control. Akilah didn't need unfounded attention.

Two hours later

Throughout his thirty years of service to Magi society, Akilah had stood in the center of the Great Hall's Gathering Circle many times. But never like this.

Although the polished tiles sent coolness through his soft

leather shoes, his face heated. Nothing about this Council meeting was normal. Its late hour. The line of questioning. No water clock to limit its duration. Heads from both the priestly and governmental divisions attending. Was this a meeting or a hearing? Akilah gazed at the hall's vaulted ceiling as if answers might appear across its cedar beams. In response, light from suspended oil lamps thrust the attendees' shadows toward him in long, rebuking fingers.

Sassanak, Head Magus of the Lower Council, scanned his notes. "How can you prove your sighting wasn't a heavenly alignment?"

"A conjunction—whether solely of planets or planets with other heavenly bodies—aligns and separates within a few days," Akilah said. "What I saw did not. And it was much brighter than any conjunction I've ever studied. It must be a new star."

"But it disappeared."

"Yes."

"When did you last see the phenomenon?"

"A year ago."

Murmurs rippled through the Magi crowding the boundary of the Gathering Circle. Sassanak's glare swept across the gathering, silencing all watchers. They shuffled uneasily in place. The brief movement roused the metallic threads in their robes to send shimmers of reflected lamplight around the Circle. Why couldn't Akilah's reasoning behind his research shine so readily?

Pain crept through Akilah's left hip, reminding him how long he had been standing before the Council. Fallout from his childhood injury resurfaced at the most inconvenient times. But he remained motionless, erect and alone in the center of the Circle.

Refusing pain's bid for attention, Akilah counted heads. Twenty-one facing him. Perhaps as many standing two deep. Far more than a routine progress report would warrant. No

New Star

proceeding of the Lower Council required so many attendees except the appointment of a new Head Magus.

Sassanak's jaw tightened. "Harbingers disappear. Not stars. Even seasonal stars reappear at appointed times." Sassanak swiveled his head as if marshaling the entire room. "What makes you think you will see this ... thing ... again?"

Within the long sleeves of his robes, Akilah fisted his hands. This "thing" was more than an astronomical discovery.

Sassanak's voice boomed. "Akilah, you are bound by oath to answer. How can you be sure you will see this phenomenon again? Ever?"

Akilah swallowed hard. Research rested on science, not religion. He was treading shaky ground. He locked eyes with his superior. "Prophecies. As noted in my progress report." His crisp answer dissipated in the meeting hall's vaulted expanse.

They can't disallow my work now. What can I say to regain their approval? I need to keep studying this star.

Sassanak glanced at the only other person seated—the head of the Upper Council. The man's expression remained as unreadable as deep water on a windless lake.

Akilah didn't dare shift his gaze in that direction. The Upper Council, Persia's governmental overseers, cared nothing about progress reports of obscure research. Least of all the Upper Council's highest-ranking member, the Chief Megistane. Why was *he* here tonight?

"Akilah, your past achievements in astronomy are unblemished," Sassanak said. "But frankly, the only 'progress' I see in your progress report is your increasing expenses—to study a missing star—if you can even call it that." This time, Sassanak let the group's muffled laughter rise and fall unhindered. He pressed his back into his chair and folded his hands.

Akilah's nostrils flared. Sassanak assumed that position

every time he made young Magi hopefuls squirm under his withering questions.

In the uneasy silence, Akilah fixed his eyes on a spot above Sassanak's head, beyond the meeting hall's hexagonal walls, across the courtyard. *Ring, tower bells. That will end the meeting if the Council won't.*

Merciful peals! Their herald to evening prayers forced Sassanak to his feet. "All in attendance are bound to silence regarding these proceedings. May Zarathustra's principles guide our words and actions in pursuing truth, fairness, and justice." He retrieved an object hidden under his chair, its outline bulging beneath an imperial purple velvet cloth.

Sassanak strode to the center of the Gathering Circle. With a glower that could impale a bull, he whisked away the cover and thrust the stone statue at Akilah.

Not the *Faravahar*.

Akilah's hand hung limp at his side. How could he in good conscience touch the sacred symbol of Persia's official religion? It would signal his agreement that the meeting—and its outcome—were just and right. But Sassanak hadn't delivered the Council's decision yet. A protocol breach that others would easily overlook due to the late hour.

Akilah remained riveted on the specter of the statue. Satisfy his scruples or risk forfeiting a year's worth of research? Endanger his career or adjust his conscience?

Lift your hand. You have no choice. Akilah's hand wavered momentarily before he grazed the head, wings, and left loop of the winged-man carving. "Wisdom, positive forces, and right direction," he said. His gaze strayed to the floor.

Sassanak turned, held the Faravahar high, and delivered a short rendering too perfect to be spontaneous.

Akilah exhaled forcefully. This meeting—and its outcome—had been rigged.

The back of his neck prickled. The ruling was smattered with

New Star

threats veiled in carefully worded conditions. But challenging it would be foolish. At least it didn't disband the study. That's all that mattered.

Akilah's inner voice said to heed his niggling concerns, but he did not. Despite the threats still ringing in his ears, he filled his mind with details of his travel plans and gifts for the child-king.

He wove his way through dispersing Magi. Their bustling chaos and preoccupation with preparations for evening prayers cloaked Akilah's exit from the Great Hall. Finally free from the crowd, he rushed through a side door to a seated figure with woolly ebony hair.

"You're late." Rashidi's faint Egyptian accent tweaked his vowels.

Ignoring the gibe, Akilah stooped to sit on the steps with his colleague. "Rashidi, what of the commissioned pieces"—he lowered his voice—"our gifts for the child?"

"Still as safe as they were yesterday. The metalworker is having trouble with the locks on the boxes that will hold the gold. Should we switch the metal?"

"No. The metalworker is a Kushite. He can handle it."

Tallis emerged from a pillar's shadow. "What of the Council's ruling?"

Akilah had to tell his colleagues. But not in front of the Great Hall, the hub of all Lower Council activities. "Meet me in my chambers."

"In short, the Council still approves of our study of a new heavenly body … and, to a lesser extent, our lengthy trip to Jerusalem." Akilah kept his tone light as he circled his reading table. He tapped the map they'd studied in planning

13

their travel route. "In all those respects, nothing has changed."

"But something *has* changed, yes?" Tallis said.

"Not for you, my friends. Only for me."

"What?" Rashidi shifted to the edge of his seat.

"Research is very important to Persia's image as a world power." Akilah slowed his words. "I'm walking a fine line between science and religion. Jerusalem's priests hold the key to all our unanswered questions about the star and the exact location of this prophesied child-king. If I don't find the child or confirm he is the eternal king foretold, I'll lose my position as a Magus. If I do find him, then it could … upset some in our society's highest circles. That, too, could jeopardize my career." Akilah grinned ruefully. "So … do you still want to go to Jerusalem with me?"

Chapter 3

Another Look

The next day: the first day of Nowruz

Gongs resounding throughout the hallways of the Magi's quarters broke the trio's concentration on the map of their route. *Karana* fanfares called across the courtyard. Torches whooshed, blazing an ascending path from outdoor walkways to the grand banquet hall. Rashidi sprinted toward the door. "We should go. Can't be late for First New Day."

"Ah, yes. Nowruz," Akilah said. "New year. New life. New possibilities. And many courses of food. I'm right behind you."

As Rashidi sped down the hallway, Akilah chuckled. "His boyish enthusiasm will buoy him through oceans of disillusionment."

He dropped his voice to almost a whisper. "Tallis, do you have the scribe's scroll with you?"

Tallis nodded and pulled something wrapped in an oiled leather cloth from a pocket deep within his cloak. His attention to detail never failed. Of course he'd take steps to protect the scroll in a way that hid its provenance.

"Mind if I have another look?" Akilah extended his hand.

"The top third is just courteous formalities and information about the scribe's ancestry."

"Help me move it to the reading table?"

"For what?" Tallis's forehead creased into a frown.

"Just another look."

"That's more important than starting our holiest festival with the rest of the Magi?" Tallis shielded the leather package behind his back.

"I won't be long. Besides, everyone will eat and celebrate until dawn."

"Then I'm taking your portion of *fesenjān*."

"That is brutally unkind." Akilah loved the ground pomegranate-walnut-poultry stew. "I won't be *that* long."

"I'll take your portion of *haft mewa* as well."

Akilah rose in half-feigned indignation. "That is sacrilege. You wouldn't dare." He knew Tallis wouldn't. The seven-fruit salad paid homage to their religion's seven deities.

The two burst into laughter. Still, Tallis hesitated at the door. Akilah shooed him away. "I'll be there before you can finish the first course."

As soon as he was alone, Akilah grabbed his box of oculars and selected the largest from its velvet-lined nest. Hovering the magnifying lens over the obliterated third of the scroll, he strained to detect remnants of letters or hints of words. The word "Daniel" was discernible in several places. Maybe more. What made this Daniel important enough for the scribe to devote so much space to writing about him? Was the Daniel prophesy about the child-king linked to the star Akilah's team was studying?

Daniel ... Daniel. Akilah's grandparents had talked about a man named Danyal. Those childhood memories were once lessons. Now they seemed more like lore. But his beloved Babayi and Mamani seemed so sure of what they and generations before them had said … moreover, believed. A Danyal who did what other magi could not. Who believed what other magi did not.

What had Mamani said about that Danyal? "He believed in the one true God."

What a foreign concept. So exclusive. So contrary to the diverse religions the Magi served in their priestly duties.

Akilah pushed through the cobwebs of his mind. Babayi had mentioned something about God's plans including a glorious king. Could that be the same eternal king in the scribe's copied words? Was it even possible for a king to be eternal? That would make him deity. Earthly kings sought to deify themselves. But could a person—a child, no less—be eternal from the start? It defied explanation.

As Akilah re-read the last lines of the damaged scroll, he rued not paying more attention to his grandparents' words. But then he was only ten. The banks of the Euphrates were within running distance of their house, and playing outdoors with his cousins was far more interesting than listening to lessons indoors. He'd rather trap a mole rat burrowed in the riverbank than snag instruction in religion.

Yet his grandparents had a way of sneaking life lessons and Danyal stories into model-boat building, hairstyling demonstrations, or whatever else Akilah and his cousins fancied at that age. Everyone delighted in the Danyal stories but quickly dismissed them—except Akilah's youngest cousin, Farzaneh. She remained attentive at his grandparents' feet long after the cousins had devoured mamani's honey almond cakes and had seen past other clever bribes to listen to elder wisdom. No, "bribe" was too harsh a word. And Farzaneh probably just liked the attention. She was barely more than a toddler then.

Despite Akilah's determination to play, something about the Danyal stories had kindled a spark in his heart, a deep-seated warmth and joy he'd never experienced from parroting his family's religion. Emboldened by childhood curiosity, Akilah had asked his father about Danyal. His father's response was a smack, a swift rebuke, and a mandate to never speak of such matters again. Many years later, he learned his grandparents' abrupt silence about the Danyal stories was the price they'd paid so Akilah could keep visiting them. It was the first of many wedges that father or son would drive between themselves—wedges that ultimately splintered the family.

Akilah discerned another word. "Fullness." And a number. Six hundred eighty-something. Only part of the stem of the last number remained. Three? Six? More important, if that was a calculation, how was it derived? Such a precise number had to mean something, but what?

Something in the prophet Isaiah's words rekindled the dampened tinder from Akilah's childhood. He re-read the passage, hungering to discern more words but also desiring to understand the words he could see. Each pass fanned a flickering flame in his heart. Akilah's whole body warmed like something had harnessed the sun's heat inside him. He couldn't explain it, but somehow he *knew* Isaiah's words and his grandparents' stories referred to the same person. That, perhaps more than anything else he'd ever done, was worth pursuing. Worth confirming, no matter what the cost.

Another karana fanfare jolted Akilah from his hunched position. His absence would be noted if he lingered longer over the scroll. Re-rolling and wrapping it with care, he thrust it into a clothing chest.

Chapter 4

Which Rule

Sassanak slipped into his lavishly appointed office off the main corridor of the Great Hall of Audiences. He needed a moment alone before making his grand entrance at Nowruz's first night of festivities. A soft creak behind him signaled otherwise.

Without looking up, he automatically said, "Hold your business until after—"

"You ruled yesterday's meeting with brilliance, Sassanak."

A half-smile played about his lips, but he quickly erased it before he turned and eyed his colleague, Azazel, with an impassive stare. "I'm the Head Magus of the Lower Council. That's my job."

"You know what I mean." Azazel brushed past Sassanak's desk but paused to hover his hand over a worn codex, propped in a place of honor on a wooden stand carved with grapevines. "I couldn't help but notice the Chief Megistane's presence at the meeting."

Sassanak shook his arms out of his Magi robe, exchanging it for an opulent ankle-length silk coat. "It was hard to miss. He was the only one in Upper Council garb."

"Quite a coup. The Chief has never attended a Lower Council meeting."

He shrugged. "He had business with Fakhri before the meeting and stayed as the Honorific's representative."

"Curious, then, why the Chief didn't change into Lower Council garb to represent Fakhri. What business did the two have right before Nowruz?"

"Azazel, the Chief sat next to me. It would have been out of order to pry information from him. We merely exchanged professional pleasantries before the meeting started. I can't presume anything about his private business or wardrobe schedule. Neither should you."

Azazel searched Sassanak's face. "Yes, Fakhri is sorely missed. His illness remains a mystery to us all."

"I'm sure our healers will find the answer soon." Sassanak slouched into his chair behind his desk and fiddled with his quill box. "Azazel, what do you make of Akilah's claim?"

He tipped his head toward the starry sky beyond Sassanak's open window. "My specialty is the history of social institutions, not astronomy."

"Don't pander to me." Sassanak studied the smoke curling from the oil lamp on his desk. He would have words with his servant for not trimming the wicks. "Akilah seems convinced this so-called new star has a deeper meaning ensconced in Jewish literature." The sentence slipped smoothly from his tongue, but its last two words smoldered in his head. "Speak your heart, Azazel."

His face clouded as he leaned across the desk. "I find his line of reasoning appalling, as I'm sure you do, especially as Head Magus. Jews believe in a pale imitation of Zoroastrianism. Why, even one of their great prophets—"

"Isaiah. I know." Sassanak snorted with disdain.

"Yes, Isaiah—wrote that Persia's King Cyrus was their god's 'anointed one' long before Cyrus was born. The Jews' prophet

Ezra wrote that Persia's kings treated them favorably. Generations of our kings—Cyrus, Darius, Artaxerxes—let the Jews survive, thrive, and rebuild their cities. Jews should forget their god and bow down to our empire instead. Look at all we've done for them." Azazel spread his arms wide. "Yet they continually cause trouble for whoever tries to rule them. They did it to Persia. Now they're doing it to Rome. It's bad enough that pockets of Jews live within our empire. Especially in Adiabene."

"That little country? It's an inconsequential vassal state in the northwestern corner of the Parthian empire."

"Adiabene is less than a day's ride from Persia, and that 'little country' is expanding its territory. It's very sympathetic to Jews."

Sassanak choked back a laugh. "You believe Adiabene is a credible threat to our empire or our official religion?"

"Yes." Azazel's hand strayed to the exquisite silver hilt of a dagger tucked in his sash.

"You personally traveled to Adiabene to confirm this?"

Azazel clenched the dagger's hilt. "I always do."

Only one thing surpassed Azazel's passion for uncovering history—his zeal for maintaining the purity of Persia's official religion. Sometimes his expeditions in the name of research blended both as he surreptitiously mapped Jewish communities throughout the empire.

Sassanak would find a way to parlay that knowledge to his advantage, but only after unhitching it from Azazel's zeal. He knew how to bridle zeal in the name of devoutness. On the other hand, Azazel's ardent practices on the shadowed edges of Persia's official religion had cost him his bid as Head Magus. Sassanak smirked. "I've never had reason to doubt your scouting abilities, Azazel. Or your unique … connections."

"Be wary, Sassanak. Akilah's study may seem an innocent curiosity, but it could create an incursion that could harm our religion and culture in more ways than the Greeks have. The Jews are immovable in their beliefs. Akilah is crossing a dangerous line in using science to investigate religious claims."

Sassanak passed a hand over his brow. During the Council meeting, he had warned Akilah in strong terms about mixing science with religion. But, in his single-minded stubbornness, Akilah would not likely heed the words. If he continued to pursue his study, that would complicate Sassanak's job.

He had hoped for that. Now, he counted on it.

Azazel turned to a shelf behind him and motioned to a leather flask, its belly embossed with a distinctive seal. "Wine from Herat. Not only the best wine region but also its best vintage. What's the occasion?"

Sassanak chuckled. "You don't miss a thing, do you? No occasion yet. But soon, I hope."

"You can't skip lines like that with a friend. This is not the time for secrecy."

"To have a secret, one first must know something worthy of concealment. Until that happens, I have nothing to share. But perhaps soon." Sassanak clapped a hand on his colleague's shoulder and pivoted him toward the door. "Many pardons, but there is more to do than cycles remaining in this day."

"Surely you don't intend to work through the first night of Nowruz."

"I would never miss our most holy holiday. But a Head Magus's work is never done. I will join the celebration soon, my friend."

Chapter 5

Of Interest

The next morning

Sassanak needed more wine. Last night's celebration had merged with dawn. He shouldn't have called a Council meeting right before Nowruz, but he'd delivered the strong message he'd intended. Juxtaposing the two events underscored urgency. His method of inquiry had cast enough doubt on Akilah's study to convince the Council to reevaluate it. That should mire it indefinitely. But the paperwork involved ... The prospect amplified the throbbing in his head. Overseeing the Magi's scholarly pursuits could be tedious.

Sassanak smiled at his unprecedented accomplishment of convincing the Chief Megistane to attend that particular Council meeting. He had waited years for that first step, so crucial to his plans. The next step was minutes away. More than enough reason to sample his wine from Herat now.

He exhaled with deep satisfaction. Yes, savoring his victory with a delicacy few other Magi could afford did make being Head Magus of the Lower Council worthwhile.

Beyond his window, the first spring flowers confidently burst with color that belied their lack of vigor. Despite the trumpeting braggadocio of red, orange, and purple inverted tulips on their tall stalks, a hard frost could crush their delicate life in a day. He enjoyed their fleeting beauty but coveted lasting esthetics—such as his favorite drinking vessel that now held his ruby-colored libation.

Sassanak caressed the *rhython's* elegant curves. Each golden slope thrilled his fingertips. With deliberate slowness, he traced its trumpet-shaped rim down to its winged-lion base. Such splendid workmanship was worthy to be crowned with a rare jewel—the choicest vintage from Herat.

Sassanak reached again for the embossed leather flask sitting next to a worn codex on his desk. He returned the volume to the safety of its stand and poured more wine. Try as he would, he couldn't ignore the codex, *The Spirit of Wisdom's Commandments for the Body and Soul*. Under his breath, he thrummed its injunctions he'd learned in childhood. "Commit no slander ..." He swirled the wine to release its full bouquet.

"Form no covetous desire ..." A more energetic swirl.

"Indulge in no wrathfulness ... Commit no lustfulness ..." Vigorous swirls.

"Choose a wife of good character ..." A vitriolic swirl freed a few drops of the precious wine from his drinking vessel and flung them onto the ornate embroidery of his Magi robe.

Choking though no wine was in his throat, Sassanak searched for a cloth. But a knock on the door interrupted him. *Collect yourself. Make the most of this short meeting.* Before he could rise, the Chief Megistane strode in.

"A pleasure to see you, Chief. Please, sit."

"I'll stand." The Chief's gaze strayed to the rhython gleaming in the morning sun. "You've always had an eye for fineness, Sassanak."

"Join me?"

"Before today's second cycle, I must leave for the royal capital. What is so urgent?"

"An investigation of sorts."

"A local magistrate can handle that."

"It is no petty civil matter." Sassanak locked his gaze with the Chief Megistane's. "More a matter of national security. That's part of your job as head of the Upper Council, yes?"

"Don't be dramatic. I haven't the time."

"This investigation needs you, Chief. In fact, I think it will interest you very much." Sassanak leaned forward. "How much do you know about Jewish prophecy?"

Chapter 6

Out with the Old

The wick in Akilah's oil lamp was almost spent. Another evening of Nowruz's thirteen-day celebration had slid into early morning.

Akilah had little time for festivities. The nation's highest holiday heralded the vernal equinox. Day and night became equal—perfect for observing nighttime and morning lights. Their positions could predict crop plantings, rains, harvests. Akilah's meticulous field notes calculating those events lay limp in his hand.

Nowruz celebrated the promise of a new year and new life. But what new information could Akilah show for his months of study? There was still no sign of the star.

He stared through the observatory's nearest alignment window. How many discoveries had he made from this high perch? Enough to carve his name in Persia's annals of history. But Akilah wanted more. A discovery that could change the world. Redraw a star chart. Or remodel the orbitus he held so dear. It dizzied him to think of finding a planet beyond the fifth one. What a coup that would be—to rewrite the great Posidonius's work on astronomy!

Akilah's ambition chafed many Persian astronomers. They seemed content to translate others' works, gaining knowledge without endeavoring their own discoveries. Why? Accepting others' work as fact was merely a beginning. The heavens whispered secrets worthy of a lifetime of discovery. Look at what astronomers from Babylonia, Greece, and Cin[1] had accomplished. Especially the one from Cin, rumored to be cataloging hundreds of stars. Akilah's heart galloped. Could he achieve something greater?

Oh, how he wanted that. Akilah knew many things, but he was certain about one thing above all else—the stars made him dream of possibilities and yet-to-be-discovered realities beyond one's imagination.

A frequent admonition from his accomplished father invaded his contemplation. "Think for yourself! But make sure they're useful thoughts. Chasing ideals gets you nothing." Pragmatism permeated every aspect of his father's life, from his governmental duties to his religious leanings.

What was Akilah chasing? An elusive star. That was anything but pragmatic.

Nippy air groped through Akilah's cloak, another reminder that yesterday's final cycle was almost over and dawn would break in less than two hours. His chilled fingers fumbled to deposit his notes in his silver lockbox, an heirloom gift from his equally accomplished mother. He tucked a corner of his cloak around the frigid metal and pulled it to his hip. Even through the fabric, he could trace the lid's familiar bas-relief ridges of stars.

With his other arm full of star charts, Akilah carefully negotiated the steep spiral descent from the observatory's thirty-cubit height. At ground level, he shelved the armload.

---

1. China

Ground … such a limited view. An endless expanse awaited those willing to make the climb.

As he crossed the open field between the observatory and the Magi's complex, smoke tingled Akilah's nostrils. Flames flickered in the distance. He quickened his pace, ignoring the cold's attempt to steal his breath.

A small man, his frame even smaller in his bent posture, was feeding a roaring fire.

"Burhan al-Din. How good to see you."

The man bobbed his head. "Akilah. Ever respectful."

"I heard you helped one of my colleagues locate a difficult-to-find text on ancient history. Let me add my belated thanks to his."

"Oh. Rashidi. Mm-hmm."

"The Council isn't overburdening you with too many recording duties, are they?"

"No. No." Burhan tittered.

"Splendid. I wouldn't want them to keep you captive in that upper room."

"No, they gave me the key," he quipped.

"So, what brings you into the cold at this hour?"

"Just disposing of outdated materials. Making way for all the new greatness that you and the rest of the Magi are working on."

Akilah coughed to hide a smirk. "That's kind of you to say, but much of our work is quite mundane. Tracking weather patterns for crops. Calculating economic effects of drought. Determining the most accurate weight measurements and converting them from units used in other countries."

"Still very important, to be sure." Burhan hastily dumped the last basket of scrolls onto the fire and stared intently into the flames. "Then there's your star project." He wagged his deformed index finger skyward. *"That's* not mundane. It's the talk of the Council."

Akilah winced. What had the Council said about him after its last meeting? Likely something about wanting practical results instead of personal convictions.

Burhan's left eye twitched as he wielded his firestick, deftly coaxing the scrolls farther into the fire. Tongues of flame licked the edges to taste their new fuel. With pleasure, the flames shot high, igniting the scrolls with a whoosh.

What was it about the recorder's servile attitude that bothered Akilah so? Of course Burhan would know of the "star project," as he'd termed it. He was an Orderal. His job was to catalog all the Magi's scholarly endeavors. Even so, a sudden shiver passed through Akilah.

Burhan smiled unevenly. "Cold?" His crooked mouth overpronounced the word.

Akilah pulled his cloak tighter about him. "Yes. You?"

A curious mixture of surprise and contempt crossed Burhan's face before he turned away to stack baskets.

Despite the smoke, Akilah stepped closer to the fire's warmth. "How often are old records purged?"

The bent man stared into the flames. "It depends. Whenever something new makes old information obsolete. Final findings replace preliminary results. Approved reports replace erroneous drafts …"

"Well, don't let me keep you from your work."

"I'm done. Just need to purify the fire with incense and douse it when it dies down." Burhan rummaged in his cloak. "Forgot the incense." Torch in hand, he hobbled toward the Magi compound.

Akilah glanced away. Watching Burhan walk was painful. His bow-legged gait, lopsided sway, and head-forward hunch seemed locked in a perpetual tug of war for his balance.

Akilah lingered by the fire, warming his outstretched hands, until a loud pop within the blaze knocked a partially consumed scroll off the pile. Sparks flew at him. He jumped back and threw a fold of his cloak across his face to shield himself. The shriveled but smoldering volume, still clinging to its spindle, rolled past. He had to get it back into the fire. He found Burhan's firestick nearby. But when he prodded the scroll close to the flames, it crackled and split, flicking ash and soot onto his clothes.

He shook his cloak, only to swirl more debris about him. "What a mess for the scourer to clean," he muttered.

Akilah's eyes flitted to the burning scroll. Why was it still on its shaft? The cold kept him from lingering on his thought. He reached for his lockbox. A singed scrap slid off the lid. From idle curiosity, he picked it up. His heart skipped a beat.

Hebrew text. An untouched corner said ישעיה. Yeshaaya. Isaiah.

Chapter 7

Memorization

"Tallis." Akilah shook his colleague's shoulder again. "Wake up."

Nestled under his goat-wool blanket, Tallis was slow to rouse. "Wha—are you—doing to my *korsi?*"

Ignoring his colleague, Akilah upended the framework, catching blankets as they slithered off. He tossed them aside and dragged the supports from the center of the room to expose the floor's sunken terracotta pot, still aglow within from its retained heat. "Shh. I'll reassemble your blanket warmer later. I need to show you something."

"Now?"

"Yes. Because we must destroy it."

"You're not making any sense."

"Look." Silvery fingers of moonlight reached through the window across the room, illuminating a scrap Akilah held.

"Isa—where did you get that?" Ignoring the cold, Tallis threw his covers aside and sprang from bed.

"Burhan was burning scrolls when I came back from the observatory just now."

Tallis dropped to his knees by the korsi's faint light and heat.

"*The vision concerning Judah and Jerusalem that Isaiah* … something, something … *during the reigns of Uzziah, Jotham, Ahaz, and Hezekiah, kings of Judah.*" Tallis squinted. "*Listen … for the L*ORD *has spoken.*" He looked up. "Spoken what? The rest is too charred. Is this—"

"An introduction to the writings of the Hebrew prophet Isaiah? I believe so."

"Burned?"

Akilah paced. "Burhan said he was purging outdated documents. Everyone knows that shaking the house starts three weeks before Nowruz. All cleaning must end before First New Day." His voice shook as he pointed to the scrap. "More important, this is no 'outdated' document."

Tallis reverently cradled the fragment in his hand. "Maybe it was a mistake. I heard Burhan had been ill again. But who would want to burn *any* religious writing? For three centuries, Magi all over Persia have tried to reconstruct the religious texts that accursed Alexander destroyed when he burned the libraries in Persepolis."

Akilah paced in front of the korsi. "Where's that pouch from the scribe?"

"Locked in one of my clothing chests."

"Does anyone other than the three of us know you have it?" Tension tightened Akilah's voice.

"No. Why?"

"Get rid of it." Akilah set his jaw.

"We had hoped it would help us find what we need in Jerusalem. That scroll and our audience with the Temple priests were going to be our strongest justifications to the Council after making our journey."

"We can't use it now."

"The Council has always been so tolerant of all religions. They wouldn't censor …" Tallis swallowed hard, his voice suddenly raspy. "You should report what you saw."

"I don't want more controversy following us."

"Surely you can trust someone with your suspicions."

Akilah sagged against the table near Tallis's bed. "I don't …" Tallis jerked his head up. "What's happened?"

"The last Council meeting. Someone from the Upper Council was there."

"Upper? Why? They deal only with governmental affairs. The Lower Council oversees our scholarly pursuits."

Akilah avoided Tallis's gaze. "The Council didn't understand—"

"Maybe they did—all too well." Tallis held out the scrap to Akilah. "People fear what they don't want to know."

Akilah laid the scrap atop the korsi's embers. The piece flamed a moment before curling to black ash. "Tallis, did you commit the scribe's message to memory?"

"Yes. Along with the other few references we found."

Akilah stirred the embers. "The Council can't question what they can't find. Get the pouch."

Chapter 8

Waterfall

What a doubly glorious evening. A cosmic hand had painted the sky with bold bands of indigo, violet, crimson, and orange—and Farzaneh could share its beauty with her husband, Ihsan-Katana, home from his latest government contract work. After a busy day managing her land holdings, a sunset stroll through her private gardens and orchards was one of Farzaneh's few indulgences. Tonight she would not walk it alone. The evening was perfect. Almost.

"You seem far away. What troubles you, my husband?"

"Have you heard from Akilah?"

She halted. "No. Why should I?"

"Rumor is your cousin is causing a stir with his study of a new star said to herald an eternal king. The king of kings, as some would say."

"What a pert notion," Farzaneh said, her tone flat and uninterested. She resumed walking. "Persian kings since Cyrus the Great have proclaimed themselves 'king of kings,' simply because they let their conquered kingdoms continue some semblance of self-rule. Our empire isn't the only one to flaunt such a title—or imperial pretentiousness."

"You are ever observant, my beloved. But I wouldn't dismiss Akilah's work so quickly," Ihsan-Katana said. "It has merit in Jewish religious texts."

Pausing in the middle of a row of apricot trees, Farzaneh dug her hand into the soil. Good. The first seasonal addition had been applied. Its nourishment would stimulate the trees' sluggish growth, transforming them into their full fruit-bearing potential.

She rolled some soil between her thumb and middle finger. Should she be irritated or intrigued at her husband's gentle command? She never talked about her cousin, and her husband knew he shouldn't either. Whatever Akilah was embroiled in, he must have brought upon himself. Regardless, she had no reason to care. But she did care about her husband. He never wasted words. The few he'd spent on Akilah piqued her interest.

Farzaneh tilted her head upward, her eyes drinking the sky's majestic but waning colors. "Does this have anything to do with your latest trip to Adiabene and the copy of the Isaiah writings you bought while there?"

"Yes." An intense undercurrent coursed through her husband's single word.

She pursed her lips. That scroll. What a contentious addition to their household.

Ihsan-Katana had spent parts of many years working in Adiabene, a region that bore the brunt of Rome's bids to control the Tigris-Euphrates basin. Parthia's defensive fighting on Adiabene's stage had repeatedly damaged the area's water supplies. Ihsan-Katana and his crews had repaired or replaced its *qanats* many times. His last trip to the region fourteen months ago had started like every other ... until he became acquainted with the area's Hebrew population. He returned home six months later, guarding several scrolls of their holy writings as though they were priceless jewels. He started practicing some of their customs. And he would occasionally say strange things like, "Even Rome's imperialism has a place in Adonai's greater plans."

His new belief in the Hebrew God had upended Farzaneh's comfortable relationship with her husband. At times, such talk drew them closer together. Other times, it threatened to tear them apart. For Farzaneh's sake, Ihsan-Katana hid his new beliefs from everyone but her. By all outward appearances, they were still a Zoroastrian couple. He would not do anything to jeopardize their community standing or family relations.

Yet the Isaiah tome seemed particularly important to him. Farzaneh had read it so they could converse about it. Some of it comforted her, but most of it confused her. Some sections seemed to speak of past, present, and future as if they were one.

Had her cousin commandeered some of Isaiah's words for his self-absorbed Magi purposes?

Farzaneh resumed walking down the row of apricot trees. She quickened her strides, a habit when frustrated. "Akilah wouldn't entangle himself with something that could cause him to fall from the Council's favor." She flung the words over her shoulder to dismiss the topic.

"Anything is possible, my dear." Ihsan-Katana matched her paces, a half-smile playing about his lips. He cradled her elbow to steer her in another direction. "Shall we visit the waterfall?"

Although a dozen urgent matters crowded her mind, she nodded absent-mindedly. "I really should—"

Ihsan-Katana pitched forward, grabbing Farzaneh's arm in an unceremonious bid for balance. She staggered. Straining to keep both of them upright, she finally steadied him, but his face had paled like a waning moon. Thankfully, no one could see them in the orchard. But no one was near enough to help them either.

Farzaneh swallowed her rising anxiety. "Husband, you are ill. I—"

"The waterfall." It wasn't a suggestion.

Farzaneh nodded and slipped her arm around his waist.

"Ihsan." She murmured his shortened name, an endearment for their ears only. A word she had said with reservation for years. "Ihsan, I am here."

He kissed her forehead.

She tried light-hearted conversation to ease his labored steps to the waterfall. "You know, if I hadn't bought this parcel of land, we never would have met. You brought life and beauty to this parched ground in a way that exceeded everything I had imagined."

She wanted to add, "And you did the same for me." But, after fifteen years, she still had trouble voicing that sentiment. Ihsan seemed to sense her thoughts and smiled big enough for both of them. That smile had taken Farzaneh years to fully accept. He truly, deeply loved her.

Being near the waterfall seemed to invigorate Ihsan. It both comforted and discomposed Farzaneh. The cascading cataract, terraced and paved on both sides, was Ihsan's crowning achievement in coaxing mountain and underground waters to their appointed places on her property. Seating near the top of the waterfall offered a spectacular view overlooking Farzaneh's gardens, orchards, and house. But tonight, Ihsan didn't climb the steps. He gazed past them. Farzaneh could not follow his line of sight. She didn't want to acknowledge the deep secret behind the waterfall.

Chapter 9

Shadowlands

The next day

Sassanak tugged on the rough-woven tunic and cloak, both gifts from grateful villagers who'd received a share of his grain allotment. Partial payment for Magi service was grain, and portions to those in the highest offices were ample. Sassanak always parlayed his share into an annual goodwill visit to the masses. Any modicum of sharing was effortless publicity.

Sassanak donned the headpiece that matched the cloak. Ugh. Scratchy, crude stuff. Although he despised the villagers' paltry gifts, today the clothes proved useful. In such rustic attire, Sassanak could move about, unnoticed, in unofficial capacities.

He had no fear of traveling alone. In this disguise, no one would consider him worthy of robbing. Especially today.

He made his way northwest to Nineveh. Posing as his own servant, he entered the great city through the only gate in the south wall. He touched a scroll in his belt. The message, secured with his official seal, ensured no one would ask questions when he conducted his clandestine transaction. Not far inside the gate, he paid a highly skilled but obscure silversmith for his craftsmanship.

Less certain of his second task, Sassanak turned toward the city's outskirts. Hopefully this risky venture could shed light on a matter of great importance to the Council. Or, at the least, a matter significant to him.

The village was unremarkable, save for its squalor. Dirt-streaked children played amid irrigation ditches dug carelessly close to waste ditches. A trash heap on the village's periphery stung Sassanak's nostrils with its pungency. The sooner he found what he was looking for, the better.

There it was, on the doorpost of the largest mud hut. A *sigil*. A symbol that reportedly harnessed the stars' energy to magnify a person's interpretive abilities. The metal circle stamped with curved lines and smaller circles eerily resembled a face with a wide-open mouth.

"This is madness," he said. Why had he agreed to this task? The thought chafed his mind as much as his clothes irritated his skin. He had been ready to dismiss Azazel's impassioned insistence on the necessity of this trip until his colleague said this astrologer could provide the ultimate key to protecting the empire's religious purity. And somehow, Sassanak could use that information against Akilah.

Akilah. Who did he think he was? His claim of spotting a star no one else in or beyond Persia had seen was audacious. But it was sacrilegious to assign the star a spiritual meaning based on some foreigners' revered writings.

Glaring at the sigil, he stepped back. The stench of dead animals mingling with sweet-but-earthy burnt myrrh wafted through the door and groped its way into Sassanak's lungs. "A *haruspex*," he muttered. "I don't need someone who reads entrails. This person had better be more expert at reading the skies than sheep livers, or Azazel will have much to pay for my wasted time."

Covering his mouth with a corner of his sleeve, he knocked on the door. A man, his skin as wrinkled and reddish-brown as Numidia's Thuri dates, answered.

Sassanak choked back his revulsion. The man's cloudy eyes tracked in two directions. One studied Sassanak's face while the other seemed to peer past his left ear. The man's stumbling walk and wasted muscles spoke of longstanding illness. An aura of excrement and sweat hovered about him.

"You came." The man snatched the sigil from the doorpost and dropped it into a basket just inside the hut. Leaning heavily on a stout walking stick, he turned and limped halfway across the room to a cushion. After easing himself onto it, he pointed with his stick to another cushion near him.

The hut's stale air reeked of entrails, incense, and secrets. As Sassanak crossed the room to the dusty seat, he dodged gourds and bundles of dried herbs hanging from the ceiling. "I hear you are an expert on conjunctions and their interpretation. I need information about both."

"How much time do you have?" The old man gaped an almost toothless grin.

"Very little." Entering the shadowy fringes of Zoroastrian beliefs sent icy shivers down Sassanak's spine. Within the religion he practiced and defended so fiercely, astrology and divination were as useless to him as mythos. Who needed superstitious fodder for senseless soothsaying? Yet here he was, consulting what he previously had dismissed.

Determined to ignore the smells threatening to overwhelm his senses, Sassanak focused on his task. "Zoroastrian astrology ascribes meaning to different kinds of conjunctions. I believe you call them magnitudes. Explain that to me. Briefly."

The old man cackled. Shrill, high notes crescendoed, cracked, then plummeted to a breathy, rattling end. "Such impatience. It has taken me a lifetime to understand the divine nature of steady stars and constellations. The demon side of wandering stars and the sun's cords that keep them bound."

"Then start with this. The sun, moon, Jupiter, and Saturn aligned within Varak during Nowruz a few years ago. Which magnitude was that conjunction? And what did it mean?"

The old man straightened and raised his hand. "You seek history in what conjunctions portend."

"Yes." Sassanak dared not say more. He couldn't reveal his true purpose for being there.

The old man twisted his neck. Was that the only way he could look directly at a person? Or could he see at all? "There are four magnitudes of conjunctions. You described a great conjunction—one of the third magnitude. It speaks of the fate and destiny of kingdoms."

Fate of kingdoms? Persia's unpopular king was about to be replaced. Furious debate had surrounded the matter for several years. The fate of his successor—and the empire's destiny—lay in the Megistanes' hands. Akilah could have been part of that, had he accepted the Megistane vacancy that still hung in the balance. But he had declined that great honor to study that infernal star ...

The man's one eye trained on Sassanak penetrated his chest like a hot poultice and made his skin crawl. But he still needed to get what he'd come for. "What of the fourth magnitude?"

The old man writhed and scooted backward, moaning.

Sassanak's mouth turned dry as desert sand. "Tell me, man."

"No ..." The wizened man's eyes rolled back in his head. "Earth, air, water, fire. Earth, air, water, fire." He whimpered, rocking back and forth.

Sassanak grabbed the man's bony arm. "In the name of all that is holy, what is it?"

His breath came hard and heavy. Frantic, he peered through the hut's dim light and dusty air. Bowls of bones lined a low shelf along the back wall. Above it, curious artifacts and incomprehensible charts hung in haphazard collections. A tortoise shell etched with astral signs dominated an adjacent wall. Symbols surrounding it formed an eerie map, but not of land. More like parts of a body. And the symbols looked like they'd been drawn in blood.

Bile rose in Sassanak's throat. He released his grip on the man's arm and threw a money pouch on the ground in front of him. "Answer me. Now!"

The man slid the pouch under his left thigh. His gaze darted across the ceiling, his eyes swimming with dread. "Have you seen a fourth magnitude conjunction?"

"No. But one of our scholars might claim he has."

The man's eyes bulged with fear. "Why does he wait to announce it? Must prepare ... Our country ..." The man pitched forward, his head to the ground.

Sassanak's heart hammered. The room tilted. "He thinks he saw a new star, but it disappeared from the sky. Based on what he described and what has been ruled out, it must have been a fourth magnitude conjunction."

Shrieking, the old man beat his head with his hands. "Pray you are wrong. Pray he is wrong." His voice shook. "A fourth magnitude conjunction brings the most upheaval of all. It brings a change of religion."

Change of religion?

Volcanic dread erupted in Sassanak's chest. Molten passion consumed him in the hiss of one thought. Persia's religion must remain pure at all costs. Nothing can be allowed to change it.

The room's heavy air closed in on him. His lungs seized. He stumbled from the hut, gulping fresh air like a man dying of thirst.

Talk of the Hebrew child-king must die. And Akilah with it. Now he knew how to make that happen. Legally.

Chapter 10

Skins

Two days later

The attendant's energetic scrubbing with consecrated urine of the white bull had done more than purify Akilah's outer body. His reddened skin tingled. Every nerve buzzed. His nostrils burned from the acrid smell, but inner and outer purification weren't complete yet. The priestly acolyte sprinkled ash into a small square container. "Drink."

Gulp it so you won't gag. Akilah downed the ash-tinged urine in one swallow.

He straddled a drainage trench in the flooring. If only he were allowed to brace himself against something for this moment. But touching anything during the purification process was forbidden.

A shower of icy water shocked Akilah head to toe. A second dousing. Then a third. Every rivulet carved more shivers through his body. The purified water, its usefulness exhausted from ceremonial washing, drained through the trench, never to be used again.

The attentive acolyte slipped his hands into silk gloves and hastened to towel-dry Akilah. Priestly robes hung at the ready. Only Akilah, now ceremonially clean, could touch the all-white garments.

He attached a filmy veil to his headpiece—his least favorite part of his priestly garb. Despite its lightweight fabric, the veil labored Akilah's breathing. But even his breath couldn't taint the sacred fire central to Zoroastrian services.

Ignore the inconvenience. Focus on the honor. I'm leading a service of the empire's official religion in the preeminent enclave of Magi society. I could have been assigned a Sumerian service in some remote city.

His preparation complete, Akilah hastened to the anteroom where Rashidi waited. "The *haoma?*"

Rashidi handed him a silver chalice brimming with a milky, greenish-white liquid. "Pressed and ready."

"Did you scour the chalice with wood ash and wash it with water beforehand?"

"Yes."

Akilah nodded with approval and covered the chalice with a gauzy white cloth. "You are learning fast, Rashidi. Ah, there's the wood."

Tallis entered the anteroom, toting a bundle of wood under each arm. One bundle would be burned, the other, prayed over. The weighty bundle, bone-dry camelthorn, juniper, and chenar would produce a pure, smokeless, sacred fire. The slender bundle, *barsom,* conveyed spiritual and physical healing in its twigs of myrtle, laurel, pomegranate, tamarisk, willow, and juniper.

"Now we are ready," Akilah said to his colleagues, also clad in white.

Two men walked ahead of the trio to clear the winding path of snakes. About half of the Magi from the Lower Council joined the trek to the hilltop location of the open-air service. As usual, Sassanak and his closest colleague, Azazel, led that group. A few Megistanes from the Upper Council joined but did not mingle with the others. Instead, they flanked the procession's rear.

Akilah veered to avoid touching an intact snakeskin near the side of the path. Dead skin was useless. Live skin was vital. Snakes had to shed their skin to grow—and rid themselves of parasites. Did the Parthian empire need to do the same? His thoughts flitted to the Chief's warning about impending disaster if the empire's half-breed heir apparent came to power. Akilah flinched. He could have been an influencer in that process.

The Magi's ceremonial robes were another skin—cherished, nourished, and maintained. More broadly, the skin of religion protected the empire and held it together. Would the empire's tolerance of foreign religions jeopardize its own?

That was a topic of ongoing debate.

Despite its outward unity, Magi society argued how stringently to enforce the empire's theology. Akilah avoided such discussions at all costs. Although Zoroastrian practices suited him and he had pledged to uphold its tenets, he didn't claim the religion his own. In contrast, Rashidi wholeheartedly embraced it despite his Egyptian heritage. Tallis didn't say one way or another.

A smattering of villagers from surrounding areas had made the trek to the hilltop. Dressed in their distinctive striped worship clothes, they clustered a respectful distance behind the Magi. Akilah admired their effort. Other than on high holy days, most villagers worshiped in their homes. Corporate worship should be for more than those paid to lead and live it as a career.

At the crest of the hill, a glorious panorama of the Magi's corner of the world spread before him. Isolated huts dotted the rugged high terrain, while villages at lower elevations interrupted spring's inaugural green carpet.

A morning breeze lifted a corner of Akilah's veil, offering

him a few moments of unrestricted breathing. As the pure, cool air rushed into his lungs, *úshtá* overcame him. Nature always harmonized his thoughts and energy.

He loved that about Zoroastrianism. Outdoor worship at open altars. No temples, idols, icons, or religious statues. No dimly lit rooms laden with burnt incense and secret incantations.

Akilah led the group in calling upon Ahura Mazda, the supreme being. Additional invocations followed for the six angelic beings that aided him.

As the smokeless fire consumed the sacred wood, the message in the damaged scroll overtook Akilah. The words from Isaiah said the Hebrews' eternal king was more than a ruler. He was Mighty God. Everlasting Father.

God. Deity. That was hard enough to comprehend. But *Father?*

Akilah could grasp the notion of worshiping one god, but Isaiah's words made the Hebrews' God sound like ... "more" than any other religion's god. "Mighty God" signified immense, perhaps unlimited, power. But *Father?* Why pick a term of endearment? Was this God more powerful *and* more approachable than the supreme entity Akilah had invoked? His earthly father was unapproachable, essentially impossible to communicate with. A deity one could call Father was inconceivable. He tried to shove his thoughts to the farthest corner of his mind. But they kept surfacing like bloated dead fish on the sea.

✡ ✡ ✡

Two hours later, the Magi finished the service. Normally they would have headed to the scourers waiting to clean and purify their sacred garments. But not today. Akilah and his team

New Star

would take the worship service to Fakhri, their Magus Honorific.

For decades, he had taught religion to almost everyone in the compound. Akilah counted Fakhri as teacher, mentor, and friend. The aged Magus was a guiding light to all Magi. He never spoke against other belief systems but maintained Zoroastrianism was the only true one—the one Good Religion, as its staunchest believers called it. It grieved Fakhri that Magi society served many cultures' gods, but he didn't challenge the empire's policy of tolerating them.

If only anyone's religion could help Fakhri now. In just three months, his mentor had become practically bedridden, suffering from an unknown ailment. Cruel by Akilah's scales of justice. What had Fakhri done to deserve such torment? His absence from services left a vacuum no one could fill.

Akilah knew well the way to Fakhri's spacious living quarters in the building reserved for the elite of the Lower Council. His door yielded to Akilah's light taps. "Fakhri, it's Akilah. Are you well to worship in your room?"

No answer.

Akilah pushed past the door and startled at the sight of the Chief Megistane sitting by Fakhri's bed. At the intrusion, the Chief drew himself up to his full standing height. Forgetting his appointed priestly authority on this day, Akilah reflexively bowed to the highest-ranking official of the Upper Council. The Chief returned Akilah's bow with a steely stare that softened when Tallis and Rashidi entered, laden with the requisites for high worship.

After all these years, how could the Chief's commanding presence wilt Akilah so? The Chief's stare always seemed to demand a confession of the heart's darkest secrets and deepest failures. Akilah had never devised a defense against that look. Instead, he diverted his attention to the *topi* on the Chief's head. To be sure, it was a prayer cap but not white like Akilah's priestly attire. The Chief's cap was satin, splashed with vivid colors.

Some people think wearing a topi strengthens their prayers. Maybe he believes a colored one amplifies his prayers. Akilah silently scolded himself for the negative thought. "Chief Megistane, will you stay?"

Roused by Akilah's voice, Fakhri stirred in his bed. A slow smile crept across the wizened man's face. "Both of you here. Good."

"Be brief," the Chief whispered to Akilah. "This morning's walk in the courtyard exhausted him."

Akilah cleared his throat. "We just finished worship on the hilltop and would like to deliver the same to you, Fakhri, if we may."

Fakhri's hand wobbled in the direction of an ornate gold chalice on a table. "Use that to hold the sacred fire." Rashidi added the torch of smokeless fire and set it within Fakhri's line of sight a safe distance from the bed.

"We honor the fire, for it is Ahura Mazda's seventh creation," Akilah started. After two more sentences, the Chief arched his eyebrows in warning. Akilah skipped the traditional service and moved directly to praying over the barsom.

"Thank you. Thank you." Contented sighs separated Fakhri's feeble words. But the brief service seemed to refresh him. "Akilah. Gadiel. Stay a moment."

The Chief froze in his chair. Akilah's skin prickled. Thankfully Fakhri's bed separated them.

After Tallis and Rashidi bowed and left, Fakhri summoned the energy to push himself up to a sitting position. He beckoned Akilah and the Chief closer. With an unusually clear look in his rheumy eyes, Fakhri said, "Someday you two will think as one."

Akilah shook his head. "If you mean the Megistane position—"

"No, no, not that." The elderly man's voice cracked. With

New Star

uncharacteristic strength, he swatted Akilah's arm in reproval. Akilah recoiled at the overt violation of touching a priest in sacred garb. Was Fakhri out of his mind?

"He's spoken of 'two as one' before," the Chief whispered. "Ignore it."

"No!" Fakhri gripped his gut in pain. "Someday," he said, panting.

With great effort, he extended one hand to Akilah and the other to the Chief. "You are opposites. Not oppositional. Opposites ... Same coin ... two sides." His reach faltered. His open hands, still empty, fell to his sides with a soft thud as he collapsed onto his pillows.

Akilah gaped. The Chief's face turned to stone. An awkward silence grew.

"Honorable Magus, be well. I will visit you again before I leave for Jerusalem." Akilah was indebted to Fakhri in many ways, but sometimes the old man said such puzzling things. Whether the words came from age, infirmity, or prophecy, Akilah couldn't tell. Without looking back, he left the room at a trot.

Chapter 11

Dinner Talk

The next evening

Burhan shifted again in his chair, but another round of pain shot through his hunched frame. Even so, he remained seated beside Fakhri. The sun had exited the sky more than an hour ago, yet the lamps in the room remained unlit save for a small one perched atop a heavily carved, standing storage chest.

"Ahura Mazda is the supreme, omniscient, omnipotent God." The Magus Honorific droned from his bed. "He symbolizes truth, radiance, purity, order, justice, courage, strength, and patience. He is the world's creator and sustainer, protecting good from evil."

After more monologue, the elder seemed to pause his stream of thought. Burhan patted Fakhri's hand. "Thank you for your training. It is both wise and good."

Burhan rose to go. Finally, some relief from pain. Standing did that—to a point. After a time, pain would seize him and pull him back into a chair. The cycle repeated without remorse.

He turned toward the door, but the wizened man resumed

his droning. "We must hold fast to the values of *Asha*: order, beneficence, honesty, fairness, and justice."

Burhan slid sideways into his seat again. "Indeed. Disturbing to see how this country is letting other religious practices dilute Zoroastrianism."

"Like fire temples." Fakhri's words gained momentum. "Litanies of other gods."

"Terrible."

Fakhri's arm wavered upward. "We must remain on the side of good and help Ahura Mazda rid evil from creation. Cultivate his qualities represented by the six Immortal Beings." He sank unkempt fingernails into Burhan's wrist. "Keep from sin by not practicing other faiths. Keep our religion pure."

Burhan winced but bobbed his head vigorously. "I completely agree. But the hour is late. As always, I've enjoyed our time together."

"Thank you for bringing my meal. My feet don't work right these days." Fakhri's voice faltered.

"You didn't eat much."

"A touch of indigestion and dizziness."

"With deepest respect, Honorable Magus, in this darkness, it would be difficult for anyone to see or desire their food."

"The light bothers me."

Fakhri's puffy, watery eyes silently questioned Burhan as he slipped his hand into his cloak. "Just checking for my keys." He patted an interior pocket. "Hard to see in the dark."

He bungled the food tray while opening the door. "Goodnight, Honorable Magus. Rest well. May Ahura Mazda bless you with *úshtá*."

Long shadows draped the dimly lit hallway. That mattered little to Burhan. His stooped slouch and attention to the tray in his hands kept his eyes cast downward until one shadow loomed larger than the others.

"Good evening, Burhan."

"Head Magus!" Burhan white-knuckled his grip on the tray, slopping soup onto his ink-stained tunic.

"What brings you to the Magi's quarters?" Sassanak's voice rumbled through the stone hallway.

"I-I took Fakhri his dinner."

"A thoughtful gesture. How is he this evening?"

"He ate some soup tonight."

Sassanak's expression could have turned the soup into stone. "Need I remind you that a cook's helper takes meals to anyone who cannot dine with the others?"

"I-I meant no disrespect. As for the hour, Fakhri started talking about Zoroastrianism. I didn't want to interrupt him."

"His favorite subject."

"Yes."

"He's probably told you the same thing dozens of times."

"I usually learn something new, regardless."

"So, you talk with him frequently."

"Only after work hours. If he feels able." Burhan's head bobbed and weaved as if dodging invisible arrows.

"I see." Sassanak scrutinized him. "Well, it's late." He pulled the tray from Burhan's grasp. "I'm headed to the cook's station, and your quarters are in the other direction. Tomorrow will arrive soon enough, and an Orderal's work is never done, right?"

Burhan nodded until Sassanak's footsteps no longer echoed in the hallway. "No, it's not."

Chapter 12

Old Friend

"Fakhri, my old friend." Sassanak warmed his elder colleague's hands, massaging each gnarled finger and smoothing every crease in his palm.

With great effort, Fakhri turned toward the touch. "Oh, it's you. Such a good student. One of my best."

Sassanak chuckled. "I'm glad you remember that instead of the grief I gave you."

Fakhri's weary smile dissolved. "I can't feel my hands and feet. "Why don't they work anymore?" he whimpered. "There's so much to do."

"Yes, yes," Sassanak cajoled. "But first, you must rest."

"I don't have úshtá. Something is wrong. Very wrong."

"Your mind and spirit can be well even when your body is not. Be at peace."

"But they aren't—"

"Shh, Fakhri. All is well."

The withered elder scratched at Sassanak's sleeve. "You won't give up, will you?"

"Never. I promise."

"Keep pure ..." The Magus Honorific fell back onto his pillow.

"What can I get for you?"

"Food makes me sick. Is it too late for a hot herbal drink?"

"Never for you. I'll make it myself if I need to."

"Maybe just water." But as soon as the words passed Fakhri's lips, he fell asleep.

As Sassanak rose, his face hardened. Retrieving the tray he left outside the room, he disappeared down the hall.

Chapter 13

A Greater Good

The next morning

Labored snorts and thundering hooves shattered the reverie of Akilah's early morning walk. Streaks of brilliant color flashed across his path, halting his steps. A breeze lifted the rider's robe into crimson-cobalt-black ripples, momentarily obscuring Akilah's gaze. Towering over him, erect and proud, the Chief Megistane sat astride his magnificent Nisean stallion, its silvery back perfectly complementing the Chief's governmental garb. Gold ornamentation on the Chief's head cap scattered the sun into countless beams, forcing Akilah to shield his eyes.

He bowed deep to hide his concern. The Chief Megistane never casually visited anyone. Riding the Nisean, a breed reserved for royalty, meant one thing—the Chief was bound for Ctesiphon, Parthia's royal capital. Royal business couldn't possibly have anything to do with Akilah. Could it?

"You know what's at stake with a transfer of power. And yet you persist in your selfish ambitions."

Should Akilah dare answer? He couldn't forget the Chief's

unprecedented appearance at the last Council meeting. Swallowing hard, Akilah lifted his chest. "The gain should outweigh the risk."

"Gain? You think too small. You would abandon the greater good for what you call a scholarly … pursuit?" The Chief spat the last sentence out of his mouth. The vigor of his words belied his age. Only his neatly trimmed salt-and-pepper beard hinted that he was twenty years Akilah's senior.

Akilah pressed his hand to his chest and bowed again. "I have devoted my life to the Magi's priestly and scholarly duties. It is an honor to serve the Lower Council in those capacities. My loyalty, as always, lies with Magi society. If the Megistanes see fit to make me one of them when I return from Jerusalem, then I will accept the Upper Council position with gratitude and will serve it with all my devotion."

"You weren't given that option. Time doesn't allow it."

He stiffened. Everything about the Chief was always yes or no, stay or go. Akilah preferred a nuanced life that explored all shades of possibilities. He folded his left hand over his right and discreetly twisted the diamond-encrusted ring on his fifth finger. How could he respond to that? What good would it do to try?

The Chief's steely eyes flashed. "A new king must replace Phraates IV—soon. His son, that wimp from a Roman slave girl's womb, cannot become king. When Phraates accepted that woman into his court and bedchamber, divine power left him. He claims he can achieve peace with Rome's emperor Augustus, but he has bedded himself and his country with the enemy." The Chief's voice gathered speed and intensity like an impending storm. "Persia has tolerated that abomination too long. Phraates's progeny cannot be allowed to reign. Roman blood cannot sit on Persia's throne."

The stark reality of the Chief's words stunned Akilah into silence. He still had no desire to be a Megistane. He couldn't abandon his study, but he wouldn't abandon his country. His lack of response seemed to rankle the Chief further.

Glowering, the Chief spun the Nisean in a tight circle around Akilah. "Our country stands alone in having a committee choose their king. *You* could be a kingmaker. *You* could be part of a pivotal point in our country's history," the Chief said with force. "Yet you would deny that opportunity—that responsibility—and risk much more on your questionable star project?" He snorted. "Most of us can't afford the luxury of idealism."

Akilah couldn't bear to meet the Chief's piercing gaze.

"More is at stake than you realize." The Chief lowered his voice. "You have no idea what a hotbed of unrest Jerusalem is. Persia can't protect you there. Don't let your persistent idealism become presumptive arrogance. It will be your undoing."

"I am pursuing truth." His eyes still cast downward, Akilah's words passed his lips in a weak trickle. "Is that not a worthy cause?"

"You know nothing about truth," the Chief retorted.

"I know more than you taught me," Akilah said under his breath. But the thunder of hooves drowned his response.

Chapter 14

Sour Words

The tartness of the steaming *rivas* stew before Sassanak titillated his senses even before he tasted the dish. Early spring rains had matured this rare fruit sooner than usual. To many, the sour fruit was sacred. To him, it was a well-deserved luxury.

He savored each spoonful. Ah, the pleasure of fine food in his private garden. Perhaps he should eat his morning meal here more often.

A shadow crossed his bowl. He paused without looking up from his delicacy. "Well?"

"No threat could convince Akilah to stay. But you should have surmised that already." The Chief Megistane's tone matched the stew's acidity.

Stirring with strokes as measured as his words, Sassanak replied, "A pity that one's bloodline doesn't guarantee the next generation will uphold the same ideals as yours."

"You're out of line."

"Still a thorn in your side, isn't it?" Sassanak said softly. "Akilah preferring priestly and scholarly duties over your path."

"Speak another word like that, and I'll have you dismissed. You know I can."

"But you won't, Gadiel. Especially now."

"Chief Megistane to you," he growled. "We'll talk when I return from the capital. Pray you have something useful to tell me by then."

Sassanak circled the table. Stooping over his garden, he cradled a cluster of cyclamen buds. "Like these flowers, impatience won't open them, but time will. I'll get you what you need ... at the right time."

The Chief sidled up to the table and spun the half-full breakfast bowl until Sassanak lunged for it. The Chief slapped his hand over it, halting its gyration. "Nothing less than the best for you, yes?" he scoffed. "And you complain about government excess." He shoved the bowl toward Sassanak.

Sassanak bowed low. In the matters at hand, the Lower Council was required to defer to the Upper Council. And, at present, he had to shelve his differences with its Chief.

Chapter 15

Retrieval

Under increased pressure, Sassanak gulped his breakfast. He needed to deliver on his promise to the Chief, or all his plans would crumble.

"The cook sends a thousand pardons for the delay." A timid voice invaded his thoughts. "Here is your *tahdig*." A young servant bowed and approached with a steaming skillet.

"I haven't time for that now," Sassanak snapped. "Leave it in my office."

"He took pains to follow your specifications, Head Magus. Ghamsar rose water, a pinch of saffron, rice cooked in coconut oil—"

"Yes, yes. Leave it, I said." Sassanak pushed past the flustered servant and hurried to the library, a massive building anchored by four cuboid towers.

Three of them held archived volumes, but part of the north tower housed records of research in progress. Treading as quickly as the twisting stone stairs allowed, he reached the Orderal's workspace out of breath. Shafts of light squeezing through vertical window slits gave shape to dust lingering in the air of the inconspicuous room. It was an awkwardly shaped space, its oddness dictated by structural reinforcements encased within the walls. Twice as tall as it was wide, the room was small compared to the large task of cataloging the Magi's scholarly and scientific research.

Sassanak skimmed his hand over the pulley system that helped Burhan's twisted body boost scrolls to the shelves' heights. That ingenuity had helped Burhan cement a spot on the fringes of Magi society.

Sassanak picked his way past scrolls spilling from baskets. As he neared Burhan's work desk, he gave a wide berth to pots of pigments scattered on a nearby shelf. "How goes the cataloging today?"

"Fine, fine," the bent man said with an amiable smile.

"How close are you to finishing your new system?"

"I already used it to reorganize the new research. With your permission, the next step will be to apply it to completed research. Then use it throughout the library."

"Well, let's give it a try, shall we?"

"Now?"

"Come, come," Sassanak chided. "If your system is as good as you claim, it will rival the *Pinakes* cataloging system at the great libraries of Alexandria."

Burhan tittered. "I-I wouldn't know about that."

Sassanak held out his hand, palm up. "Ways to increase grain yields." He barked it as a command.

Without hesitation, Burhan pulled a scroll from a shoulder-height shelf.

"Zurvanism versus Zoroastrianism."

The bent man winced but quickly produced another scroll.

"Medicines that can heal or harm."

Burhan drew a long breath, pulled a stool close to the wall, and reached on tiptoe to pull a scroll from a shelf half again his height. With his arms full, he presented all three scrolls to Sassanak.

He unrolled one, smiled, and tapped the papyrus roll on the Orderal's hunched shoulder. "Well done. We'll talk when I return these tomorrow."

Although Burhan's exhale exuded relief, his hands flittered toward the research he'd relinquished. "Bu-but no one should have access to new work until first results are recorded."

"You know the rules well. Tomorrow." Sassanak left in a hurry.

Chapter 16

Enlightenment

Although darkness had descended four hours earlier, Sassanak's breakfast tahdig remained untouched. Its formerly crispy top layer now congealed and sticky, it sat, forlorn, on his reading table opposite the borrowed scrolls and a globe lamp. The day had been too full of interruptions to study what mattered until tonight.

Resolute, Sassanak bent over the latest research on medicines that can harm or heal. But the longer he read throughout the night, the more harried he became. What he had counted on to help him had failed him. "Useless. Rubbish." He dashed the scroll to the floor.

He grabbed the tahdig and stepped back, his arm cocked. Reconsidering, he slammed the bowl onto the table and hurled an empty drinking vessel at the wall instead.

Long ago, he had learned the meticulous art of healing with plants. Now he regretted setting aside that knowledge for other priestly disciplines. Achieving the office of Head Magus had come at a high price, but he never imagined it would include this pain.

His prayers had not healed Fakhri.

Maybe plants could.

Sassanak donned a turban and headed to the library as sunrise streaked warm colors across the sky's indigo canvas. Rose and orange rays weakly lit the shelves he browsed furtively in solitude. Where were the seminal volumes on Zoroastrian herbal remedies? Apparently misfiled. He rifled through every shelf designated for works on the five types of Zoroastrian healing: justice, goodness, surgery, prayers, plants. Odd that the librarian wouldn't notice the comprehensive scrolls regarding healing with plants were buried among scrolls on healing with goodness.

But Sassanak's concern for his old mentor far exceeded his frustration with the librarian's negligence. What was sapping Fakhri's life? Four months ago, the Magus Honorific was in such good health for his age that he still taught Magi inductees twice a week. Now he could barely walk or string sentences together. Sassanak needed to confirm his suspicions quietly. If necessary, he'd conjure a reason to go to Nineveh's library.

Satisfied with two scrolls, he retreated to a corner behind the interior bulge of the north tower. But muffled voices within its stairwell stopped him before he could unroll either volume. He shoved the scrolls onto the nearest shelf and flattened himself against the cold stone wall.

"Encouraging news about your cataloging system, Burhan." The head librarian's voice squeezed through chinks in the stones' grout. "Perhaps this warrants more, ah, spring cleaning before you implement it. No need to catalog dead weight, right?"

Burhan snickered. "Especially Jew—"

"How dare you?" The chief librarian's sharp reproof sliced the air. But a hearty slap, brief scuffle, and laughter negated his words.

"I did you a favor by finding those Jewish references for Rashidi." Burhan's pinched voice slipped between the stone's mortar cracks. "His combing through the Books of Moses gave us time to dispose of other writings that would have been more enlightening—like those of Isaiah and Micah."

"Indeed." The door handle creaked. "The west tower is still ... overfull. But don't get greedy. Otherwise, we won't be able to conceal the gaps in the volumes."

Sassanak squeezed his eyes shut and turned from the sound. Cheek pressed to stone, he willed himself invisible.

Beyond the wall, a door latched. Two sets of footsteps separated. Uneven, light steps shuffled westward. Heavier, steady steps strode southward, presumably toward the head librarian's office.

Sassanak waited until echoes of two more doors creaking open and shut reached him. He grabbed his scrolls and exited a side door, finding uncommon vigor in his feet.

Chapter 17

Sacrifice

Breathing hard, Sassanak sagged over the reading table in his quarters. No one should have been in the library until the end of morning's first full cycle. With difficulty, he shelved his newfound knowledge of the head librarian's clandestine purging. He had to find a way to help Fakhri.

He worked feverishly between the reference volumes and the new research on medicines that can harm or heal. But the sun climbed faster than he could read and cross-reference so many technical details. He needed more time. Keeping the library's scrolls wasn't a problem, but the new research he'd wrested from Burhan was. By law, duty, and his own words, he had committed to returning it today. Magi society protected its members' research with the same ferocity as a mother safeguarded her child. Punishment was swift and harsh if research was handled improperly for any reason, including loaning works in progress. No research was to leave the Orderal's office until finalized. Sassanak couldn't make Burhan a scapegoat for what he'd coerced from him.

Resolute, Sassanak swept all the scrolls into a storage chest.

He had to act quickly. He paused in front of his polished copper mirror for a long, hard look. A pity. He liked these clothes, despite their creases from two days' wearing.

He made one stop before fulfilling his obligation to Burhan.

✡ ✡ ✡

Sassanak lounged in the open doorway of Burhan's workspace. Such a diligent little man. That should prove useful. "Burhan, I can stay only a moment, but I wanted to keep our appointment to tell you I fully support the implementation of your new cataloging system for all research as well as the entire library."

Burhan spun toward the open door of his cluttered space. His smile contorted into a grimace as the smell of wet camel pellets filled the room. Backing to the closest window, he yanked open its bamboo-and-reed blind. Gusts of wind jumbled loose papyri on his desk. He dove to retrieve his scattering notes.

"I would tell the head librarian myself"—Sassanak ignored Burhan's dilemma—"but you did all the work, so that honor should be yours. Together, I'm sure you two can make everything work as it should."

In a curious mixture of nervous attentiveness and avoidance, Burhan alternately ducked, dived, and bobbed as Sassanak talked.

"Now, if you'll excuse me, I must visit the fuller." Sassanak headed toward the stairs.

Burhan exhaled forcefully, hunched to the window, and gulped outdoor air. Crossing the room as fast as he could, he called down the stairwell. "Th-thank you. But wha-what about the scrolls you borrowed?"

The fading echo of Sassanak's footsteps was his only answer.

Chapter 18

The Side of Kindness

Assur

Ihsan murmured his thanks to the servants and their careful efforts to change his withered bedsheets without moving him. When they left, he turned his head toward Farzaneh. "Continue studying Isaiah, my beloved. The scroll has much to say."

She forced a smile. That was as close to a command as she'd heard him speak since he'd fallen ill. She smoothed the fresh linen across his chest, inwardly shuddering at how quickly his vigorous body had become weak and gaunt. "Rest, my husband."

Ihsan's hand flopped but never quite lifted off the bed. The flaccid gesture ended in a soft thump. Whether it was intended to dismiss her words or attempt to stroke her cheek, Farzaneh couldn't tell. She closed her hand over his.

He swallowed with difficulty. "Nothing is more important. Understand?" His uncharacteristically impatient words croaked through his dry throat.

She lifted a cup of water to his lips. "I will have dinner

brought to you so you can bless it from the comfort of your bed. Shall I share the meal with you?"

"Dear Farzaneh, always deflecting my questions." Ihsan grimaced as he shifted his weight and tried to push himself upright.

A stone dropped in her stomach. She drew back. "I will send for the *asu*."

"I don't need another physician to tell me what I already know." His tone softened. "But I admit the pain is worse today. Could you mix some camphor with *qunabu*[1] for me?"

Her husband's habit of understatement didn't fool her. He needed a stronger painkiller than qunabu but continued to refuse poppy juice.

Hopelessness rushed over her in a torrent. Since childhood, she had groomed a calm exterior to counter every seemingly hopeless situation she'd faced—abandonment, intimidation, fear. But the sight of her husband weakening before her eyes evaporated that calm exterior. Her throat tightened. "What else can I do for you?"

"You know what to do when the time comes. All is in place. And you need not worry for me."

His peaceful composure strangled her heart. She didn't want to entertain thoughts of his meticulous funeral arrangements or ponder his confidence in the afterlife. She wanted to snap at him, say something endearing, and cry lakes of tears all at once. Her heart welled with gratitude—even love—for this man who had shared fifteen years with her. She regretted that she had never fully given her heart to him. The stern sentinels of her traumatic childhood and repressed young adult years still relentlessly guarded her emotions with exquisite jealousy.

She grieved for the times they could have enjoyed together. Walks ... talks ... travels ... possibly even children.

---

1. Cannabis

She watched Ihsan drift off to sleep and wept silently. Maybe the pain cream could wait. Tonight, she would wait with him. She settled into a cushioned chair by his bed.

Their relationship had started simply. She had bought a parched parcel of land behind her residence and envisioned orchards flourishing from its barren ground. He was the region's foremost expert on qanats, so she hired him to build one along with an irrigation system to bring life to the land.

She had approached the project with the same circumspect attitude she had for any business matter. She was a successful land manager. Accustomed to dealing with shifty or shrewd businessmen, she was always on her guard. But Ihsan presented her with a baffling new challenge—kindness.

She had scrutinized his early work for signs of cutting corners. Instead, she found he demanded two things of his building crews—excellence in their tasks and extra safety measures. He recognized the work's inherent dangers to life and limb. He monitored his crew's hours to avert mistakes borne from exhaustion. Farzaneh was pleased but surprised he cared as much about his employees as he did his qanats' structural details.

Early in the project, Farzaneh's first husband died when a tree fell on him during a storm. Then tragedy and opportunity visited Farzaneh arm in arm.

Ihsan was fourteen years her senior and a long-time widower, immersed in his career as deeply as Farzaneh was in hers. When she approached him three days after the requisite Zoroastrian mourning period had ended, he agreed to her marriage proposal. He enjoyed her company. She found him fascinating. Ihsan had a brilliant mind and enough government connections that he could have deduced her reasons for her bold proposition. If he did, he never mentioned it. If he considered her action merely a business offer, he didn't seem to begrudge it.

Regardless, the marriage was Farzaneh's choice—unlike previous ones forced upon her.

Ihsan's work sometimes separated them for weeks or months at a time. That didn't deter either of them. Both settled into a comfortable arrangement of living apart but together.

Halfway into Farzaneh's qanat project, she shared with Ihsan her full vision for the land—personal gardens and a waterfall surrounded by well-watered orchards. His eyes had lit up with something more than architectural imagination. She didn't understand that look until much later.

It was love growing in the fertile soil of kindness.

At his own expense, he changed her qanat plans. Later she learned he had forfeited a lucrative job to devote his time to fulfilling her desires. He could have hired a second crew to finish her work, split his time between jobs. His skills in the precise science of qanat construction garnered him many government contracts and distinguished business influence. Yet she'd rarely witnessed him wield either. His unassuming actions spoke a different language. Especially to her.

She didn't deserve kindness or favor, nor was she accustomed to it. Orphaned when six years of age and thrust into an arranged marriage when twelve, she was a lonely child lost in an adult world. Her first marriage, marked by stricture, would have been far worse if not for her guardians' intervention. They taught her how to make her way in the world. She was grateful for the years they'd groomed her to learn a trade she was surprisingly good at. But their early kindness toward Farzaneh the waif changed when she became a teenager. Compassion became contractual, contingent upon meeting their expectations. As her experience in land management increased, so did her discernment of people's motives. In the business world, overtures of kindness always cloaked a darker agenda.

The notion of being kind without expecting anything in

return was beyond Farzaneh's grasp. Although she learned in time to give it, she couldn't receive it without reservation.

In contrast, Ihsan's favor and affection toward her deepened every year. He genuinely cared for her. When she would ask why, he'd sidestep his answer.

In all their years of marriage, Ihsan had asked little of her—until his latest return from Adiabene. Saying no to him or his plans was impossible, although she didn't fully understand his request at the time.

Ihsan moaned in his sleep. Why must agony chase him to the farthest recesses of his mind even while he rested? Perhaps she should leave just long enough to make his pain cream.

Instead, she lingered by his bed, mulling his comment about studying Isaiah. In the past six months, he had shared other Jewish holy writings with her but kept returning to Isaiah. It seemed to hold more significance than a favorite read.

Ihsan moaned again. She slid her hand into his and stroked it. With long, smooth motions, she moved along his forearm, past his elbow, up to his shoulder. She had no idea if that truly helped, but her touch seemed to calm his fits of pain, whether awake or asleep.

A light knock on the door brought Farzaneh to her feet. She cracked the door open to find her head servant fidgeting in the hallway. "A thousand pardons, master. Sundown has passed, dinner is cold, and it *is* that special day of the week …" He jerked his head in the general direction of Ihsan's bed.

Farzaneh's eyes moistened. "Thank you for your attention to the time, Javad. My husband and I shall not be dining tonight. Reserve half the food for tomorrow, then share the rest with any servant who has not yet eaten today or is saving food for an ill member of their household."

Javad bobbed his head. "As you wish." He thrust a folded cloth into her hands before he hurried off. She lifted a corner of the cloth. Honey almond cakes.

Chapter 19

The Side of Right

Elegant silver handle, exceptionally sharp blade. Sassanak's new knife from Nineveh cut through fruit as if it were warm camel butter. Fine craftsmanship was such a heady pleasure.

He was methodically quartering an apple in his private quarters when the Chief Megistane appeared in his doorway.

As usual, the Chief ignored courteous formalities. "What do you have for me?"

"Surprisingly, I went searching for one thing and found another." Sassanak rhythmically pricked the air with his knife point as he uttered each word. "Can you guess how many Jewish prophecies exist regarding their Savior they call Messiah?"

The Chief glared. "I don't have time for riddles."

"Several hundred. Or so I've heard. But Akilah's team found only a few. Curious, don't you think?"

"Because?"

"The writings weren't ... available to them."

"You *hid* them? To thwart his study?"

Sassanak clutched his chest. "Oh, that hurts, Gadiel. I did

nothing of the sort. But I did discover certain Jewish holy writings had been disposed of."

"How?"

"Unsure. Hidden or burned."

"That's a civil offense. A direct violation of the empire's religious reclamation project. Your duty is to submit inquiry papers to the local magistrate or the province's satrap, as the offense warrants. The court will punish those responsible according to Persia's Books of Law. This still doesn't involve me." The Chief Megistane turned to leave.

"Oh, but it *does* involve you." Sassanak weighted each word like a dredging anchor restraining a ship. "The offense itself, no. What it represents, yes."

The Chief paused, his hand on the door.

"Please, sit. Fruit?" In one hand, Sassanak held aloft a deep bowl brimming with apples, sour plums, and cucumbers. In the other hand, he balanced a squat, sealed clay container. "Perhaps your religious studies are rusty, Chief."

Good. He'd piqued the Chief's curiosity enough to lure him back into the room.

Sassanak thumped the hilt of his silver knife on the sealed container. "Let me refresh your memory." Another thump and red grapes, still fresh after six months' storage, spilled from the cracked clay.

Sassanak set the fruit and two ornate, double-handled salt-boxes between them. Pushing three apple chunks to one side of his plate, he continued. "Zoroastrian prophecies speak of three *Saoshyants* that will be born miraculously to three virgins impregnated with Zarathushtra's seed. More than mere benefactors, they will be saviors. One for each of the last three millennia of the world. Eventually, they will defeat evil."

The Chief thrummed his fingers on the table. "Your point."

Sassanak stabbed the fourth apple chunk and twirled it at eye level. "The Jews talk of a single Savior, born to a virgin, who

New Star

will do more than defeat evil. He will save people from their sins and reign eternally. *A person already born.* Akilah and his team aim to find that person. What do you think will happen to Zoroastrianism if this idea of a Jewish Savior catches on here while Persia waits thousands of years for its saviors?"

Sassanak bit into the fourth chunk of apple. "Let's just say people are impressionable—and impatient." He flicked his fingers.

"You've seen what Greek influence has done to Zoroastrianism. Jewish influence could do infinitely more damage." He studied the Chief's inscrutable face. Had his words penetrated that stony exterior?

"The Jews' high court tribunal, the Sanhedrin, reportedly wields as much influence as you Megistanes in your Upper Council," Sassanak continued. "And Jewish Pharisees are much like our Lower Council."

"Measuring your competition?"

"We're talking about our empire's security, not a footrace," Sassanak snapped. "Persia is the heart of our empire, and its Magi society is its heartbeat. *We* shape the empire's spiritual direction. *We* cannot let Jewish influence defile our religion."

"Yours. Not mine." The Chief Megistane shoved the plate back.

"Our country's *official religion*, Chief. You of all people should appreciate its value as a rallying point. Religious convictions shape an empire's destiny more than its politics. The masses cling to religion even when they lose everything else. With the right king in place, he—and we—will be lauded for strengthening the empire. Unifying and protecting its religion from outside influences. Especially Jewish."

He mounded granules of common white salt on one side of his plate, rare blue salt on the other side. "So, my esteemed Chief, good religion must exist, if for no reason other than to eliminate bad religion. Wouldn't you agree?"

The Chief met his gaze with granite silence.

Sassanak's lips curled. "Let me put it in terms you'll appreciate. A strong empire will have the fortitude to withstand *Rome*—especially if the Jews' prophesied Savior fails to overthrow its rule." He spat on the ground. "Those Roman pigs think they're the gods' gift to civilization. The only society worthy of world dominance."

"What's in it for you?"

He rolled a sour plum between his palms. "I'm just as dedicated to Magi society as you are. We simply function in different capacities."

The Chief's mouth tightened into a thin line. "I repeat my question."

"Me?" Sassanak shrugged. He dipped the sour plum into the blue salt and bit into the fruit with zeal. "Chief Religious Overseer has a nice ring to it," he said, studying his suspended oil lamps pooling light on the ceiling.

"The Lower Council has no Chief rank. And neither Council division has such a title."

"Not yet."

With a dismissive snort, the Chief rose and turned toward the door. Perhaps only one thing could convince him to ally with Sassanak.

"You want proof of this religious threat to our society?" He leaned forward, his tone blistering. "Someone is poisoning Fakhri."

The Chief's gaze flickered momentarily. "How do you know?"

"Fakhri's odd copper skin color. Numbness in his feet and hands. Indigestion. Confusion. Disorientation. Symptoms of slow arsenic poisoning. Arsenic is tasteless. Easy to slip into food and drink." Sassanak pounded the table. "Fakhri is Zoroastrianism's staunchest supporter and most venerated teacher. If they will try to kill him to further their agenda, what else will they do to dismantle the empire's official religion?"

"Who is 'they'?"

"That's the real question, isn't it?" He leaned back in his chair and interlaced his fingers behind his head. "Unknown. But that criminal offense is undoubtedly linked to the destruction of Jewish texts. To which I say, let them do it."

"You're withholding evidence."

"To snare a larger prey, yes. Those people may be … ah, misguided … but their motives are not." Sassanak grabbed a cucumber, his voice throaty with intensity.

"Think beyond the present danger to a large-scale casualty, Chief. You specialized in history. You know how many civilizations crumbled from within due to moral decay. Long-held beliefs descend into myth when another belief system usurps them. If Zoroastrianism doesn't remain pure, today's religious favor will degenerate into tomorrow's tolerance. Tolerance will descend into indifference, then prejudice. Prejudice ignites persecution. Like when that accursed Alexander persecuted Zoroastrians and the Magi three hundred thirty years ago."

He thwacked the cucumber in half. "Religion can tear a country apart through civil war. Or, when used rightly"—he arranged sour plums around the halves—"religion can peacefully unite a country. And preserve Magi society."

The Chief's jaw softened.

Taking that as a hint of an agreement, Sassanak plunged ahead. "Besides, the Jews are nothing but trouble." He waved his hand as if dispersing a stench. With his knife pointed at the Chief, he added, "Remember what happened thirty-five years ago when our empire fought Rome on the Jews' behalf in Jerusalem?"

"*Herod …*"

"Exactly." He skewered a cucumber half. "He built Herodium

solely to flaunt his victory over Persia." Sassanak fiercely carved slices. "Well, Herod can have his Jews."

He checked himself. "Ultimately, Chief, we want the same thing. A king who will maintain a strong, independent empire in every way. One free of outside influences. Hellenistic. Jewish. Especially Jewish."

The Chief's eyes narrowed. "If Jewish prophecy is true, no power on earth would be able to stop it. Anyone who tried might come to ruin."

Sassanak scoffed. "Don't pretend to be soft with me. You enjoy the privileges of Magi society just as much as the rest of us. And you're not above political maneuvering—even when it involves religion." He dipped a cucumber slice in blue salt. "Akilah refused his promotion to Megistane, so you must choose another to fill the position. One who will appoint the right king to maintain religious purity and Magi influence."

Sassanak waved the cucumber slice in front of him. "As for our petty thieves, they'll become cocky when they think they can destroy more scrolls. When we catch them in their carelessness, we'll learn who's poisoning Fakhri and stop this religious incursion at the same time. See? Three goals achieved with one action."

With a roar, the Chief knocked the cucumber from Sassanak's lips. "You would wait and let Fakhri suffer?" The Chief lunged. His hands closed on Sassanak's throat. The plate of fruit crashed to the floor. Sour plums bounced in every direction.

Choking, Sassanak croaked, "Fakhri may already be beyond help. Healing through prayers hasn't helped. Healing through plants hasn't helped. Even the strongest haoma hasn't helped. Healing through justice may be the only healing we can offer him."

A shove sent him into the wall. Reeling and gasping, he crumpled in a heap. Dimly, he saw his silver-handled knife close to his face. "I uphold Magi society's tenets over all." The Chief's voice floated above his head. "Even if I must investigate you. You are on dangerous ground. See that it doesn't collapse on you."

The elegant knife clattered to the floor atop a green footprint.

Chapter 20

Soup Pot

Twenty minutes later

"Sassanak?" The muffled call and repeated knocking reached him from a great distance. His head throbbed. His ears rang. Why was one side of his face cold? Groping for his bearings, his hand braced against flat stone. How long had he been lying on the floor? He instinctively felt his throat.

The other side of his face burned as if pressed into hot sand. He rubbed that cheek and yowled as blue salt fell from his hand. What wasn't already ground into his face crunched underneath him amid salt-box shards. With a groan, he rolled over. Sour plums skittered across the room. He staggered to a wash basin, dampened a cloth, and wiped his face. In his haste to sponge off the salt, he got some in his eye.

He slid on smashed cucumber and stumbled into his overturned chair.

The knocking continued.

"In a moment." His thin voice struggled past his tight throat. He lunged for the fruit within arm's reach and fell again. Dazed but angered, he swept his arm in an arc to shove what he could out of sight.

Sassanak pressed his full weight into the chair to tip it sideways. Inhaling deeply to muster strength and focus, he managed to right his chair. "Coming."

He was returning the knife and plate to his table when Azazel burst through the door.

"Are you well? What happened to your face? It looks like—" Sassanak's scowl silenced his fellow Magus.

"Yes, ahem." Azazel's gaze fell on the knife. "Stunning workmanship. Looks almost like my new dagger."

Sassanak folded a napkin around the knife on the pretense of wiping it. Admitting any covetousness or his methods in finding the creator of Azazel's dagger was beneath him. "We both have impeccable taste, yes?"

Azazel leaned against the doorframe. "Any luck with the Chief Megistane?"

"Not yet." Sassanak rubbed the back of his head. "It'll take some time for him to come to our side."

"Time is not our ally." Azazel's voice sizzled. "We must increase our vigilance in repelling other cultures' advances on our empire's religion, just as the empire has repelled so many countries' takeover attempts."

Sassanak nodded. Their mutual hatred for anything that threatened the empire's official religion was part of the glue that bonded the two Magi.

Azazel paced, his eyes flashing. "Persia should have let the Jews rot in exile in Babylon. Or let them fail in trying to rebuild Jerusalem on their own. But Persians are so dedicated to the protocol of law ..." Azazel's words dripped with sarcasm. "If Governor Tattenai hadn't involved King Darius, Jewish culture would not exist today."[1]

---

1. Ezra 5 and 6

Although he agreed with Azazel's assessment, Sassanak needed to fetter his colleague's zeal, lest it derail his plans. "We can't correct the past—only change the present. Today's matters require delicate handling." He folded his hands. "Otherwise, our actions will be perceived negatively. Magi society can't afford to suffer another crushing blow like it did long ago."

His hands tightened into a clench to keep them from shaking. Inwardly, he shuddered. Persia's King Darius had indeed financed the Jews' rebuilding of Jerusalem. But later, he beheaded countless Magi when a few became too greedy in their bids for governmental power. Darius's deed remained so cruel and infamous that, to this day, no one dared speak of it directly.

"If I were Head Magus—"

"But you aren't." He shot his words like arrows at Azazel. No need to plow that ground again.

"Well, your position as Head Magus does make you more adept at … maneuvers."

Sassanak gestured for them to sit. "You have your skill set. I have mine."

"Yes …" Azazel sat but almost immediately jumped back up. "I can't abide other influences diluting our religion." He spat on the floor. "If it doesn't remain pure, all we'll have is soup. An end-of-week pot of whatever is on hand."

Sassanak grimaced disarmingly, his hand over his ribs. "Don't remind me of your mother's leftovers. I tolerated them when you added more spices." He lit another oil lamp. "That, and good company, saved the food."

Azazel waved the compliment aside, but his face relaxed. "I still wonder if Mother knew when we tinkered with her cooking. If she did, she never said anything. She did appreciate us helping her in the garden."

Sassanak laughed. "Maybe that was our penance." His smile dissolved into pensiveness. "Would that everything could be fixed so easily. The world is changing, Azazel. I am grateful you and I are of one mind about religion."

"We never disagreed on that. It's too important." Azazel rose. "But, as Head Magus, you are in the best position to champion the cause. I am but one in the ranks."

He clasped Azazel's arm. "My greatest supporter."

Azazel withdrew from the grip and moved to the doorway. "You walk a fine line every day between your beliefs and your priestly duties."

"I have prayed to Ahura Mazda about that. Those other religious services mean nothing to me," Sassanak said.

"Indeed. The job you fought so hard to get comes with certain ... paradoxes."

"I am not conflicted."

Chapter 21

Stocky but Sturdy

Four days later, the end of Nowruz

With great satisfaction, Akilah rubbed mud from his hands. *Sabzeh*, the ritual of planting sprouted grasses and bulbs by the river, marked the end of Nowruz and its celebration of new life. Sabzeh was a good sign. Now he could embark on his venture to find the prophesied new life.

As he headed to the stables, he reflected on his team, grateful for their complementary interests, talents, and experience. Tallis had been his calm, steady research and travel comrade for the past ten years. Rashidi was youthful, passionate, relentlessly thorough, and determined to prove himself despite his lack of field experience. Akilah wouldn't have gotten this far in his study without them. And the servants … He quickened his pace. Packing was a challenge to keep on schedule.

"Instrument cases go here. Clothing trunks over there. Food

New Star

supplies in that corner." From a distance, Akilah watched his most trusted personal servant, Hakeem, direct traffic.

This journey was really happening.

With precision, Hakeem crossed details off the list. "Where are the tents and rugs? The flints and tools? That crate is for the observatory. Leave that with me."

Under Hakeem's watchful eye, servants scurried to comply, placing each load with care in its designated spot. From there, everything would be divided and re-sorted. For that task, one side of the stables sat empty except for numbered signs, each corresponding with a pack camel.

Akilah trusted Hakeem to solve the enormous puzzle of packing. His head servant had a keen eye for envisioning how gear would be used and which supplies packed together easily. He would mentally divide loads among camels by the gear's poundage, shape, use, and the animals' constitution. Any misstep in this planning could be disastrous. An overly heavy burden could injure a camel, lengthen their travel time, or both.

Akilah waited until the swirling stream of servants dissipated.

"Excellent job so far, Hakeem."

"Master, are you sure the Magi should ride camels instead of Arabian stallions? The horses are excellent for endurance riding —faster and more comfortable. And, if I may be so bold, more indicative of your status."

"True, the horses are faster. But we need to get there the same time our gear does." Akilah smiled. "The camels are fine. And they'll be carrying the comforts of home."

Surveying the neatly stacked gear, he added, "That's the easy part."

Although Akilah said the words in jest, he knew the work that lay ahead. After weight allocations came test runs to hitch, load, and unload the camels. The servants had to execute their tasks flawlessly, safely, in minutes—for they would do it countless times during the trip.

"You're spreading our provisions among many camels?"

"As always, master."

"You have things well in hand, Hakeem. I'm heading to the observatory, so I'll take the crate." Akilah turned about the stable. "Where is the camel we bought a month ago?"

Hakeem pointed to two animal healers leading a shaggy, drab-tan, two-humped camel. "We checked him thoroughly. He seems healthy. He's stocky, sturdy, and young. Well suited for the long trip."

"As far as you can tell, is he ready to carry a full load?"

"Yes."

"Good." Akilah nodded. "Add the observatory crate when calculating his load."

"Yes, master." He scribbled notes. "In case you're interested, the former owner calls this camel Kani."

Chapter 22

Withdrawn

Akilah ran his hands over the camel's neck, then down his back and legs. "He seems of good constitution. But Kani? That sounds like a nickname."

"His full name is Kaniel, but he responds only to Kani. I can't say why," Hakeem said.

"Any territorial problems with the other camels?"

Hakeem shrugged. "The Arabians never seem to like having Bactrians around. You know how it is."

"Unfortunately, yes. Like some humans." Akilah muttered the sentiment under his breath. He hoped the long trip ahead would diminish those differences.

He dipped his hands into a wash basin to loosen the dirt from Sabzeh. The stubborn mud resisted. When he finished scrubbing, Hakeem was still lingering over Kani. "Something troubles you?"

Hakeem had an uncharacteristically distant look in his eyes. "Do you suppose camels understand anything other than commands ... and duty?"

Akilah grunted. "Some people don't even understand that.

But your dedication to duty has made you head over many servants. Duty does have its rewards."

Hakeem nodded curtly.

Akilah left the stables with a light heart. His path to Jerusalem finally seemed as clear as the spring sky.

Until a shadow crossed his path.

"Akilah, I have some news that you should hear from me first," Sassanak said. "Regrettably, your trip to Jerusalem is canceled. Its funding has been withdrawn."

The words yanked him to a stop as abruptly as a rider shanking a horse's reins. He flung his head back and bit his words to curb his anger. "No one can decide that without the Council convening an open meeting to vote."

"True. But, on occasion, for security reasons, a closed session may be called."

Feet planted wide, Akilah faced his superior. Only one person had that authority. Sassanak.

With difficulty, he bridled his tongue. "What do you mean by 'security reasons'?"

"It seems someone has been trying to sabotage your venture by disposing of Jewish texts that might have aided your efforts. We've launched a quiet, private investigation to right this wrong. We have no desire to besmirch anyone's reputation, but this is a serious matter and must be dealt with swiftly."

"Why should that affect the trip?"

"Magi don't pay the head tax or agricultural tax, so we must fund our investigations privately unless they become a matter of national concern. Protracted processes can become costly, so the funds for your trip have been diverted to those coffers. The supplies you have already purchased will go to our central stores. Rest assured, nothing will be wasted."

Sassanak handed Akilah a parchment emblazoned with his seal as Head Magus of the Lower Council. "You aren't under investigation, but you may be questioned. You understand. Protocol."

Akilah clenched the parchment until it buckled in his hand. "Respectfully, I do not."

Sassanak squared his body with Akilah's. "I know what you are thinking. You're right. I never approved of your star study. But I have done nothing to stand in its way, despite how unprincipled it was compared to your prior years of outstanding research. I'm sure you'll continue to make significant contributions with worthier projects in the future."

Chapter 23

For the Want of Money

Akilah watched Rashidi pace the room. "Defunded? That is so ... I don't even have a polite word for that." Waving the Council's notice in front of him, Rashidi muttered an expletive in Egyptian.

From his reclining couch, Akilah reached for Rashidi's sleeve. "Don't wear out my favorite rug." His clipped words belied his attempt at humor.

"Canceled?" Tallis sat rigid in his seat. "What can we do?"

Akilah rubbed his forehead. "If we had more time, we could solicit a private sponsor to fund the trip. But that would take months of negotiations to secure a contract. We're almost ready to leave. Letters have been sent. Schedules finalized. The commissioned workers expect final payment. All I can do is appeal to the treasury."

"How would that help? They already seized our funding." Tallis fumed.

"Maybe they'll listen to reason."

"Doubtful. All they care about is counting *tetradrachms*." Tallis rubbed his thumb against his fingers like a money-grubber.

Rashidi clapped his hands. "We could get an advance on our pensions. Pool our money."

"I'm the only one of us with enough years of service to do that," Akilah replied. "Even so, pensions are linked to taxes from annual grain yields. No one is allowed to use more than a year's worth of pension in one year's time. Ever. It wouldn't be nearly enough."

Tallis frowned. "We need a wealthy benefactor—a saoshyant. How can we find one on short notice?"

Rashidi heaved the Council's notice at Tallis. "Ha. We need more than that. We need a savior."

"Be practical, Rashidi." Tallis set the notice aside. "If someone outside of Magi society funded the trip, the Council couldn't stop it. It wouldn't be under their jurisdiction anymore."

"From the start, we straddled a line with this study," Akilah said. "The Council supports research largely to the extent that it will increase Persia's status in the world's eyes. In some ways, it's a miracle we have gotten this far."

"Then we need another miracle," Tallis said.

"Bureaucracy tires me." Akilah sighed. "We *must* go to Jerusalem. I just don't know how."

Tallis's hand strayed to the hilt of his favorite short dagger, almost hidden in his thick sash about his waist. "We must consider something else as well. If we pursue private funding, we won't have Magi protectors traveling with us."

Rashidi grabbed Akilah's sleeve. "We can't undertake such a long journey without them. And we don't have funds to pay for private protectors."

"A journey is many steps," Akilah said. "I will not let our efforts die because of a money issue."

Rashidi glared. "You are avoiding my question."

"You didn't pose a question. You voiced an opinion. One that offers no help for our present situation."

Rashidi let go of Akilah's sleeve. "Let's say we somehow get the funding. Then what?"

"Little by little, wool becomes a carpet. Not every detail must be settled at once." Impatience tinged Akilah's voice. "And, if we must, we will ... improvise." He waved the air.

"Improvise?" Rashidi turned to Tallis and shook his head.

Covering the room in six long strides, Akilah spun around in front of the door and drew himself up to his full height. "Gentlemen, what are your intentions? Are you still as committed to this as you were two seasons ago? We risked our reputations to study a star that defied understanding." He pounded his chest. "My heart burned when I read the prophecies about the birth of a divine child. Did yours? We accepted those prophecies as truth. And we did not make that leap of faith lightly."

He punched the air in the direction of the Great Hall's Gathering Circle. "If I had explained all *that* to the Council, they would have said the hand of an evil deity had touched my mind."

Every sinew in his body tensed as he measured his colleagues with his eyes. "Persians avoid oaths, as swearing one would make the words a religious matter. But I must ask you to come close to that. Are you still committed to seeing this to its end—whatever that may be? If you say yes, there's no turning back."

"Yes," Tallis said with finality.

Rashidi nodded.

"Good. Then we press on, no matter what lies ahead."

His colleagues' consensus uncorked the tension in Akilah's body. He sagged against the stand that held his orbitus. "I'm heading to the observatory. I think better there. Where is my lockbox?"

Tallis reached to a shelf behind him. "Here."

From habit, Akilah's fingers traced the lid's familiar outlines. In the doorway, he stopped.

"What?" Tallis rose from the reclining couch.

"Continue with our plans. Act as though nothing has happened. I'm going to Assur." Akilah nodded with decisiveness.

Tallis shot Akilah a guarded look. "Parthia's administrative capital? What—"

"Speak of this to no one until I return."

Tallis followed Akilah to the door. "Do *not* tell me you intend to appeal to the national treasury's comptroller. We would be barred from Magi society for such insubordination."

Akilah waved aside Tallis's concern. "I should be back in a day."

Chapter 24

Farzaneh

Assur

Akilah shifted his weight on the stone bench in the courtyard. Arched entries perfectly framed the lush garden surrounding him. Fig and pomegranate trees hovered over a carpet of pink, purple, and white Persian lilies. A central pool sparkled in the sunlight. His cousin had done a masterful job of turning this area into a little paradise. This setting was pleasant, but the sun warming Akilah's neck reminded him how long he had been sitting there.

Someone in attire resembling that of a head servant passed him, walking fast. Akilah stood and waved to catch his attention. "Kind sir, can you tell me when the *arashshara* will meet with me? I have urgent business with her that cannot wait."

The servant bowed. "Soon, my lord. Soon." He hurried through a side door.

Akilah had resisted announcing himself as Farzaneh's cousin. Given the time between past visits and the nature of this one, it seemed inappropriate to prevail upon family ties. This meeting was regarding business. But, after three hours of waiting, he questioned his choice. Perhaps she was truly as busy as he imagined a person of her status would be. Or perhaps she had seen Akilah and was forcing him to wait as punishment for his distant past actions.

After another half hour, the servant reappeared and ushered Akilah into a reception area, its two longer walls impeccably decorated with stucco motifs of urns and vines. A floor carpet spanning the room echoed the vine pattern. The pleasant surroundings didn't abate his rising impatience. "Please tell your master that her cousin still awaits her audience."

"She will see you soon," the servant said, as preoccupied as before. "We will prepare for your visit."

Akilah had pushed as far as he dared. He should have sent a messenger a day ahead of him to announce his coming, but there had been no time for that. He hoped his cousin would deem his visit more urgent than at least one of her scheduled appointments for today.

The servant reappeared and bade Akilah to follow him. They passed a banquet room and traversed a hallway almost as grand as those radiating from the Magi's Great Hall. When they passed outdoors again, the servant pointed toward a paved walkway and motioned upward.

Expansive private gardens spread before Akilah. He paused, savoring their sights and the cool breeze rustling through dense plantings of cypress and pine trees. Paved walkways meandered on either side of a waterfall, flanked by beautiful terracing. Farzaneh had expanded her gardens since he was last here. He didn't remember the waterfall or side paths with groves of olive, date, and mulberry trees. Akilah hastened up the left walkway.

When had he last visited his cousin? It was during Nowruz, but which year? Regrettably, his childhood memories of her were more numerous than his recent recollections. But they all faded at the sight of the stately woman seated on a bench under a pergola at the top of a hill, at the waterfall's prominence.

Her dress was immaculate, a turquoise silk outfit adorned with silver and gold embroidery. Such silk could come only from Cin, a costly purchase but befitting her stature in society. Most of her hair tumbled in loose waves across her shoulders, an odd counterpoint to the formality of her dress. An elaborate silver comb attached to a veil pulled some of her hair from her face, but the touch seemed unfinished. A light breeze lifted the edges of her veil, revealing more of her uniformly ebony tresses.

Akilah collected himself. Why would he search for signs of graying? His cousin was eight years his junior.

His throat went dry. "Peace and prosperity to you, Farzaneh."

She motioned to a seat adjacent to her and poured a hot drink. Akilah found it strange a servant did not attend to that task. He fumbled his words. "Are you well, cousin?"

Farzaneh sipped from her cup before responding. "Persia's postal relay system is unparalleled. Yet you arrive with no advance announcement. Your business must be most urgent."

"I ... heard your husband has been ill."

Farzaneh's face remained inscrutable, though her gaze never left his. "My husband is dying. There is no cure for his affliction."

Akilah's intentions couldn't have been more ill-timed or ill-advised. "I am most grieved to hear that." At a loss for what to say next, he gulped his rose petal tea. Maybe if the hot brew burned his throat, the heat would jolt his mind into more adept conversation.

During a seemingly interminable silence, Farzaneh seemed to test Akilah's words, appraising them as he imagined she would assess a parcel of land. Then she acknowledged his sentiment with a slight nod. She motioned to his cup. "If your tastes have changed, my servants can bring you something else.

An herbal infusion ... honeyed wine ... a cucumber-vinegar drink."

"No, this is fine. Excellent," Akilah said.

She unwrapped a cloth to reveal a short stack of honey almond cakes. Their sweet smell transported Akilah back to his childhood. He and his cousins ... everyone's grubby hands reaching for his grandmother's signature treat. He resisted the urge to grab one like he did when he was a spindly youth.

Farzaneh offered the snack again, as was Persian custom. Pleased to accept a cake, he smiled and nodded. But Farzaneh's next words shattered his fond memories. "Akilah, you know little of my present life or my husband. What compels you to travel here today?"

A trickle of sweat slid down his back. Although her question lacked daggered undertones, he may as well have been a lamb roasting on a spit. He had to admire his cousin's unruffled demeanor. He could imagine her bidding on land or arguing for water rights. And winning each time.

"I do want to hear about you. And your husband. But I also have a request. A rather unusual one. I deeply regret its timing." The cake grew sticky in Akilah's warm palm. He shoved the whole piece into his mouth.

Farzaneh pulled a wax writing tablet from a pouch at her feet. She poised her stylus over the wax, beautifully framed in ivory. "I am listening."

Akilah outlined his study, his team's findings, and why the trip to Jerusalem to consult with the priests was central to the study's success. He tilted his explanation toward the science of the star while underplaying his desire to find the eternal child-king. He discreetly omitted two details—the Council's threats and the time gap since he'd last seen the star.

Farzaneh listened intently, jotting notes and making calculations. "This sounds auspicious. Why would the Council not fund it?"

Akilah dusted invisible crumbs from his lap. "Persia is intent on funding only what it is reasonably sure will further its position as a world power. Young researchers are having difficulty getting established in Magi society because of that. I offered my allocation of funds for the Jerusalem trip to be redirected to them instead. I have not forgotten how people supported my early research efforts. I want to do the same."

Farzaneh's eyebrows arched. "Who in particular are you encouraging to become the next shining star?"

At the double entendre, he choked on his rose petal tea. Had his cousin wielded those words intentionally? He mumbled a fictitious name, praying she wouldn't ask for details.

Her eyes brightened, but not with a smile. "That is remarkable. Near the apex of your career, you are willing to lay it down for the sake others ... while still finding a way to satisfy your needs. By coming to me."

The words were not a compliment. Another rivulet of sweat snaked its way down Akilah's back. An uneasy silence followed.

"Your funding was reallocated, but not by your choice."

Farzaneh's powers of discernment sucked the wind from his lungs.

She tilted her head to one side and draped an arm over the bench's backrest. "Lies sprinkled with truth are more readily believed. You are unskilled at lying. I do not recommend further practice of it."

His face heated as if he was a contrite schoolboy. Suddenly, his needs seemed so selfish. Why should Farzaneh listen to them? She had no motivation to help him unless it benefited her.

Was her attentiveness laced with cunning? In that moment, he didn't care. He poured out the truth of the matter. His words tumbled over each other, racing like a raft on a swollen river, heedless of the dangers ahead. Only when he paused for a breath did he worry whether she might exploit his predicament.

Her expression remained stoic as she agreed to help him. "You are pressed for time. Let's finalize this arrangement with a simple contract." She wrote it the spot and penned a copy, which she handed to Akilah without hesitation. He marveled as he read it. Clearly, her years in land management had perfected that skill.

The sun's waning light reminded Akilah he had consumed much of her day. "Farzaneh, this is most generous. I ... words fail me." He shook his head in disbelief. "Thank you for helping me."

"I'm not doing it for you." A hint of sharpness edged her words. "I will help you—on one condition." She continued with complete composure. "A non-negotiable requirement." She pulled a single half-sheet document from the pouch at her feet and held it out to him.

A *stūrīh*? Akilah cringed. He had to sign *that* to receive her money and resources?

Oh, she was clever.

The stūrīh described a form of custodianship, an agreement to safeguard and cohabitate with Farzaneh. Not exactly marriage, unless the couple desired more than what the arrangement required. The verbiage was standard for such a contract. But it was more than a legal document. Stūrīh was a religious obligation.

Religious obligation.

That's where she had him. Akilah gritted his teeth. Farzaneh knew his priestly responsibilities with the Lower Council would compel him—no, bind him—to sign. He'd be shamed, if not cut off, from Magi society if he didn't fulfill all his religious obligations, including this. But a stūrīh could end his career as he knew it. What choice did he have?

Why did his cousin insist on this? Was she exacting revenge for what happened thirty years ago? Or, less likely, did she need companionship or protection? If protection, from what?

Farzaneh snapped her wax writing tablet shut, interrupting Akilah's thoughts. "Surely you understand what this is."

He straightened his spine. She had made a calculated move. A business transaction she must have planned months ago. She had no way of knowing he would come today.

Akilah bristled. She had made him an acquisition—like another plot of land. Why? Despite his rising anger, something nudged him to think beyond himself. Farzaneh couldn't execute a stūrīh on her own. For such an authorization, her husband first had to grant her the freedom to be her own guardian. How long ago had that happened? When he first became ill? Akilah's self-directed questions dissipated much of his anger but little of his fear of the arrangement's consequences.

A new thought struck him. Did she fear something enough to ensure protection for herself? "Farzaneh, are you in danger?"

She smiled unevenly, the corners of her mouth weighted with a heaviness that kept them from wholly turning upward. "Is anyone ever truly free from danger?"

"If a tenant or vendor is harassing you—"

"Stop." She held up her hand. "Anyone who lives with passion of conviction is in danger. Like you, Akilah. People with less conviction challenge, even detest those who stand on the firmness of their beliefs. That is why you are here. The Head Magus believes in your study less than you do, so he has found a way to withdraw your funding. I can respect that."

She rose. "It's late. I must attend to my household. Sign both copies of each document, and I'll do the same." She handed him her quill and silver inkwell.

Chapter 25

Help from Assur

The next day

Akilah slid behind a column in the Great Hall of Audiences and stared across the Gathering Circle. He smoothed his Magi robes, a tangible reminder of what they and the Circle embodied—the Magi's unique contributions within their societal unity. All robes of the Lower Council resembled but did not mirror the Circle's tiled design. Each element was present in everyone's robes, but the embroidery differed—acknowledging one's individuality. The circles woven into the robes echoed the Gathering Circle's missive to seek unity with each other for greater community and to progress toward unity with the Supreme Being of their official religion.

Surely Sassanak would emerge from a meeting soon. When he skirted the Circle, Akilah could intercept him. His superior would know his business intentions as soon as he saw Akilah's formal attire, but that mattered little. All he needed was enough time to obtain a signature.

Soon Sassanak's voice carried across the hall. Careful to circumvent the Gathering Circle's hallowed borders, Akilah reached his superior in fifteen long strides. "Head Magus, a word with you privately, please."

At his superior's lack of comment, Akilah cut in front of him. Holding a scroll at arm's length, he bowed, slightly winded from the counterpoint his pounding heart played against his racing thoughts.

The Head Magus glowered at the scroll in Akilah's outstretched hand. "That's not a royal or administrative seal. Whose seal is it?"

"A sponsor's."

"Five minutes. In my office."

Amazement, then anger, filled Sassanak's face as he read the scroll. "Your orphaned cousin is sponsoring you. How lucky for you to find a saoshyant. To offer herself as a benefactor must mean she's doing very well with the business your mother bequeathed her."

"My cousin owns many lands and oversees many people," Akilah replied. "She is an *arashshara*." He immediately regretted his defiant admission.

Sassanak jerked ramrod straight as if someone had thrust a hot poker up the back of his tunic. "So ... now she's so skilled and high-ranking that she is considered a 'great chief'?" He white-knuckled the arms of his ebony chair but just as quickly relaxed his grip and eased into a slouch.

"An intriguing, if not slightly outspoken, lady. Women owning land. A law almost unique to Persians. She is fortunate to have a husband who condones her ways."

Akilah rankled at Sassanak's patronizing tone. *Show enough courtesy to speak her name. Even if it doesn't suit you.*

Sassanak pressed his back into his chair and folded his hands. "Such a tragedy to hear her second marriage will end in sorrow. As did her first."

New Star

The words pierced Akilah as surely as an obsidian arrow. How could Sassanak know such a detail? What business did he have with Farzaneh's affairs? How could he be aware of her husband's grave condition but not her community status?

For an instant, a smirk twisted one corner of Sassanak's lips.

Long ago, the Head Magus had perfected the sport of using people's fear or anger to off-balance them. In that vulnerable state, they would surrender information they otherwise would never divulge. Akilah ran his clammy palms down his robe on the pretense of smoothing its folds. The pressure crinkled the half-sheet papyrus in his pocket. He silently swore. He should have emptied his pockets before this meeting. All could come undone if Sassanak discovered what that papyrus said.

But the Head Magus seemed consumed with other thoughts. He pushed aside the contractual scroll and exhaled deeply. "Well, it appears you have your cousin's blessing and a loan of considerable resources, including some protectors. A prudent, commendable measure—although they could never equal the expertise of the *cataphracts* assigned to the Magi. And the entourage will certainly be smaller than what representatives of Magi society ... deserve." He cleared his throat. "Your little expedition will launch after all."

"Head Magus, if you will sign and date the scroll to confirm the trip is now funded privately, I will leave you to the remainder of your day."

"According to tradition and this agreement, you must start the trip from Assur," Sassanak said. "That could set your schedule back a bit."

"We will manage."

"A clause in this sponsorship states that, to not overburden our facility, you will utilize only one-fourth of the Magi resources you intended to take. Servants, camels, supplies. Unusual. Even magnanimous. As is your willingness to withdraw a year's pension early. Your commitment—or convictions—regarding this venture are admirable, if not misplaced."

"Your signature, please?"

Sassanak grudgingly reached for his quill.

Five minutes later

Azazel slid into Sassanak's office. "Any news about Fakhri?"

"I can't say how he fell ill, but I may know what caused it. Unfortunately, no one has any idea how to cure him," Sassanak said.

"You'll figure it out. You always do. Your past never really leaves you."

He knew Azazel better than to accept those words as an unqualified compliment. "I suppose you overheard my conversation with Akilah."

"Enough of it. How could you approve such a transaction?"

Sassanak shrugged. "It was legally binding. Besides, we stand to gain more by letting them go. They will never reach Jerusalem."

"How do you know?"

"They'll be traveling without Magi protectors." A half-smile played about the corners of his mouth.

Azazel stepped back. "You wouldn't."

"Any journey of that length is perilous. Floods ... nomads ... mercenaries ... Perhaps crossing paths with some people you know?" He tidied his desk while stealing a sideways glance at Azazel.

"On our friendship, I vowed to help you discredit Akilah. Not kill him."

New Star

Sassanak stood and glided around his desk. "Still your thoughts. I suggested nothing."

"Save your smooth words for someone else." Azazel seized Sassanak's shoulders. "Your years as Head Magus have made you a master in the art of evasion. Your tongue never ceases to find new ways around Persia's stricture against lying and oath-taking." He fisted his hand close to Sassanak's face. "Dismiss your dishonorable thoughts at once and cover yourself tonight with extra prayers."

Sassanak drew Azazel's arm down to his side. "Life is prayer in action."

Azazel cast a withering look over his shoulder as he stormed from the office and slammed the door.

Sassanak returned to his desk but kept his eyes on the door. "I've always been better than you at making hard decisions. That is why I'm Head Magus. Akilah will see Jerusalem from a distance. But he'll never reach it."

✡ ✡ ✡

Three days later

A sweaty man from the postal relay system raced into Sassanak's office and dropped a mail pouch on his desk.

"Close the door."

The man scurried to comply.

Sassanak rifled through the pouch's contents. Only administrative notices. "Is this all? For your sake, I trust you have more."

"Yes, Head Magus."

"Go on."

"The lady in Assur that you've had me watch … I believe she

is no longer with a spouse. In the marketplace, I heard rumors of his demise. It seems her servants are under pressure to keep the matter quiet."

"Are they now?" Sassanak flashed a smile and tossed a small, tinkling pouch toward the postal carrier. "Well done."

Chapter 26

Snake in the Grass

The next day, in Assur

"Master, you have a visitor."

Farzaneh didn't move from the comfort of her couch in her darkened sitting room. "Give them my regrets and inform them that I am not receiving visitors."

"Many pardons, master. Someone from the Council is here for you."

She rose mechanically and drew the curtains aside. When she turned toward the door to greet her guest, her eyes widened. He was the last person she wanted to see.

Sassanak bowed before her. "Your beauty is veiled in mourning. I have come at the most unfortunate time. My deepest apologies. I did not know. If I had sent word ahead to schedule a visit, I would have avoided this awkwardness that adds to your sorrow."

Either fatigue or anger loosened her tongue. "Head Magus, you are in your official robes. If you did not plan to visit me, then you surely planned to visit Assur." She swallowed to avoid saying more. Her thoughts must not travel past her lips. *Only* your official attire got you past my servants. Otherwise, they would not have let you enter unless I allowed it.

"You are as wise as you are comely. Yes, Assur is one of my stops on my routine rounds to visit Magi in this jurisdiction."

Farzaneh steadied herself on the arm of the nearest chair. Her painful childhood had taught her to distrust Sassanak. Time had not subdued that memory—it had heightened her wariness. Even if he had not yet met with the local Magi, Sassanak would soon learn she had not called upon them to perform final rites for her husband.

"You understand that I must attend to many matters. Regrettably, I have no more time for visitation today. Thank you for coming."

He ambled toward her, his hand scooping air toward his nostrils. "You are burning frankincense and sandalwood … a Zoroastrian practice to cleanse a home after a death. Yet I smelled meat roasting in your cook's outbuilding. Zoroastrian law forbids eating meat for a week after a death." His voice dropped. "Farzaneh, where is your husband?"

Still gripping the chair for support, she met Sassanak's gaze. "Dead. You paid your respects. You may leave."

"You called no professional corpse-bearers. Your husband's body is not in the Tower of Silence, is it?" He clicked his tongue at her stolid gaze. "It seems you have strayed from the laws of our religion—the one Good Religion. Those laws protect us from spiritual and physical corruption."

Farzaneh's stomach heaved. A plume of bile rose in her throat. How dare he turn her mourning into a weapon against her?

Her disdain for him eclipsed her fear of what his power could do to her. She moved half a dozen paces away. Fingering a colorful bouquet of flowers on a side table, she said, "Persia acknowledges many religions while honoring its official religion. Surely the Head Magus would uphold no less than that. To do so would dishonor our government's great wisdom."

The corners of his mouth curled. "So, your husband wasn't a Zoroastrian? How clever of you to hide it. My concern for you is deeper than it was even a moment ago. But you must know I have always been concerned for you. Let me help you."

Farzaneh's throat constricted. "I do not need any help. Thank you."

Sassanak closed the space between them. "Think of what we could do together. Magi society owns vast lands. So do you. If we combined my position with your land management skills, we could—"

"Good day to you. Leave now."

His face darkened. "You *need* but have no real protection. I can give that to you." His eyes narrowed to slits. "Consider this: even as we speak, the Council is reviewing a proposal to build a Fortress of Oblivion for those who require ... spiritual redirection. It has the magistrates' full support."

Fear threatened to overwhelm her. But Akilah's father had taught her to cloak her emotions, especially fear, when transacting business. Despite her thundering heart and shallow breathing, she needed to stand on her own, as she had many times before. She dismissed the notion of showing the stūrīh she had forced Akilah to sign. She refused to give Sassanak reason to know the contract existed, let alone an opportunity to search for a loophole in it. He could twist the spirit of the law when the letter of the law didn't serve his purposes.

She rang a bell to summon her head servant. "Leave, or I will have you forcibly removed."

"Be very careful, Farzaneh. You are in great danger."

With a deep bow, Sassanak followed the servant from the room.

Only when Javad confirmed that Sassanak had left town did Farzaneh dare leave the house. She fled to her private garden, past the babbling waterfall, to the pergola at the crest of the hill, now wrapped in sundown orange and indigo. She collapsed on the bench where she and Akilah had met less than a week ago.

"My husband," she whispered. "It was easier to be a God-fearer when you were still here. We hid that truth so we could live in peace with others. You said peace might not always be possible, but Adonai would always be my protector. Will I ever know true peace or protection?"

If Sassanak knew the whole truth of who she was and what she had done, he would surely arrest her. The stūrīh might not be enough to protect her. Would Akilah, with his openness to many religions but unwillingness to partner in her agreement, understand her reasons for the stūrīh when she fully revealed them to him?

Her shoulders shook. She lifted her tear-streaked face and spoke to the darkened sky. "When Akilah came to me for help, I thought my assistance would let me be a silent partner in something that would pay tribute to my husband's belief in the one true God. Something wonderful beyond the world's expectations. Perhaps, more than anything, I had hoped it would bolster my flimsy faith as a God-fearer. What have I gotten myself into?"

She lapsed into silence, straining for an answer. But the only reply was the joyful tempo of tumbling water. Like the waterfall, her life seemed swept into a current she couldn't swim against —only follow to its end.

Farzaneh squared her shoulders. No matter what happened next, no one could know what was under her feet. The gardens and manmade waterfall were designed to keep its secret forever. Hidden in the bowels of the hill was her husband's tomb. A Jewish tomb. The antithesis of Zoroastrian practice.

Chapter 27

Poisonous Intent

The next day

Sassanak carved a serpentine path around overflowing baskets of scrolls in Burhan's disordered office. "Part of the cataloging transition, I presume?"

"Yes, Head Magus. Please pardon the mess." Burhan's bow was little more than a bob as he steadied a stack of codices by his elbow.

"An exciting time for you. Congratulations again."

Burhan beamed and bobbed again. "Thank you. Thank you."

"Oh, I almost forgot. The research scrolls I borrowed. A little late. Time escaped me." Sassanak thrust three scrolls into Burhan's arms. "Well, I must go."

But he paused halfway out the door. "Ever heard of Antiochus IV Epiphanes?" he said in an offhanded tone. "Messy business trying to exterminate Jerusalem's Jews."

A scroll slipped from Burhan's hand. In his bid to catch it, the tie opened. Its contents billowed to the floor, unrolling before Sassanak.

"Antiochus called himself God Manifest. Quite the title for

a man to assume. Of course, the Jews had a much different name for him. An interesting read. I'm sure you can find it in the west tower ... unless your cataloging reorganization required moving the library's collection of ancient Jewish writings."

Shaking, Burhan dropped another scroll while fussily trying to roll up the first.

"Here, let me help you." Sassanak bent and picked up a scroll. "Oh, look. An analysis of Zurvanism versus Zoroastrianism. What's your opinion on that?"

"I-I just catalog the Magi's research. It's not my place to say." Burhan snaked his neck as if recoiling from icy water poured down his tunic. Scrunching his face didn't quell his eye twitches. His hands shook as he dropped all three scrolls into a basket.

Sassanak caught Burhan by the arm. "But surely you have your own thoughts on the subject. Come now, don't be modest. We're alone and you can speak your mind—as one Zoroastrian purist to another."

Burhan's face flushed, but he spoke with uncharacteristic self-assuredness. "Zurvanites are heretics that should be eliminated because they insist on interpreting Zoroastrian writings in their own way." He fisted his hands and exhaled forcibly.

An emboldened response. Exactly what Sassanak had hoped to hear. He glided his hand down Burhan's arm to his fist. "Like you eliminated some Jewish writings?"

Sweat beaded on Burhan's brow.

"How did you do it?" Sassanak lowered his voice and circled Burhan like a wolf stalking a wounded fox. "Burn them?"

"I did only what I was told."

"So, you *did* burn them. How resourceful. Tidy, though hardly original. Who ordered you?"

"I-I can't say."

"You can, and you will. Or we can start talking about how you poisoned Fakhri."

Burhan's twisted body crumpled. "Poisoned? N-No, I'd never do that."

"Then who?"

"I don't know."

"Of course you do. Think hard. Because the evidence against you is strong. You took him dinner many times. Spent countless hours with him. Ingratiated yourself to him to gain his trust."

"No ..." Burhan inched toward the door.

Sassanak grabbed Burhan by his rounded, uneven shoulders and spun him into his desk. "You tempted him with his favorites, didn't you? He'd be more likely to eat them despite how poorly he felt. It was so easy to slip something into his food."

Burhan gasped. "I'd ne-never do that."

"Of course you would. To divert suspicion from your other dealings."

"No!" Flailing with uncontrollable nervousness, Burhan knocked a pot off the shelf. With a splat, globs of red pigment mottled the research scrolls Sassanak had returned.

"Fakhri knew what you were doing, didn't he? But he couldn't report it if he were dead. How convenient. There's just one problem. He isn't dying fast enough."

Burhan's face turned ashen. "Fakhri doesn't approve of other religions, but he would never condone violence against them."

"But you do. You already have. Who knows how far you'll go?"

Terror filled Burhan's face. "Please don't do this. I have no family. No other means of support."

Sassanak hovered over the quaking Ordeal. Time to go for the kill. "This isn't going well for you, Burhan. If you don't help me, I can't help you." Sassanak's iron stare kept Burhan pinned to his spot.

He thrashed against his desk, his eyes wild with fear. He glanced in vain toward his only exit route, but Sassanak remained planted between the doorway and him.

Burhan's face contorted as if to squeeze memories from his mind. In a barely audible, trembling voice, he said, "I-I'm not the only one who took Fakhri his food."

"Who else?" Sassanak's thunderous words drove Burhan to the floor, writhing.

"Azazel. Maybe others."

Sassanak took a half step back. Momentarily off balance at the name, his movement afforded Burhan enough space to shrink into his seat.

"But if Fakhri's food had been poisoned, Azazel would have gotten sick too." Burhan whimpered, his left eye twitching.

"Why?" Sassanak's question cut the air like a knife.

"I saw Azazel taste Fakhri's rivas stew right before the cook's helper took it to him."

"What else?"

"Sometimes when I'd sit with Fakhri, he'd talk about food. But I couldn't tell whether he was remembering the past or talking about the present. All I know is Azazel wanted to make sure Fakhri had the best of everything. Rivas stew, hawthorn leaf salad, wine from Herat." Burhan sniffled. "I heard Azazel tell the head cook that's the least he could do for Fakhri."

Sassanak studied the cringing figure before him. "You want to make all this go away, Burhan?"

His body heaving, the Orderal bobbed his head.

"Actually, I think we can … in a way that might also give you another shot at Magi status." He measured his words in full Head Magus fashion. "'Third time pays for all,' as they say."

Burhan rocked his rigid body. "How?"

Hiding a smirk, he patted Burhan's knee. "It's simple, really. First, keep this little incident about burning scrolls between you and me. It'll remain our secret *if* you stop destroying them."

New Star

Burhan looked up, stunned.

"Second, your Magi candidacy thesis. Very important." Sassanak's hands skimmed the pigment-splattered scrolls near him. "You weren't born into Magi society, so it's harder for you to break into it. You've applied twice already, yes? This time, your thesis needs to be exceptional. Timely and relevant. Well-researched and passionate."

He whirled around and held up a finger stained with red pigment. "How about the effects of outside influences on national religion? That suits your passions. As a starting point, may I suggest Alexander's persecution of the Zoroastrians and the Magi three hundred thirty years ago? And look into Antiochus's tactics one hundred fifty years ago. In both cases, you'll find deleterious effects and failed efforts. Good arguments for maintaining the purity of a national religion, don't you think?"

Burhan stared, slack-jawed.

"I'm sure you can find other historical examples to round out your view." Sassanak waved vaguely toward the west. "You could even go all the way back to Abraham and his opposition of Nimrod's fire worship."

He flicked his fingers. "That ancient history is rather murky. But it should be in the west tower—unless overzealous spring cleaning swept it away."

Burhan fidgeted, his hand twisting the edge of his worn, ink-stained sleeve.

"The most important thing is to demonstrate the necessity and unifying strength of a pure national religion," Sassanak continued. "Bring your work directly to me. But don't delay." He rapped his knuckles on Burhan's desk. "Finish it in less than a month, and I'll push for its review at the next Council meeting."

He grazed Burhan's cheek, leaving a streak of red pigment. "Think of your writing in a broader view. It might prevent history from repeating itself. That is a noble cause, yes?"

"Yes," Burhan whispered.

Chapter 28

Prepare Your Heart

"Akilah, may we enter?"

"Yes, of course." Akilah beckoned Tallis and Rashidi inside his quarters. "My apologies. I'm better at expedition planning than personal packing."

Tallis and Rashidi picked their way past open trunks and disorderly stacks of clothes, equipment, and scrolls.

Akilah paced, his hands clasped behind his back.

Tallis leaned toward Rashidi. "Here it comes." His mouth twitched with something between a grimace and a smile.

"What?"

"Just wait."

"My friends, our preparations are almost complete. We have worked hard to see this day come. But we must prepare for one more thing." Akilah paused, his brow knit in concentration. "Change."

Rashidi beamed like he was enjoying the world's most sumptuous banquet. "The highest aspiration of any Magi study is to pursue truth that can change the world. I am honored to be part of it."

Akilah fingered his Magi robes, draped over the lid of an

open trunk. If only touching the cloth could summon the words he sought. "Yes, truth can remodel many things. It also can change *us*. We need to prepare ourselves for that."

Rashidi frowned. "How?"

"By keeping an open mind. Discovery often changes one's perception of truth."

Rashidi shrugged. "As you say, 'We don't assume, we learn. We don't judge, we seek to understand.' Many discoveries have changed truth as we know it. All Magi studies seek to find and report truth."

Akilah raised his index finger. "We report *facts*. Facts become truth after people confirm them. Then others choose whether to accept the facts as truth."

He resumed pacing. "That's the paradox. Truth requires facts *and* faith. A personal reckoning, if you will. The question is what we will do with what we learn. Do we embrace it as a new truth?" Akilah looked away. "I feel the burden of those questions more with this expedition than any I've ever undertaken."

Noting Rashidi's quizzical look, Akilah said, "Let me put it another way. Do some truths never change?"

Rashidi shrugged. "Our religion won't change."

"We'd like to think so," Akilah replied. "But what if another empire conquered Parthia, outlawed our religion, and demanded we worship their gods?"

"That doesn't change the truth of our religion. It only makes it harder to practice." Rashidi bristled. "We're investigating a claim in the Hebrews' religion. The assertions in their writings don't make their claims objectively true. And examining them doesn't obligate us to embrace their beliefs."

Akilah pursed his lips. There were no limits to what Rashidi could achieve if he embraced his potential as an engineer as zealously as his penchant for philosophy and religion.

"No, it doesn't," Akilah said. "But we wouldn't have come

this far or risked this much unless we had more than an academic commitment to this undertaking. We believed in a star that didn't move across the sky. We believed what the Hebrew texts said."

He halted his pacing. "Our convictions point to one thing—we are trying to find the Divine contained in a person. If we find what we seek and it is true, it will be unprecedented—a new truth that could bend every norm we've subscribed to all our lives. The question is, what we will do with it."

Rashidi rolled his eyes. "Every religion espouses some version of a supreme being—or beings. Or many gods, each with different attributes."

Akilah nodded. "Does that make religion culturally relative? In fact, has anyone actually seen a god?"

Rashidi's body grew taut as a bow loaded with a nocked arrow. "Akilah, if people outside this room heard your words, they'd charge you with blasphemy." His words flew with an archer's precision.

"Then it is my good fortune to speak with you in private." Akilah plunged ahead with abandon. "We are doing more than finding a person. We are finding *truth*—about the One whom the Hebrews believe is the only true God. The God who doesn't change. Who can say they've seen an unchanging truth?"

"Akilah, you go too far." Rashidi's words smoked with heat. "Superlative truth does not exist. You said as much yourself—"

"What truly never changes?"

Rashidi shrugged. "Night always follows day."

"But a total eclipse turns day into night."

Rashidi turned to Tallis. "Is he always this way before a trip?"

Tallis shushed his young colleague. "Temper your tongue."

"Don't you see?" Akilah's voice rose. "What if this child embodies a new truth—perhaps an immutable truth? Does that not awe you? Have we been entrusted with some grand task beyond understanding? If so, why us?"

Rashidi rolled his neck in a circle as if tossing the idea around in his brain. Tallis seemed glued to the floor.

"My earliest memory of my grandfather was the wide armband he always wore ... here." Akilah clutched his right arm halfway between his shoulder and elbow. "It was a silver piece with a large, rectangular, red-orange carnelian set in it. The stone was inscribed with 'truth always.'" He smoothed his robes again. "This journey seems to have a higher purpose than investigating the veracity of some religious writings. It's hard for me to put into words." He turned away from his colleagues.

The whirlwind in his mind refused to slow long enough for him to sort his thoughts further. The Danyal stories, the Isaiah text, the Balaam prophecy, the star. All consumed his heart with a blazing desire. This trip could be his career's finest moment. But he had passed the point of wanting to go to Jerusalem for the recognition it would gain him. He *had* to go—regardless of what awaited him.

Akilah spun on his heel. "That is all I have to say on the matter." With uncharacteristic curtness, he gestured toward the door.

Rashidi opened his mouth to protest, but Tallis steered him from the room. "Talk's over," Tallis whispered. "Do with it what you will."

✡ ✡ ✡

Akilah waited at least ten minutes after his colleagues left before he circled to an obscure corner of his meditation room and snatched a cat figure from a shelf of curios. The wooden carving was crude, the proportions distorted, the gray stain made from ash. Instead of the tail coiling about the cat's feet, it oddly spanned the entire length of its body, arching over the cocked head. Rudimentary paws snugged into a tightly fitted base. Akilah had bought it years ago from a trinket dealer. The itinerant tradesman had no idea he possessed an important Egyptian artifact.

He pulled the figure from its base and flipped the hinge hidden in its paws. He reached two fingers inside its hollowed interior, the perfect hiding place for what he didn't want anyone to see—the second contract from his cousin, Farzaneh. The stūrīh. His hands shook as he re-read the crumpled half-sheet.

Thirty years ago, he had avoided this kind of entanglement. Back then, orphaned Farzaneh was eleven and under the guardianship of Akilah's father, a newly minted Megistane and rising star in Magi society. Farzaneh had been of marriageable age for two years, and Sassanak had set his sights on her. However, an authorized marriage required the couple's consent as well as the guardian's sanction. Akilah didn't know his father's reasons for his swift action against Sassanak, only the results of it.

Persian law required girls nine to twelve years of age be allowed suitors. Akilah's father had tapped Akilah, expecting him to agree to *pādixšāyīhā* with Farzaneh. It would have been a temporary marital arrangement, not unusual in Persian society for women in her position. But Akilah was nearing twenty and singularly intent on becoming a member of Magi society's Lower Council. He refused to entertain any notion of marriage —even a provisional one for a limited, mutually agreed period. It was a distraction to his career. No. A hindrance.

He covered his face. If only he could block the memories of his father's fury and his family's shame. Through his father's maneuvering, Farzaneh was wed to a distant relative. But the event opened a rift between Akilah and his parents. One that widened when Akilah's Magi aspirations with the Lower Council ran counter to his father's career path with the Upper

Council. His mother still supported Akilah's dreams but lavished her time and attention upon Farzaneh.

Feeling orphaned by his parents' distance drove Akilah to excel. He attained early acceptance in the Lower Council, distinguishing himself as its youngest inductee to date. Yet that did not erase the family's shame. He was ignored as if he were dead. His father would not speak to him. When his mother died a year later, she left all her possessions, including land holdings, to Farzaneh. Whether from grief, duty, or honor, Akilah's father immersed himself in coaching his niece to succeed in business.

Akilah's misgivings about marriage seemed justified when he was chosen over married Magi for projects that required extended absences from Persia. Those deeply satisfying ventures had earned him early recognition in astronomy. Magi society was the only home he needed. He thrived while making a name for himself there. In those days, Sassanak had supported Akilah's aspirations and encouraged his travels.

As a land manager, Farzaneh succeeded beyond everyone's expectations. But her first marriage ended tragically when her husband died in an accident during a storm. She hastily remarried a man fourteen years her senior—who now lay gravely ill in Assur.

Akilah's visit to Farzaneh had unsettled him. She showed no undue signs of weariness from her husband's illness. She was the consummate businessperson in discussing her role as saoshyant for Akilah's trip. Was she truly that composed—or cold—in every matter of her life? Then again, why had she insisted on the stūrīh? Why would one so accomplished and self-sufficient need it?

By definition, the stūrīh had stipulations Akilah didn't even want to think about. He slumped into a chair. The document slid to the floor as exquisite pain surged through him. His chest heaved. Tears meant for his eyes flooded his heart. Was his choice thirty years ago a grave mistake borne from his stubborn single-mindedness? And what of his recent rejection of the Megistane promotion? Maybe his father was right. Idealism was a luxury he couldn't afford.

Were Akilah's lofty ideals and his relentless pursuit of this star largely fueled by rationalization or pride? Perhaps his choices had cost him all too dearly. Especially the price his cousin required him to pay now.

Discovery often did change one's perception of truth.

Chapter 29

Adiabene

Farzaneh settled onto the bench near the waterfall. She dreaded returning to this spot, but Hadi had come with her to bolster her courage.

"You are my shield and protector, Hadi." She whispered to the muscular dog at her feet. The cream-and-tan Sarabi, a magnificent Persian mastiff almost twice Farzaneh's weight, swung his massive head into her lap. "But I must leave you for a while." She stroked Hadi's head. "Guard the household well. That includes Javad. You and he are in charge while I'm gone. Do we have an agreement?"

The Sarabi shot a baleful look at her.

She chuckled softly. "You know what I mean. Don't let any intruders in. You can tell whose presence isn't wanted."

"Many pardons, master." Javad approached with a drink tray and warily eyed the Sarabi. The two had a tenuous relationship, but today the huge dog simply yawned in his direction.

Farzaneh held out her hands to accept the cool drink.

Javad inched within range and bowed. "It is a good day to enjoy the waterfall, as well as sir's favorite *sharbat*. I am pleased to see you drink it again. I extracted the seeds for it myself."

"Thank you." She sipped the fruit-and-herb drink reported to strengthen the constitution. If only she could bottle strength. She would have to find it somehow. Otherwise, she knew not how to navigate her newly imperiled life. She inhaled to fill her words with as much strength and confidence as she could muster.

"I have some tasks for you ... Mekonnen."

Javad stood straighter, his eyes glowing like embers. His reddish-tan skin turned a shade darker than usual. "You have not uttered that word in many years."

"Mekonnen" was Javad's native name, the only thing he still possessed of his homeland deep in Africa. A land he hadn't seen since he was a teenager. Farzaneh's first husband had purchased the teen from a slaver's auction block on impulse. She couldn't forget the *titulus* around the boy's neck—a plaque summarizing what some slave trader deemed pertinent for attracting a buyer. The oddity of Javad's homeland was one of many flights of fancy that her first husband had soon tired of. Frustrated at the boy's inability to communicate in Persian, he told Farzaneh she could do whatever she pleased with the slave.

Under her clandestine tutelage, Javad learned to read and write Persian. Although she wanted to keep Javad's Kushite name and culture alive, her husband had forbidden it, among many other things. As Javad's skills grew, so did difficulties with Farzaneh's first marriage. Javad's native name, Mekonnen, became a private code—Farzaneh's signal to Javad for help whenever she couldn't say aloud what she feared someone in the household might hear, report, or use against her. As she gained more independence and skills in land management, "Mekonnen" became her secret signal for Javad to execute tasks that required the utmost privacy and care, particularly carrying messages of business transactions when she was not allowed to travel. Javad had rewarded her trust in him with unfailing loyalty. In return, she eventually freed him from slavery and promoted him to the household's head servant.

"Master, I will do whatever you ask of me."

"I need to travel north to settle some of my husband's final affairs. I will leave soon, traveling light." She squared her gaze with his.

"If visitors ask why you are gone, what shall I tell them?"

"Only that I am fulfilling my husband's final wishes to the people he designated." She regretted not being more forthcoming but tried to reassure Javad. "If pressed, you may say that my husband's final request was for me to transact some out-of-town personal business for him." Seeing her servant's doubtful look, she added, "Don't worry about how long I will be away. At present, I cannot say." She withdrew a small scroll from a pocket in her sash. "That is why I have executed this. It gives you authority to conduct business on my behalf—except to buy or sell land. No one will be able to force a change of hands for any of my property while I am gone. The legal details are in this scroll."

Javad stepped back, shaking his head.

"You have run my household for years. Now, my business is in your capable hands until I return. To that end, I am promoting you to head steward of my entire estate."

"But master, I do not—"

"You know more than you realize. You'll be fine."

"What of your cousin Akilah and his caravan?"

"When he deigns to arrive, give him all the supplies and servants he and I agreed to. He should have that contract with him. If he forgets, my copy is in my silver lockbox with the stars on the lid. I hid the key where you can find it."

Farzaneh bent to pet her mastiff. "Keep Hadi with you at all times. Inspect the grounds and the qanat every day. The walks will do both of you good. Hadi will protect you. And take him with you when you go into the heart of the city to conduct business on my behalf."

Javad's face clouded. "Master, are you in danger?"

She rose from her seat. "Sometimes convictions can be our biggest peril." Her tone brightened. "If anyone from the Council questions you about me or my husband, rest in the fact that you cannot comment on what you do not know." She smiled. "And I forbid you from speculating."

"May your trip be productive." Javad's countenance sagged, but he kept his tone light. "May it bestow you with peace. And may the unexpected be a happy discovery." He bowed deeply and turned to leave.

Farzaneh knew he suspected she had more motives for her trip than she'd voiced. But, for his safety, she couldn't share them—not until she got some answers. Who were those God-fearers in Adiabene, and what about them had changed Ihsan? She had so many questions. But none that could be asked in Persia. She would not do anything to endanger her household.

"One final task." Farzaneh's volume dropped to a whisper, even though no one was nearby. "I sorted through the leather trunk that sits in the corner of my bedroom near the window. All that remains inside the trunk needs to be burned. Today, Mekonnen."

Chapter 30

Redistributing the Wealth

Later that day

Akilah fumed on his walk to the stables. Creating a severely pared checklist was enough of a chore. But his most urgent task was to squelch the servants' speculations. He didn't blame them. Who in their right mind would cut three-fourths of their staff during the final weeks of preparing for such a lengthy trip?

Before he addressed the servants, he had to talk with Hakeem. "Any questions about the revised plans?"

"No, master," he replied. "I'll prepare a smaller caravan. An escort from Assur will meet me beyond the Magi complex."

"Mix the crate from the observatory with mundane supplies, such as my tent and rugs," Akilah instructed. "And my instruments, if that's not too much."

"Kani would be good for that. He can carry a heavier load."

"Excellent. Pick the sturdiest camels from the ones we intended to use. We're allowed only one-fourth of what we had planned to bring. Tallis, Rashidi, and I will follow on horseback as soon as we finish our administrative duties. If we're delayed for any reason, wait for us in Assur."

Hakeem nodded. "May all your plans unfold as you intend."

"Are all the servants here?"

"As you requested, master. Waiting behind the stables."

Akilah circled to the back of the stables and strode into the crowd. Scores of questioning, wary faces watched his every step. *Maintain unity. Calmness. Trust.* "Thank you for your dedication in working so hard to prepare for the upcoming trip. Changes in its scope and funding have regrettably forced me to make some concessions."

Angry murmurs rippled through the ranks.

Akilah gestured for silence. "But I want to assure you that you all still have jobs. In appreciation for all you've done, I am paying you two months' wages in advance."

He waved aside the men's cheers. "While my envoy is gone, you likely will be assigned to other Magi. When I return, I will have much more work for you to do. But, for the next few days, you have a little time off with pay. Enjoy it, knowing you'll be able to feed your family with this advance. I trust you'll use it wisely and make it last."

The less-refined servants surged to the front of the crowd with outstretched hands. Amid excited chatter, all the coins quickly disappeared from Akilah's money pouch.

"Master, I've never seen anyone do what you just did." Hakeem shook his head as servants streamed from the building.

"Most servants live only in the immediate. I want them to work with purpose and loyalty to my team. That is worth the extra cost."

"But some will not be loyal. Perhaps many."

"A risk I'm willing to take." He clapped Hakeem on the back. "I trust you'll finish everything here, yes?"

Hakeem nodded.

"Two more things." Akilah lowered his voice. "Unfortunately, your job has become larger with this latest development. Although you would oversee all servants regardless, it will be a more challenging matter with my cousin's servants comprising most of the help. They aren't accustomed to the rigors of long treks. They won't appreciate you drilling them in matters they assume they know. But attention to every detail is critical. Grooming. Saddling. Loading. Our camels will be heavy-laden. We can't afford any carelessness that would risk injury to them."

"Understood."

"One more thing. Keep a keen eye on Tahrea. He's one of my cousin's servants, a rather unfocused young man with an unusually rough past. My cousin thinks the change of pace will mature him. I'll grant him the benefit of that good thought for the present. But if he—or anyone else—causes any trouble, squash it immediately. Hot tempers and discord have no place in my caravan."

"Yes, master."

"Good man." At that, Akilah trotted to catch up with his colleagues heading toward the Magi's quarters.

Chapter 31

Simurgh

"Akilah, wait!"

He pivoted to find Fakhri, stooped with infirmity, his bed robe dragging the ground, shuffling as fast as his feet could carry him across the courtyard. "Fakhri, did you shortchange your morning prayers to come see me?" Akilah chided fondly.

The wizened Magus raised his withered arm. "Fire has moved to water," he intoned. "The sun no longer lives in the first point of the ram *Varak* at Nowruz. The sun is now in *Mahik*. Two connected, but opposite-swimming fish. A dual reality is rising. A bridge between life and death."

Fakhri's face creased into a thousand crinkles of concern. "Your trip is in danger."

Not the send-off Akilah expected.

Fakhri fumbled in a pouch. "Take this." His hand shook as he extended a palm-sized gold medallion emblazoned with a Simurgh, the immortal Persian winged creature believed to be present since creation. The detailed bas-relief rendering exquisitely captured the scale-covered body, dog's head and foreparts, lion's claws, and peacock's wings and tail. "It will protect you. Mediate your messages between the Sky and Earth."

Akilah eased the elder's gnarled fingers over his medallion. "Fakhri, this is most kind. But I can't risk losing something so valuable on our trip."

"Take it. Take it." The old man's voice shrilled. With uncommon strength, he gripped Akilah's wrist. "You are heading into harm's way."

"Is everything ready?" Tallis clapped a hand on his shoulder. Rashidi appeared on the other side of him. Both were blessed interruptions to this disturbing conversation.

Akilah extricated himself from Fakhri's grasp and patted his hand. "Please excuse me a moment."

He pulled his colleagues aside. "Did you hear any of that?"

"It would be rude to refuse his offer," Tallis whispered. "Just give it back when we return."

"I can't accept something I don't believe in," Akilah hissed.

"Why not?" Rashidi crossed his arms. "It's a revered Persian symbol. If there's even a grain of truth in it, how can it hurt? Besides, Fakhri knows more about Persia's history and religion than anyone here."

"Pardon the interruption, but I thought you might need some extra writing materials for your trip." Seemingly out of nowhere, Burhan appeared by Akilah's side, swaying as he held a box the size of a small crate.

"Why, thank you, Burhan." Akilah accepted the gift.

The bent man twitched. "If I may, you'll have difficulty conducting all your priestly duties while you are gone. Perhaps a reminder of them wouldn't hurt?" He bobbed his head toward the Simurgh in Fakhri's hand.

The silence thickened. "I overstepped my say." Burhan rubbed his twitching eye. "I must get back to work." He patted the box before he hobbled off. "Safe journey."

Shuttling it to Tallis, Akilah reluctantly took the Simurgh but clasped Fakhri's hand as he did. "Blessings on you, Fakhri. May great úshtá surround you."

When the three Magi headed toward their quarters, Fakhri remained where he stood. Akilah turned twice to wave goodbye. He pressed the Simurgh to his chest, his heart strangely unsettled.

On the far side of the courtyard, Akilah turned a third time. Rashidi nudged him. "That wasn't so hard, was it?"

Akilah shook his head. "You have much to learn, Rashidi. I deeply respect Fakhri's knowledge. He was one of my earliest teachers. But the Simurgh appears in holy writings in the context of medicine and healing. Only tradition assigns the Simurgh protective attributes. And the heavenly phenomenon Fakhri referred to occurred sixty years ago—a decade before I was born. The years have dulled his memory."

"All the more reason to humor him."

"Perhaps." Akilah slid the medallion into a concealed pouch sewn into his sash.

Chapter 32
Ready?

Akilah surveyed Rashidi's living quarters. Despite Akilah's mandate to pare what they packed, his younger colleague's room was considerably bare. "Are you ready for this?"

"Absolutely."

"This will be your longest away trip, yes?"

"Mm-hmm. Oh, forgot my combs." Rashidi tucked them into his pocket.

"Akilah, how will we perform worship services when we travel?"

"We pray facing fire or the sun while we ride. We can't stop the caravan five cycles a day to pray. Of course, the first and last prayers of the day are easier. We won't be riding then."

"We won't have a pure fire."

"That's right, Rashidi."

"Do you take sacred bundles with you?"

"The barsom, yes. The other, if space permits. A benevolent god will understand our practical limitations in how we worship."

"What about keeping my *sudre* and *kushti* clean?"

Akilah coughed to stifle a laugh. "The caravan includes two scourers and a fuller. They'll wash all our garments—outer and under—including the sacred ones." Extended fieldwork tended to redefine what was sacred.

Rashidi fidgeted, looking as though he would burst.

Akilah smiled. "More questions?"

"May I ask you something personal? Answer me truthfully."

"Of course. Persians prize honesty above all else."

"I'm practically half your age."

Akilah uttered an exclamation that ended with a groan. "That makes me sound old."

"Pardon my poor word choice. What I mean to ask is, why did you pick me over more experienced Magi?"

Akilah crossed his arms and laid an index finger over his mouth. "Do you remember the first time you presented here?"

"Sadly, yes. You and Tallis were the only attendees. My topic must not have interested anybody."

"Well, a 'brief' comparison of world religions is an oxymoron."

Rashidi laughed ruefully. "So why did you come?"

"I heard the Council had recently welcomed a promising young scholar. I was certain he'd try hard to impress with his first topic. And indeed, he did—try, that is. Despite how far he overreached, his presentation spoke volumes about his passion and thoroughness. That is worth a great deal to me."

Rashidi stared at his feet. "Are you sure I wasn't simply an object of curiosity to you?"

Akilah snorted. "Why? Because you bested me as Magi society's youngest inductee? That is dim."

"So ... my passion and thoroughness were enough reason for you to add me to your team for the star project?"

Akilah rested his hand on his young colleague's shoulder. "Rashidi, your name in Egyptian—your first language—means 'wise.' In Arabic, it means 'rightly guide.' That is exactly what you did. Your research uncovered the first prophecy linking the star to a king. It guided everything we did this past year. That is no small feat."

Rashidi's tense posture relaxed. He smiled.

"But please, let's drop Burhan's nickname for our study." Akilah moved with brisk steps across the room. "This is about something bigger than a star—even if what we saw actually is a star."

"What do you think it is?"

"I truly don't know."

"Are Magi allowed to admit that?"

"The humbler ones do. Come. Assur is waiting."

Chapter 33

Detained

"I'm afraid you won't be going."

Akilah whirled around to face Rashidi's doorway. The Chief Megistane loomed large in it, a grave expression on his face. "Come with me. You're under investigation."

"For what?"

"Undermining Persia's national religion and security."

"That's preposterous! On what grounds?" Akilah's words exploded ahead of his thoughts. He was no political or religious enemy of the empire.

How could the Chief make such serious allegations? And why wasn't he in his Megistane robes? Any legal act by the Upper Council required its members to wear the agency's *ex officio* attire.

"Your colleagues acted at your direction. They are free to go. But you are under house arrest until further notice."

Akilah's blood boiled. None of this made sense. "House arrest. For how long?"

The Chief Megistane gripped Akilah's arm. "As long as it takes." He pushed Akilah toward the door.

"You will be sequestered. No one is allowed to speak to you unless I authorize it." The Chief's words rolled off his tongue. "Fortunately, everyone expects your imminent departure for Jerusalem. They'll think nothing of your absence, regardless of where you are. As for your colleagues"—he glared at Rashidi—"it's in their best interest and yours to not speak of this to anyone. In fact, they should leave *now* to avoid that temptation." The Chief pulled Akilah into the hall and motioned to two guards waiting at attention. One stepped toward Rashidi. The other disappeared down the hall.

"Rashidi, do as he says," Akilah called over his shoulder. "Wait for me in Assur. We *will* go to Jerusalem."

Chapter 34

New Rules

The Chief Megistane adroitly steered Akilah away from well-used walkways in the Magi complex. As they skirted its boundaries, no one seemed to notice their exit from the surroundings Akilah held so dear.

The walk to the Megistane complex seemed interminable. Out of sight and far removed from all other Magi buildings, it was shrouded in mystery. Few people other than the Megistanes had been inside its walls. They took pains to separate their lives and affairs from everyone else's, presumably due to their involvement in sensitive governmental matters. Akilah had no desire to enter their world. Especially not under these circumstances.

Akilah and the Chief descended a hill, then scaled a rise. Unbidden, Akilah's mind filled with his childhood debacle of trying to prove he was a man by riding his father's horse. Not just any horse. One of the Megistanes' prized Niseans, a breed ridden only while on official business for Persia's king. Akilah had trespassed by simply entering the breeders' stables. But, in "borrowing" the Nisean, he had broken half a dozen other rules —and two bones.

Limping from pain and tight splints, he had walked in silence with his father to the court. On a good day, he could double-time his childhood steps to keep up with his father's long strides. But on that day, he lagged behind like a servant or concubine.

Persian justice was particular in exacting retribution for every offense, regardless of one's age. Akilah had dreaded what was to come. Then, he was too young to understand his father had taken most of the penalty upon himself. Years later, Akilah realized he would have been barred from consideration in Magi society if not for his father's intercession. But no one could intervene for Akilah now. The charges were too grave. And his inquisitor was none other than the Chief.

His father.

They walked in silence, save for their footfalls crunching pebbles in their path. Was this narrow path reserved for prisoners being led to their fate?

As they climbed the hill, a citadel rose before them. Akilah looked away. "Will I be tortured?"

The Chief's stride wavered half a step. Or maybe his foot bent sideways on a stone.

"The course of your questioning depends entirely upon you." The Chief's tone was eerily neutral and resolute. The rhythmic crunch of pebbles underfoot resumed. This time Akilah's step faltered.

They crested the rise. The Megistane compound loomed, stern and foreboding, over them. Akilah and the Chief passed through a double barrier of fortified walls, the second higher than the first. Inside, the Chief's steps quickened so much that Akilah caught nothing more than glimpses of stark buildings before they entered a maze of conical structures resembling small *yakhchāls*. Was his holding cell a Persian ice pit?

The Chief pushed through the only door to one cone-shaped

structure and motioned inside. "Your quarters until the investigation is completed."

Despite the sunny day, the circular room was dark, save for brightness from a single opening in the center of the high ceiling. The small circle of light illuminated the only furnishing in the room—a sleeping mat. The walls sloped to the ceiling at a steep enough angle to preclude leaning against any wall.

"Are all Megistane accommodations this Spartan?" Akilah quipped.

"You will remain here except during interrogation. Meals will be brought to you. No personal effects are allowed. Guards are posted outside your door. Any attempt to leave will be met with force."

Such chilling, well-rehearsed words. If that was a requirement for Megistane service, Akilah would rather remain in blissful ignorance of that arm of Magi society. He was grateful he'd declined the invitation to become one of them.

"Empty yourself of all belongings on your personage."

Akilah fumbled in the inner pocket of his cloak and handed the Chief a few coins and a small, blank scroll.

Without comment, the Chief left. The end of that uneasy exchange was nothing compared to the finality of metal clicking in the door lock.

He eased onto the mat. Something hard and curved jabbed his rib. When he rolled onto his side, he felt a lump. Fakhri's Simurgh.

✡︎✡︎✡︎

Akilah was dozing when clanking keys roused him. Dull scraping of wood on stone signaled someone had left something on the floor. Before Akilah could rise, a key clicked in the lock. The circle of moonlight above him shed no light on the rest of his cell. He rolled off his mat and plunged into utter darkness. Disoriented, he crawled toward the sound of the lock and bumped his knee on a tray. Its clatter warned that he'd probably strewn his dinner across the floor. As he groped for morsels, his hand and sleeve dampened. He must have spilled a bowl of soup. What he consumed from his foraging was cold and bland, seasoned only with the floor's grit.

✡ ✡ ✡

The next morning

A pair of rough hands pulled Akilah to his feet, startling him from a fitful sleep. The manhandling continued as a silent sentry dragged him across a barren courtyard. The sudden sunlight seared his eyes, closing them to slits. He alternately stumbled against the sentry and let himself be hauled until the man shoved Akilah into a small room.

He did not wish to see where he was. Through burning, watery eyes, Akilah could distinguish an oversized table in the cramped room. He blinked until his vision cleared enough to see people instead of blurs.

Seated at the table, the Chief Megistane and a prelate, both in governmental robes, attested to the gravity of the matter. A scribe in the corner sharpened his quill. The Chief gestured to the only empty seat. "Let us begin."

Chapter 35

Questions

A week passed. Akilah couldn't shake the chill from his body. Only his mind seemed afire, stoked by the Chief Megistane's measured, methodical questions—paced with enough deliberate silence after each to make Akilah squirm. Rehashes of previous Council meetings. Motives for Akilah's study. His decisions and setbacks. Questions about every family member and acquaintance, their knowledge of his study, their religious affiliations. How Akilah's religious convictions affected his work. The religious questions particularly prickled Akilah's sensibilities.

In the shrouded solitude of his cell, he determinedly pushed thoughts of his interrogation aside. *Focus on what you can control.* Although the Chief had wrung many details from Akilah, one remained untold. Tallis's contact with the scribe and the message he'd sent. Akilah aimed to keep that secret. It would raise too many questions, especially why Akilah had chosen to burn the pouch and its contents.

For three days, Akilah was questioned for many hours. Two days only briefly. One day not at all. His hollow stomach remained empty. The unidentifiable, meager meal he received once a day only heightened his hunger. He remained unwashed. The waste bucket in his holding cell overflowed with an unbearable stench. How could they ignore Zoroastrian rules of hygiene, even if he was a prisoner?

When not facing the Chief, Akilah replayed the two bits of information he had discerned from the damaged third of the scribe's message. "Fullness" and six-hundred-eighty-something were still a mystery to him.

But hunger and weariness overtook Akilah on the seventh day of interrogation. Unbidden, rambling thoughts surfaced while he drifted in and out of consciousness. He jolted awake to a sharp jab that knocked the wind out of him. The Chief had shoved the table into Akilah's gut.

"Do you have reason to believe someone was sabotaging your study?" The Chief's terse voice demanded Akilah's compliance.

He pulled his grimy cloak tight about him as if it could protect him from more questions. "I can't say."

"Can't or won't?"

"I don't know enough ... to comment one way or another."

"It's a simple question."

"I have no answer," he said in a hoarse whisper.

"Who disapproved of your study?"

Akilah licked his parched lips. "I suppose ... anyone who thought it wouldn't yield practical results."

"Did the Head Magus approve of your study?"

"No."

"On what grounds?"

"He questioned its usefulness. If results don't add to the existing body of knowledge, they aren't useful."

The Chief jotted more notes. "And he took measures to stop the study?"

"You would have to ask him."

"But you were at odds with each other about it."

Akilah mustered all his strength to answer. "Differing opinions can coexist within the boundaries of collegiality. Without differences, we wouldn't question what could be. There'd be no new thoughts. No research."

The Chief spread his hands. "He defunded your study."

"Yes."

"For what reason?"

"He said someone had tried to impede my study by destroying Jewish writings ... and a private investigation was the best way to handle the matter. It had to be paid with Magi society funds from my—from the Jerusalem trip." Woozy from hunger, Akilah struggled to focus.

"You saw Burhan burning scrolls late one night. One scroll might have contained information pertinent to your study."

Akilah's heart raced with alarm. "Yes."

"Did you confront him?"

"No."

"Why not?"

"I had no reason to. He said he was disposing of outdated information. I was unaware of the scroll's contents until after he left the fire to get purifying incense."

The Chief frowned. "You didn't wait for him to return?"

"No. It was late, and I was cold."

"You were standing next to a fire."

Akilah couldn't afford to show fear. "I had been in the observatory for hours. Morning stars were in the sky. I was cold and tired."

"Did you talk to Burhan the next day?"

"No."

"The next week?"

"No." How much longer could Akilah force his brain to work? It was as slow-moving as a chariot stuck in mud. "I was making final preparations for the trip to Jerusalem." He grimaced. Jerusalem seemed only a distant dream now.

"Did you find anything odd about Burhan's behavior that night by the fire?"

Anger pushed Akilah's posture straighter. "Burhan has many behaviors. Some are due to his unfortunate past. Only he knows his motives."

"Don't dodge the question. What was odd about Burhan's behavior that night?"

Would these questions never end? Akilah couldn't give in to his fatigue or bias about Megistane duties, but both were clouding his thinking. By definition, default, or drill, the Chief's governmental tasks seemed to assume the worst of people. In Akilah's scales of justice, that defied Zoroastrianism's foundational tenets. Perhaps that was idealistic. The Chief had certainly accused him of that when he had declined the offer of promotion to Megistane. A pang of conscience pierced him. Was he manipulating his view of Zoroastrianism to justify his own selfish motives in this investigation?

"Answer me. Burhan's behavior by the fire." The Chief's scrutiny sifted Akilah.

Whatever lapse in judgment he may have had that evening, Akilah would not let himself be manipulated into implicating Burhan of anything. "He may have been twitchier than usual. But the smoke or the cold could have caused that."

"What else?"

"The scrolls he burned were still wound around their rollers. Normally the shafts are reused."

"And?"

Akilah willed his sluggish brain to keep working. "When I thanked him for helping a colleague find an ancient text, he knew I was talking about Rashidi, even though I didn't say his name or specify the text."

"Tell me about Burhan's religious convictions."

The stuffy room suddenly became unbearably hot. "His beliefs are his own. I can't see into his heart."

New Star

"Burhan and Fakhri are Zoroastrian purists, are they not?"

"All Magi pledge to maintain the tenets of the empire's national religion."

"Burhan is not a Magus. Don't try to sidestep me. That will only work against you." The Chief's steely gaze knifed Akilah. "What do you know of a movement to keep our country's religion pure?"

Akilah stared blankly at the Chief.

The Chief folded his hands over his writing tablet. "Are you aware of the punishment you are facing?" His voice remained neutral, but his face clouded.

Akilah's throat closed. His answer escaped as a raspy whisper. "Death ... if found guilty of undermining Persia's national religion or security."

He grew faint, but not from hunger. Until this moment, he had never truly feared for his life. What could save him if the truth wasn't enough? Unbidden, his thoughts flew to his cousin's insistence on his signing the stūrīh. He had assumed it served only Farzaneh's needs. Could it do more? Even save him from a death sentence or a life sentence? Had Farzaneh somehow reckoned the danger Akilah would face? Or was that wishful thinking borne from his desperation? He murmured, "So ... Far—"

"You dare think about Jerusalem now? The only distance you'll travel any time soon will be back to your holding cell."

For once, the Chief was wrong. Not the farness of Jerusalem. Farzaneh.

The Chief snapped shut the lid of his writing tablet. "Has anyone threatened you since you started your study?"

Akilah startled at the word. "Threatened? No. Frankly, I can't see how my work could be perceived as any kind of threat, let alone one of national security."

"Idealist," the Chief said. "Your findings could antagonize

those who are intolerant of any religion other than the one our empire officially sanctions."

"Antagonize who? Burhan?" If Akilah had more energy, he would have laughed, but the Chief's granite face silenced the urge. How could the Ordeal be a threat to anyone—unless Akilah had grossly misjudged him?

"Chew on this morsel. Burhan threw your precious pouch under a diplomat's chariot as it left the Magi compound."

Akilah's eyes bulged.

"Don't look so surprised," the Chief said. "Things are rarely as they seem. Especially truth—and men's hearts. Burhan guessed the pouch was important to your study when he saw its messenger in such a hurry to find Tallis. Burhan took it, said he knew where Tallis was, and promised to deliver it directly. Instead, he made sure the pouch's contents were so damaged that no one could tell he'd read them. He has more than one way of reading other people's mail. We've been watching him for some time. He will pay for that violation."

Akilah caught his breath. If Burhan had read the entire message, did he remember what it said? Akilah wavered between the thrill of that possibility and the dread of what the Chief would do to Burhan. "Surely you won't impose the full sentence."

"You are in no position to make demands." The Chief's words cut the air like a knife. "You have no rights while under investigation."

"I only meant—"

"For his cooperation, I will recommend that Burhan be dealt with leniently."

Akilah sat back in his chair and exhaled slowly. "How did you know about the pouch?"

"You *are* an idealist. I wouldn't be doing my job if I didn't question all your colleagues. Your friend Tallis has an impeccable memory. You wouldn't need the pouch even if you still had it."

Akilah groaned inwardly. Either the Chief had ordered his guards to detain Tallis the same day he did Rashidi in the Magi complex, or the Chief had spent a day in Assur questioning them. He must know every plan Akilah had taken pains to hide. A more disturbing thought arose. Had the Chief questioned Farzaneh too? If so, he might already be aware of the stūrīh. Akilah shrank in his chair. "You talked to ... others?"

"Of course." The Chief's voice was bland as if reading an accounting of a grain harvest.

"Where are Rashidi and Tallis?"

"Tell me what you know about Fakhri being poisoned." The Chief's tone didn't shift.

Something seized in Akilah's chest. His hand pressed against the Simurgh in his sash pocket. "Nothing," he whispered.

Chapter 36

Tables Turned

Sassanak's office in the main Magi complex

"Head Magus, come with me."

Sassanak ignored the unfamiliar voice. "Can't." He didn't bother to look up. "Reviewing Magi candidacy theses. Come back tomorrow."

"It isn't a request." A more authoritative voice filled the opulent office.

Two officers parted in the doorway. The Chief Megistane crossed the room in a few long strides and dropped a dual-sealed scroll on top of Sassanak's stack of reading materials.

Frowning, Sassanak studied the unmistakable seals. They conferred both administrative and royal authority to the Chief.

"According to Magisterial Law and the Law of Accusations, you are under investigation. You are relieved of your duties as Head Magus until the investigation is complete."

"What?" Sassanak sputtered. "You can't override the Lower Council in ecclesiastical matters. That's my jurisdiction."

"If the matter were purely a religious one, that would be

true. But you also alleged wrongdoing against Persia and the Parthian Empire at large. That obligated me to open a governmental investigation—which takes precedence over yours," the Chief Megistane said. "Because you voiced your earliest allegations during Nowruz, you have the freedom to present your complaint to the High King himself, if you choose." The Chief continued, his voice smooth as silk. "All proceedings and judgment papers will go to the Board of the Lord High Chancellor. Or the Chief Judge of the Empire, if you want to pursue the matter all the way to the top."

The Chief ran his finger over the dual seals. "I am obligated to inform you that no one is allowed to defy or frustrate Persia's principles of justice. But the severest penalties are reserved for those who violate the sanctity of justice by its intentional miscarriage." He picked up the scroll. "Now that we have those formalities out of the way, I advise you to not make a scene."

"Take him out the back way." The Chief nodded to the officers. "Directly to interrogation."

✧✡✧

How many more days did he have to spend in this cramped interrogation room? The Chief Megistane stretched his long legs under the table. With the prelate, a scribe, and a detainee in the room, there was barely space to move. Moreover, the room seemed too small for this investigation, which had grown far beyond its original boundaries.

Two officers shoved Sassanak into a chair in the barren space. *This should be interesting.*

"How long will you detain Akilah?" Sassanak's tone was almost cocky. "Both the Upper and Lower Council need to question him. You on governmental issues, me on religious issues."

"My investigation. My questions. Sit." The Chief opened his wax writing tablet framed in ivory.

"I have important information that can help your cause, Chief."

"Indeed." The Chief Megistane rankled at the phrase "your cause" but limited his reaction to smoothing the folds of his governmental robes.

"Head Magus, did you purposely withhold information regarding an alleged national threat?"

"You knew why—"

"Did you make any attempt to stop alleged illegal activities related to hiding or destroying our library's Jewish writings?"

"It was for—"

"Think carefully before you answer, Head Magus. Every recorded word will remain in Persia's annals."

Sassanak glanced at the scribe. "I ... am continuing to gather information about those activities and the suspects involved."

"You."

"Yes."

"Did you or did you not say, 'Let them do it' when referring to the destruction of Jewish writings?"

Sassanak swallowed. "I—"

"Yes or no?"

"To—"

"Under Persian law, what would you call that?"

"I am not an expert in Persian civil law." Sassanak leaned back in his chair.

"When you learned the library was missing some of its holdings, did you engage a private investigator?"

"That's confidential."

"As are these proceedings—for the moment. Answer the question," the Chief commanded, tapping the summons scroll.

Sassanak cleared his throat. "If necessary, I will initiate a private investigation."

"But you haven't."

"No."

"So, you needlessly withheld funds from Akilah's trip."

"Re-allocated. Based on the strong possibility of requiring them."

"Need I remind you that lying is a capital offense?" The Chief's words exploded like a thunderclap across the room.

The seriousness of that threat seemed to roll over Sassanak to no effect. "I was doing my job."

"I'll deal with the ethics of your money management later." The Chief glanced at his notes. "You alleged someone was poisoning Fakhri. And you alluded to a religious motive for doing so. Your findings?"

Sassanak leaned forward. "Azazel. He's been poisoning Fakhri."

"Your proof?"

"An eyewitness told me he saw Azazel handling the food he sent to Fakhri's room."

"Did that witness actually see poison added to the food?"

"No. But—"

The Chief Megistane slammed his fist into the table. "Enough! I'm through indulging you. You know nothing." The Chief thrust his index finger at Sassanak's face. "You want to wade through more conjecture? Then try this. Azazel set you up to take the blame for Fakhri's poisoning."

Sassanak flinched. "What?"

"I questioned everyone who handled Fakhri's food. Burhan's survival instincts won over his religious convictions when I got to him. He confessed to hearing Azazel talking to the cook about the food. Azazel is a slippery one. So far, he'll admit only that he directed the cook to make the rarest, most expensive foods for Fakhri as a way to honor him. Coincidentally, they are also many of your favorite foods. I suspect Azazel requested those on purpose. I just can't prove it yet."

Sassanak reeled as if hit with an invisible blow.

The Chief flicked his fingers. "My guess is Azazel tasted the food in the presence of others to put himself above suspicion. Then, he or an accomplice added the poison immediately after. By having the cook's helper take the food to Fakhri's room, everyone who ordered, cooked, carried, or served the food would become suspects.

"An ingenious way to plant seeds of doubt," the Chief said. "Azazel would bide his time, dropping hints about the foods Fakhri had eaten until people started to suspect you. He always wanted a shot at your job. Some rivalries never die."

The Chief pulled a small vial from his robe. "Hold out your hand."

"What?"

Before Sassanak could comply, the Chief grabbed his wrist and poured some of the vial's grayish-white powder onto his open palm. "We found this arsenic hidden in Azazel's quarters. Of course, he has a strong alibi for having it. He said he was treating himself for an ulcer ... which will also be investigated."

Wresting his hand from the Chief's grip, Sassanak violently shook the powder off his palm. For good measure, he scraped his hand against the table's edge. He gaped at his inquisitor. "Azazel would frame me?"

"It wouldn't surprise me. You and he are two hours of darkness in the same night. You did the same to Burhan." The Chief Megistane pulled a half-finished document from his governmental pouch. "Look familiar?"

"No."

"But you used extortion to get Burhan to write it."

"I told him if he'd try one more time to apply to become a Magus, I would help push his candidacy thesis through the Lower Council. I was doing him a service."

"Odd word choice. You'd expedite his candidacy if he wrote what you coerced him to. A topic that would further your agenda—and set up Burhan as a religious conspirator. A convenient scapegoat, should you ever need one. You'd simply use Burhan's own writing against him. If his thesis wouldn't suffice to convict him, you'd leak word of his scroll-burning activities. You'd stay clean, and he'd suffer the consequences. Very tidy. By the way, I already indicted the head librarian on three accounts: conspiracy, destruction of property, and collusion."

Sassanak rose from his seat and leaned across the table, a vein bulging on his left temple. "There is nothing wrong or illegal about condoning undefiled religion. My office and duty require that I keep Zoroastrianism pure. I am proud to do so. The empire is stronger for it."

"Spare me your speech. You exalt Tiridates for being Zoroastrian, even though he was little more than a Roman vassal who drove Phraates from Parthia's throne for a time."

Sassanak opened his mouth, but nothing came out.

"Sit. Down." The Chief shoved his chair into the wall and drew himself up to his full height. His glare impaled Sassanak. "You can't question a suspect without a prelate or other impartial witness present. Otherwise, the answers can't be used as evidence. You knew that, but Burhan didn't. The minute you started questioning him, he should have invoked a Council meeting. But that could have exposed you. So you preyed on his fears and ignorance of Lower Council law. What's most disturbing is you would create or foment a conspiracy to further your agenda. And then take credit for stopping it."

The Chief Megistane leaned over the table. "Your sense of justice needs overhauling."

Sassanak's eyes narrowed. He gripped the table's edge, ready to stand again. But the Chief's menacing glower drove him farther into his seat.

"You have two choices," the Chief said. "Undergo an Imperial investigation or resign your position and be excommunicated from the Parthian Empire and Magi society forever."

Sassanak gaped, thunderstruck. Drawing a shaky hand across his mouth, he shivered as if a viper had slithered up his spine.

"Have you ever gone before the Imperial Ministers or the Grand Senate?" the Chief said icily. "They aren't afraid to pass the death penalty in such matters." Still standing, he pushed a document toward Sassanak. "Investigation or excommunication. Choose wisely."

Sweat poured down Sassanak's brow. "Is there a third option?"

"According to the letter of the law, you shouldn't get two."

Swallowing hard, Sassanak read the document.

More documents appeared in front of him. His hand trembled as he signed each one. He glanced at the Chief, a pleading look in his eyes. "Gadiel, we were classmates …"

"Competitors."

"Our combined strength could reach new heights in Magi society. In Parthian society."

"The government may legislate a national religion, but it can't legislate morality." The Chief's voice dropped to an ominous rumble. "You masqueraded religion as nationalism. Misused your status. Morally bankrupted your office. Manipulated people to further your agenda. Miscarried justice. You went a distance too far."

Chapter 37

Rise and Go

Akilah's holding cell

"Get up."

The voice reached into Akilah's slumber. Dozing during the day had become the easiest way to shut out many things. Cold. Hunger. Isolation. The cell's chill, its gray monotones, its perpetual darkness, broken only when the sun aligned with the ceiling's small opening, all vanished when Akilah slept. But this time, when he opened his eyes, the room wasn't uniformly gray. Black, punctuated by crimson and cobalt, hovered over him.

"Up, I said."

He uncurled his wooden legs and forced his stiff arms to push himself up to a kneeling position. Strong arms pulled him to his feet and covered his face with a damp towel. Choking, Akilah fought back. He pulled free of the grip and yanked the towel away.

"Wipe your face. Put this on." In one swift move, the Chief Megistane removed his governmental robes and head cap. "Listen carefully." He thrust his Magi attire at Akilah's chest.

"The guard is gone. Walk out this door. To the right is a Nisean. Saddled. With a blanket, food, and a waterskin in a pouch. Ride through the north gate as fast as you can, straight to Assur. Don't stop for anything. No one should question you when they see the Nisean and the robes. Understood?"

"How ... Why?"

"Explanations must wait. You are free to go."

Akilah hesitated, his eyes questioning.

"Yes. Legally. *Go.* Your friends are waiting." In two strides, the Chief reached the door. "A warning. You are leaving some dangers but will face greater ones in Jerusalem. Temper your idealism with prudence."

Akilah shimmied into the Chief's governmental robes. "You're giving me your Nisean?"

"Idealist."

Chapter 38

What Are The Odds?

Arabia, two weeks later

Stiffness in his left hip woke Akilah. Like a nagging, repetitious schoolmaster, the hip's early arthritic aches again reminded Akilah of his brash childhood attempt to prove he could ride a Nisean horse. His pride and his bones had mended, but not the joint tissue. Tonight's pain recalled how long it had been since he'd slept in a real bed. Heavy rugs on bare ground could cushion and comfort only so much.

Tallis stirred as Akilah tried to slip out of the tent. "We could have stopped at a *kahn* three *parasangs* back," Tallis whispered. "The inn would have been much more comfortable for everyone. Pressing on like this won't shorten our trip much—a few days at most."

Akilah's decision to camp instead of lodge had less to do with speed than his colleague assumed. Thankfully, as the leader of this venture, his word was final. That helped defuse such questions.

He smiled at Tallis. "Just hedging our bets against the unexpected ... bad weather and such."

Akilah glanced at Rashidi, snoring softly and sleeping as soundly as if he were on a stack of mattresses. "Ah, the advantages of being twenty years younger."

Tallis propped himself up on one elbow. "Akilah?"

"Hmm?"

"Thinking about where this trip will take us?" Tallis, the quietest of the three Magi, was often the most insightful.

"Akilah, you have been 'One of Four' to princes." His tone shifted from collegial to crisp. "In fact, the most eminent 'One of Four.' Remember that during the uncertain times."

"Thank you, Tallis."

As encouraging as his colleague's words were, they brought little comfort. Tutoring Persian princes when they turned fourteen was an honor but largely an academic exercise for four appointed Magi. The "most just" taught government, the "most temperate" taught sobriety, the "bravest" taught courage. And the "wisest" taught worship of the gods. Akilah had been called upon twice as the wisest.

He shook his head. He had been so confident in teaching those privileged boys. So careful in crafting his words. "Many smart men lack wisdom. A man can be wise without education, but an educated man cannot be wise simply from his education. Scrolls contain only knowledge. Knowledge without wisdom is useless. Wisdom applies knowledge for the greater good of the people. When you can do that, you will be wise indeed."

But history was fraught with leaders who misused knowledge and judged unwisely. Who was wise enough to always choose the right course of action?

The scribe's words from Isaiah said the child would be Wonderful Counselor. For months, Akilah had wrestled with those words to rightly reckon them. He could conclude only one thing. The child would be an advisor without peer. He would have wisdom no one else possessed. And that wisdom—or what he did with it—would inspire wonder.

A pang of jealousy shot through Akilah. That child would be infinitely wiser than the wisest men, including the Magi. Akilah's status, studies, and experience had elevated him to One of Four. But was he truly wise? At this moment, he wasn't even sure what that meant.

Reluctantly, he had to rely on a wisdom beyond human knowledge. Wisdom that somehow rested on writings of a long-dead prophet named Isaiah. And, if Daniel and Danyal were the same person, that was the same wisdom Daniel had possessed. Wisdom imparted by the Hebrews' God. Akilah prayed his personal convictions and ambitions hadn't clouded his reasoning.

Tallis touched Akilah's shoulder. "A Hebrew writing, attributed to their prophet Daniel, says that their God changes the times and the seasons, removes and raises up kings, and *gives wisdom to the wise and knowledge to those who have understanding.*[1] Akilah, you are wise. Whatever you need to know, you will find."

Akilah inhaled sharply. The Daniel that the Babylonians took captive? The same Danyal his grandparents had talked about? Just as quickly as that thought entered his mind, pain shot through his hip.

"One of our healers can give you medicine if your hip is bothering you that much."

"Thank you, but that's not necessary." Akilah turned to Tallis. "There's one thing I never told you about my injury."

Tallis cocked his head.

"The first time I sneaked into the Niseans' stables, it was on a dare from Farzaneh. We wanted to see if it was true that the royal breeders had a white Nisean. We knew of the rare silver Niseans reserved for the king and the Megistanes. My father

---

1. Daniel 2:21 (ESV)

rode one. But a white Nisean supposedly belonged only to the gods."

"Childhood curiosity. Did you find what you were looking for?"

"No. But getting past the guards and stablemen without being caught gave me false confidence. A couple years later, when I was particularly angry with my father, I decided I would ride a silver Nisean to show him I was a man. I didn't know the one I chose was still untamed. I was as willful as that horse. I ignored Farzaneh's warning to not act on my impulses." Akilah laughed ruefully. "Maybe she could have ridden it. She was always a better rider than I."

He rubbed his throbbing hip. "I suffered the consequences. Still do. But it all started with trying to find something unattainable."

"Akilah, you're cold and tired. If you're worried that you've been reckless about pursuing this trip, perhaps that is good. No one is so wise as to be able to trust himself all the time. That kernel of distrust keeps you humble." Tallis clasped Akilah's arm. "And if this is your way of wondering if we'll find this child, then calm your misgivings. The people who fear what you've already found have tried to stop you in more ways than we can count. There is untold value in what those people *don't* want you to discover. Rest well."

"I will. Soon."

All his hopes rested on finding answers in Jerusalem, the heart of Jewish culture. But that wouldn't be the end of their journey. He was counting on the priests knowing the location of this child-king. Otherwise, the trip would be for naught.

Wrapped in his camel-hair cloak, Akilah wandered outside, coughing as he inhaled the cool night air. The clear sky was ablaze with stars—stippled pinpoints of white on a sapphire canvas. The countless spots glittered with so many tantalizing secrets. No wonder astronomy was Akilah's favorite subject. He had studied and taught it for decades. Refuted lesser men's postulates about it. But now?

We have reviewed your findings. While they are interesting, we question their value. A heavenly body that doesn't move daily or seasonally cannot be used for navigation, time, or any other purpose. Although it is curious, it does not appear to be useful, and therefore, not productive use of your considerable talents. You admitted that you haven't seen this phenomenon in a year. What are the odds that it will appear again?

Chapter 39

Final Word

Persia, the Magi's complex

T he Chief's quill scratching across papyrus marred the silence of Akilah's meditation room. Administrative work was the bane of the Chief Megistane's duties, and Sassanak's excommunication had doubled it. Now, the Chief was tasked with the logistics of transitioning Sassanak's successor as well as escorting the deposed Head Magus out of the country. Although the former required intensive time with the Lower Council, it came with an advantage. Until his oversight of those activities ended, the Chief would remain in Akilah's vacant quarters—close enough to visit Fakhri daily.

A morning breeze from the open window adjacent Akilah's reading desk rippled the tapestry behind the Chief. Sunlight shifted, dappling his Magi robes draped over a reclining couch. He paused his quill. "This is a pleasant place," he mused. Subdued light. Beautiful wall hangings. Shelves of knowledge interspersed with mementos of Akilah's travels and accomplishments.

An unfamiliar pang shot through the Chief. Regret? Today's

circumstances, not desire, had brought him to these quarters for the first time. Its extra rooms spoke of how well Akilah had done for himself. Had the Chief ever acknowledged any of his son's accomplishments? He could remember only one, Akilah's induction into the Lower Council. The Chief loathed to attend the ceremony but was obligated to appear. After all, another generation of his family was becoming a Magus—although not in the manner he would have preferred. He had hoped his gesture of passing down his heirloom Magi ring to Akilah might sway him to reconsider a career of service in the Upper Council. At the least, the inductee gift would distract from the Chief's grudging attendance. Surprisingly, Akilah's open delight at seeing his father seemed to eclipse his appreciation of the prized gift—a Persian diamond ring he had worn on his fifth finger ever since.

The Chief's conscience dimmed as daylight pushed with greater insistence through the window. The morning sun was climbing, and he couldn't be late for today's vote. He donned his Magi robes and hurried to the Great Hall's Gathering Circle.

It seemed the entire Lower Council was present to elect Sassanak's successor. "As your impartial moderator, my purpose is to ensure procedural adherence," he said. "Your vote will be weighted equally with the person's qualifications and all other considerations as already outlined. So, let us—"

The *ashipu* assigned to caring for Fakhri tumbled through the Magi circle and prostrated himself before the Chief. "A thousand pardons for this breach in protocol, Chief Megistane." Ragged gasps punctuated the tribal healer's words. "But the Magus Honorific is asking for you."

Not again.

"A quarter cycle recess," the Chief ordered.

Although he doubted the ashipu's skills and knowledge, the man was attentive, if nothing else. A week ago, the ashipu had summoned the Chief, maintaining Fakhri was breathing his last.

But Fakhri had rallied and asked the Chief to deliver final rites when the time came. Fakhri also had made an unsettling prediction about Akilah.

The ashipu's interruption and wide eyes told a grimmer story today. The Chief flung his robes at the tribal healer and sprinted across the open courtyard to the audience hall of the senior-ranking Magi. He bounded the building's steps at a run, slowing only to turn down the hallway to Fakhri's quarters. "Where is the *asu*—the physician?"

Panting like a horse finishing an endurance race, the ashipu caught up with the Chief. "Gone. Said he'd done all he could."

The Chief threw open the bedchamber door. Although the day was bright, Fakhri's room was dark.

"Gadiel?" A trembling hand groped the air.

The strong hand gripped the failing one. "I am here, Fakhri."

Minutes passed as Fakhri struggled to form words. His eyes, now robbed of sight, were void of the *úshtá* that had always filled them. The Chief pulled a chair flush with Fakhri's bed and waited.

"Forgive." One word, barely a whisper.

"What?" The Chief leaned closer. Perhaps his old mentor was not in his right mind.

"Greater than justice," Fakhri mumbled. "No limits."

The Chief had never heard Fakhri talk that way. Forgiveness was not a Zoroastrian tenet. Forgiveness was unique to the Hebrews' religion.

For the first time in his life, the Chief struggled for a response. Behind misty eyes, his mind blanked. His mouth turned to cotton. "Honored teacher ... my friend ..."

"Forgive." The whisper escaped Fakhri's lips with his final exhale.

Chapter 40

Prudence

Near Judea's northern border

As the sun's light and heat increased with each week of travel, the tempers of the caravan shortened. This was a dangerous stretch of the trip. Akilah worried, but not for the caravan's physical safety. With so many weeks behind them but their destination not yet before them, the not-yet time always tested everyone's morale.

"I could use a real bath," Rashidi griped. "One that uses more than two ladles of hot water."

"Think about something else," Akilah said.

"All right. What do you miss the most about home?"

"Beds," Tallis chimed in. "You?"

Rashidi grinned. "*Faloodeh.*"

Tallis shook his head. "You miss frozen sweets?"

"Yes. And the yakhchāls that let us freeze water and make confections like faloodeh are a brilliant engineering feat. We didn't have anything like that in Anatolia. Well, we had *kümbets*. But those were houses. Shaped the same and ventilated at the top, but they couldn't make ice."

Akilah smiled wryly. "Rashidi, as always, I admire your zeal for engineering. But I can't say I'll ever look at a yakhchāl the same way again."

Rashidi's face reddened. "Many pardons." He scanned the surrounding hills. "Where's our next stop?"

"Susita, in Israel's northern district, on the east side of the Sea of Galilee," Akilah said. "We'll rest and get fresh supplies there. Should be easy to spot. It's on a flat-topped hill."

Rashidi craned his neck behind and before him. "We're still on low ground. Does that concern anyone besides me?"

Akilah shrugged. "It's a Roman road."

"A minor one," Rashidi said. "We haven't seen any outposts for three days. And with heights all around us ..."

"We're making good time. But it's always prudent to stay alert. Complacency is never a traveler's friend."

Chapter 41

The Price of Dates

"Susita. Finally." Akilah twisted to look behind him as he slid from his saddle. "That was some climb."

Susita sat tall and proud like a crown atop a flat, diamond-shaped mountain. High fortifications constrained the rectangular metropolis that hugged the contours of its lofty perch. Far below the mountain's craggy brownness, carpets of green spread toward blue in the distance.

Tallis gazed at the panorama before them and the path behind them. "This is so isolated. Only one access—up the mountain's western slopes and across that narrow saddle bridge. No cities nearby. No wonder they're heavily fortified."

Akilah smiled. "Ever the tactician. Yes, it's quite the city on a hill. But think of how close we are to Jerusalem. It's only twenty-five parasangs away. Look—you can see the Sea of Galilee. If I squint, I can almost see Jerusalem."

Tallis laughed. "Your imagination may help you see things no one else can find in the stars, but it won't help you see Jerusalem from this distance. Not even with squinting." Still, he followed Akilah's finger pointing southwest.

Rashidi craned his neck the opposite way, down Susita's

main street. "This place seems to be thriving. We should be able to find everything we need here."

Akilah turned to the caravan. "This is a quick stop. We will water the camels and get a week's worth of provisions. With luck, we'll arrive in Jerusalem long before then."

"Too bad we couldn't quite make it without resupplying," Tallis said.

Akilah frowned. "I must have miscalculated our food rations."

Tallis laughed again. "Don't be hard on yourself. Maybe your cousin's servants eat more than ours do."

"Swine! Get back." Rashidi tackled his colleagues, sending them tumbling into a display of bagged dry goods. He popped up, his flushed face streaked with revulsion.

"I thought Susita had trade connections with Hebrews." He kept his voice low but unapologetic.

"We do." A stumpy man who seemed to be the shop's keeper approached the Magi. He motioned in the swineherd's direction. "Don't mind him. He's taking that sounder of swine to Kursi. The Gerasenes enjoy eating pork."

"Gerasenes?" A sickly pallor spread across Rashidi's face.

The vendor laughed. "Gerasenes are more Greek than anything." He wiped his hands on his tunic. "We get all kinds here. Romans, Jews, Aramaeans, Ituraeans, Nabataeans." He wagged a thick index finger at the Magi. "I advise you avoid those last two. They're nomads … predators living by their own rules."

The man sized up Rashidi. "You practice one of those religions that doesn't eat swine?"

Rashidi nodded.

"Well, to each his own beliefs. But where are my manners?" He clapped his hands together in front of his face and bowed deeply. "Nakal at your service. If you need supplies, I am your man. For twenty-five years, I have served traders and travelers on this route. I am the most successful—and well-stocked—supplier in this area."

A scowling, scrappy man appeared from behind the storefront. "I'm still waiting for my payment. Perhaps you need more help, Nakal. Or more reliable help."

"Did my daughter inspect and log your shipment?"

"Yes, but then she disappeared." The scrappy man paced impatiently and glowered at the Magi.

"Wait here. I will pay you directly." Nakal shrugged his apology to Akilah. "I will be but a moment."

Nakal returned with a jingling pouch in one hand and a date in the other hand. When he bit into the fruit, his eyes lit with rapture. "Fresh as always. You are a good man, Sarbaz. Here is your payment."

Sarbaz grabbed the pouch. "You've delayed my other deliveries." He waved his payment in the air. "If I didn't get so much business from you, I'd hate you." In his haste to leave, he bumped into Akilah, sending coins flying from the pouch.

Rashidi dove to retrieve them.

"Humph." Sarbaz snatched the coins from Rashidi's outstretched hand and scurried off.

Akilah returned his attention to Nakal. "Can you direct us to someone who repairs camel saddles? Two of ours are unsteady. We've done what we can, but we need someone to make a stronger repair and rebalance them."

"Of course, of course. I know just the man. I am sure you need other supplies as well. Please, start your selections or write a list of your needs." Nakal motioned toward a generously sized storefront behind him. "My daughter Keket will assist you. She'll add the cost for the bags of lentils and chickpeas you broke." He laughed and slapped his thigh. "I will return shortly with the best carpenter in Susita." Before the Magi could reply, he disappeared down the street.

Rashidi touched Akilah's sleeve. "Nakal just paid that man

with clipped coins. He cheated his vendor. Maybe we should …" A strikingly beautiful woman stole the rest of his words as she stepped through the doorway of Nakal's shop.

She bowed deeply. "I am Keket. How may I serve you?" She spoke Aramaic but finished her vowels with a hint of Egyptian.

She straightened and studied the caravan in a cool, calculating way until her eyes met Rashidi's. As her gaze lingered, something struggled deep within her hazel eyes … eyes that seemed to change from green to brown to gold in the sunlight.

"We will tell you if we have any trouble finding what we need." Akilah nodded curtly to Keket.

She dipped her head and resumed studying Rashidi. "You must be traveling far."

"Yes …"

Tallis frowned Rashidi into silence.

"Well, not so far," Rashidi added.

"Please show our servants where to draw water for our camels." Akilah stepped on Rashidi's toes hard enough to make him scowl.

Keket's bow of acquiescence tugged her veil from her forehead. Thick waves of hair the color of sunlit autumn leaves tumbled around her face as her veil fell to her shoulders. Flustered, she quickly covered her head.

Rashidi stepped around Akilah. "I will go with you. To supervise our servants."

"Tallis, can you take care of our saddle repairs and supplies while I stretch my legs?" Akilah rolled his eyes toward Rashidi.

Tallis nodded. "Certainly."

"This way." Keket pointed toward the city's center.

Akilah knew what distance and time could do to men's desires. He meandered toward the market stalls but remained within hearing distance of Rashidi.

Twenty paces later, Keket turned to Rashidi. "You are Egyptian."

"Yes."

"How have you come to be so far from home?"

"I could ask you the same. I see Egypt in your skin."

Keket ran a hand down her arm and looked away. "My mother was an Egyptian of high standing." She resumed striding with purpose over the street's flagstones. "But nomads overtook her caravan. They sold everyone as slaves to the Romans. When the Romans passed through Susita with their new 'property,' Nakal saw my mother. He bought her for twice what the Romans paid. After a time, she became his wife ... in an imperfect way." Keket looked down, but not before a tear escaped her eye.

Rashidi stuttered without saying anything intelligible.

Akilah winced and feigned interest in a stack of mangoes. *All Rashidi remembers of his childhood in Egypt is a string of painful losses. What is this woman stirring in his heart?*

"Nakal is all I know of my mother," Keket said. "She died when I was very young. Nakal said it was from homesickness. He could have sold me then—either into slavery or to Baal worshippers for child sacrifice at Mount Zaphon. But he didn't. Much to his friends' dismay, he kept me—and my Egyptian name."

"That is fortunate for all of us," Rashidi said in Egyptian.

Without breaking her stride or responding in kind, Keket continued to the city's forum. "A large reservoir lies underneath our feet." She stopped and pointed. "Your servants may draw water freely over there. I must return to the shop."

"I'll go with you."

Keket cocked her head. "But you must stay and supervise."

A sheepish grin crossed Rashidi's face. "Yes."

"Perhaps you'll learn how to lose your chaperone next time."

Rashidi whirled as Akilah turned away.

"Weigh carefully what Nakal says." Keket raised her voice as if to include Akilah in what she said next. "He is not as well off as he would like you to believe. He has unpaid debts. The more you buy, the more ... grateful we both will be."

She hurried off.

Akilah waited until Keket was halfway down the street before he started back toward Nakal's shop. When he reached the storefront, she was not in sight.

"That is unacceptable." Tallis's voice, uncharacteristically agitated, wafted from the back of the shop.

Akilah rounded the corner. "Do we have a problem?"

"My deepest apologies." Nakal bowed. "I did not know the carpenter left yesterday for Raphana. Apparently, his sister there has taken ill. Or so his neighbor tells me. However, I happen to know another person who can repair your saddles. And I can say with certainty that he is in town." Nakal slapped his thigh.

"You?" Akilah sighed.

"Yes, yes. And I can start on them right away."

"We need tamarisk wood for the repairs. Do you have some?" Akilah barked his order.

"Of course, of course."

"Make pegs from the same," Tallis said.

Nakal grinned broadly. "That too." He headed out the back door of his shop.

"And for the price you quoted, we keep all cut-offs and castaway pieces for firewood," Akilah called after him.

Nakal walked away with an over-the-shoulder wave.

Akilah huffed. "Tallis, does he strike you as almost too solicitous?"

"So much so that you could put a watermelon under his arm. But we can't risk having a saddle break in these mountains."

"Watch him. But don't let him see you."

Tallis nodded and slipped away.

Akilah walked toward the front of the shop to see Rashidi

New Star

unsuccessfully trying to talk further with Keket. Under different circumstances, they might have made an arresting couple. Both Egyptian, both intelligent, both about the same age.

She was all business as she measured and tallied items for the Magi. "You must have traveled far." She turned to Akilah. "Your saddle pads are packed down. Shall I add extra *teben* for restuffing them?"

Akilah nodded.

"And it wouldn't hurt to have a few extra side straps and hind straps in case one breaks."

Another nod, another sale.

Keket seemed unfazed by his curtness.

"Why should you treat her with disregard like common travelers do?" Rashidi hissed in his ear.

✡ ✡ ✡

Surprisingly, Nakal worked quickly and seemed to be well versed in everything related to camel saddles. His bragging aside, the saddles were ready sooner than Akilah expected. He inspected them thoroughly and charged Hakeem to do the same. When they both finished, Akilah pronounced them satisfactory.

"Thank you," he said. "Here is something extra for your work."

"I can't accept that." Nakal thrust the small money pouch back into Akilah's hand.

"I insist."

"And I insist you pay me only what I charge you."

Keket touched Nakal's arm. "Father, we have talked about receiving kindness from strangers. Do not let the years behind you harden you to that."

Nakal looked adoringly at Keket and sighed. "Right, right.

But ... I will accept the extra money only if you accept my hospitality."

"Thank you, but we need to travel farther south today." Akilah studied the mid-afternoon sky. "We must pass beyond the shadow of this mountain while daylight still favors us."

"I insist." Nakal scowled and crossed his stocky arms over his broad chest. "You would dishonor me if you refused."

Akilah hesitated. Persian courtesy refused a kindness several times before accepting it, but he was at a loss regarding Nakal's customs. "Regrettably, we must leave without delay."

Nakal paced. After several circuits, he threw up his hands. "All right, all right. But you will take something of mine with you, yes? Dried toot-mulberries. Good for traveling—and to sweeten any drink."

At Akilah's lack of reaction, Nakal steepled his fingers in front of his face. "No, I have something better. Early dates, very fresh, the sweetest you have ever tasted for this time of year. Today's shipment is not yet unpacked. A special treat so early this year. You couldn't find fresher dates unless you picked them yourself, which"—Nakal laughed—"you most assuredly don't have time to do. But it is no trouble at all for me to offer them. Your whole caravan can enjoy them now or later. Yes?"

Across the room, Keket's stare engulfed all three Magi. "Take them," she mouthed. "Please."

Rashidi nudged Akilah. "If taking the dates will get us on our way, then accept them."

Akilah handed Nakal the money pouch again. This time he took it, a hunger glistening in his eyes. "Quickly, quickly, Keket. Bag the dates before our guests change their minds. I will help you."

"I can help," Rashidi said.

"No." Nakal shook his head. "This is our job, not yours."

Keket set her jaw. "It would not be right for someone of your status to enter a commoner's storeroom. Wait here. We will return shortly."

Chapter 42

Improvisation

The next morning

Surrounded by mist, Akilah stretched his hands toward the sun's first glimmers. Gold and orange rays squeezed between the mountains as he finished his first cycle of prayers. A breeze danced with the carpet of red, purple, and white wildflowers at his feet. He lingered, savoring the serenity and the sun's hints of a glorious day to come in this beautiful land.

Yesterday's trip to Susita was more profitable than he'd anticipated. And the closer they got to Jerusalem, the more welcoming the land became. The refreshing climate beckoned them onward. All were good omens for what lay ahead. Ushtá flooded Akilah's soul. He inhaled deeply, the cool air invigorating him almost as much as his anticipation of the last leg of the journey to Jerusalem.

"Akilah!" The chief healer's voice shattered the morning's silence.

Akilah turned. Sadiq was never that informal. Yet there he was, signaling frantically from the edge of the clearing. Without

New Star

hesitation, Akilah raced across the meadow, trampling flowers with every pace. He made a mental note to do penance for that later.

As Akilah neared Sadiq, the healer dropped to the ground. "A thousand pardons for interrupting your prayers. But your men are sick."

"How many?" Akilah's chest heaved with each word.

"Almost all the servants."

"What? How could that happen?"

"I'm still trying to determine that."

"But yesterday we stopped only at Susita. And we all ate the same food for second meal."

"Pardons again, my lord. But not everyone ate the dates."

"Dates?" Akilah seethed. He grabbed Sadiq's vest. "Did anyone feed dates to the camels?"

"No. The servants have been faithful in following your order to not give dates until foraging becomes sparse."

"What kind of sickness is this?"

"It starts with nausea and ... progresses."

"Can you treat it?"

"Possibly."

Akilah twisted Sadiq's vest tighter in his fists. "What does that mean?" He had no time for this complication.

"I can't tell if the sickness is from a poison or contagion. Mithridatium would treat poison, but we don't have enough to treat everyone. A silver preparation would treat contagion. But, again, we have a limited supply. Enough for everyone to have one dose but no more. If you would allow me and an escort to return to Susita immediately, I could purchase supplies of both."

"No." Akilah surprised himself with the force of his words. An unholy scenario swirled in his mind. Whether it arose from caution or paranoia, he could not tell. He swallowed the words he wanted to say. "We can't be certain that Susita has what we need. And we have no time to go back. We must press forward.

Make a note to fully supply the caravan with both medicines when we get to Jerusalem."

"But the men—"

"Will receive care here, in the best way we can give with what we have. If that means you must improvise, do it."

Sadiq bowed. "I can ... but it will mean staying here for at least a day. No traveling."

"Explain."

"We give everyone warm camel dung. But we must collect it as the camels expel it. The dung can heal many digestive ailments—but only while it is still warm." Sadiq shrugged his shoulders in apology. "It is readily available and addresses both poisons and contagions."

"A spear for the work of a scalpel." Akilah snapped to his full height. "I'll announce your plan to the caravan. Start the collection. Tell Hakeem to gather all the dates and bury them. Then have him search the saddlebags and gear. Do it quietly."

"Ah, yes. Some of the servants may have tried to hide dates for themselves."

"More than that. Poisoning the caravan might not be the full extent of our woes. We need to look for anything that isn't ours. We can't afford to be stopped and accused of stealing. Hakeem has a full account of our supplies."

While Sadiq raced back to camp, Akilah engrossed himself in more prayers. But he doubted their effectiveness. Dark thoughts of Nakal disrupted his petitions as he stomped up the rise to his caravan.

Moans floating over the crest of the hill greeted him. Urgent moments had eclipsed all semblances of Zoroastrian sanitation practices. He shook his head. This would be a long day.

Chapter 43

Taken

The next morning

A kilah paced in front of Sadiq. "Are the servants well enough to walk?"

"Some are still weak from fluid loss. Many have not slept."

"We can't afford another day without travel. We will go slow and rest as needed. Tell me if you see overt signs of distress. We have plenty of water. We leave in a half hour."

Packing commenced as Akilah ordered, but the absence of banters or complaints told him how poorly most servants still felt. He considered resting one more day but dismissed the notion.

For two hours, the only sounds coming from the caravan were saddles creaking and animals plodding. He reached into a pouch attached to his saddle and pulled out a map. Where should they stop next? Mountains surrounded them. He needed a clear, high spot to take measurements for their bearings.

Something zinged past Akilah's ear and knocked the map from his hands.

Before he could retrieve it, blood-curdling shrieks erupted from the hills. Seemingly from nowhere, nomads descended in a swarm. Farzaneh's protectors had time to release only a few volleys of arrows before the throng overwhelmed the caravan. Brandishing short swords and yelling gibberish, the nomads herded the terrified servants into a tight circle.

"*Gladius* swords," Tallis whispered to Akilah. "Only Roman soldiers have legal access to them."

What bandits would be so brazen as to attack a Roman contingent? Or perhaps they'd traded with people who had. Both scenarios sent ice down Akilah's spine. What chance of survival did his caravan have?

Camels gurgled and moaned, their mouths wide with fear as robbers dragged four of the animals over the crest of the nearest hill.

Akilah tried to cut through the rising chaos. "What do you want?" he yelled in Aramaic, Parthi, and Elamite. He glanced at his protectors. Vastly outnumbered, they had already been stripped of their bows and arrows.

Amid shouting and sword-waving, the brigands forced the Magi off their horses. One sunburned robber pointed to a case strapped to Kani's framework.

Akilah waved his arms. "Just instruments." He tried three other languages and cupped his hands upward to imitate stargazing.

With his dagger pointed at Akilah, the marauder eyed Kani's gear again. The sweaty man circled the camel and yanked a strap on its framework. In response, Kani landed a swift back-leg kick to his stomach, sending the man sprawling and Kani's load tilting.

Akilah reached to steady the camel's saddle but backed off when the thief scrambled to his feet, yelling something unintelligible and shifting his dagger between his hands. He lunged at Akilah and ripped the turban pin from his headwear.

Another ridded Tallis of his. The next instant, the Magi's horses squealed in terror as another thief grabbed their reins. Roaring and trumpeting followed as more thieves dragged the protectors' horses away. The noise almost drowned Rashidi's cry for help.

Two other robbers must have sneaked behind him. Rashidi struggled in vain while they tied his hands behind him. Jabbering incoherently, they grabbed his hair, jerking his head back as they pushed him up the hill behind the rearing horses.

"Rashidi!" Akilah started toward him, but the tip of a gladius stopped him. He could only peer through churning dust that almost obliterated any view of his young colleague.

Suddenly a high-pitched keen pierced the chaos. Raucous but retreating noises sounded beyond the ridge.

In that momentary distraction, Rashidi twisted and kicked his captors with all his might. They stumbled and loosened their grip. Another violent twist and Rashidi fell to the ground. He threw himself down the hill, the unforgiving rocky terrain cutting him as he rolled.

Stunned, the caravan watched him tumble to the road in a cloud of dust.

The robbers vanished as quickly as they had appeared.

"Everyone get to your assigned camels," Akilah ordered.

Had someone come to their aid? Or was the caravan about to be beset by a greater threat?

Akilah attended to what he could control. He hauled Rashidi to his feet. "Slow, deep breaths." He untied Rashidi's hands and leaned close to his ear. "Do a head count. Make sure all the servants are still here. Then have a healer tend you."

Dazed and shaken, Rashidi could only nod. He paused, dropped to his knees, and vomited.

"That's one way to release fear." Tallis pulled Akilah a few paces away. "Good idea to keep him busy. What did we lose?"

"Besides all the horses, at least three camels carrying food.

Maybe some gear and camels without loads. Hakeem will do a full accounting of our supplies. Seems the robbers' needs were mostly utilitarian."

Tallis shook his head. "So much for comfortable riding."

"Oh, the Nisean ..." Akilah's stomach lurched. The elite horse, used only for royal business, was valued as much as members of the royal family. He would have to compensate both his father and the government for the loss.

Tallis shrugged. "Given what just happened, let's be grateful that we still have our personal camels. But it looks like the nomads took most of what we bought in Susita. We'll need to resupply again before we reach Jerusalem. We have only one spare camel left for carrying gear and supplies. We might need to load our saddle camels, too, but their saddles aren't designed to carry such heavy loads."

"Resupply again?" Akilah's concerns mounted. He couldn't afford to buy more horses, and protectors on foot wouldn't be much help as sentries. Their extra bows and arrows remained safely stowed, but they couldn't afford to lose more.

Tallis scanned the rocky heights around them. "What do you think they were looking for?"

"Speed. And a quick way to acquire money. They didn't find our money pouches, so they took the next best things—our horses and Rashidi. His ethnicity and age would have fetched a high price. But some interruption convinced them otherwise."

Akilah walked around a cluster of camels. "Where is Hakeem? I need to know the status of our supplies."

Rashidi tapped him on the shoulder and held out a trampled, torn parchment. "I hope you have another map of this area." He winced and held his side. "All the servants are accounted for."

"Good. Go see the healer."

"Akilah, I am sorry. This was my fault."

"In what way?"

"I gave in to Keket's suggestion to take the dates. Keket—if that's really her name." Rashidi snorted. "And, if she's Egyptian, she's forgotten how to speak it."

Akilah arched his eyebrows in mock surprise.

"I urged you to accept the dates," Rashidi said. "They made us sick and weak. An easy target for ambush."

Akilah shrugged. "Taking the dates seemed a good decision at the time."

"Not a good decision. An expedient one."

"Then we will be more careful to avoid expediency in the future." Akilah signaled Hakeem.

Rashidi trailed after Akilah. "What about Nakal? Shouldn't we—"

"If he was involved in a larger scheme to slow our progress, then he deceived all of us. But you give yourself too much credit, Rashidi. I could have said no to your suggestion. Regardless, we can't afford to mire our progress with conjecture." Akilah trotted toward Hakeem.

"That's it?" Rashidi threw his hands in the air.

"You are alive. We can replace what we lost. Thankfully, all that is most important is still safe."

Chapter 44

Crossing the Jordan

The exuberance of rushing waters filled the air long before the caravan reached the Jordan's swollen banks. Akilah turned a deaf ear to the servants' mutterings. All of them shrank back except Kassim, Rashidi's personal attendant. Standing in between the Magi's camels, he seemed unafraid of the roiling muddy water. Even so, as he scanned it, his forehead sank into a frown.

Rashidi leaned across his camel to Akilah. "Are you sure this is where we should cross?"

"Yes," Akilah said, unperturbed. "Half a parasang south of the mouth of the Yarmuk River."

"It's still flooded from spring rains." Rashidi craned his neck downstream.

Surging water knotted spray around rocks. Plants and branches tumbled helplessly in the current. Driftwood, buffeted to sharpened points, impaled debris in its downriver rush.

"It looks fast but shallow. We'll test it." Akilah summoned Hakeem. "Get our longest length of rope. Pick a tall servant who can swim. Have him secure a rope across the river for safety.

Then cross with a pack camel to see if it can handle the current with its load. But don't use Kani."

Behind the Magi, the servants' murmurs grew.

"Maybe we should look for another crossing," Rashidi said.

But Akilah was resolute. "We need to press on. Here. Now."

"We could wait a few days for the waters to subside," Tallis suggested.

"We don't have time to spare," Akilah said.

Tallis shifted in his saddle. "Our camels are heavy with the weight of new supplies. We can't afford to lose any provisions to the river. And surely you can sense the servants' fears. They're not ready to cross. Not like this."

Akilah set his jaw. "You surprise me, Tallis. You led men into situations far more dangerous than this. Besides, it doesn't matter if the servants are ready."

"Your zeal approaches recklessness," Tallis said through clenched teeth. "Do not invite danger. It will be all too happy to travel with us. Besides, not everyone can swim."

"I can swim," Kassim said. "I'll go across and secure the rope."

"No." Rashidi dismounted and grabbed his personal servant's arm. "You're too valuable."

"I'm not afraid."

"Other servants can do it," Rashidi hissed. "Do your job."

Hakeem approached, one arm guiding Omid, a lanky man who seemed burdened with a weight far greater than the coils of rope on his shoulder. He shuffled forward, his head down.

"Everyone stay clear of the bank," Akilah called. "Give him room."

"If this doesn't work …" Tallis whispered to Akilah.

"Then we'll head south to the ford of Damiah near the mouth of the Jabbok River."

Tallis shook his head. "That takes us through a deep gorge—and into Samaritan territory. Mountainous and contentious."

Akilah shrugged off the concern. "We have no quarrel with the Samaritans. We don't share their ethnicity, culture, or religion."

"The mountains hide many robbers. They care only about what they can steal. Didn't we just learn that?" Tallis looked pointedly at Akilah.

He had no time for such talk. Focused on the moment at hand, he barked orders. "Secure the rope first. Then try fording the river with a camel."

Omid lashed one end of the rope to the stoutest tree near the bank and tentatively stepped into the racing water. It churned between his legs, challenging his balance. Akilah waved him on.

Kassim remained by Rashidi's side but strained to look upstream. "Omid! Watch out for driftwood! And snakes!"

Rashidi glared. "Mind your place."

Waist-high water seethed around Omid, its current an insistent tug on his tunic. He stopped.

"The current is too strong," he shouted. "And the river looks wider than the length of this rope."

"Go on," Akilah called.

Trembling, the servant hitched the coils higher on his shoulder. After a few more timid steps, he slid.

"Keep going." Akilah crossed his arms.

Another step. Water rose to Omid's chest.

Omid never saw the tree trunk and driftwood spikes tumbling toward him. He reeled from their impact. Rushing waters swallowed his scream as the current pulled him under.

Along the bank, the servants' muttering swelled to frenzied chatter. The protectors, brandishing their weapons, forced the servants away from the bank. Akilah started toward the river's edge, but Kassim beat him. Omid surfaced twenty paces downstream, a ribbon of blood circling him. Although his head was above the water, his glassy eyes stared vacantly ahead.

New Star

"Hang onto the rope!" Kassim yelled. "We'll pull you in!"

Omid disappeared again under the water. Rope uncoiled like a snake behind him.

As Kassim raced down the bank, Akilah prayed he would catch sight of Omid again.

"Omid, swim to the rope." Kassim's directive was barely heard between the servants' chaos and the noisy waters.

Akilah turned toward the river. Except for his hair moving with the water, Omid was strangely still.

"We have to get him!" Kassim shouted.

Ignoring Rashidi's "I forbid you," Kassim jumped into the water and half-swam, half-rode the current downstream. Dodging rocks and straight-arming branches in his path, he lurched his way forward.

Omid's body rolled face down with its left elbow bent upward, poking out of the water like a toy sail on a lake.

Akilah's pulse raced. What had he done? He couldn't bear the thought of losing one servant. Now two lives were at stake.

He struggled to watch the water's careening weight buffet Kassim. Plant debris slapped and slashed him. Spray drenched him. With strong strokes, Kassim cut across the current toward Omid. When a tree trunk rolled past, Kassim threw himself on it and slung one leg over the trunk to straddle it. Huddling low, he held on while the river hurtled him toward the unresponsive servant.

Omid's seemingly lifeless body rolled and drifted toward an eddy. Kassim leaned forward as far as he dared and paddled toward Omid, but the trunk slid from under him. It reared up and grazed the back of Kassim's head. Staggering, he managed to grab Omid before he lost his footing and went under.

Akilah barely realized what he was doing as he shouted orders and ran to the bank. Somehow, the strongest servants followed him and helped haul Omid and Kassim out of the water.

"Breathe!" he commanded. He rolled Kassim onto his side and motioned for the nearest servant to do the same with Omid.

Kassim opened his eyes.

"Don't move," Akilah said.

"Where is Sadiq?" His voice thundered above the water's roar. "Fetch him or another healer. Now."

The healer raced to the bank and slid to the ground with a leaf in hand. He poised it over Omid's nostrils for what felt like an eternity to Akilah.

When the leaf fluttered, relief flooded Sadiq's face. "He's breathing." He tossed the leaf aside and assessed Omid's wounds. "Lie still. Your arm is bad. And I need to pull splinters from your back."

Sadiq held up his hand in Kassim's direction. "Tell me what you can see."

"Your face, but it's fuzzy."

Squinting through the afternoon sun, the healer laid his hand on Kassim. "Omid is alive, thanks to you. Rest. You need almost as much attention as he does."

"I must attend to my master's camel." Kassim tried to rise, but Akilah pinned his shoulder to the ground with his muddy foot.

"No duties for you the rest of the day. I assigned Malachi your tasks for tonight." Akilah kept his foot on Kassim's shoulder until the servant nodded in acquiescence.

Akilah motioned to Sadiq and drew him a dozen paces away. "How badly are these two hurt?"

"No lifting or hard work for at least a month after I set this one's arm. I don't know about his leg yet. He may have to rest from walking. As for the other, he needs to rest for at least a day. I can tell you more tomorrow."

Akilah instructed Hakeem to oversee making a sledge for Omid. Being dragged behind a camel would be an uncomfortable ride, but it seemed their only option. All the camels were carrying supplies and gear.

Like purified water that is exhausted and drained away after priestly ceremonial washing, Akilah's energy left him. He sagged against a tree trunk, all self-sufficiency spent. He had just risked two people's lives for something he believed in. Would he be as willing to risk his own life for his convictions?

He circled back to check on Kassim and Omid but stopped within earshot as she saw Hakeem talking with them.

"You are lucky, my friend." Hakeem bent over Kassim.

"What happened?"

"A tree trunk hit you. But somehow you held on to Omid," Hakeem said. "My master started a human chain so we could pull both of you from the river."

✡✡✡

"We'll stay here at the Jordan for second meal," Akilah announced to the caravan.

As the throng of servants scattered to their evening duties, Rashidi, his face etched in granite, headed toward Kassim. Akilah moved with speed to divert his colleague. Pressing his hand into Rashidi's back, he said, "Leave him, my friend. He conducted himself well."

"He disobeyed me."

"To serve a greater good."

"Should I allow my servant to defy me? That's a short journey to chaos."

"Or a short walk to greater trust and mutual respect."

"They're servants. Obeying without question is what they do. And you—you broke Magi protocol in—" Rashidi stopped, abashed. "Thank you for helping save my servant."

Tallis appeared between them. "Speaking of servants …" He

jerked his head toward six of them listening to a young but hardened-looking servant.

"If Omid had been one of the masters' servants, they would have been quicker to try to save him," the servant said.

"Tahrea." Akilah exhaled the name. Tahrea was Farzaneh's "reclamation project."

"How can you know that?" another servant replied. "We couldn't see everything that happened."

Tahrea scowled. "Hakeem did. But he doesn't count. He may as well be one of them, the way he orders us around. And did you see how his boss tried to revive Kassim first?"

"Our evening routine hasn't changed." Akilah's voice boomed over the group. "Camel grooming and feeding before second meal." Servants always found something to complain about, but he'd need to keep a closer eye on Tahrea. Perhaps on all the servants.

Akilah looked for Kassim. The waterlogged hero, a ruggedly fit young man, was propped against a tree, still dazed from the day's ordeal.

Akilah crouched in front of him. "I must ask ... When you were at the river's edge, it looked like you could read the water."

Kassim nodded and looked down. His damp hair, still matted with river refuse, fell over his face in wavy, loose curls, like grape vines dangling from a trellis.

"Few people are such strong swimmers. Did you grow up near water?"

Another nod. "On an island ... between Anatolia and Greece."

"You performed a great service today. Thank you." Akilah patted the servant's shoulder. "Now rest."

Chapter 45

Conflict of Interest

"Tallis, help me search for that map." Akilah wriggled into dry clothes while shuffling through a trunk. "After second meal, we'll continue south to the ford of Damiah near the mouth of the Jabbok River."

"We would have to travel well into the night to reach the Jabbok River. Tired, distracted servants make dangerous mistakes. Camp here for the night. Let everyone enjoy their second meal at leisure here by the Jordan, even if it's morning leftovers."

"We must keep moving."

"No, *you* feel we must keep moving. This isn't a military march. What is driving you so?"

Akilah couldn't divulge his true reason. Money issues aside, he couldn't shake the urgency burning in his heart to find this child before … Before what? He couldn't say. He didn't want to lie, but how could his colleagues understand what he couldn't understand himself? "I … Time seems … short."

"Your words say one thing, but your eyes tell another story. Which one is truth?"

"Our finances are lower than they should be, and every

unexpected cost worsens our situation." Akilah lowered his voice to a whisper.

"Understandable," Tallis said. "But I've traveled with you for ten years. This isn't the first time our finances have run low. Something deeper troubles you."

"The letter you received from the Hebrew scribe mentioned six-hundred-eighty-something years. Why would he write such a specific number—then talk about 'fullness' right after that? Did he mean 'fullness of time'? What if he was telling us about something momentous predestined to happen *now*? Something we can't afford to miss?" Akilah grabbed Tallis's arm. "You know more about genealogy than all of us. Did you learn anything else about the timing of this eternal child-king's birth?"

"Nothing I could confirm."

"But—"

Tallis motioned toward a murmuring throng of servants. "Time is not your biggest enemy. You are."

Akilah recoiled in anger, but Tallis ignored his reaction. "You need to unify the caravan. Your cousin's servants claim we're treating our servants preferentially. Omid's rescue added fuel to their fire."

Recalcitrant servants and raging waters could not ruin his plans. "Maybe you should lead this expedition," he snapped. "You were good at rallying people around grand causes."

"Don't you *ever* mention my past. You took an oath." Tallis's words seethed like the churning Jordan River that had defeated them.

Akilah winced. In his anger, he'd almost violated a sacred boundary he had vowed to keep with Tallis. He couldn't risk that. Too much was at stake for too many people.

Tallis jerked his head toward the servants. "Listen."

"The camels get to rest. When do we?"

Akilah cringed. Tahrea again. Would he be a perennial

troublemaker? Was his cousin's "reclamation project" beyond salvaging?

"Don't think about it," another servant said. "Makes it easier. Come on. We have to feed and groom the camels."

Tahrea shoved the other servant and pointed to the animals. "They get to eat before we do." The rising pitch in his voice indicated he was just getting started.

A few servants laughed weakly. But complaining, like snow on a mountain, can quickly gather strength and destructive power.

"Look at the masters' saddle camels. They eat better and even dress better than we do. Neck collars. Halters with tassels. More status than we'll ever have."

Akilah glanced at his camel, Dain. Five rows of crescent-shaped silver ornaments sewn on scarlet cloth encircled his curly golden mane. His multicolored woven halter sported oversized scarlet, blue, and gold tassels. Even Dain's *mahawi* was regal. The highest-quality leather saddle, cushioned by fine wool pads and thick, elaborately woven blankets. Tahrea had a point.

"And have you noticed how the masters prefer to talk with their own servants?" Tahrea continued. "Their servants look down on us—"

"Because you're *gardas*," a Magi servant taunted.

"We are *not*."

"You aren't here willingly. Someone paid to press you into service. That makes you a garda. A slave."

With a roar, Tahrea hurled himself at his insulter, tackling him at the knees. The servant buckled and hit the dirt. The two rolled over and over, wrestling to pin each other to the ground.

"We are servants just like you are." Tahrea spat the words through clenched teeth. His right hook connected with the Magi servant's jaw. The servant yowled and lunged for Tahrea's throat.

Hakeem, who had been watching from a discrete distance,

sprang into action. "Get off!" He heaved one servant aside and hauled the other to his feet. "Explain yourself."

His fists still clenched, Tahrea spat at his adversary's feet. "You Magi servants act like you're the only *bandags* here. You treat us like gardas."

"Enough. No one here is a garda," Hakeem shouted, shoving the two farther apart. "All of us are servants, not slaves. The next one making that accusation will be punished—with striping."

Hakeem barked commands for the Magi servants to return to their duties. Then he addressed the on-loan servants. "On this trip, your masters are the Magi. You follow *their* rules. They are fair, but they do things differently than you're used to. Your job is to obey them and make every moment of your work count."

"How?" Tahrea seemed more concerned with dusting himself off than listening to instruction. "Say we saved a few seconds packing and unpacking each day. What difference will that make?" He shrugged. "It won't get us where we're going any sooner."

Hakeem glared. "Over a few weeks, that could mean enough time to stay ahead of a storm and reach safety. You won't appreciate that until you experience it. I don't advise learning it that way."

Although Hakeem was handling things well, Akilah groaned. What more could he expect from Tahrea? Yet Akilah didn't want to judge the servant from one scuffle.

Scanning the circle around him, Hakeem continued. "Just as important, make sure the camels stay strong and healthy. If you see any sign of limping, sores on their legs, feet, or backs, you tell me or one of our healers immediately. Yes?"

Hakeem prodded the servants from their sullen silence with a more forceful "Yes?"

When the servants saw the Magi in the background, they mumbled their agreement and dispersed like autumn leaves in a strong wind. Rushing to their stations, they gave the Magi a wide berth.

Akilah sighed and turned to Tallis. "Why the fuss about slavery? Persians don't own slaves."

A shadow crossed Tallis's face. "Yes, they do. They're just out of sight."

"What?"

"Captives of war," Tallis said, his eyes dark and brooding. "Traded like loot ... treated like chattel ... mutilated so they can't run away. Serving royalty and government officials as disposable labor. Punishments lorded over them that make dying a mercy. Persians have perfected the art of prolonging death. Scaphism, crucifixion—"

"Stop." Akilah shuddered. Every time he learned more about Persian government, he regretted it. The Megistanes directly served the highest levels of government. Did Megistanes also harbor slaves? The Chief never talked about that or any aspect of his work. Probably best. Akilah didn't want to know.

Once in their tent, Akilah approached Tallis. "Many pardons for what I said out there. I spoke out of frustration and fatigue. I did not mean to resurrect the past."

Tallis paused over his clothing chest and bobbed his head. "Anything else?"

The halting cadence of Akilah's words mirrored the struggle in his heart. "Before we started this journey, I talked about preparing our hearts for what we might learn. I think I'm learning that this trip is more than a search for knowledge." He stopped. Rashidi seemed frozen, bent in half over his clothing trunk. Akilah was acutely aware his words might change his young colleague's perception of him forever. But he had to unburden his heart.

"Knowledge is a conquest for me. Master one topic, then move on to the next."

"I can appreciate that." Tallis shrugged into his cloak.

Akilah plopped on a cushion. "But now ... we are pursuing knowledge we may learn more of but never conquer." He glanced at Rashidi, also pulling a cloak from his clothing trunk.

But Rashidi straightened and clapped a hand on Akilah's shoulder. "We'll just have to wait and see. All part of the journey, yes? That's a measure of being a Magi scholar."

Akilah couldn't bring himself to admit he might not have the skills or wisdom to make the unprecedented decisions needed for this endeavor. Leading the caravan through dangers he couldn't anticipate was just a fraction of the risk. Three-fourths of the servants had no loyalty to him. He didn't know their destination, but he couldn't tell the caravan that. If they caught even a hint of that truth, chaos would ensue. Even with his colleagues' help, how could he succeed?

Tallis touched Akilah's other shoulder. "Don't you still need to take readings for tonight? We'll go with you."

Akilah had never been so grateful for that show of solidarity. Whether the Jordan's waters had drowned his self-sufficiency or not, he would need to rely on his colleagues more.

Wrapped in their cloaks, the three ascended the closest hill with their oil lamps and instruments. As the camp shrank behind them, its fire dwindled to a miniature ball of light in the darkness. Silhouetted against the sky, Akilah pulled out his astrolabe and cross-staff. He caught his breath. When they were finished, the three descended in a hurry.

"Not long now," Akilah whispered as they crossed the camp. But his enthusiasm dwindled as he overheard the servants' mumblings.

"They said the same thing two days ago. So what?"

"Does anyone know where we're going?"

"Jerusalem, I think."

"I'll bet that Hakeem fellow knows more. He's the caravan master."

"He wouldn't say if he did."

New Star

Akilah connected with Hakeem's gaze, but his head servant looked away and vanished into his tent. Even collective Magi wisdom might be inadequate for this trip. A more disturbing concern crossed Akilah's mind. What if the priests in Jerusalem couldn't or wouldn't help them? Would they have to rely on the God of the Hebrews to reveal their destination?

Chapter 46

Religion versus Science

Two days later

Akilah huddled before the fire, quietly saying evening prayers. He was grateful for religion he could practice outdoors, especially when traveling. Outdoors simply made sense to him. A truly powerful god couldn't be contained in a building, so why erect one? Yet most religions did.

Disturbingly, some of those practices had crept into the Parthian Empire's national religion. Regions north of Persia now used enclosed temples with interior altars. Was that area so remote from the empire's capitals that it felt it could do as it pleased? Or had that area capitulated to Hellenism? Either way, it seemed to be a step toward the excesses Akilah had seen of other countries' temples and trappings.

Religion without edifices and statues suited him just fine. *I sound like a religious purist like Fakhri. Or Sassanak.* The last thought disgusted him. Over the years, Sassanak's faultless but rigid diligence in honoring Persia's official religion had become a platform for intolerance toward anyone who dared deviate from its beliefs in any measure.

New Star

Distance from his superior and the Council's affairs afforded Akilah the space to ponder Sassanak's agenda behind his actions. Had Sassanak's religious diligence helped his meteoric yet controversial rise to Head Magus? Was such vigilance justified—or even needed?

Alone with his honesty, Akilah had to admit Sassanak's stern warning to not mix science with religion had only strengthened his resolve to pursue his "star study" as far as Jerusalem. He had prided himself on tolerating his superior's gibes for more than a year. Regrettably, he'd used that pride to rationalize his growing resentment of the man. He would need to wrestle more with that before he could banish it.

Whether Sassanak's office compelled him to uphold a larger agenda or not, he was still Akilah's senior in years and rank. To identify with him in even the smallest measure unnerved Akilah. He'd grown so accustomed to being against anything his superior promoted that doing otherwise seemed a conflict of interest. But the heart of Zoroastrianism was good thoughts lead to good words. Combined, they lead to good actions. What principles had Akilah neglected while studying this star? Was he loyal only to the parts of religion that were convenient or comfortable for him to practice?

Akilah returned to the Magi's tent and settled onto his favorite rug, a token of home from his meditation room. The vivid cypress tree motif, a Persian symbol of death and life, reminded him to keep pressing on to find this new life foretold.

If only the scribe's message hadn't been so heavily damaged. But it had roused something deep within Akilah. That memory inspired. A competing memory irritated. A memory from that fateful progress meeting before the Council.

We are concerned about how much value you are placing on writings that link this object in the sky with a larger purpose. Astrology and mythology are replete with such inferences.

> *Moreover, Jewish history and its writings are full of controversy. One would be hard pressed to correlate disparate writings spread over so many hundreds of years. Furthermore, in the larger scheme of things, we must be careful to not confuse religion with science ...*

In his pursuit of this prophesied child, had he muddied science with religion?

The Council's words weren't the only reason he questioned himself. He slipped his hand into his inner cloak pocket to once again feel the two small papyri he'd found in the extra blankets Farzaneh's head servant had given him at the last minute before they left Assur. Should he tell his colleagues about them?

The first papyrus contained two sentences, both attributed to the Hebrew prophet Isaiah.

> *The people who walked in darkness have seen a great light; those who dwelt in a land of deep darkness, on them has light shone.*[1]

> *The spirit of the LORD shall rest on him, the spirit of wisdom and understanding, the spirit of counsel and might, the spirit of knowledge and the fear of the LORD.*[2]

The other papyrus contained only one sentence, constructed almost like a lyric, also attributed to the prophet Isaiah.

> *Lift up your eyes on high*
> *And see who has created these stars,*
> *The One who leads forth their host by number,*
> *He calls them all by name;*

---

1. Isaiah 9:2 (ESV)
2. Isaiah 11:2 (ESV)

Because of the greatness of His might and the strength of His power,
Not one of them is missing.[3]

Akilah's heart raced every time he read the words. His inmost being told him the phrase "seen a great light" referred to the star and the child they were seeking. But how could a centuries-dead person speak of a light Akilah had seen a year ago? Similarly, "The spirit of the Lord will rest upon him" described a person—echoing the words in the scribe's message to Tallis.

The other papyrus scrap catapulted Akilah's astronomy senses to dizzying heights. How could this Hebrew God know, name, and keep track of *every star* in the sky? Were the words merely poetry, or was the Hebrew God truly that powerful?

Most important, who wrote those papyri? The two scraps were separate thoughts. How had they gotten tucked into a blanket that someone in Farzaneh's household had possessed?

Akilah shook his head. If only the note had come with some explanation. Or a signature.

He ran his fingers across the letterforms. The handwriting seemed familiar, even comforting. It contained extra flourishes like Akilah's mother would add in correspondence to close friends and family, but the strokes weren't quite the same. Or were they? His mother's body had been laid in the Tower of Silence twenty years ago. Moreover, she had never professed an interest in Hebrew writings. In her final year, she had devoted her waning energy to helping Farzaneh become self-sufficient.

Farzaneh.

Akilah hurled open the lid of one of his clothing trunks. Plunging his hand to the bottom, he fished until he felt his cat statue. His excuse for packing it was that the secret

---
3. Isaiah 40:26 (NASB)

compartment might prove handy for hiding sensitive documents. His true reason for bringing it was he didn't want to leave Farzaneh's stūrīh behind where probing eyes might find it. Packing the statue before he was incarcerated was a great serendipity. No. A blessing.

He extracted the stūrīh from the hidden cavity. If his hunch was right, Farzaneh would not have entrusted such a personal contract to be scribed. She would have written it herself.

Akilah's hand shook as he unrolled the stūrīh next to the sentences from Isaiah.

The handwriting was identical.

That raised as many questions as his musings of the words' meaning. What did Farzaneh know of Isaiah's writings? What message was she trying to convey in the sentences she chose? What had constrained her from giving them directly to Akilah?

No otherventure he'd undertaken had been fraught with so many questions he couldn't answer.

The Hebrew prophet Isaiah seemed to hold the key to many details about the child the Magi sought. As fascinating and frustrating as that was, it also brought the Council's warning into sharp relief. But taking words out of context was dangerous.

Akilah slid the stūrīh back into its hiding place and buried the statue in his clothes just as Rashidi and Tallis returned from their evening inspection of the camp. Tents offered little privacy, so Akilah kept his voice low. "Gentlemen, are religion and science mutually exclusive?"

Rashidi stabbed at the dirt with a dry stick. "Yes. Maybe." He shrugged.

"No," Tallis said firmly. "If the goal of both is to find truth, how can they *not* intersect? And if you accept the idea of an all-knowing God, then mankind simply discovers what God already knows."

Rashidi's eyes narrowed. "Does this have something to do with the Council?"

"They cautioned me to keep religion and science separate in our study."

"They'll have our heads if this is a wild goose chase." Rashidi snapped the stick in half.

"We wouldn't have planned, done, and risked all of this if we didn't believe the Hebrews' writings," Akilah replied. "As for the Council, some maintained our study stretched the limits of their scholarly guidelines. But due process prevailed." Inwardly, he groaned. Circumstances compelled him to whitewash the Council's words and actions.

"Still, our reputations are at stake."

Rashidi, the overachiever. Such weighty worries for one so young. Matched only by his almost obsessive dedication to research. But risk? Rashidi was risking nothing compared with Akilah.

His throat tightened. His colleagues knew his career was in double jeopardy, but not to what extent. "We all want to be Magi for life. But this is different from our other studies. It has more ... purpose. Hard to put into words."

"I wonder if anyone else is pursuing this," Tallis mused.

Rashidi scratched his head. "If we find this child—"

"*When* we find this child," Akilah corrected.

"We could witness history in the making." Tallis stroked his beard.

Akilah nodded. "It's hard to know what to expect."

"We haven't seen the star this whole time," Rashidi said. "And we still don't know exactly where to go."

"We'll figure that out in Jerusalem."

"How?"

"We ask."

Chapter 47

Jerusalem's Splendor

The day dawned as all others had during this trek. Everyone rose early to walk in the morning, rest during the hottest part of the day, then walk again. Since entering Jericho, the road had been one long upward climb. Now another ascent. The camels' labored steps mirrored everyone's fatigue.

"The hills of Jerusalem!" The protector's cry from the head of the caravan pierced the late afternoon drudge.

Their destination was in sight.

So were thick, dark clouds gathering in the southwest to meet them. The caravan's last parasang seemed interminable as they toiled uphill against gusts of wind.

Hakeem eyed the sky. "Looks like rain."

Akilah followed his line of sight. A slate overcast shrouded the heavenlies above them. How could any stars pierce that cover—especially *the* star he hoped to see again? "We should reach Jerusalem ahead of it. Let's quicken the pace. Everyone is tired. We don't want to be tired *and* wet."

Just when the caravan's pace faltered, a wide plateau opened before them. And upon it, Jerusalem.

"Is that the Temple of the Hebrews' God towering above the whole city?" It's ... astounding. Awe-inspiring." Rashidi exhaled his astonishment. "But where do we enter the city?"

"Our instructions say to approach from the east, through what the Hebrews call the Golden Gate—or, in our language, the Gate of Mercy," Akilah said.

The gate wasn't difficult to find. The Temple rose behind Jerusalem's walls like a beacon pointing to the Golden Gate. The name belied the gate's grandeur—two grand arches decorated with friezes, each arch harboring a doorway wider than two men's height.

As Akilah conferred with one of the gate guards, the exhausted caravan collapsed against the city's outer wall. Akilah wanted to do the same. Instead, he patiently answered question after question and heard a second time that they must wait. Resigned to foreign bureaucracy, he joined the caravan by the outer wall. Its colossal limestone blocks were an engineering feat Rashidi would find worthy of study. Akilah leaned against the massive wall and let its coolness sooth hundreds of parasangs of weariness. He looked up to give thanks and gasped. Standing against the wall's base, he couldn't see its top. Ground level was such a limited view compared to their first glimpse of the city when they summited the mountains rimming Jerusalem.

"What's the delay?" Tallis said.

"Not sure," Akilah replied. "All the questions seemed standard until I said we were here to see the new king. Did you see the guards' blank looks? As if they didn't know what we were talking about."

Tallis shrugged. "Or maybe they think we're spies. Parthia controlled this area more than thirty years ago."

Akilah hoped that wasn't the case. Although the caravan's size was more modest than he'd originally planned, it was still flanked with protectors, and their Parthian clothes were the exception in this crowd.

Finally, one of the immense wood and iron doorways groaned open.

In defiance of the gathering darkness, the city was aglow with torchlight and the buzz of people in its streets. One sight, higher and brighter than all others, dominated the caravan's view. A tiered complex on the highest hill, its walls reaching more than one hundred fifty cubits toward heaven. On the top tier, a resplendent building glistening with white marble, bronze doors, gold columns and a gold-studded rooftop.

"The Temple of the Hebrews' God," Tallis whispered.

"Good thing it's dusk," a servant said. "I heard you can blind yourself if you look at the Temple when the sun's out."

Another servant scoffed. "Mind the camels. Don't let them run off like your imagination has."

The caravan skirted the colonnades of the Temple's outermost courtyard, briefly stopping at one gate.

✡✡✡

"Well, that didn't go as planned." Rashidi sighed with frustration.

"We didn't know the extent of the priests' purification requirements. Or what they're not allowed to do on certain days of the week. Or that we would have to purify ourselves so we could stand in their presence." Akilah bit his tongue. Purification rituals were a part of every religion he served. But the Hebrews' rituals barricaded him from finding the answers he'd traveled months to find. To literally stand on the doorstep of those answers and be denied the chance to satisfy himself was a bitter pill to swallow.

"We can't fault ourselves for that," Tallis said. "We knew only what we could find about their traditions and what they mentioned in their letters to us." He shifted in his saddle. "That presents a problem of time. The Levite said we would need days to become ceremonially clean. Plus, the priests won't receive us until after they conduct their weekly public service and Shabbat ends. Maybe someone else could tell us how to find the child. But who?"

"Honored servants of the Most High, you seek the One of Three." As if on cue, a voice called from the shadows.

Akilah scanned the darkness. His vantage point astride his camel should have enabled him to see far into the shadows, but he couldn't discern anyone. "Who are you? Show yourself."

A woman cloaked in scarlet and black stepped into the torchlight. Her attractive curves, marred by a hardness in her face, made it impossible to guess her age. Copper bangles glinted against a string of strange symbols on her headscarf. A heavy snake-skin collar sewn with cowrie shells wrapped her neck. The same motif adorned the hems of her sleeves, sash, and long tunic.

An unholy dread gripped Akilah. The woman grabbed his leg, letting her sleeve slip back to reveal a henna-stained tattoo on her forearm. "Honored servant of the Most High—"

"Who are you?" Akilah shook off her grip. "Why are you bothering us?"

"You seek the One of Three. He is not here. But I can tell you where he is."

A chill coursed down Akilah's spine. "Information that no doubt comes with a price. What is yours?"

She pulled a pouch from her sash. "You cannot pay for what is beyond price. I cannot charge for what cannot be bought." Her dark eyes glowed with reflected torchlight as she opened the pouch. "I can only show you. Come. You will see." Bones with etched markings rattled into her hand. She stretched her open palm toward Akilah and beckoned him down from his camel.

As a youth, Akilah had seen Chaldean seers interpret bones

and entrails. That form of divination had repulsed him. But when he saw mediums conjure apparitions, an otherworldly dread had descended upon him. Despite how much he wanted to revolt against all his father stood for, the experience had driven him to his family's religion—his country's official religion. A safe, comfortable place in a society full of its followers.

He hadn't felt that same otherworldly dread until now.

"Leave us, woman. You have no part in our business."

"Honored servant of the Most High—" Her voice rose.

"In the name of the Hebrews' God, be gone," Akilah roared.

The woman writhed as if a scorpion had stung her. As quickly as she had appeared, she shrank back into the shadows.

Akilah gathered his wits. Did he just swear an oath or speak a declaration? Where had it come from? Somewhere deep inside his gut. Uttered without thinking. But with a power beyond his understanding.

He shook off the event. He needed to get his caravan to its lodgings without further delay. Beyond the Temple, the caravan passed elegant villas gleaming in torchlight. Arched bridges, opulent villas, and other splendid buildings rose before the caravan.

"Jerusalem is more magnificent than I ever imagined," Rashidi said.

Jerusalem's streets were bursting with sights, smells, and sounds. People jostling. Vendors hawking. Gamblers cajoling. Falbins fortune-telling. Snake charmers fluting. Chanters thrumming. Dancers jingling. Guides shouting. Camels moaning. Goats bleating. Donkeys braying. Braziers sizzling. The clamor swelled to a cacophony that threatened to swallow the caravan halfway through the Upper City.

Abruptly, the noise ebbed. The crowd parted effortlessly like a silk drape drawn back.

"You three. Come." Soldiers motioned the Magi away from their caravan.

Chapter 48

Opulence and Unease

Akilah shifted uneasily atop his saddle camel. Once again, the Magi waited, this time outside of Herod's palace complex. Before them rose a citadel-like wall studded with towers, enclosing who-knew-what beyond. A lookout must have seen the Magi arrive with the soldiers because the weighty gate before them inched open, scratching a shallow groove in the ground.

Tallis turned to his colleagues. "Speak only Latin when you address Herod and anyone in his service." His voice was tight.

Rashidi swallowed hard. "I'm not well versed in Latin."

"Then tonight's conversation will not wind you."

Rashidi's eyes remained riveted on the gate. "Are you sure the courier got the message right?"

"No one keeps a king waiting, especially when he sends you an escort." Akilah sniffed his sleeve and hoped for the best.

Tallis gripped his saddle horn. "This is wrong. We needed to talk with the priests first, to ask them about Isaiah's writings."

Rashidi grimaced. "Do you think one of those guards sent a message to Herod?"

"It seems so." Tallis's posture remained stiff, as if on high alert.

"We shouldn't have been so open about our business." Rashidi glanced nervously around.

"Too late now." Akilah shrugged.

The gate's groaning ceased. A soldier motioned the Magi through the slit in its inward swing. Akilah suppressed a gasp as staid metal and wood gave way to a stunning panorama.

A sprawling complex defying description spread before them. Royal guards ushered the trio across a colonnade-shaded walkway into gardens punctuated with exotic trees and babbling bronze fountains. Peacocks meandering through the gardens studied the group. A couple of males fanned their feathers, but not to impress the humans.

The Magi passed between grandiose twin buildings. Ahead of them, high on its own plateau, Herod's palace gleamed in white marble, its huge stones fitted with such precision that the entire edifice appeared to be made of a single stone. Its splendor was second only to the Temple of the Hebrews' God.

In a fluid exchange, the guards left when someone dressed in linens befitting a head servant appeared. "Herod the Great, king of the Jews, bids you welcome and awaits your attendance in this banquet hall." He gestured to one of the twin buildings. "But first, he invites you to prepare for dinner. This way, please."

Soon the Magi found themselves in an opulent bathhouse.

"Undress here," The head servant ushered the Magi into a room covered with mosaic tiles of undulating wave motifs. Akilah stopped to gawk, but the servant was all business. "Ahead is the heated bath. To the right, the tepid pool. Beyond, the cold room. Slaves will scrub you with olive oil. Others will guide you to each bath. When you have soaked long enough, the slaves will scrape dirt and oil from you. The head servant lifted his chin. "You may need more than one cycle of baths."

"Just like a Roman bathhouse," Tallis whispered.

"I will prepare fresh clothes for you to wear in the presence of the king." The servant turned to go. "When you are cleansed, your final preparation will be an anointing with noble oil. King Herod rarely orders this. Consider it a high honor. He must be preparing quite a feast for you." The servant bustled from the room.

Two hours later, refreshed and clean, the Wise Men entered the expansive dining hall, its ambiance dripping with opulence. Gleaming floors reflected marble columns soaring to the cedar-beamed ceiling. Elaborate frescoes and inlaid artwork rich with multicultural imagery graced the walls. Exotic trees and foliage gushed from glazed ceramic pots. And tables. Not ones where diners reclined, but tables with chairs to sit upright. Three massive, intricately carved tables, situated in a U shape, opened to the center of the room.

Akilah peered past the servants enveloping him. He could almost guess who were family, statesmen, and other guests by the way the servants seated them. From a few guests' jealous glances, Akilah surmised the Magi had garnered a spot of importance in the middle section of the U, to the left of an oversized, ornate chair that likely was where Herod would sit.

Herod entered the room, flanked by two servants leading cheetahs on heavy metal leashes. Everyone rose and bowed.

"Welcome to our special guests tonight, our neighbors to the east of our great kingdom," he proclaimed with a flourish.

The evening unfolded with rehearsed precision. The servants' attentiveness was impeccable. The food far more abundant and elegant than the Magi had eaten in months.

Bejeweled guests swathed in fine linens and silks chatted in a mélange of languages, but not with the Magi.

As Akilah waited to be spoken to, he traced the carving on the arms of his chair and stretched his long legs under the table. He guessed the table could seat fifty. A seemingly endless procession of servants had borne so much food that the feast spread across the table's entire length.

"They just brought in a roasted boar," Rashidi whispered to Akilah. "We don't eat swine, and neither do Hebrews. What should we do? We can't offend the king."

"Perhaps our host is being all-inclusive. Fill your plate with other food and pretend to be full if some is offered to you." Akilah leaned into Tallis. "This could feed our entire caravan for many days." Months of travel and lack of sufficiency now stood in stark contrast to this affluent banquet. Despite his hunger, he resisted the urge to indulge until Herod began eating with abandon.

Herod glided effortlessly from one subject to another, pausing strategically to emphasize a point or ensure a response. "Have you been to my port city of Caesarea? Its harbor is larger than Alexandria's."

"My fortress at Machaerus is impenetrable. You would appreciate its architecture."

"Have you attended an Olympiad? The games are much improved since I started financing them."

The king's edacity for food seemed as voracious as his passion for his building projects. "Try this garum on your fish. I import the garum from Hispania."

"These bananas are from Aksum."

"You must taste the roasted ostrich; I brought the birds from Northern Africa and bred them here."

He pointed to a stew-like dish exuding ginger, garlic, and turmeric. "Have some of this." At a snap of his fingers, a scantily clad female server slid halfway onto his lap and ladled a steaming spoonful from the double-handled serving bowl into his mouth. He traced the server's bare thigh as he chewed.

Whether food or flesh delighted the king more, Akilah could not tell.

Herod momentarily closed his eyes in rapture. "Delicious.

Made with coconut milk," he exulted. "Coconuts are impossible to get here. I import them from Hindustan. I'll send a crate of them with you. No, three. How many crates can you carry?"

Rashidi almost rose from his seat. Anger stoked fire in his eyes as he turned to Akilah. "In Egypt, coconuts are food of the pharaohs. The world beyond Judea knows about coconuts. If he wants to give us a rare gift, persimmon oil would impress."

Akilah silenced his younger colleague with a scowl. This evening had to be more productive than an exercise in international etiquette. Before Akilah could respond to Herod's offer of coconuts, the king moved to another topic.

"Learning about different governments is one of my passions. How do you select a king?"

"By committee," Tallis said.

Herod's eyes gleamed. "Are you part of that committee?"

"We are not part of the division that concerns itself with governmental affairs." Akilah shot a warning look at Tallis.

"You have no ties to your government?"

"We are priest-scholars, great king." Akilah bobbed his head in lieu of standing and bowing.

"I see." Herod's eyes once again shifted to the banquet hall's door.

Did Akilah dare voice what he would have asked the priests? If so, he should ask soon. The king's conversation was growing more self-aggrandizing with each course served. Whatever was on the other side of the door must have been detained. Was now the best time?

Akilah opened his mouth, but Herod's hand silenced him. He motioned to a servant, who set small silver vessels in front of Herod and the Magi.

"Drink. It enhances the experience." Herod lifted his vessel and imbibed deeply as throbbing music started.

Experience? Akilah brought the vessel to his lips but only sniffed the slightly syrupy liquid. Poppy juice. The bitter smell was unmistakable. Careful to not let his lips touch it, he pretended to drink. He raised his eyebrows to Tallis and Rashidi and shook his head ever so slightly to deter them from consuming it.

Dancers streamed into the room, their bodies undulating with hedonistic abandon. Herod downed the rest of his drink with a capsule that Akilah surmised was pressed poppy leaves or petals. More "enhancement." Or a pain killer.

With each swirl in front of the Magi, the dancers' lithe, perfumed bodies engulfed the trio in a mesmerizing mixture of lilies, calamus, spikenard, myrrh, and balm. Three more dancers circled past the tables, their spins arcing incense burners on chains. The sweet scent of qunabu wafting from the burners simultaneously sickened and calmed Akilah. The room grew brighter, its colors more vibrant. Every sound intensified. In another pass by each table, the dancers spritzed each diner with rose water.

The music swelled to a frenzy. Matching each beat, the dancers converged in front of Herod, their thighs quivering. On the final chord, they flung their shimmering skirts at his feet and fell to the floor.

Herod rose from his seat, arms open wide. "Oh, this gives me *great* pleasure." He lingered over each word. He turned to the Magi. "Would you agree, my honored guests?"

Unsure of what to do or say, Akilah rose and bowed to the king. Tallis and Rashidi scrambled from their seats to follow suit.

The dancers exited as quickly as they'd entered, but their redolent scents remained, along with their skirts. Most of the diners acted refreshed by the rose water and unaffected by the heavy perfumes, but Akilah's dizziness grew. This was unlike any intoxication he'd encountered. He must ask Herod now, while his senses were intact—or he might miss his opportunity.

"Great king, in your wisdom, you must know of many Jewish teachings."

Herod, now reseated in the comfort of his heavily cushioned chair, tilted his chin down and smiled. "Of course. After all, I *am* king of the Jews."

"Then may I prevail upon your great knowledge to help us solve a puzzle? We are looking for the whereabouts of the One who has been born King of the Jews."

"I can forgive your lack of familiarity with our history and customs," Herod said. "One is born a Jew. My father was a Jew. I am a Jew. And I am *king* of the Jews. You are looking at him."

Akilah was at an impasse. Say no more and he'd leave empty-handed, with Herod's guard likely tracking his group's every move. With a deep breath, Akilah launched into uncharted waters, praying his gamble would pay off. "Great king, may you live forever. The information we have speaks of a future king. A new star heralded his birth. Our information was incomplete as to the location. We have traveled far to give reverence to this king."

"I see." Herod motioned and whispered to someone who appeared to be his head attendant. The man scampered from the room as if running from a fire. Then, with words of polite regret, Herod dismissed his family, other guests, and servants from the dining hall.

He turned to Akilah. "It would be my greatest pleasure to hear more about this king."

When the dining hall was empty, Herod leaned forward, his eyes flashing. His words, still full of aplomb, now pulsed with a new undercurrent of single-minded intensity. "Tell me what you know. I will help you find this king."

Unlike Herod's earlier polite questions to the Magi and his listless attention to their answers, the king sifted every word Akilah said until the head attendant returned. "Please excuse me for a moment," he said. "I must attend to an urgent matter of state. Remain here, and my servants will bring you whatever you desire until I return."

Akilah's gaze followed the king until the Magi were alone. He turned to his colleagues and switched from Latin to Elamite, a language that bore no resemblance to the universally spoken Aramaic. "Speak only in this language until our host returns. Pretend you're continuing to enjoy yourself. Smile but say nothing of consequence—unless you can suggest how we can leave this dining hall with grace and favor. Think quickly."

His thoughts strayed to Hakeem, waiting patiently for hours without supper at the edge of Herod's complex. He slid some fruit into his cloak's inner pocket.

Fifteen minutes later, Herod returned. "I apologize for the interruption. You did well in coming this far. And your wisdom has brought you to the right source for obtaining what you still lack. A Jewish text, one you must not have had access to, mentions Bethlehem as the birthplace of an auspicious child. If he was born there, someone should be able to tell you if his family has moved. Bethlehem is a small town. Of course, I cannot guarantee the child is who you seek. If you are relying on prophecies to guide you, their interpretation can lead you in many directions." He rubbed his left thumb and two forefingers together.

Akilah rose and bowed to the ground. "Thank you, great king."

"What will you do when you find him?"

Akilah stopped short. His own Council had proved untrustworthy. How much less should he trust this foreign king, despite all he'd given the Magi this evening? "We will do what we can to confirm this information. If it is accurate, we will honor the child then return to Persia."

Intent on speaking with the utmost care about the child, Akilah almost neglected his manners. "We wish to honor you with gifts as well, great king."

Something in Herod's posture faltered. He turned away from the Magi. "Your presence is the most unexpected gift I have received in a very long time. Go and complete your journey." He dismissed them with a wave.

That was too easy. Herod could have insisted we stay at his palace until we left for Bethlehem.

After expressing his profound gratitude, Akilah and his colleagues left the complex. But fifty paces beyond its formidable gate, Akilah alit from his camel. He gave the reins to Hakeem and slid the fruit from his pocket. "You haven't eaten. This is the least I can do for your service tonight."

Hakeem reminded him of the impending weather.

Akilah nodded and glanced at his colleagues. He gestured northeast toward the Temple. "Let's walk." Walking was the best way for him to sort deep thoughts.

Tallis and Rashidi hurried to match Akilah's double-timed leggy strides. After several minutes, he broke the silence. "Did you find anything odd about tonight's time in the palace?"

"Besides eating indoors?" Rashidi quipped.

"The reception was flawless. The ambiance beyond opulent. But Herod …" Tallis shrugged apologetically.

Akilah could supply a few words. *Disingenuous. Calculating.* But his concern eclipsed Herod's character profile.

"Herod seemed inordinately interested in Magi being 'kingmakers,'" Rashidi offered.

"Yes. Perhaps because he became king in a much different way," Akilah said. "But why would Herod allow a servant to interrupt him in the middle of entertaining after he expressly told all of them not to disturb him? What would prompt a king to excuse himself without punishing the servant's disobedience?"

"He said it was a matter of state." Rashidi shrugged. "Maybe he had to relieve himself."

"Rashidi!"

New Star

"Well, he ate more than all three of us. What's your point?"

Akilah stopped and glared at his colleague.

Rashidi ducked his head. "If this is a test of deductive reasoning or observational skills, could we have the night off?"

Rashidi's impudence warranted a rebuke, but tonight Akilah ignored it. "When we first arrived, Herod engaged in customary polite conversation about who we are, where we're from, and so on. Nothing unusual there."

"Except his boasting. And his talk about Rome consulting Magi regularly—as if he knew all about Magi." Tallis tipped his head.

"True," Akilah said. "But when we said we were searching for the one who would sit on the throne of David as King of the Jews, he said *he* was the king of the Jews and Augustus Caesar was the world's savior."

Tallis snorted. "No divine authority made Herod king. The Roman Senate did."

"Did you notice what happened next?" Akilah didn't wait for an answer. "Everything about him changed—his body language, his tone. He pressed us for details regarding when we first saw the star and exactly how long we'd been traveling. That was the only time he sat forward in his seat. Right after that, he jerked his head, and a servant left the room. That's the only sudden movement he made all night."

"Kings signal servants all the time." Rashidi pursed his lips.

"True. But think about the timing. That's also when Herod dismissed everyone from the room. Then he practically demanded information from us about the prophetic writings. When we explained what we'd found and that we believed the child had been born recently, a servant appeared and Herod excused himself. No one summons a king. The king does the summoning. So, who did he talk to?"

Tallis smiled. "I'm sure you'll tell us."

"Herod is clearly no scholar of Hebrew literature. But priests and scribes are. Herod must have summoned them—maybe even the high priest—to compare what we said to what they know. Why would he be so anxious to do that?" Akilah's words gathered speed.

"They must have told him something valuable. Something he didn't know before. How else can you explain that, only *after* Herod returned, he specifically told us to search for the child *in Bethlehem?*"

The three exchanged glances.

Akilah set his jaw. "We have come too far to jeopardize this trip."

Tallis kept his eyes forward but drew his lips into a thin line. "Have you noticed anyone following us?"

Akilah knew that tone. Something must have prickled Tallis's instincts, honed from past training.

"No. Why?"

Tallis fingered the gold-and-black serpentine embroidery on the fine linen the Magi had donned in the bathhouse. "Any gift from someone like Herod comes with … obligations."

"What should we do?" Despite the darkness, Rashidi's face paled.

"We haven't found the child yet. We must trust that we'll know the right path to take when the time comes," Akilah said firmly.

The Magi walked in silence, heads down. What did this mean for the last leg of their long journey? Akilah had no experience in subterfuge.

"You there!"

Akilah looked up—and froze. Two men, their hands on the hilts of their swords, stood in the Magi's path.

Chapter 49

Clothes Make the Man

The younger of the two men circled behind the Magi while the other blocked them from the front. They were surrounded. By Herod's guards.

Six hours prior, the Magi had seen those guards' attire up close as they'd walked through the palace grounds. Unlike the body armor of centurions or tribunes, the royal guards wore segmented iron carapaces. Only royalty could afford that.

What had those men heard?

"Why are you walking through the city unaccompanied?" The older, more hardened-looking guard barked his question.

"Pardon?" Akilah's heart pounded. He hoped his question would buy him time to think. And breathe.

"Every member of Herod's household must be escorted at all times."

"Oh. We're not ..." Akilah shook his head. "We were simply his guests tonight."

"But your clothes. They're—"

"Loaned. Sometimes servers can be so clumsy." Akilah forced a laugh.

"They spilled food or drink on all three of you?"

"It was good for a laugh afterward."

"Our king must have thought very highly of you to give you those clothes."

"He was a very gracious host." Akilah bowed deeply so he wouldn't have to feign a smile.

"You are at risk walking alone this late. We will see you to your quarters."

"Thank you for your kind offer, but that won't be necessary. We know the way. It's not far." Akilah gestured in the direction of their inn.

"What did you have for dinner tonight?" The guard's tone shifted.

This conversation needed to end. And it could—badly.

With relish, Akilah launched into details about the meal, the banquet hall's décor, and Herod's entertainment. Throughut his monologue, the guard waited, his face impassive.

Still expressionless, he drew his gladius sword. "Come with me."

"Good sir, we are very tired from months of travel—"

"You can rest in prison." The tip of his short sword pointed dangerously close to Akilah's heart. One thrust would silence the Wise Man forever.

Before Akilah could protest, Tallis stepped between him and the guard. "Prison is for people awaiting trial or execution. You have accused us of no crime. If you must detain us, then take us to Herod and demand he issue orders for our house arrest. When you do, tell him why you are impeding a mission he entrusted to us."

"Mission?" The guard scoffed. "Rumor is you've been talking nonsense about a child king. Sounds like treason to me."

"Herod is king of Judea," Tallis countered. "Everyone serves at his pleasure. Even dignitaries who spend an evening in his company. Now dispatch your companion to Herod to confirm we are acting at his behest. We will wait."

New Star

The guard paused, inches away from Tallis. Akilah prayed his colleague's boldness would somehow be their salvation.

"Move." He jerked his head toward the palace.

Tallis nodded once. "You are just doing your duty. Pray it doesn't cost you your life."

"Stop talking."

Mercifully, the guards didn't make a spectacle of marching the Magi through Jerusalem's streets at sword-point. In the dark, with the soldiers' swords at their sides, few people noticed the group.

Their second walk through Herod's complex was brisk and unceremonious. The guards herded the trio through the gardens straight to the reception hall of Herod's palace.

"How dare you disturb my chamberlain at this hour, demanding he summon me for a matter a vizier could handle?" Echoes of the king's rumbling anger preceded him down the marbled hallway.

Herod swept into the reception room, his eyes flashing, a corner of his bedclothes visible under his royal robes.

The Magi bowed low before him.

"Do not speak," Tallis whispered to Akilah.

"You have been wrongly detained." Herod's tone was as oily as his blackened hair. "That guard has been dealt with and serves me no more. I have many guest rooms in my palace. You will stay here tonight for the trouble my guards have caused."

"Thank you, great king," Tallis said. "But, as one who commands many, you will understand the servants we command would worry at our absence and come looking for us. They are simple men, not refined in the ways of a mighty metropolis such as yours. We have no wish to further disrupt your evening nor your guards' duties. But we will accept your gracious hospitality again when we succeed in our search. Thanks to your guidance, we are confident of its outcome."

"Indeed. I richly reward success. Not failure." Before Herod could say more, a page appeared in the doorway. Bowing low, he whispered to a guard and motioned toward Herod.

"What is it now?" the king bellowed.

The guard fell at Herod's feet. "Great king, a man named Hakeem is waiting at the royal gate." His voice trembled. "He said his masters were with you this evening."

"My head servant and caravan master." Akilah tried to hide his admiration for Hakeem's courage.

"Such loyalty. Most commendable." Herod extended his words like letting out lengths of a lasso as he circled the Wise Men. He stopped in front of Akilah. "Go. Find the child and report his location to me so I may worship him. Then we will celebrate the auspicious occasion with a banquet, and you will sit at my right as my guests of honor."

✡✡✡

While trying to act casual, Akilah had put at least a hundred paces between them and the gate of the palace complex before Rashidi broke the silence. "'Servants can be so clumsy?' I didn't know you could lie on cue like that, Akilah."

"A skill every Persian should be loath to acquire. Obviously, I need practice. My lie did not keep us from danger."

"And you, Tallis." Rashidi's voice dissolved into a tremulous whisper. "Did Herod ... The guard who questioned us ... Is he ..."

"Dead? Yes. We're running out of time to find the child."

Chapter 50

Who Wants a Lamb?

In his haste to return to the inn, Akilah ignored a jumble of talk until it was upon the Magi. Arguing men in rough-woven tunics and animal skins collided with, then quickly separated from the Magi. With mumbled apologies, the rustic men edged past the trio.

"Ugh. Now I smell like sheep." Rashidi sniffed his spotless sleeve. "Filthy animals."

The unrefined group, still dickering, leapfrogged from one rant to another, seemingly unconcerned who might hear them.

"I don't get it. We swaddle them, separate them, even protect them in a feed trough away from other animals. And somehow the priests still find a reason to reject a lamb."

"No use arguing with them. Part of their purity rituals."

"If I could be anything but a shepherd …"

"How? No one trusts us."

"Wolves probably got that lamb I couldn't find. But I still had to pay for it."

"Shepherding is even lower than dung hauling."

"But just as smelly." The shepherds roared with laughter and punched each other's arms.

"The only difference is the gate we have to use when we enter the city." More guffaws.

"I don't know who's the bigger hypocrite—the high priest or Herod."

Herod? Akilah pulled his colleagues away from the street's torchlight. Touching a finger to his lips, he beckoned his colleagues to follow the shepherds at a distance.

"The high priest is worse. Worship at the Temple is a racket. First the tablers pocket a commission from changing everyone's money to Tyre's silver. As if that money is special. Then the merchants charge the pilgrims five times more than what they paid for the sacrificial animals. The high priest knows all that—and does nothing."

"Herod is worse. Says he's king of the Jews, but he isn't even Jewish."

"You want to die? You will—if the wrong people hear you."

"The high priest seemed upset about more than lambs tonight."

"Who cares?"

"Weren't you carrying your lamb?"

"He was walking with the others."

"You should have carried him. Then he wouldn't have gotten scratched."

"Not allowed. Remember?"

"Who would have known? You could have put him down before we got to the gate."

"Well, I'm carrying him now. Here in my girdle."

"At least our flocks know us and accept us."

A tender bleat close to the shepherd's chest stopped him in his tracks. Running his hand over the cosseted lamb's fine-textured fleece, the shepherd's rough voice softened. "Others did ... one night."

"Yes. Mmm," the rest murmured.

"Angels ... the family ..."

"Like we heard hope. Then saw it."

"And that light ..."

"Will never forget that."

"Heard anyone else talk about it?"

"No. We may be the only ones that know."

"How can that be?"

"Come on. We have to get the flocks into Migdal Eder before it rains." One shepherd's tone changed from jovial to stern. "The storm must be close. We can't see the stars."

"And I have two sheep about to give birth. Jedaiah, will you help?"

"I need to check on my mother first. And give her part of my pay."

"Any change in her condition?"

"No."

Chapter 51

The Star's Song?

The shepherds hurried down a side street, their voices fading into an indiscernible hum. One man zigzagged another way into an alley.

"Let's go." Akilah started down the alley. Upon realizing his colleagues weren't following, he doubled back. "Where's your sense of adventure?"

"Standing on the outside, sitting on the inside," Tallis said.

"Already asleep at the inn." Rashidi yawned. The palace's food and drink seemed to be working their way into his thoughts. "It's dark, it's late. We're on foot in a foreign city we've never visited. And what if we come across those guards again?" He shook his head. "What's so interesting about shepherds, anyway? You see one, and you've seen them all."

"They mentioned the high priest," Akilah whispered. "Those shepherds must raise sheep for ceremonial slaughter at the Jews' Temple."

"And they had a bad night. So?" Rashidi shrugged.

"They also mentioned a star." Akilah could hardly contain his excitement.

"No, they said a *light*."

Count on Rashidi to split hairs. But he was right.

"What if it's the same thing?" Tallis pushed Rashidi just enough to off-balance him.

Rashidi pursed his lips. "You don't chase an approximation of what you hope to discover. As you say, 'Semblance is shadow, not substance. Semblance is counterfeit truth.'"

Akilah fisted his hand over his chest. "A star started us on this journey. What we saw ... studied ... tried to track ... but haven't seen since. We've traveled so far, hoping to see that star again. If those shepherds tend flocks outside of Jerusalem and they saw a star or light worth remembering, it might be what we're looking for. It could lead us to our destination."

Akilah quickened his pace. But the shepherds were nowhere in sight, and soon the streets became a dizzying maze of dark, narrow alleys.

After half a dozen twists and turns, their effort seemed wasted. Even Akilah had to acknowledge his exhaustion. As the trio turned down a south street, the midnight blue sky turned inky black. Thunder rumbled in the distance. Gusts of wind billowed the Magi's clothes.

Suddenly Akilah stopped. "Do you hear that?"

Wondrous words
Sudden light
Quickened steps
Humble plight
Sleeping child
God's foresight
When angels sang
And heaven rang
On that holy night.

Carried on the wind, a man's husky singing wafted over the Magi's heads.

Akilah strained to locate the voice. It seemed to come from a silhouetted man on a rooftop balcony. He was bent over something, perhaps a person.

Chapter 52

Denial

"Let's ask him about the star." Akilah's voice sizzled with energy. He started down the street, but Rashidi pulled him back.

"Wait. How do you know that's not just some nursemaid story set to song?"

Normally, Akilah appreciated Rashidi's debate skills. But not now. "Songs memorialize events that aren't written down." He shrugged out of Rashidi's grip and trotted down the narrow street, scanning the rooftops and houses for exits.

Rashidi matched his pace. "Do you think it's wise to ask a perfect stranger about his singing? How would you react if a foreigner asked you that?"

"He probably wouldn't talk to us. Not dressed the way we are." Tallis fingered the gold-and-black serpentine embroidery on the finely woven, snow-white tunic he was wearing. "After all, we *are* in clothes Herod gave us. He insisted."

"Ooh, Herod's bathhouse ... its mosaic floors ... and bathing chambers big enough to hold hippos." Rashidi's face radiated delight.

"What moves the heart wags the tongue." Akilah's sarcastic

words distracted him long enough to miss the rooftop singer's exit. Where did he go? There must be a back stairway to the street. From the corner of his eye, Akilah detected motion. He hurried after it and caught up with a rough-hewn man in his forties.

"Pardon me, good sir. Might I have a word with you?"

"No." The man turned away, walking fast.

"Were you singing about a star just now?"

"No."

"I'm sure I heard you. The song was lovely."

"You must be mistaken," the man said over his shoulder.

"I study the stars. Were you singing about a particular one?"

The scruffy man whirled. "Do I look like I sing? Go away, court diviner." At the sight of Akilah's clothes, he backed away in dread and bowed awkwardly. "Forgive me. I did not ... I must go. Good night."

"Sir, I am *not*—"

"We can sort this at our lodgings." Tallis laid his hand on Akilah's shoulder as the man vanished into the night.

"Or sleep on it," Rashidi said.

Akilah shook his head with resolve. "But we must do one thing yet this evening."

Chapter 53

Secrets of the Box

After thanking Hakeem and bidding him goodnight, Akilah tiptoed through the stable.

"Quietly now." He motioned to Tallis and Rashidi, then pointed to the row of camels. "Skirt around them. Carefully." Camels dozed more than slept and could do both lying down or standing up. Either way, they didn't appreciate being disturbed. "Find Kani."

They reached the end of a row.

"There." Tallis pointed to a long box near the camel.

Rashidi grabbed one end of the box and pulled. The scratchy dragging roused Kani.

"Pick it up," Akilah hissed.

"It's too heavy," Rashidi mumbled.

"We'll lift it together. We don't have to move it far. Just into the corridor so we have space to open the box." Grunting, Akilah raised his end.

"Kani looks content," Tallis whispered as the camel opened groggy eyes.

"He's earned a rest, but not yet," Akilah said.

The Magi huddled tightly about the oblong box the Bactrian

had been carrying for more than two months. Amid the glow of terra cotta lamps, they unlocked the box.

"Everything intact?" Tallis said.

"Hard to see," Akilah replied. "Rashidi, hold the light up."

They rummaged through layers of straw.

Akilah sighed in relief. "All safe."

Before leaving, he stroked Kani's neck. "Sleep well tonight. You have a big day tomorrow."

"We still don't have a solid plan for finding this family," Rashidi said.

Tallis nodded. "Now would be a good time to see that star again."

Chapter 54

True Destination

The next afternoon

Akilah hurried to the inn's stables to find his trusted head servant. "Is everyone still buying supplies?"

"The ones with Malachi are," Hakeem said. "The rest are grooming or feeding the camels."

"Good. Ready our saddle camels and Kani at sundown. Take extra care to load him with all that needs to go with us."

"Your camels probably wonder when they can have a day off," Hakeem said.

"Soon." Akilah's thoughts churned. How to find this child? Head toward Bethlehem and hope for the best? *God of the Hebrews, please protect and guide us.*

A few hours later, as the sun slid behind the mountains surrounding Jerusalem, the Wise Men met behind the inn, dressed in their finest garments. Elaborate turbans pinned with jeweled fasteners. Silk tunics. Braided, ornamented belts. Robes embroidered with stars, flowers, and vines, framed by geometric patterns. Threads of gold and silver shimmered amid the indigo, burgundy, flaxen, and umber fabric of their robes. Magi robes. The embodiment of who they were.

Hakeem bowed to the ground before their splendor. As pre-arranged, he would accompany the Magi on this final leg of their journey to ensure Kani's load stayed secure. Malachi and Kassim would remain at the inn to oversee the other servants.

The terrain outside of Jerusalem became rougher, the road full of stones. Although the rain had stopped earlier in the day, Akilah worried the camels could lose their footing on the dark, wet path. But their way seemed exceptionally bright.

"A full moon tonight," Rashidi said.

"Mm." Akilah appreciated its light but wished for divine guidance.

"Doesn't look like we're being followed," Rashidi added.

"Herod is smarter than that," Tallis said. "He'll let us do his work for him."

The Wise Men rode in tense silence for an hour. Akilah had to lighten their mood. What would reassure his colleagues? "Bethlehem should be—"

Light exploded across the sky, rending night's curtain in half. Trees bent. The ground shook as if the light bore the power of a storm. Brilliant white overwhelmed all other lights in the sky, then completely banished the heavens' darkness. In the blinding brightness, the Magi flattened their faces against their camels' necks. The camels curled to the ground. What was this terror?

Hakeem prostrated himself. "Master, what's happening? Save me!"

Akilah dared look up. An invisible hand seemed to gather the light, narrowing it to a spot ahead of the group. Within a few moments, the indigo sky and night lights returned. But now, one light burned infinitely brighter than the others—with pulsing, pure-white fingers reaching earthward and upward at the same time.

"'Sudden light!'" Akilah gasped. "What the shepherds saw."

New Star

Trembling, he pointed to a spot in the distance. "That's where the child is."

Hakeem remained motionless, hands flung over his head, face and torso pressed into the dirt.

Akilah took his servant by the arm. "Get up. Don't be afraid. This is very good news."

Soon they reached Bethlehem. Such a small, nondescript town. The Magi's robes were a stark contrast to the humble stone and mud houses they passed. The houses became smaller and sparser, dimly lit by the uneven yellow-orange flicker of oil lamps. Then no houses.

As the Magi continued southwest toward the light, tantalizing scents of fruit blossoms and fresh spring water wafted over Akilah. Was another town nearby? If so, it was out of sight.

They turned down a side path. The light they'd followed poured over a spot beyond the end of the path, tucked behind a grove of trees. Akilah signaled the others to stop. A palpable but indescribable thickness hung in the air, surrounding and filling him. Not dread, but anticipation that his life would never be the same again. He had to press on.

In breathless awe, he followed the path to a small stone house, little more than a hut. It was so insignificant, so drab, so perfectly ordinary that anyone would have missed it if they hadn't known to look for it. Except now. The simple dwelling was awash in snow-white radiance.

"Oh, praises—we're here." Akilah could barely breathe the words. Should he nudge his camel into the extraordinary light? What would happen if he did?

Words failed him. Akilah had seen many splendors in the heavens but nothing nearly as glorious as this. This was celestial beauty he could touch—if he dared. He slid to the ground and gingerly stepped into the light like he would test water in a pool. His heart bursting with wonder and reverent fear, Akilah prostrated himself on the ground in silent worship. He wasn't sure *what* he was worshiping, only that it was worthy of worship.

After a few minutes, he straightened. Struggling to find his voice, he managed, "Hakeem, announce our arrival. Tell them we studied a star that brought us from the East, and we want to pay homage to the child that the star foretold."

Hakeem knocked on the door and spoke briefly with someone inside. "The master of the house asks our patience while he makes room in his stable for your camels."

Chapter 55

Servanthood in a New Light

A few minutes later, a medium-build, twenty-something man with dark, wavy hair and a neatly trimmed beard greeted the Magi. The man's humble, worn clothes hinted at years of hard work. "*Shalom aleichem.* I am Joseph. Please, rest your camels behind the house."

"Thank you for receiving us at this hour." Akilah matched Joseph's Aramaic.

The Wise Men stooped to remove their shoes in the entryway. Akilah couldn't help but gawk at the room. Where were the homey touches? The room was so bare and so ... common. Sleeping mats, a water jar, some baskets, a few dishes and cooking pots. What else did this family have? Anything?

As the Wise Men huddled in the doorway, a teenage girl approached them with a large basin. "Peace be to you. Welcome. I am Mary. Here is water for your feet."

Tallis shuffled, his discomfort obvious. "Our servants aren't here to wash them."

Joseph gestured to a bench by the door. "Please, sit. Let me wash your feet. You have come so far."

Akilah and his colleagues shared incredulous looks.

Abashed, he nodded assent. Only servants had washed their feet. Until now.

In these simple surroundings, almost everything about Akilah and his colleagues felt out of place. Their elaborate garments. Their extensive education. Their high status. But their gifts?

Through the room's small windows, pure white light poured into the house and washed over the Wise Men. But the light also seemed to fill the room from within. How could that be? The metallic threads in the Magi's robes shimmered as the light touched the fabric.

How could this incredible light be equally as bright everywhere in the house? *And how could the light not create shadows?* The tiny hut was completely devoid of them. Every space below shelves, behind jars, even the room's farthest corners and the insides of the Magi's leather shoes by the door, were filled with light. Light alive with almost touchable joy. It wrapped Akilah like warm blanket.

What *was* this light? It emitted no heat but exuded warmth and peace. Dare he say, a Presence? Jumbled emotions tangled his thoughts.

Tallis nudged Akilah. With fresh eyes, he scanned the tiny house, dismayed that the box of gifts they'd taken such pains to deliver wasn't there. "Many pardons, Joseph. My servant should have brought a large box into your house. I fear he isn't nearby now."

"Perhaps he went to get water for your camels," Joseph said. "We are close to Artas. Its four springs supply Jerusalem and all the nearby villages with water."

"Artas. Is that where the wonderful smell of fruit blossoms is coming from?"

"Yes. Artas has many orchards."

Akilah drew a sharp breath. In Persian, "Artas" meant

"truth." Did the light in this house point to the Truth he sought?

"How may I help you in your servant's place?"

He collected himself. "Thank you for that kind offer. I believe what we are missing was unloaded in your stable. Could you help me find it and bring it inside?"

"Of course."

The stable was more like a simple shelter with a branch-and-twig roof abutting the back of the house. Fences and feed troughs defined the area of tamped-down ground strewn with fresh straw. "There's the box. Near Kani." Akilah pointed.

The camel pressed into the fence when the men reached for the box. Joseph stroked Kani's neck in appreciation. "Thank you for making room for us, my friend."

"Careful now," Akilah said. He and Joseph lifted the box in unison. Joseph's end wobbled as he shouldered it. Painstakingly maneuvering it through the house's back entrance, Joseph freed one hand long enough to close the door. But it didn't latch.

Chapter 56

Unforgettable

As Joseph changed direction to guide his end of the box into the house, a toddler with tousled dark hair slid past him into the stable. "Mary?" Joseph called. "Can you get Yeshua? He's in the stable again."

With another pang of conscience, Akilah realized what an imposition their visit must be, coming unannounced near the toddler's bedtime. Outwardly, Mary and Joseph seemed to take the intrusion in stride, but what were they truly thinking?

Mary reentered their house with the toddler on her hip. "Yeshua, we must stay inside now. We have visitors. They have traveled very, very far to see you."

Akilah smiled at the motherly admonition. Apparently, even an eternal child-king had a knack for being anywhere other than where his parents wanted him to be. The toddler in her arms seemed riveted on something behind him, but his curiosity shifted to the three royally clad men as Mary crossed the room.

The Wise Men hastily relinquished their seats so the young family could sit in front of the oblong box Kani had hauled over so many miles. A box that now served as a makeshift table for the gifts spread before the family. Gifts for a king.

Akilah's carefully rehearsed questions melted from his mind as he gazed at the toddler on his mother's lap. With happiness and gratitude too deep for speech, all he could form was one thought. *We found the child.*

Akilah hadn't known what to expect. But this was more than he could have imagined. In unison, the Wise Men knelt and bowed to the ground in worship.

He wiped his damp eyes to compose himself before he lifted his head from the dirt floor. Words stuck in his throat, so instead, he swept his hand over three bas-relief gold boxes adorned with purple tassels. No shadow fell upon the boxes, but the distinctive triangular grain of the glassy rare-metal locks bent the room's light into ripples. "Gold—to honor the King Above All Kings."

Tallis, also maintaining a posture of worship, spread his hands over three intricately carved olivewood boxes with ivory marquetry, jade inlay leaves, and silver clasps. "Frankincense— for the High Priest Above All Priests," His voice pitched higher than normal.

Mary and Joseph looked on, speechless.

Rashidi's hands shook as they hovered over three amber-colored, crackled glass jars with ornate openwork bronze lids. "Myrrh—for your sacrifice will be for all."

Color drained from Mary's cheeks. Swallowing hard, she drew Yeshua close to her. She turned to Joseph, her eyes wide. "That sounds like what Simeon said to me in the Temple when we presented our purification offering." Her voice was hoarse and tight.

"Remember what Anna said as well." Joseph rested one callused hand on Mary's shoulder and held out the other to Yeshua, who wrapped his tiny fingers around Joseph's.

"Your gifts are most kind," he said.

Joseph's gentle squeeze on Mary's shoulder seemed to rouse her from a troubling memory. She handed Yeshua to Joseph and placed a bowl of dates amid the gifts on the makeshift table. "Please, noble lords, have some refreshment."

"*Barukh ata Adonai Eloheinu melekh ha'olam borei p'ri ha'eitz,*" Joseph said, blessing the food.

Akilah swallowed hard. Such simple, selfless hospitality. What a stark contrast to Herod's ostentatious banquet.

Akilah knew eight languages, yet now he struggled to find the right word for this visit. Perhaps a Greek word, *koinónia*, came closest—intimate fellowship and communion. Feeling so close and connected to perfect strangers … how could that be?

The Wise Men graciously accepted the dates. While they ate, they tried to talk with Mary and Joseph. The couple was more interested in hearing how far the Magi had come and where they lived than in sharing information about themselves. Akilah sensed this family's story was beyond what anyone would know for many years.

Despite his musings, he couldn't take his eyes off Yeshua. Something in the child defied naming. Was this innocent one truly created for a singular purpose?

Soon Akilah signaled his colleagues. He murmured his thanks to the young couple for receiving them, unannounced, at this late hour. In a more distinct voice, he said they must leave to prepare for their return journey.

"*Barukh ata adonai elohenu melekh ha'olam, shehecheyanu, v'kiyimanu, v'higiyanu la'z'man ha'zeh,*" Joseph said.

"What did he say?" Rashidi whispered to Akilah.

"Blessed are You, Lord our God, Ruler of the Universe, who has given us life, sustained us, and allowed us to reach this day."

"Yes," Joseph said. "It's how we thank Adonai for enabling us to experience a new or special occasion."

A special occasion. Such an understated phrase to describe the evening. Akilah fumbled for an appropriate response. "May we meet again," he said, bowing low.

"If Adonai wills," Joseph said. "Safe journey."

Akilah paused at the hut's front door. "Joseph, many pardons, but may I ask? This light. Have you—"

"Seen it before? Yes. Once, from a distance, when Yeshua was born. We received unexpected guests that night too." Joseph smiled at Akilah's discomfiture. "Adonai must have brought you here for a special reason. *L'hitraot.*"

"Yes." Akilah returned the smile. "Until we see each other again."

Chapter 57

Duty or Purpose

As the camels picked their way through the rocky path back to the inn, Akilah strained to see ahead, for the light no longer led them. Darkness cloaked their return to Jerusalem. The camels' soft plodding played counterpoint to Akilah's pounding heart and racing mind. Had he really seen an eternal king? It still was inconceivable.

Their intent to pay homage had become worship. Worship with new meaning. Real. Natural. Personal. Not a ritual, but a relationship—a presence in a child that seemed so "other" and so utterly common at the same time. How could that be? And if that child did embody the Hebrews' God, then the Wise Men had worshiped a God not their own.

That was too extraordinary to grasp.

Moreover, the child's family took no credit for being part of something wondrous. They seemed to have only awe and gratitude for the Wise Men's gifts.

What would Joseph and Mary do with the gifts? They seemed to need everything. Did the couple recognize the gifts' significance? They were what a subjugated country gave a conquering king. Rashidi had initially deemed that idea excessive. But the prophecies—or something deep inside Akilah that defied naming—had compelled him to pay their high price. A king without peer deserved the best of the best as an expression of homage. Had he made the right choice?

They had risked much and had given much. But who had received more?

Were his colleagues wrestling with similar thoughts? Perhaps some thoughts were best left unsaid. At least until they could be sorted.

✡ ✡ ✡

The Wise Men returned to the inn to find their servants counting and organizing fresh supplies. Packing lasted well into the day's last cycle. When they finished their duties, everyone could rest.

But Akilah and his colleagues weren't resting.

In the privacy of their lodging room, they repeatedly started to say something but stopped each time. The light had been more than a guide. The child more than prophesied words. Was it sacrilegious to talk about such a sublime experience?

"What should we tell the Council?" Rashidi was the first to break the silence.

His question wrested Akilah from the sublime into the ordinary. Despite the trip's external funding, the Magi were still obligated to provide the Council with an exhaustive account of their activities and findings. But, if they dutifully chronicled the breadcrumbs they'd followed, the venture would sound unreasonable. Unscientific. Unscholarly. Swift consequences would follow.

The first Jewish prophecy they'd found about a star heralding a king had sparked academic inquisitiveness. Seeing the star itself had fueled something far beyond curiosity. Comparing

Jewish writings with astronomy texts had become an obsession. Understanding the meaning behind the holy writings, a compulsion. Commissioning the gifts, a passion.

Now, distanced from the Council, he could appreciate its misgivings. Had fate or divine intervention moved the Council to approve the study? Akilah had justified the trip to Jerusalem as a science consult. In most cultures, priests were the most knowledgeable astronomers or astrologers. He had counted on the Jewish priests to know of a unique star and who wrote the first words about it. What would the Council say of his failure to talk with them? Akilah could only surmise Herod had spoken with the priests. But whatever had passed through Herod's filter to the Wise Men didn't include any mention of a star.

Despite everything, the pursuit had led them to far more than Akilah had bargained for. Dinner with a king instead of discourse with a priest. A star that others hadn't seen. A child-king no one knew of. None of it made sense. Unless one believed.

But reports couldn't be based on beliefs. Or descriptions of a poor young couple with a toddler. That was as far from royalty as a family could get. Yet Akilah somehow knew—but didn't understand how—the child was part of a greater purpose. Because in that child's presence, heartfelt, unrehearsed worship had poured from their hearts.

Worship.

How could he ever explain *that*? The gentle tug on his heart seemed a compelling call to something beyond fealty or allegiance.

"Whatever we write, the Council will circulate its official version of our findings." Tallis's comment brought Akilah back to the present. "Their stance may not align with our experience, but what we saw won't change."

"You're right," Akilah said. "Our task is to report objective facts."

"But the Council could reject our report. We could face censure—or expulsion," Rashidi said.

Akilah's heart flopped in his chest. The Council had the power to do both, but he would not admit either possibility. "Our report must simply speak the truth of what we found—even if the Council tries to create its own truth. What we know of Yeshua seems like only the beginning of a larger truth that exceeds our knowledge."

Akilah startled at his words as if they had come from another person. Persia's official religion was touted as absolute truth, yet the Magi served many religions. How had he lived with that dichotomy for so long? Could all religions be true? Or only one?

Did the Council perceive this prophesied child to be a threat? Although Sassanak maintained he acted on behalf of the Council in accusing Akilah of undermining Persia's national religion, did the Head Magus harbor a darker agenda behind the charges? Moreover, if the Council was determined to squelch all knowledge of this child, what reception would greet him when he returned? The Council had already threatened sanctions against him if the results of this trip didn't suit them. But that would be only the start of what they could do to him. He may not have a future in Magi society. Or any future at all.

A more urgent concern disturbed the ripples of his thoughts. *How should they respond to Herod?*

The night brought no rest for the trio.

Chapter 58

Warning

Akilah's mind churned through the night. Sleep eluded him until a drop in temperature sent him burrowing deeper under his covers. But his fitful slumber was short-lived. Something stirred in the room. He sat up and stared through the darkness. No shadows shifted. Although the fire had dwindled to embers, his arms warmed. Then his face. The warmth expanded, driving coolness from the room. What invisible force could defy the laws of nature like that? As the heat intensified, dread gripped Akilah's chest and choked his windpipe.

The wall before him dissolved in a blaze of snow-white light. A being, taller than human, stepped through the light and stopped at the foot of Akilah's bed. Light flowed from the motionless figure. When it turned its head, translucent shimmers of silver and gold rippled through the room, dispelling stale air. Akilah's lungs filled with something purer than mountain breezes after a spring storm.

Who was this mighty being with bronzed skin and hair like the sun? And why was it carrying a sword? Mesmerized, Akilah momentarily forgot his fear. The sword appeared weighty, yet the blade was virtually transparent. Beams of light ricocheted off it, confirming its mass. But it exuded a strength beyond weaponry. A power deeper than its material essence.

Akilah trembled. What was he thinking? This being could, with a stroke, turn the sword on him. Frozen in fear, the Wise Man cowered in bed.

"Do not be afraid."

Amid translucent, swirling shimmers, the figure spoke. Or maybe Akilah felt its words in his heart like one feels the rumble of thunder before hearing it.

"Do not return to Herod. Flee danger."

Akilah dared to look directly at the being

It turned its head to its sword and rested a hand on the hilt. The blade glowed crimson. Distant screams emanated from it. As the sound faded, the blade darkened to a dried-blood mahogany, then returned to its transparent state.

"God is with you."

In a blinding flash, the figure vanished.

Akilah shrieked and shielded his eyes. The sudden coolness in the room stole his breath. He dropped to the cold stone floor, but he couldn't see his hands. Or anything else. He gulped air to call Tallis and Rashidi, but no words came out.

He crawled across the room, groping for his colleagues' beds and praying his sight would return. His floundering reach finally touched blankets. Clutching them for guidance, he frantically shook the bedframes.

Both men shot straight up, gasping.

"I had the most vivid dream—or vision."

"Me too."

"An angel?"

"Light."

"Warmth."

"Warning."

Their words tumbled over each other like a waterfall—jumbled but with the same elements.

When they stopped for breath, the three spoke as one. "We can't go home the way we came."

Chapter 59

Which Way?

"Get up." Hakeem roused another servant.

"It's at least half a cycle before daylight," one grumbled.

"Our day off," another mumbled.

"Quickly." Hakeem kicked feet and slapped arms sprawling from the rows of sleeping mats. "The masters require you to work today."

Most servants turned away from Hakeem's prodding. "We were promised rest."

"Plans change," Hakeem said. "Hitch and load your assigned camels. Hurry. The masters are here." He dug his foot into another servant's rib cage.

The servants scrambled to their feet at seeing Akilah in the doorway, then rushed to their assignments as he strode through their sleeping room into the stable. A gurgling, growling camel swung its neck toward him. The attending servant looked equally disgruntled. Akilah hurried past. He didn't want either of them to spit on him.

"Thank you for rising early." At the center of the stable,

Akilah lifted his voice above the chaos. "We have urgent business beyond Jerusalem. First meal later."

"Hopefully that will defuse any questions," he whispered to Hakeem.

It didn't for long.

The caravan had traveled only an hour when the sun broke the horizon to their left—alerting everyone they were headed south—opposite of the way they'd entered Jerusalem.

"Aren't we going the wrong way?" a servant asked.

"It's not our place to question," another replied.

"They said they had business in another city before returning to Persia."

"They didn't say anything about that when we started out."

"Don't be so suspicious."

"I can be anything I want to be."

"Suspicions won't get you anything but a sour stomach."

"Maybe so, but I don't want this trip to last any longer than it has to. Our duties in Assur were a lot easier than this."

Akilah cringed at the comments he could hear from the two servants. He presumed more unrest was brewing behind him, out of earshot, but he kept his eyes forward. How many more half-truths would he need to conjure on this journey? A bigger concern crowded his thoughts. *Herod didn't know about this child until we dined with him. What avalanche of consequences would follow?*

After two more hours, Akilah signaled the caravan to stop at a well. Normally, they wouldn't rest until twice that time had passed. He hurriedly retrieved the Magi's roll of maps from a cylinder strapped to Kani's framework and motioned to Tallis and Rashidi.

"How do we avoid Herod?" Akilah said as he passed maps to his colleagues.

Shuffling through the lot, they whispered while they pored over one particular map.

"Coastal route?"

New Star

"Ridge route?"
"No—no main route."
"Twice as long."
"More provisions?"
"Must keep moving."
"It's settled."

Chapter 60

What is our Duty?

For many miles, the only sound at the head of the caravan was the Magi's saddles creaking with the sway of their camels' side-to-side gaits. Akilah didn't dare speak his thoughts. He had always wanted a fulfilled life. But he had assumed each achievement would enrich the life he had. Not turn it upside-down. He had always been confident he could shape his future. Now, something beyond his understanding seemed to be shaping it for him.

He had to admit that seeing an angelic being was a compelling push in a different direction. But most disturbing was how readily Akilah had discarded thoughts of his future and had taken for granted that he had to risk everything to protect the caravan *and* the Wise Men's knowledge of Yeshua. The former was a given, but was the latter necessary? Would he be willing to risk everything for Yeshua's sake if called upon to do so?

"What should we tell the servants?" Tallis's voice broke Akilah's train of thought.

"For now, only that we're taking a different route back," Akilah said.

"They'll insist on knowing more. Soon."

"When they do, we should have better answers for them than we do now."

"We can't tell them about our dream last night. They're already superstitious enough."

Rashidi cleared his throat. "Do we have enough money to get where we're going?"

"Not a concern." Akilah twisted the diamond-encrusted ring on his fifth finger. He couldn't answer directly. The truth was too discouraging.

Although Tallis and Rashidi were as committed to this venture as he was, Akilah had borne the greatest burden of this journey. The gifts were a disproportionate cost compared to the trip's other expenses, so he had made do with less than the fourth allowed from the Magi's resources—including their servants. To keep his cadre of left-behind servants intact, he had paid them the advance from his pension fund. That money could have cushioned them against the unexpected. He had counted on his cousin's sponsorship to compensate for his shortfalls. But he hadn't counted on Herod.

Now much more than money was at stake. Yeshua and his family were in danger, and the caravan couldn't help him. Would an angelic being warn them the way it had warned the Wise Men? Akilah hoped so.

The threat of danger crushed Akilah's chest. What would happen if Herod hunted them? His caravan was in danger because of his actions. Three-fourths of the servants on this trip were Farzaneh's. Extended travel was difficult even for seasoned, loyal servants. His cousin's servants were neither. Their cooperation was contractual, not consensual. How could he earn their loyalty despite an uncertain future?

Even if he did manage to return the rest of Farzaneh's property and servants intact, he was still obligated to fulfill his cousin's second contract. That alone could jeopardize his career, but it paled in comparison to Akilah's current decisions. A lengthy, unscheduled absence from Persia would result in disciplinary measures against his colleagues but would have far direr consequences for him.

He steeled his mind. So many variables, most of them beyond his control. His immediate concern was how to get the caravan to safety—wherever that may be and however long it would take. Would the remaining money last longer than the detour? Despite his frugality on the way to Jerusalem, his measures might not have been enough. More drastic measures would be necessary. Eventually.

What if he couldn't solve every future problem, even with his colleagues' help? The only comfort he had was his vivid memory of that majestic being and its parting statement, "God is with you." If only the being hadn't been so short on words. Akilah appreciated details.

Every time he recalled that memory, an uncommon peace settled over him. If that powerful being served the Hebrews' all-powerful God and God was with Akilah, then lesser matters like money were inconsequential. He resolved to remain focused on the message in that memory. *Yes, the Hebrews' God—and this eternal child-king—would be worth risking everything for.*

✡ ✡ ✡

The caravan halted at the welcome sight of a palm grove and a well. At last, the Magi could talk among themselves at a distance from the servants.

"Akilah, how do we get word to the Council?"

"We don't, Rashidi. We can't. Not for now."

"We're breaking protocol."

"Gentlemen, what is our duty?" Akilah's voice dropped.

Rashidi wiped his brow with a dampened cloth. "To report our findings."

"When duty is plain, delaying it would be foolish and hazardous. When duty is unclear, delay can lead to wisdom and safety," Akilah said. "True wisdom is doing the right thing when no precedent exists for it.

"What we witnessed is a threat to some people in high places," Akilah continued. "Others may feel the same way. Threat is a beast with many heads. How does that change our duty?" He held his breath. He couldn't openly declare his newfound conviction of trusting the Hebrews' God, no matter the cost.

"As Magi, we are accountable to our Council." Tallis spoke slowly, as if choosing his words with utmost care. "But our actions also unintentionally endangered the caravan. Our visit may have created more ripples than we know. Our first duty is to keep our caravan safe. The fastest route to safety seems to be south, beyond Idumea's border."

"Well said, Tallis. But is there also a greater purpose to our actions? Our belief in what we read and saw in the heavens led us to a child. We acted on faith more than reason. Perhaps now a higher purpose should temper our decisions—including when and what we say about our experience. For safety's sake."

Rashidi fidgeted. "We did witness something truly wondrous. But it doesn't mean we should assume that family's safety as our personal cause."

Those words roiled Akilah's soul.

"Besides, philosophizing about duty versus purpose won't change the Council's rules," Rashidi added. "Wait. Are you saying we shouldn't talk to anyone about what we saw—especially the Council?"

"Yes. It's best for now. We seem to know something the rest of the world doesn't. In the short term, it may cost us some inconvenience."

"Inconvenience? That's a honey-drenched word for it. It's already cost us more than we could imagine," Rashidi said. "Look around. We're renegades."

"Renegades?" The word strangled Akilah's throat.

"You heard me."

"Well, in a manner of speaking ... circumstances being what they are ..."

Tallis arched his eyebrows, but the corners of his mouth relaxed. "Don't trip over your Magi robes with semantics, Akilah."

Rashidi paced. "How do we live until it's safe to return? We don't know survival skills."

"Tallis does." Realizing his slip, Akilah hastened to add, "A wise man never borrows trouble."

"What will the Council think when we don't return when expected or send word of our delay?" Rashidi's words galloped ahead.

"We can't control that. I will vouch for our actions. They'll understand when they hear the full story." In his heart, Akilah doubted his words. Given what had happened, his word would carry little weight in convincing the Council to not curtail his colleagues' future studies. But the Council would not be lenient with him.

The Council will permit you to study this object in the sky as long as it doesn't interfere with your other duties. We grant you that based on your past exemplary work. However, it is our opinion that this study constitutes undue risk-taking. Further, we have serious misgivings that your efforts likely will not yield a return commensurate with the initial, substantial investment you've made. Your actions affect the Council's reputation and finances. You may choose to proceed. But, if your final results are not justified in the Council's eyes, you will be stripped of your Magi office.

Chapter 61

What if God?

Akilah hoisted himself onto his camel again. The first prophecy they'd found was the Magi's basis for preparing gifts for a king. He and Tallis had been in the company of kings before. But something more had prompted Akilah to lavish unprecedented creativity, care, and cost on the gifts' containers and contents. With his colleagues' help, he'd commissioned materials from Greece, Egypt, Kush, Saba, and Cin. He, Tallis, and Rashidi had exercised an abundance of caution with the craftsmen, ensuring they never met each other and never knew the real purpose or destination of their work. He'd hidden the gifts from prying eyes. Now Akilah was grateful for each decision.

The implications of Isaiah's words in that tattered scroll—eternal superlatives about a child who would be king—justified every choice in Akilah's mind. Their trip became a pilgrimage. They *had* to see the child, no matter what the cost. A child! Child-kings were extremely rare, but detailed prophecies about a child who would reign without end ... that was unheard of.

So was everything else about this undertaking. All of Akilah's past studies had either supported or refuted his theories. Obtaining results ended the study. But this wasn't the end. It was just the beginning. Because their finding was a *person* —not a thing.

The distance lengthened between the caravan and Jerusalem. Would Akilah recognize the child if he saw him again? Would the boy grow to be all that was said of him? Only time would confirm or disprove the prophecies. The future was beyond everyone's horizon.

On the other hand, the star that had hovered above the predawn horizon was imprinted indelibly on the Magi's past. Its first appearance had ignited their imagination. Its second appearance had shed light and direction when they needed it the most—the last two parasangs of their journey. Incredibly, it seemed to appear just to them—foreigners. And, almost two years earlier, to a group of outcasts—shepherds.

Could the Hebrews' God control the stars?

Or was the star something other than a star?

Akilah jerked upright in his saddle. To think that the star could be a glimpse of God Himself was almost too fantastical. Hebrew writings talked of God's glory, but what *was* that?

What had he really witnessed yesterday? Most importantly, what did it mean for his convictions? His purpose in Magi society?

Chapter 62

About That

The sun's height prompted the caravan to rest at the next shaded dot of an oasis. While most of the servants curled up to nap by the camels, Hakeem approached Akilah. "Should we stay or press on?"

"I will watch the sun. Everyone needs to rest."

"Very well. If you don't need me ..."

Akilah shook his head. "Thank you, Hakeem. Go rest."

Tallis nudged Akilah. "Walk with me." The two circled the caravan, their silence broken only by the soft crunch of pebbles underfoot.

"Something troubles you." Tallis turned to Akilah.

He stared at the ground. "Is it possible that I have spent all my life learning about religion without knowing what religion is?"

"Anything is possible."

"That's not what I asked."

"Only you can answer your question, my friend."

"That doesn't help, Tallis. All my life, religion and worship were transactional. We approached the gods, asked for what we or our people needed, and we hoped they'd answer. When we saw Yeshua, we didn't worship to get something. We simply acknowledged something truly worthy of worship. At least I did. What about you?" Akilah searched Tallis's face, pleading for affirmation.

Tallis clasped his hands behind his back and kept walking. "Only when we face extraordinary circumstances do we truly learn what's in our hearts."

"Like what happened when you left your first career?"

"Something like that."

"Where does that leave us?" Akilah stopped and faced him. "Do you believe religion can be more than ritual?"

"What I believe and what I do in service to Magi society are sometimes two different things. Everyone must come to terms with their contradictions—and their convictions."

"But can religion be a relationship?" Akilah grabbed Tallis's shoulders. "This child ... What if God isn't a principle but a *person*? If this child is more than a sign of deity but actually has the presence of God living in him, is this child the only way to understand God?"

Akilah's anguished thoughts tumbled in a torrent through his mouth. "Just as unfathomable ... If his government will be without end, then he must be more powerful than the three Zoroastrian saoshyants predicted to come in the distant future. This Hebrew child will be able to do more than eliminate evil. But what? I don't understand. This child—is he a *personal* Savior? What is he saving me from? Can the child we saw do all that?"

Tallis's eyes bored into Akilah. "The world is big enough to hold many religions. But the heart can hold only one."

"I ..." Akilah let go of Tallis's shoulders.

His colleague never minced words. When he spoke, it was always with authority and deep meaning. Now more so than ever. More importantly, Akilah had never seen his eyes flame with such passion.

Tallis covered Akilah's hands. "Before yesterday, had you ever come face to face with something more personal and powerful than religion? Before yesterday, what did you trust more than anything? What gave you hope beyond all understanding?"

Akilah's stomach knotted. That sounded dangerously close to how common people reacted to religion. They were all too eager to believe in the first hopeful thing that came their way. He didn't want to count himself among them. He was a man of reason, immune to the ebbs and flows of popular beliefs, too self-sufficient to rely on religion for heart matters like hope. But this was different. "Is my dedication to logic getting in the way of believing in this child? We believed before we saw him. Why is believing harder now?"

"Maybe because what we saw wasn't what we expected."

"But—"

"Your mind doubts. What does your heart say?" Tallis's eyes bored into Akilah. "Do you still believe what you saw?"

"Yes."

"Yet you don't understand it."

"No."

"If you could explain it, would you more readily accept it as truth?"

"Yes."

"Maybe more explanation must wait."

Tallis's echo of the Chief Megistane's final words when he freed Akilah from his holding cell jarred him. "Wait? For what?"

"For your head to reconcile with your heart."

"How?"

"Only an all-knowing God can answer that," Tallis replied. "You have a choice. Adjust your conscience or change your life. The first is easy. Your conscience can rationalize anything to distract you from truth or numb you to it. Rationalization is an illusion. Illusion fades. Truth doesn't."

Tallis clapped a hand on Akilah's shoulder. "Life moves in one direction, my friend. Forward. Whether we are ready for it or not. We embrace it or not. Simple as that."

"Mm." If only he shared Tallis's reductionist attitude. What his colleague called simple was far from easy. Maybe Akilah's penchant for a nuanced life was a barrier to embracing a new truth. Something completely counterintuitive and countercultural. He groped for a reply but found none.

"Shall I have Hakeem draw water for you?" Tallis said.

They had walked full circle back to their camels. Time for another private discussion would have to wait until nightfall.

"Tallis, about changing your conscience or your life … My life has already changed. I believe in this Hebrew God. So, it follows that I believe He and this child-king are worth risking everything for."

Tallis eyed Akilah as a hardened military officer would. "Everything? You just admitted to a life choice. Will the strength of your conviction withstand harder circumstances than we're facing now? This is but one test. Before the stakes get higher, settle with yourself whether you will continue to embrace that truth no matter what the cost." He trotted off before Akilah could answer.

He buried his head in his camel's curly golden mane. "How can I calculate the cost?" If only Dain could answer him. Joy, turmoil, dread, and peace swirled inside Akilah. Only the heavenly being's final words brought Akilah any measure of clarity and assurance. "God is with you," he repeated to himself.

Roused by another thought, he reached into a side pouch on his saddle. "Ow!"

"What's wrong?"

Akilah whirled around. How long had Rashidi been behind him? "Nothing. I'm fine."

"You don't act fine."

"Just a touch of arthritis."

"You'll have to do better than that. Arthritis doesn't make fingers bleed. What's in the pouch?"

"Nothing of consequence. Only sentimental value."

"We can cushion it. I'll get a servant to—"

"Not necessary."

"If you don't want to talk about it, as the youngest Magus on this trip, I must defer to your wishes." Rashidi fumed. "Otherwise, would you let me look at your finger ... and what's in the pouch?"

"Would you have Hakeem bring me water, sap, and a small bandage? I should take care of this, even though it is but a minor nuisance."

"You don't always have to carry the entire burden of this caravan on your shoulders, you know." Impatience bled through Rashidi's voice. He inhaled as if winding up to say more but respectfully looked downward. "I've been doing some calculations. I don't think we have enough funds to—"

"Thank you for fetching Hakeem for me." Akilah threw his thanks over his shoulder as he turned away.

Hearing a humph, Akilah turned back. There Rashidi stood, arms crossed, feet apart and rooted to the ground as firmly as a hundred-year-old mulberry tree. "I will learn from you. I will obey you. But I will not live like you," he said, his tone hot.

From weariness, Akilah chose silence over a reply. When he was sure he was alone, he slumped against his regal camel. Unfastening a pouch hidden under the kilim blanket beneath Dain's saddle, Akilah headed to one of his clothing trunks. "Now is not the time for this," he muttered. "It needs to stay out of sight."

He peered inside the pouch, relieved to see its contents were still intact. But the next time he would see them would likely be to say goodbye.

Chapter 63

Revelations

Akilah sank the pouch through layers of clothes until he reached a veil folded around the Simurgh medallion. Farzaneh had insisted he carry one of her veils to ensure his safe return. He had balked at her sentiment almost as much as Fakhri's gesture in giving him the Simurgh. Only now did he appreciate their significance and how important both people were to him.

Despite the veil's protective layers, Akilah still could trace the Simurgh's bas-relief shape. As crazed as Fakhri's words sounded months ago, now they rang with truth. The caravan *was* in danger. More importantly, if Yeshua would be king forever, he would be a dual reality— temporal and eternal. He obviously had been born into a temporal, time-bound world. If he were also eternal, he would bridge life and death. Either he would never die, or somehow he would overcome death. What else could "everlasting" mean? Isaiah's words were so precise.

Akilah shook his head. *Impossible. No human being can bridge life and death.* But after seeing Yeshua bathed in that incredible light, all things seemed possible.

Surely the Hebrews would dedicate tomes to this singular

person. Yeshua would be unrivaled in history. Worthy of following above all others. Such loyalty could topple other religions. *Including Persia's.*

Akilah's breath caught in his chest. Was that the true reason for his arrest? To silence him before he could learn enough to find this child and spread the word about him? If the Parthian empire abandoned the prophecies about its three saviors, its official religion would crumble. So would the foundation of Magi society—and all its influence.

What have I done?

His heart twisted. In Persia, if he dared to speak of the child despite government disapproval, much worse than imprisonment could befall him. Had his study set something in motion he couldn't stop?

He replayed Herod's paranoia and the Council's investigation. If both entities knew of Isaiah's words, they would take extreme measures to protect their interests. How else could they feel about a government without end? If the prophecy was true, *their* governments wouldn't last, but the child's would.

Akilah's thoughts flitted back to Balaam's prophecy, the first clue they had found about the child. *A scepter shall rise from Israel, and shall crush through the forehead of Moab, and break down all the sons of Sheth.*[1] Akilah tried to picture a grown Yeshua standing tall and proud, one foot resting in triumph on the rubble of an idol statue in the midst of a demolished city. Somehow that image seemed ill-fitting for him.

Fear may have moved the Council to censor Hebrew holy writings, but Akilah resolved not to let fear censor him. He would study the Hebrews' religious writings further. Under a guise, if needed. And, if he must, outside of the realm of Magi

---

1. Numbers 24:17 (ESV)

society. He needed to learn more, especially about the prophet Isaiah.

If he lived long enough.

First things first. They had to get out of Judea. Fast.

Chapter 64

Burned and Buried

Normally such a long journey would have ended with ample rest before returning home. But not this one. The caravan had to keep pressing south. It stopped for the evening much later than usual.

The servants drifted to their tents before the Magi did. The trio stared into the starry night, full of questions. But they asked only one.

"Was it worth it?"

"Oh, yes."

Silence wrapped that sentiment like a comforting blanket until Akilah reluctantly said, "It's late. May we be favored with better dreams than last night."

But he remained outside their tent. "I'll retire soon."

He couldn't stop mulling his duty versus his growing sense of newfound purpose. By birth, he was part of Magi society. By choice, he served in it. From duty, he had followed its official religion. From duty, he had studied many religions and officiated their services. All had to meet strict standards. Worship was loyal adherence to rules, drenched with human effort to reach up to a distant, detached god. Do it right, and maybe that god would reach down to ease one's plight.

But transactional religion wearied even devout followers. It didn't help that humanity muddled it. Many leaders claimed descendancy from deity or deified themselves—presumably for personal gain and to unify their country. If an earthly king *could* become a god …

Akilah sighed. Again, that detached distance.

Perhaps that's why he had never truly claimed any religion as his own. Too much human agenda. Too many manmade rules and uninvolved, impersonal gods. But if this Yeshua child was truly God's appointed Savior or had God inside him, then God had reached down to mankind.

A God who initiated the reaching. An act of wanting a relationship with humanity. And now, incredibly, reaching through a child involved in everyday life. A child who would grow and experience everything mankind experienced. That would change the very fabric of religion. The core reason for worship.

That was unique. Radical. Threatening to other religions. Even more cause to keep quiet about what the Wise Men had seen. For now.

Threats. How many more would the caravan face?

Akilah could mitigate one. He woke Hakeem and drew him aside. Soon his faithful servant slipped away from camp, laden with a knife, a bundle, a box, and a bag of camel dung pellets.

The servant returned two hours later with only the box. Akilah inspected its contents and nodded in approval. "The rest?"

"Burned and buried."

"Good."

Chapter 65

The Star's Secret

In solitude, Akilah watched the clear night sky twinkle with countless lights. For as long as he could remember, their secrets had tantalized him. Now they taunted him—winking as if to say their biggest secret was just out of reach. "If only you could tell me how logic and belief fit together," he whispered. "It's a most difficult puzzle for me."

Akilah wistfully turned north toward Bethlehem and gasped. The same pure-white light that had led them the last hour of their journey to the child hovered low in the sky, beckoning him from afar.

He grabbed his strongest ocular and pulled his cloak about him. Planting himself on the nearest rise, he resolved to remain there until he was certain the star didn't move like other night lights.

How could he describe this star? He'd seen it in different months of two different years, so it wasn't seasonal. It was visible in both night and sunrise skies, much like Sothis, the brilliant blue-white star to which the Egyptians aligned their pyramids. Yet this Bethlehem star—if it was a star—was infinitely brighter. And closer.

It couldn't be a comet. Comets portended death, war, destruction. Everything the Magi had read and seen of this light spoke life.

A conjunction? Inconceivable. He had argued cogently against that in the Council meeting. The brightest, most spectacular conjunctions happened hundreds of years apart—not a year apart. Moreover, this star was magnitudes brighter than anything he'd ever seen. And it had moved only when it guided the Wise Men to Bethlehem's outskirts.

Akilah stared at the ocular in his hand. Was this activity an excuse to avoid a new reality he wanted to accept? His thoughts turned to Yeshua. God in a child. How could it be? Even the idea of a *child* ... Every culture's gods were created fully grown and fully capable. Ibis. Bull. Eagle.

But those religions also said those animals weren't gods—only vessels the gods used when they visited Earth. The same with statues that remained hidden until festivals, when the gods supposedly manifested themselves on cue, embodying principles to emulate or appease. The notion of animals or statues giving form to gods was absurd to Akilah. But a child who would grow and live among mankind as an approachable person ... Why didn't other religions do that?

Maybe because they couldn't.

Akilah had seen a *child*. Divinity incarnate. God in the flesh. That is, if he took Isaiah's words literally. What else could he do? Isaiah had written, *"And His name shall be called Mighty God."*[1]

If Akilah embraced that as truth, should he continue his priestly service in Magi society? Would he be allowed to?

The star. The child. God. His musings wearied him more than the trip's length or the night's chill. He retired to his tent.

An hour later, something awakened him. He circled the camp but found nothing. The night was calm.

---

1. Isaiah 9:6 (ESV)

New Star

With the future's uncertainties weighing on his mind, he headed for his tent. Still, something made him pause and turn once more in the direction they'd come.

There was the light! And it still hadn't moved.

Without restraint, Akilah wept. "Why did we see this wonder? For what purpose were we chosen?"

More of Isaiah's words coursed through his heart. *Lift up your eyes on high and see who has created these stars, the One who leads forth their host by number, He calls them all by name; because of the greatness of His might and the strength of His power, not one of them is missing.*[2]

Through Akilah's tears, the star blurred but did not dim. It seemed to speak into his heart. *What do you believe?*

Akilah mouthed, *You.*

As he watched, transfixed, the light withdrew. Like a shimmering thread pulled through the fabric of space, the light disappeared from the canvas of night.

"God, who are you?" he cried.

---

2. Isaiah 40:26 (NASB)

Chapter 66

Do You Feel That?

Thirteen days later

B eyond the inhospitable desert, rose-colored mountains rose, their beauty a receptacle for more heat. Somehow the caravan had found the *siq* hidden in them—a narrow gorge, in some places barely wide enough for servants to walk next to the Magi's camels. The winding passage twisted five times before a sliver of stacked columns came into view. The siq ended abruptly, depositing the caravan into a city like no other.

Slack-jawed, Hakeem turned in all directions. "What is this place?"

"Petra," Akilah said.

Hakeem's amazement rippled through the caravan. "The whole city is cut into rock." "Never seen anything like it."

Every turn revealed another stunning edifice. A columned mausoleum chiseled into the side of a sandstone cliff. Houses stacked in rock faces. A massive amphitheater, its seating carved into a hillside. And, if rumor could be believed, a mountain temple soaring above eight hundred fifty stone steps.

New Star

Petra's beauty was both elegant and stark, a testimony to the battle of wills between man and nature. Determination and ingenuity had forced solid rock to yield to stoneworkers' wishes.

While the tired caravan surveyed their surroundings, Akilah prayed silent thanks that the servants had accepted his vague explanation of having "king's business to the south." Here, they could rest before wending their way back to Persia via a circuitous southeastern route.

After he dispatched Tallis and Rashidi to find lodging, Akilah addressed the servants. "The people here are Nabatu, or Nabataeans. We don't know their language or customs, so say little and be very polite."

Akilah longed to lose himself in Petra's sites, but he needed to replenish supplies first. That should be easy. The people walking Petra's main thoroughfare attested to the city's success as a flourishing trade hub. Residents dressed in silk and translucent fabrics. Silver jewelry encrusted with precious stones adorned their foreheads, necks, and arms. Metalworkers smelted materials from abroad. Street vendors sold food redolent with exotic spices. But oddly, Petra had no diversity. A trade hub should teem with a mélange of people groups and languages. Not so here. Only one language was discernable—a strange, perhaps ancient Arabic dialect.

Yet, the first person Akilah approached spoke with him in his homeland dialect.

Perhaps heat or exhaustion had dulled his senses to question such an oddity. He stroked his camel's back. It was far too hot. He dug his fingers through the golden curls of its protective wooly coat. Dain's skin was equally hot. The camels needed water.

The caravan's hasty retreat from Jerusalem had tested everyone's limits. But now they were beyond Judea's borders and King Herod's reach.

Or so it seemed.

Much about Petra unsettled Akilah. Red earth abounded underfoot, but pottery seemed scarce. The city's transcendent architecture reflected no national signature. Instead, it held Assyrian, Egyptian, Greek, and Roman influences captive in stone. Were those silent sentinels a wordless registry of Nabataean conquests or opportunism?

He scolded himself. Fatigue was the language of worry. But Tallis and Rashidi seemed edgy too.

Still, Akilah's thirst for knowledge brought a smile to his face. He was eager to learn if the rumors he'd heard were true—that the people of Petra controlled water in ways no one else could.

Dinner didn't offer him a chance to ask. The inn's servers whisked silver bowls and cups in front of the Magi, then left with haste.

"Look at this." Akilah turned his cup toward Tallis. The dinnerware was gilded with designs disturbingly similar to Parthian patterns.

In the evening sun, Petra's sandstone mountains glowed ruby red. The wind brought only mild relief as it stirred the sandy expanse sifting into the city. What a contrast to Jerusalem's white limestone mountains, rippling breezes, and lush vegetation.

After dinner, the Magi checked on the camels, stabled in a manmade cave. Akilah eased his back against the cool stone, a welcome change from the sun's relentless rays.

Tallis walked the length of the cave-stable. "It has plenty of feed, but where's the water?"

The Magi's servants looked up from their grooming chores. "We tried to get it, but they won't show us where the water is. We think they said they must bring it to us."

"Who is 'they'?" Akilah said.

The servants shrugged.

No matter. Soon row after row of jugs appeared at the cave's entrance. Akilah had never been so happy to see water. The servants filled two huge troughs hollowed from rock, but the parched camels barely let the water hit the trenches. They guzzled gallon after gallon until they couldn't hold any more. In fifteen minutes, all the water was gone.

Chapter 67

Plans in the Night

Two hours after the servants retired, the Magi returned to the cave-stable. Its stone mass mirrored the weight in Akilah's chest. As leader of this venture and supposedly the wisest of his team members, he should have been able to justify what he sensed. But he couldn't. Maybe Tallis and Rashidi could confirm his concerns. "Are we certain we're alone?"

"I think so," Tallis said. "Just us and the camels. And they're not talking."

Akilah ignored the joke. "Gentlemen, what do we really know about the Nabataeans other than they're here in the middle of this desert?"

Rashidi pulled two coins from his pocket. "They have their own money system."

"Tallis, the lamp, please?" Akilah studied the coins. "What did you buy?"

"I'm not sure," Rashidi said, a sheepish grin on his face. "Medicines, I think. One is called *guda*. I chipped off a piece of it; it tastes sweet. It might be from Hindustan. The other is from Soqotra. Resin from something called dragon's blood tree. I thought, why not? Maybe they'll come in handy sometime."

Akilah scratched his head. "Interesting souvenirs. Did they write you a receipt?"

"Yes. But not in Nabataean." Rashidi's voice rose with excitement. "It's written in the language of the people of Harran."

"How do you know?"

"I grew up in southern Anatolia, remember? Harran is on the main caravan route in that region. When my family moved from Egypt to Anatolia, Harran's language became my second childhood language. It's an unusual dialect."

"Harran … where the Parthian Empire defeated Rome fifty years ago." Tallis's smile hovered near a smirk. "Before your time, Rashidi."

Akilah cleared his throat. "Before my time as well. That happened the year I was born." He grabbed the receipt. "Why write in someone else's language? That makes no sense. The Nabataeans clearly have their own oral language. But they have no library. No writings carved into their temple walls. No homages on monuments to kings."

"They have wine presses."

Akilah eyed Tallis with amusement. "Do you need more refreshment tonight?"

Tallis scowled. "Think about it. Why build wine presses unless you can grow grapes nearby? Who grows grapes in the desert?"

"I can tell their cotton isn't imported from Egypt," Rashidi added. "It must be grown here."

"Exactly. Grapes and cotton require abundant water to grow. So where does it come from?" Tallis pointed to the empty water troughs. "And did you notice that no one hauled water to their homes this evening? Everyone from the elite to the lower class seems to have plenty for their household. How do they do it?"

"Their past and present seem cloaked in secret," Akilah said. "Surely we can find something about them in the records of history and wisdom we brought with us. Hold the lamp up, Tallis."

"We should have brought more than one."

"Safer with just one."

Scrounging like rats looking for food scraps in the dark, their task took longer than it should.

They finally picked two metal containers and divided their contents. The Magi unrolled and scanned papyri as fast as the dim light allowed. But after fifteen minutes, they shook their heads.

Akilah thumped his knee and sighed. "Nothing we have with us tells us anything about these people. Not even where they come from."

"I ..." Tallis turned away to re-roll his stack.

Akilah gripped his colleague's arm. "What do you know? Tell us."

"Mostly rumors. Some say the Nabataeans came from Mesopotamia long ago."

Akilah paused, his hand on one cylinder. "Your homeland?"

"I consider Persia my homeland. But yes, I was born in Mesopotamia." An enigmatic longing flickered across his face. "My beautiful Persia."

"We miss Persia with you," Akilah said. "I promise you we will see it again. Together. Tallis, you know more about geography and genealogy than the rest of us. What else do you know about the Nabataeans?"

"Word is that, after a conflict six hundred years ago, they started infiltrating Edomite territory." Tallis kept his voice low. "Then they became two groups. One group settled south of Judea. Today, they are the Idumeans. But the other group, the Nabataeans, remained nomads—with a twist. They move like ghosts. They are opportunists. They pitch their tents outside of towns, then take advantage of them. No one knows the boundaries of their territories. Rome's rule doesn't touch them. They form no alliances."

Rashidi's eyes widened. "What if Herod's mother was Nabataean?"

"Herod mentioned only his Jewish roots through his father, Antipater," Tallis replied.

"But Herod talked about how influential his father was," Rashidi countered. "He could have married outside his country to gain wealth and political favor. Kings do it all the time. Look at Herod. Marrying a Hasmonean princess gave him another tie to Judea."

Akilah closed his cylinder. "Herod did say he'd surpassed anything his father had accomplished. But conjecture is pointless. We've already seen how secretive the Nabataeans are with their water supplies. Understandable in this location but very concerning."

"This place has a bad feel to it," Tallis said. "Like how we felt after leaving Herod's palace—even before we all had that same dream. We should go."

Akilah paced. "Tomorrow morning, we will tell the servants to watch for what kinds of trade goods and supplies people take with them when they leave the city. Then we'll have our servants buy the same. But only part of what we need. We don't want to draw attention to ourselves."

"We must travel farther than we'll make it appear," he continued. "No one can know where we're headed. Including our servants. That way, if anyone asks, they can truthfully say they don't know our destination. We leave tomorrow evening."

Rashidi shuffled in place. "Which way should we go?"

"Southwest. To Ayla."

Tallis looked up sharply. "Our backs will be to the sea. Is that wise?"

"It's a short journey. We can rest there and evaluate our options."

Rashidi crossed his arms. "What about Nabataeans? We saw enough of their goods to know they engage in sea trade."

"The months of safest sea travel are not yet upon us. Nabataean traders would be a minimal, transient presence in Ayla this time of year. It's an acceptable risk." Akilah spread his hands. "Our caravan is beyond tired. I am counting on us to find shelter and safety there."

"But east of Ayla is desert and west is wilderness—"

"One problem at a time, Rashidi. We must trust that the answers will unfold as we need them."

Akilah stretched his back. "We have work to do before tomorrow evening. Rashidi, I want you to buy another souvenir. Something with writing on it. Get creative if you need to. We need to learn more of the Nabataeans' language than what is on their coins and sales receipts—in case we cross them again."

He rested his hands on his colleagues' shoulders. "My friends, we are still fugitives. Herod probably has a price on our heads. We are wise men in many ways. But, on this journey, we must be wise in a different way. Wise as serpents. And it seems wise to rely on this God of the Hebrews—that He will lead us to what we need, when we need it. Just like He did at Bethlehem."

Chapter 68

Answered Prayer

Akilah slipped through the darkness to the servants' sleeping room near the stable. "Hakeem, wake up," he whispered, motioning his servant outside. "Our plans have changed. What news of the water situation?"

"I found a canal or conduit," Hakeem said. "It's concealed—covered with flat rocks that look like steps up a hill. The conduit may lead to a cistern, but I couldn't tell in the dark. Even so, we should be able to draw enough water for ourselves without anyone seeing us."

With glee, Akilah slapped his servant on the back, then stifled his excitement. "The God of the Hebrews must have given you the eyes of an eagle to spot a water source. Blessings on you for that, Hakeem. You are a conduit, too—a conduit for answered prayer. Come. Wake two others to fill everyone's waterskins while darkness can hide them. Tomorrow we have much work to do."

The next day, under Akilah's watchful care, the servants worked in shifts. Some scouted. Others browsed. Some bought food and supplies. Others packed. After two hours, they rotated tasks. Maybe the locals wouldn't notice who did what. Maybe they wouldn't guess the caravan's imminent departure.

That evening, the caravan slipped out of the city. Petra's natural fortifications were so strong the city seemed to have no need for a contingent of guards. Would anyone follow them? Was the caravan's agenda still a secret? Only time would tell.

Chapter 69

Family Mission

Herod the Great's palace in Jerusalem

With their torches held high, the royal guards rapped on the ornate double-wide door to the anteroom of Herod's private chambers. "Come." A voice issued from the darkness beyond the room.

Antipas hesitated to cross the threshold. His father—the man whose first name Antipas bore—had never permitted his son to enter this inner sanctum. Until now.

In fact, Antipas rarely saw his father unless it suited the king's agenda. Father and son shared little except their bloodline and their desire to build. So why summon him now? What could his father possibly require that necessitated Antipas's immediate attendance under cover of night instead of the preparation and pomp that always preceded a royal audience?

Herod the Great emerged from the darkness, carrying a globed lamp. "Antipatros."

The salutation snatched a sharp breath from Antipas. His father never called him by his formal personal name. In fact, the king promulgated his son's nickname, Antipas—not as a term of endearment but as a hint that his son was too young or ill-equipped to rule. Antipas often wished he could grind his nickname into the dust much like he ground those hideous, oversized Jerusalem crickets into the city's stone pavements.

But he had just passed his teen years and his schooling in Italia. Did his Roman education, with its inculcation of Rome's ideals as well as its hedonistic pleasures, now make him Antipatros? Perhaps, if only for this moment.

"Yes, my king?"

"I must go to Jericho soon."

Antipas clenched his teeth. Whatever whimsy had wooed Herod to venture to his winter palace on the cusp of summer was no reason to summon him. As usual, Antipas would bide his time until his father's real agenda emerged. He bowed. "May your travels be swift and safe, my king."

Herod turned away without acknowledging his son's well wishes. The king appeared lost in thought, although he passed his hand over his gut several times. Apparently no medicinal could halt the putrefaction consuming his inward parts. After several minutes, he turned back to Antipas. "Foreigners from the East dined with us two weeks ago. Do you remember them?"

"Yes. They were seeking a child prophesied to be a king."

"King of the Jews." Herod wheeled to face his son. "More precisely, king of my kingdom. *I* am king of the Jews."

Antipas bowed deeply.

Herod returned to the anteroom's window as if staring through it would extract a secret from the starry sky. "Competition for the throne can come from unexpected places," he said, his voice low and menacing like a wolf's growl. "But *every* threat to the throne demands a decisive response."

The king circled a table and drew closer to Antipas. "No one can do what I can. But you can do some of it." Herod turned abruptly. "That child will not live long enough to learn what a throne is."

Antipas's heart thundered like a rampaging rhino. His father had no compunction about killing anyone who stood in the way of his plans. His orders had sent nameless armies and appointed officials to their deaths. In the past three years, Herod had executed two of Antipas's older half-brothers. Now Herod's firstborn sat in prison, awaiting conviction and sentencing by Caesar Augustus. Was Antipas next? He stole a sideways glance at the bowl of fruit on the table, relieved to see none that required paring—and no knife present for doing so.

Herod continued his stream of thought. "A decisive response leaves no loose ends. Remember that." He turned to his son. "That brings us to the matter of those who were seeking the child."

"Explain."

"Antipatros, the time has come for you to prove yourself worthy of ascending the throne. Find the Magi."

"My king, they treated you with utmost deference. I found that surprising, given your ... engagement with their country's army thirty-five years ago."

Herod's teeth flashed through lips curled in a sneer. "Persia is *not* my ally when it fights for the Jews. The world remembers Persia's defeat every time it looks upon my fortress at Herodium."

His voice leveled. "By now, you must know that everyone has a hidden agenda." He paced, furiously rubbing his thumbs against his forefingers. "At first, I thought the priests' information might have been wrong ... that it had led the Magi astray. But since then, I have consulted the chief priest and all the scribes. They confirmed Bethlehem as the child's prophesied birthplace."

His face contorted in a snarl. "Those Magi betrayed me. They promised to bring word of the child when they found him.

Bethlehem is a small town. The surrounding villages even smaller. Even if the Magi had to widen their search, they should have returned by now." Herod's words raged like waters straining against a failing dam. "Find them and dispose of them permanently." He paused. "I guarantee you will become a successor to my kingdom."

Herod's face lit with a charm bordering on rapture. Antipas had seen it often. His father had perfected that instantaneous transformation whenever he needed information, approval, or unlikely allies. It was heady to watch, nearly impossible to resist. The king's allure made people surrender their allegiance and better judgment as inexorably as Baia's attendants turned a hot-springs bath into a communal sensual experience. Still, Antipas sensed something deeper, more personal, lurking behind his father's expression.

Antipas exhaled slowly, hoping his heart would decelerate as well. "Those scholars are one step below royalty in their society. Any inordinately long absence would be noticed and investigated."

Herod plucked a handful of grapes from a bowl. "The Pax Romana can't quell everything in this corner of the world. Accidents, mercenaries, nomads ... so many unfortunate fates." He laughed, but it emerged as a throaty growl ending in a strangled cough. He squared himself in front of Antipas. "I have pushed you hard because I see your potential. You are destined to make an indelible mark on history."

The king studied his son. Antipas would not give in to that look. He would be rebuked or worse if he showed any reaction other than loyalty.

Roman schooling had taught him the price of loyalty. His father's actions had taught him the expediency of it. Proximity to power was its own education, and survival in this family hinged on learning to play its power game. Antipas was keenly aware that he hadn't been his father's first choice of successor, yet his father's recent jailing of his firstborn on charges of attempted poisoning had paved the way for him.

The words *an indelible mark on history* sent fire and ice coursing through Antipas's veins. The two exploded in his heart, a sizzling mix of desire and dread. The fire of desire extinguished the ice of dread. He met his father's gaze.

Herod bit hard on a mouthful of grapes, sending a red trickle down his chin. "To aid your effort, I will grant you use of a few of my royal guards while others complete a ... cleansing task for me."

Antipas nodded and turned to leave.

"One more thing."

The calculated coldness in his father's voice commanded Antipas to turn back, although he dreaded doing so. That shrewd tone resonated with some requirement of a more profound obligation. Acid rose in his throat as he faced his father. "Yes?"

"The death of this child won't kill the prophecies about him."

Who was this child that troubled the king so? Antipas would very much like to meet him. The son stepped closer to his father, searching his face for answers. The next moment, Herod pulled his son to him, gripping Antipas's head with such intensity that his jaw shifted. Shock stole his breath. Oil from Herod's dyed locks grazed Antipas's forehead in an unwanted anointing.

"Engrave my words on your heart, Antipatros. This so-called King of the Jews—and anyone who promotes prophecies about him—is nothing but future trouble for you. Jewish history is full of prophets, mostly false ones. But they all have one thing in common. They stir the Jews to rebellion. Jerusalem is a smoldering fire, always close to bursting into flame."

There was no escape from Herod's fetid breath or iron grip. Antipas held his own breath as potent aromas of frankincense and myrrh shrouded him. His skin crawled, just as it had when his childhood self had gotten lost exploring a burial cave.

Herod let go, panting. He stroked Antipas's cheek then slid his fingers down his neck. "A challenging but exhilarating place to be. Especially now." Herod's hand stopped in the center of his son's chest. Antipas could not quell his heart's pounding. He prayed to the gods that his father could not feel it.

The king spun around, arms spread wide. "Rome is in its golden age. Judea is prosperous. "Progressive Hellenization is replacing Jewish isolationism." His tone approached glee.

Herod swiveled toward the window. "I did all that. One child from a backward town will not stand in the way of my plans. And when he is gone, I will look down from Herodium on Bethlehem with satisfaction—forever."

For an eternity of two minutes, the king seemed lost in thought. Antipas waited. The king had not yet dismissed him.

Herod turned back to his son. "Now swear on what you hold most dear that you will eliminate those Magi. Permanently. And pledge you will commit the rest of your life to defending this throne against *any* prophet or Jew who would speak of that child, even after his death. Jewish culture is a poison to everything Rome stands for. Always remember. No loose ends."

Herod's granite missive left Antipas only one way to exit the antechamber alive. But, at that moment, he felt invincible.

The son knelt. He clasped his father's hand, kissed the gold ring bearing the king's royal seal, and pressed it to his forehead. "It shall be as you say," Antipas whispered.

Chapter 70

Where Will You Go?

Persia, the Magi's complex

Sassanak scowled at the Chief Megistane lounging in his doorway. "It's bad enough that guards stand outside my quarters day and night. What do you want? Let me guess. You're here to help me pack."

"No. To escort you."

"I don't need an escort."

"Yet you have one," the Chief said. "To see you safely beyond Persia's borders. By decree of the Lord High Chancellor."

"Government excess."

"Government prudence." The Chief strode into the room. "Give me all your seals and stamps."

"They were confiscated the day you arrested me, remember?" Sassanak sneered.

"If I have to sift through every item in your trunks, I will," the Chief replied. "Or I can summon the guards outside your door to do that for me. They will not be careful handlers."

Sassanak plunged his hand into one trunk and retrieved a

small gold box. Opening the lid under the Chief's nose, he said, "Look all you want. Just my personal seal. Happy?"

Indeed, it contained only that seal and a small bar of wax. Even so, the Chief rummaged through a clothing chest nearest him. Without a word, he moved to another trunk.

With vigor, Sassanak wound a paisley-patterned, silk-and-wool tablecloth around a pair of ornate silver candlesticks and shoved them between layers of bedding. "Any word from Akilah?"

"He is no longer your concern."

"Just making conversation."

"I know you better than that."

Seething, Sassanak slammed the trunk lid and moved to a chest to refold clothes that the Chief had mussed from his rummaging.

"Now, for your agenda—where you will go. I must file a report. Your destination?" The Chief opened his wax writing tablet.

"Undecided."

"Unacceptable. You've had a month to plan and pack. Granted, Parthia's borders are vast. Any trip beyond them will be long. So, what will it be? Thessaly? Caucasus? Saba?"

Sassanak punched his clothes. "Vilazora," he said between clenched teeth. "In Macedonia."

"Interesting choice, Macedonia. Friendly with Persia. But steeped in Hellenism and Gnosticism. A challenge to your religious sensibilities." The Chief turned to block Sassanak from seeing what he'd jotted on his wax tablet. "The fastest route is a sea trip to Athens, then inland travel. We have passed *mare clausum*, the months of closed sea. But we are not yet beyond the most dangerous months for sea travel. Nonetheless, your choices dictated the timing."

"We should go overland instead. Travel Parthia's Royal Road to Sardis."

"Too lengthy and too easy for conspirators to track you. Also, it would still require water travel from Sardis to Greece."

"Government talk for 'not budgeted.'" Sassanak suppressed a snarl.

The Chief continued his notes.

Sassanak humphed. "I still need horses."

"You will have use of Magi society's camels to transport your luggage as far as Sidon's harbor. You may keep your personal camel and horse if you wish, but you may have to sell both to set foot on the ship we engage. Every merchant ship has its own policy about carrying animals. Our choice of ship will be limited this time of year. When we dock in Athens, the rest will be up to you."

"What about my furniture?"

"Any that you purchased will ship separately at your own cost. If it's not moved within a full moon, it becomes property of the Lower Council. First rights of ownership will go to your successor."

Sassanak reached for his Magi robes.

"No. Those stay here." The Chief deftly snatched the robes from his reach.

"That is so ... and I can't live without my Magi pension," Sassanak raged.

"Others do. As they say, 'much coin, much care.' Now you have less of both. And you don't need money to have úshtá." The Chief handed Sassanak his worn copy of *The Spirit of Wisdom's Commandments for the Body and Soul*.

Livid, Sassanak stuffed the codex into a corner of his clothing trunk. "How dare you touch that? You don't even subscribe to those beliefs."

A sneer curled the corners of the Chief's mouth. "Isn't judging others' beliefs contrary to Zoroastrian tenets of choosing to 'think good thoughts, speak good words, do good deeds'?"

"Don't quote me Zarathustra's principles. You have no right. Just because you were with Fakhri when he d—"

"And you weren't? You were under interdict."

"When Fakhri was sick, *I* visited him, prayed for him, diagnosed him, tried to cure him. All my life, I have ardently believed and practiced everything he taught. What did *you* do for him?"

"Unless you can see everything at once, how would you know?"

Sassanak set his jaw but swallowed more harsh words. "Did Fakhri ask about me?"

The Chief moved with purpose about the room, measuring luggage dimensions, calculating weight estimates. "Yes."

"Did he know why I was away?" If he played this right, his question could provide an opening for him to redeem himself. The chief wouldn't dare heap dirt on his head.

The chief paused in his tally but didn't look up. "Fakhri was told you were attending to urgent administrative duties in Assur."

Sassanak froze, an armful of scrolls poised over a trunk. "You covered me." A half smile played across his face. "What did he say in the end?" His voice softened.

"He asked me to oversee his funerary rites. Final whispered prayers, haoma, lighting fire in the censer. Now his body rests in the Tower of Silence, according to Magi and Zoroastrian practices."

"Besides that."

"The schedule of remembrance prayers continues."

"You know that's not what I mean."

The Chief immersed himself in his notations. "Sassanak, my only obligation to you is to see that you reach Vilazora."

"Back to that, are we?" His anger exploded. "You make me sick."

"I'll have the cook boil some ginger for you. No, wait. Maybe an infusion of peppermint or chamomile leaves?"

"That is dim. You—"

"The guards and I will wait outside your door for one cycle. Then you must leave, packed or not."

Chapter 71

Disrupted

To find the Magi, Antipas dutifully dispatched couriers to alert Roman guards along all the main roads a caravan would use. He also ordered four palace guards to fan through the countryside. Despite his low expectations for their success, his display at their send-off seemed to please Herod, if only briefly.

After that, the king appeared more agitated and paranoid than usual.

In the past few years, Herod's crown had become a gruesome mathematical equation of subtraction. The king's last step in eliminating all the sons from his first two marriages would soon end. For the past year, Antipas's oldest half-brother had languished in prison on charges of attempting to poison the king. The high-profile case required Augustus Caesar to officiate the trial. Herod would ensure no evidence was produced contrary to his allegations, and Caesar would no doubt follow Herod's wishes for a guilty charge. The sentence would be execution. Then Antipas would become heir apparent to the throne.

He knew what he was getting into. He had already talked to

palace advisors and listened to military briefings. His first priorities would be to stabilize Galilee and Perea. Squash the Jewish dissidents in the north. Appease the Romans, Nabataeans, and Jews in the south. Perea, which bordered Nabataea, had to remain part of Herod's kingdom. No. Antipas's kingdom. It was in his father's will. Antipas would wear the crown.

He deserved a day off to celebrate.

Full of pride and confidence in his future, he retreated to Caesarea. Getting out of Jerusalem always cleared his head. Perhaps that was part of the reason why his father spent so much time at his other palaces. Until Antipas inherited them, Caesarea would substitute nicely. It was so Greek in exalting the human form, clothed or not.

He took his time exploring the curves of the nubile courtesan he had engaged for the day. He reached her neck and unpinned her silken, perfumed hair. In response, she swept her waist-length tresses across his chest, then slowly toweled her hair over his entire torso to infuse the fragrance into his skin. Inhaling deeply, he pulled her to him. She melted into his arms without resistance. It pleased him how well trained she was in satisfying his desires. Enraptured, he spun her onto the bed, only to stop short at a door creaking open. "I said no one disturbs me unless Jerusalem is on fire and the king is trapped in it," Antipas bellowed.

His personal servant flattened himself against the door. "Countless pardons, but a man outside says he's from King Herod's legal entourage and insists on speaking with you immediately."

Antipas feigned surprise and ignorance, but the unwanted visitor could be only one person—Varinius. Antipas knew him better than anyone imagined. The jurisconsult had been feeding Antipas insider information of Herod's legal dealings for more than a year. If anyone were to discover their conclaves, they would simply appear to be private tutelage—Varinius familiarizing Antipas with legal matters. As a bonus, it would strengthen his persona as the attentive son who could "ensure" his father's failing health did not cloud his kingly decisions.

Varinius was reliable—and well paid. But today, he would pay for his visit.

Antipas wound a sheet around himself, dismissed the courtesan, and turned to his personal servant. "Tell the man that, for his interruption, he must pay the woman three times her fee. If he does, send him in. Remain outdoors until I join you." The sum wouldn't empty Varinius's deep pockets, but his compliance would demonstrate his loyalty to his future king.

The dust on Varinius's riding clothes spoke of urgency. Antipas motioned for his informant to sit. The lanky, serious man folded himself into a corner of a reclining couch.

"You risked much to find me here." Antipas poured himself more wine. "What news could be that important? Speak."

"My lord, your father has changed his will again."

"What?" Rage instead of wine reached Antipas's lips.

"King Herod has made your brother Archelaus his heir and ethnarch over Judea, Samaria, and Idumea. He has designated you and your half-brother Philip as tetrarchs."

"*Tetrarch?*" What had possessed Herod to accord Antipas such an inferior title and responsibility? Had his you-are-destined-to-make-an-indelible-mark-on-history speech been merely manipulation? Or worse, had Herod toyed with Antipas for sport?

He replayed the exchange in his mind. With disgust, he recalled Herod's exact words. "I guarantee you will become *a* successor to my kingdom." What subtlety. In the moment, that tiny word had escaped Antipas's notice. He had let his guard down, let himself be charmed into thinking Herod's will was final in naming Antipas as king. Yet that conversation implied Herod had already changed his mind. Again.

Apparently, the king didn't deem anyone worthy of wearing his crown. An ethnarch was a national leader. A governor—not a king. And a tetrarch was no more than a leader of a minor principality. An inconsequential cog in the vast machinery of the Roman Empire. Antipas glowered at Varinius. "What proof do you have?"

"Ptolemy, keeper of Herod's seal, attested to it. When Ptolemy was summoned for the seal, he saw Herod's hand was too unsteady to handle wax safely. While Ptolemy melted the wax, he scanned the will. He alone affixed Herod's seal to the document."

Varinius's access to Ptolemy and the seal keeper's slyness weren't lost on Antipas. But Archelaus as national leader? Antipas seethed with contempt. His brother's name meant "leading the people," but Archelaus didn't know how to lead a goat on a rope. Antipas resolved to contest the will. But, for the present, perhaps he could leverage his lot. "Tetrarch over which territories?"

"For you, Galilee and Perea. For Philip—"

"Galilee and Perea?" Antipas ground his teeth. They weren't even adjoining territories. The Decapolis, an area not under family rule, divided them. And Galilee? Herod had labeled it the most troublesome and "insufferably Jewish" of all his lands. Antipas slammed his fist into the side table that held his libation. Wine leapt from the chalice onto the sheet covering him. The ruby liquid quickly weakened to a dusky indigo.

Varinius bowed. "My lord, King Herod is days from death. If you return to Jerusalem at once, your presence may change his mind again about the will."

Chapter 72

I Spy

The Negev Desert: Day 1

Akilah contemplated the sandy expanse before him. Petra's wares proved its people could move freely across vast stretches of inhospitable land to conduct trade. That wasn't possible without ready sources of water. If his calculations were correct, the Nabataeans would need to water their camels and herds every few days while traveling such distances in hot weather. But where could the water be? Certainly not near Roman roads. How could anyone hide water in the desert's shifting sands? Or beyond, where barren mountains rose?

The Negev's negligible annual rainfall was common knowledge. But the weighty responsibility of forcing his weary caravan to cross the forbidding land unnerved Akilah. Survival hinged on water, and they already needed more of it.

"Maybe we should lighten our load." Tallis interrupted with a practical concern. "If we carried fewer clothing trunks, we could redistribute the gear. The caravan could move faster."

New Star

Rashidi jerked around and almost tumbled off his camel. "Not the embroidered robes and turbans."

"They're our heaviest clothes. And they identify us as Magi," Tallis said.

"What do you propose we do?"

"Burn them so people can't track us."

"Burn? That's rash."

"I don't think so. We did it before."

"Those weren't our clothes!"

Akilah swallowed a smile. What remained of the clothes the Magi were given at Herod's bathhouse would serve the entire caravan when needed. In a most humbling way. As bandages.

"A greater good—"

"We earned the right to wear our Magi robes," Rashidi blustered. "They were custom made for us, to remind us of the unique contributions we would make to Magi society."

"Would we be content if we didn't have them?" Akilah interjected. "They signify what we do—not who we are. We could have done without our Magi robes in Bethlehem."

Silence marked the next few minutes of their day.

"What if we buried them instead? And marked the spot so we could retrieve them later?" Rashidi seemed pleased with his suggestion.

Tallis snorted. "Like the Nabataeans hide their water?"

"Well, why can't we do the same?"

"How good are you at treasure hunting?"

Akilah couldn't deny the significance of their Magi robes. Presented with high ceremony during their induction, the heavy, ornate garments symbolized the weightiness of being set apart for priestly and scholarly service in Magi society. Some said the privilege was a calling. Regardless, it was an honor. A treasured accomplishment.

Burying the robes might serve a future purpose if they could be recovered. But the logic was flawed. Rather than voice his concerns, he diverted his colleagues' energy and attention. "Why don't we scout for something that would serve as a marker?"

As the three focused on their surroundings, Akilah's camel swerved. "What is it, Dain?"

Akilah scanned the sandy expanse. As the caravan crossed a sand dune, a lone *Pistacia*, exuding the unmistakable smell of terebinth, appeared ahead of the caravan. he raised his hand to halt the group. "Don't pistachios grow farther north, in milder, wetter climates?" He frowned at his colleagues.

The Magi surveyed the scrawny specimen. More the height of a large shrub than a tree, it didn't look worthy of their attention. But it did seem out of place.

And inspired.

Akilah clapped his hands. "Get the shovels! Dig, but not right here. Four paces out. Don't disturb the tree."

Six servants scrambled to comply.

A few minutes later, one shovel clanged against metal.

All six servants dropped to their knees, furiously scooping sand with spades and hands. Amid eager chatter, they uncovered a forged handle secured in cement.

Akilah could hardly contain his excitement. "Find the borders." The servants plunged their hands downward, groping for a seam. As fast as their burning hands allowed, an outline emerged. After more shoveling and scooping, a pale, thick slab appeared.

"Wedge the seams."

The sweat-glazed servants, their arms caked with sand, scurried to deploy the caravan's largest adzes. Groaning, the servants strained their legs and backs to dislodge the weighty slab. Stone grated on stone as everyone held their breath. Then cheers and whoops drowned the gravelly sounds. Water!

Tallis stroked his camel's neck. "Why didn't the camels smell this? Normally they can detect water half a parasang away."

Akilah waved off Tallis's concern. "Look. A hidden cistern. The Nabataeans must have other secret water sources in the desert. With markers that shifting sands can't obscure—but subtle enough so others overlook it." He looked to the horizon. "This can help guide us through unmapped territory." Turning from the others, he added under his breath, "And help us survive."

With the protectors standing as lookouts, Akilah ordered the servants to rotate filling waterskins while others drank or urged the camels to drink their fill. Although water should be for everyone, it clearly wasn't meant for sharing. The caravan had trespassed.

Tallis solemnly watched the servants cover the cistern and trowel sand over the spot. "At least we didn't have to pay for this Nabataean water. Not yet."

Chapter 73

Think Like Nabataeans

The successful sleuthing invigorated Akilah. Privately, he tasked Tallis and Rashidi with drawing a map of their route, encoding the location of every water source and whether it was hidden. He never dreamed a crude map would become their most guarded treasure.

Publicly, Akilah charged the caravan to look for anything that might seem odd or out of place. It could be a marker for a well, cistern, or spring. The Magi on their camels could see what was beyond. The servants could see what was near. Akilah needed both perspectives.

He half-jokingly code-named the effort "concealed."

Think like Nabataeans.

Think secrets.

He regretted not having time to study the remarkable structure they'd found. An underground cistern made of waterproof cement. With a filter to separate silt. And a hydraulic system. Such knowledge, if made public, could revolutionize travel across inhospitable lands and make safe drinking water available to everyone.

But he did take a bit of the structure with him. Alone at the edge of camp, he unfolded a cloth containing scrapings from the cistern's interior. What *was* that waterproof coating? Gazing through his strongest ocular, he could only guess. It looked nothing like Persia's water-resistant *sarooj* that coated the interiors of yakhchāls. That mortar was greyish-brown, a mixture of sand, clay, lime, ash, egg whites, and goat hair. In contrast, the cistern's shavings glistened white. Was silica the main ingredient?

That evening, Akilah inched his quill pen across papyrus. With meticulous strokes, he recorded his impressions of the cistern's structure. Perhaps when the Magi returned to Persia, Rashidi could use his engineering expertise to construct his own version of the cistern. That is, if they could safely hide Akilah's notes that long.

He paused his quill. How many secrets would they need to keep in order to survive? Their knowledge of Yeshua. Locations of hidden water sources. What next?

Akilah fished his cat statue from the depths of his clothing trunk. He crushed Farzaneh's stūrīh into the far end of the cavity inside the head, then carefully slid his rolled-up sketch into the opening.

But the excitement of the discovery didn't keep the caravan's waterskins filled. In the heat and drought, everyone needed more rest. And more water.

A day later, they found an oasis. At last, the Magi could relax a little. Oases were for everyone.

Chapter 74

To Act on It or Not

Southeast of Crete

Once again, Sassanak retched over the side of the heaving ship. The Chief Megistane smirked. *That's one form of justice.*

Despite the satisfaction he got from Sassanak's discomfort, the Chief hoped the weather wouldn't worsen. Blustering winds and turbulent seas stymied the ship's progress. Every mast and rigging groaned in the ship's struggle against nature, a potent reminder of why this roiling body of water was called the Great Sea. If the weather wouldn't break, the captain would have to port in Crete. Otherwise, the ship could run aground on any of the islands dotting the sea south of Athens.

A delay ... extra time with Sassanak ... The Chief's groan joined the ship's lament.

Sassanak staggered toward the Chief, unceremoniously wiping his sleeve over his mouth. "You know, excommunicating me won't stop the movement. Others will continue the cause for keeping Persia's religion pure."

"Get below. In the ship's center, away from the sides. You'll feel fewer effects of the sea."

The Chief's words were kinder than his thoughts. But larger concerns occupied him. His mind roiled with Fakhri's murky prophecy about Akilah—that he was destined for greatness but no one would appreciate it for many years.

The Chief was alone with Fakhri when he uttered those ominous words. What kind of honor was that? Moreover, what was he to do about Fakhri's final word to the Chief? As much as he wanted to charge that moment to a failing mind, he couldn't dismiss its significance. Instead, he banished the memory from his consciousness. If he recalled it, he would have to act on it.

Another wave slammed the side of the ship and knocked him to the deck's floor. The last thing he saw was a wave's curling arm sweep Sassanak overboard.

Chapter 75

Discretion and Discernment

The Negev Desert, Day 3

"Let's pitch the tents to rest during the sun's height. May we be favored with entering Ayla this evening," Akilah told Hakeem.

His servant nodded and disappeared into the caravan with Akilah's orders.

Akilah summoned his colleagues to what little privacy the Wise Men's tent offered. "Rashidi, show us what you bought that contains Nabataean writing."

Rashidi shrank back. "It's not much."

"Anything will be more than we know now." Akilah's smile faded at Rashidi's stricken look. "You do have something, don't you?"

"Yes." He slowly pulled two small parchments from his cloak.

Akilah stared at the first sheet then his colleague in disbelief. "Lists?"

Tallis peered around his shoulder. "Looks like a cargo list

with an inscription at the bottom. Perhaps an invocation to the gods to protect the goods."

Akilah weighed his frustration against his younger colleague's discomfiture. "Did you really buy these?"

"I left coin for it." Rashidi clipped his words.

Tallis slapped him on the back. "You stole travel manifests?"

"No. Not technically." Rashidi withered under Akilah's gaze. "It was all I could find in the time we had. Did *you* see any codices for sale?"

Tallis poked Akilah's ribs. "You must admit Rashidi did as you asked."

Akilah gritted his teeth. "This could cost us in ways we can't possibly imagine."

"Pray the Nabataeans aren't nearly as diligent recordkeepers as the Persians are," Tallis said. "Regardless, it's done. At least the words will have practical value if we can decipher them."

Akilah studied the first parchment. "But this is Akkadian. That's strange."

Rashidi looked at the list then at the ground as if willing the earth to swallow him.

Tallis grabbed the second sheet and sucked in his breath. "This is a Latin dialect." His face clouded. With a howl, he whipped his short dagger from its sheath and slashed the parchment. The pieces flopped to the ground.

"Why did you do that?" Rashidi's shoulders and voice shook.

Akilah knelt to retrieve the pieces, but Tallis ground them with his foot. "The Nabataeans—or at least their tradesmen—must still write in the language of whatever people they do business with." His voice could have iced water. "They are unusually ... adaptable."

Rashidi gulped. "That must be why the Nabataeans wrote the receipt for my purchases in the language of western Anatolia. I tried to hide our identity by conducting my transaction in the tongue I grew up speaking."

Rashidi drew from his cloak a scrap of parchment no bigger than the palm of his hand. "I have this, too," he said. "I found it on the ground, not far from the lists. It may be nothing. Graffiti. A reminder. I don't know."

Akilah pulled the scrap close to his face. "Ah. This we can use. Letterforms with elements of ancient Arabic and Aramaic. No vowels," he said. "Looks like you found some Nabataean writing. Let's see what we can learn." He nodded to Rashidi. "Keep the other sheets to learn what you can about what was bought or shipped."

Rashidi's hand trembled as he reached for the slashed parchment fragments still under Tallis's foot, but Tallis stepped back.

Akilah paused his scrutiny of the scrap. "Tallis, you had trade dealings with the Nabataeans?"

"You could say that. It almost cost me my first career. It did cost me dearly in other ways."

Chapter 76

For a Good Cause

The caravan reached Ayla in the late afternoon. A welcoming breeze wafted over the group. Despite everyone's exhaustion, Akilah directed the caravan to the southernmost part of the city. Everyone needed to see and feel water.

The picturesque seaport perched on the banks of the Gulf of Elat, a deep saltwater channel to the Red Sea. The servants danced like giddy children at the sight of the gulf's sparkling azure waters. A few camels ventured to the water's edge and tasted the brine. Two-humped Bactrians could drink saltwater if needed. But most of the camels remained huddled together near the shoreline, heads tilted upward toward the cool breeze.

Everyone was too tired to enjoy the scenery for long. Before the sun set, Akilah had to secure lodging for his caravan. The answer lay just outside the city's southwestern border—a *caravansary*. He beamed with satisfaction. "Just what we need. Walled, gated, guarded, and private."

The weighty-looking stone structure held simple but comfortable lodgings for people on the second floor, storehouses and stables on the first floor. An expansive open courtyard paved with flagstones burst with foliage and flowers. A hidden gem inside the architecturally bland but massive walled construction.

Akilah pressed an ornate silver cloak pin into the caravansary owner's hand. "Will this pay for everything for a week?"

The owner, a bronzed, forty-something man named Hesed, stared at the oversized pin in awe. "I've never seen anything like this. It's stunning. Are you sure you want to part with it?"

"My caravan needs a good rest."

Hesed turned the cloak pin over and over in his hand, his thumb tracing its shape. "This upside-down triangle and notched arch joining it to a half-circle ... That must mean something special to you."

"It was going to commemorate a trip. But plans ... changed." Akilah tried not to think of the private celebration he had planned, the jubilant end to their successful journey, capped with him presenting identical cloak pins to the trio. His highly symbolic design of the pins would have been an enduring reminder of their extraordinary trip. Now the face value of one was paying for lodging in a foreign land that lay in the opposite direction of home.

Sunlight caught the polished glass and brass mirror inlays in the triangle. For a moment, light danced across the cloak pin, setting red spinels aglow amid lapis lazuli in the half-circle ringed by tiny silver balls.

"This is plenty." Hesed folded a cloth around the pin and tucked it into a lockbox.

He looked up. "We don't have all the luxuries of a khan, but we do offer one meal a day. Most caravansaries don't. We also sell bags of teben for your camels. The short straw packs so well for a long trip."

"Good. We'll buy as much as we can carry," Akilah said.

"Done." Hesed smiled.

Akilah nodded. No matter what direction they traveled next,

the terrain would be difficult and foraging sparse. Teben would supplement the camels' diet.

"I'll show you where you can stable your animals."

The caravansary was more than adequate for Akilah's needs, and Hesed was a gracious host in every way. He seemed to have a smile and a kind word for everyone—whether greeting visitors or hunching over his cooking fire in a corner of the quadrangle. The courtyard's beauty and Hesed's savory dinner dissolved the desert's harshness into a memory.

Chapter 77

Trouble with Travel

The next day, after leaving Hakeem in charge of the servants, Akilah had the Magi split up to learn what they could about points east and west of the gulf. Either direction would mean an extended, circuitous route home, but he hoped a best choice would emerge from the information they gathered. The trio agreed to reconvene at the start of the day's third cycle to compare notes and settle on a travel plan.

Akilah's long strides quickly covered market streets abuzz with far-flung languages: Phoenician, Greek, Sabaean, Amorite, Hadhrami. He listened for unfamiliar tongues, thrilling at the thought of visiting whatever region their dialect represented. Ayla's lucrative copper production and seaport location brought trade from countries beyond Akilah's travels. Despite the bustle, the city seemed tranquil compared to Petra's tension. Even so, Akilah remained guarded. His caravan needed rest, but he feared staying too long in one place. The longer the stay, the more questions people asked.

After two hours of unproductive sleuthing about westward routes, Akilah wandered past a merchant's stall stacked with dark bricks of something redolent with spices. After months of Spartan living conditions and dangerous travel, the thought of sampling something new seemed a safe enough adventure.

He stared vacantly at the table covered with the odd bricks. If this was food, the abundance of choices overwhelmed him.

"I'm pleased my wares intrigue you so much. I'm the first vendor in this region to sell this." The shopkeeper spread his arms to encompass the table. "In a few years, everyone will want to buy this."

"Indeed." Akilah shook his head, puzzled.

"Customers are waiting. Are you still looking?"

"What would you recommend?"

Akilah hastily purchased a pressed brick of something the owner described as having a secret ingredient. He stepped aside with his purchase to inhale the aroma. A contented sigh escaped his lips.

"You like?"

Akilah opened his eyes to the shopkeeper hovering over him. "Very much. I can't quite place one of the spices. Cinnamon, coriander, and something else. May I ask what?"

A sly smile brightened the owner's face. He leaned close to Akilah's ear. "Nutmeg."

"Nutmeg? I've read about it. This will be my first time to taste it."

The shop owner clamped his hand on Akilah's shoulder so hard that he almost dropped his purchase. "You should get out more. Travel."

"Travel. Yes." Akilah's mouth went dry.

"Nutmeg—hard to come by. Very expensive." The owner punched the air with his fist, oblivious to all the customers staring. "Own a bag of it, and you'll be a rich man." He winked. "And it can improve the romance in your life."

"I'll remember that." Akilah wanted to ask what he'd

purchased, but that would have drawn too much attention to him.

The shopkeeper moved on to another customer before Akilah could ask about maps or a guide.

No matter. He wasn't sure what he'd bought or how he'd use it, but it was a comfort to merely tuck it under his arm and walk through Ayla's streets in obscurity. No one needed to know his business.

Uncertain of where to go next, he paused.

The words "Wilderness of Paran" reached his ears. Who had said that? Paran was west of Ayla. It might be a sign the Magi should choose a westward route. Straining to match a face with the voice, he finally placed it with an older gentleman across the street. He was gesturing broadly as if telling a tall tale.

Akilah watched the man leave. He moved fast for his age. Akilah dashed after the older man as he turned into a side street. Half a dozen streets later, winded and holding his side, Akilah caught up with him.

"Ahem. Excuse me, sir. I couldn't help but hear that you are familiar with the Wilderness of Paran."

The man's eyes narrowed. "The 'great and terrible wilderness,' as people call it."

"Indeed."

"And it deserves its reputation." The tall, deeply tanned man stroked his graying beard and eyed Akilah.

"Is it not a dwelling place of the Hebrews' God?" Akilah said.

"There is much history to learn about the Wilderness of Paran." The man's eyes narrowed.

"Forgive me for being so bold. My curiosity overtakes my manners sometimes. I mean no offense. I simply find the stories fascinating."

The man scowled. "They are not stories."

"Of course." Akilah cleared his throat. "I must travel through that area on a ... pilgrimage. Regrettably, I have no map or guide. Do you know where I might obtain one or both?"

"No, but I can get you where you want to go." His eyes pierced Akilah like one testing cooked meat to see if it still oozed blood. "No one traverses that wasteland lightly. How confident are you about the necessity of this ... pilgrimage?"

"I most assuredly require it."

"I see." The man's shoulders relaxed slightly. "I know ways to get through the mountains that other people don't know of."

Akilah's eyes widened. "Secret passes?"

The man nodded.

"That's very interesting." Akilah hesitated. Could he trust this person? Or was Akilah in danger of walking into another Nakal scenario? He scanned the elder's weathered face and chiseled cheekbones. His eyes seemed to reflect dignity despite harsh disappointments. Still ...

Akilah flinched.

"What's wrong?" The man looked around and over his shoulder.

"Pardon me, but lunch did not agree with me. I don't mean to be rude, but I regret I must take my leave of you." Akilah bowed in haste. "Until we meet again. And thank you." He hurried away.

His meal had settled just fine, but what he saw and heard behind the man didn't sit well with him at all. Nabataeans. And a glimpse of iron armor.

Chapter 78

Alexandria's Lure

Tallis and Rashidi were waiting at the rendezvous point when Akilah arrived, out of breath. Without asking for their reports, he announced they must leave.

"Agreed," Tallis said. "The northern part of this city contains a large, permanent settlement of Nabataeans." He bit into an apricot. "They must have trade relations with Rome because the vendor I talked to said a Nabataean traded him an Imperial cast bowl for a crate of his fruit—and any information he had regarding the whereabouts of strangers from the East. Thankfully, the vendor had no knowledge of such visitors. Of us."

Akilah turned west toward the caravansary and quickened his pace.

"We can still get word to the Council before we leave," Rashidi said, pulling on his satchel. "I bought this." With pride, he produced an elegant wax writing tablet. "I can fit this with a false bottom and put a message in it. We can send it as a gift to someone in the Lower Council or to your cousin. If I nick a corner of the false bottom, they should figure out there's more to the tablet than meets the eye."

"There's no time, and it's too dangerous." As soon as the words left Akilah' lips, he wished he could snatch them back. "I applaud your engineering expertise and creativity. It's a good idea. But not now. Keep it for later." Someone might be monitoring the postal relay system for their whereabouts. He couldn't take that risk. He couldn't trust the Council, and he certainly didn't want to entangle Farzaneh in his problems. He double-timed his steps.

"Then you may be more inclined to use what I heard," Rashidi said, an edge in his voice. "An incense merchant told me Nabataean territory extends three weeks' ride southeast of Ayla. Its far eastern capital is Hegra—a second Petra, if you will. That merchant rambled on about how he had no love for the Nabataeans or Herod. And he mentioned Herod's mother. She *is* Nabataean."

Akilah halted mid-step. "So, your hunch was right. If the Nabataeans truly have no loyalty other than to themselves, they could try us as criminals for using some of their secret water supplies—or worse, turn us over to Herod if they knew we defied him. My friends, we are fugitives twice over. Our knowledge of Yeshua may cost us more than we imagined."

"Heading west appears to be our only option," Tallis said.

"Agreed." Akilah nodded.

Rashidi seemed glued to the ground. "West?" He clutched his throat, his face mixed with pain and delight as if choking on supremely delicious food. "Egypt? Alexandria?" He swayed as though the earth had quaked.

"Rashidi, are you ill?"

Rashidi's legs buckled. He landed hard on a bin of wild radishes, still clutching his throat. "It's been so long ... I hadn't dared to hope ... three generations of—"

"You're damaging my produce. Are you going to pay for that? Get out!" An irate shopkeeper ran at Rashidi, cracking a leather whip that whistled an inch away from his ear. He ducked and tumbled over the side of the bin.

Akilah caught him and pulled him into an alley. "Are you intact?"

Rashidi looked up, stunned.

Akilah shook his young colleague. "Yes, Rashidi, we shall go west—to your ancestral land. It makes perfect sense. For years Tallis and I have talked about studying in the great libraries of Alexandria. What better time than now?" His voice rose. "Can you imagine? More than seven hundred thousand volumes in one place—at the apex of Egyptian, Roman, Greek, Hebrew, and Persian culture."

Akilah stopped at Rashidi's stricken look. "What troubles you?"

"The library burned."

"Yes. Thirty years ago. But rebuilding is well underway. And at least a third of its volumes have already been replaced. Likely many more by the time we get there."

Rashidi slid to the ground, shaking his head.

"Do you not believe me?"

For the first time since Akilah had known Rashidi, his young colleague seemed at a loss for words. "It's just … my great-grandparents worked in Alexandria's libraries until …"

"Until what?" Tallis crouched next to Rashidi.

Rashidi gulped and looked at his hands. "Almost three hundred years ago, Ptolemy started a national quest to gather knowledge for Alexandria's libraries. Collect or copy every codex, scroll, and tablet in existence. Can you imagine?"

His eyes glistened. "My great-grandparents were promised research positions in the most prestigious part of The Musaeum —the division devoted to thought and discovery. Instead, they were assigned to acquisitions." A thin, rueful laugh escaped Rashidi's lips. "A kind word for harbor duty. Military inspectors searched every boat porting in Alexandria. If they found a codex or scroll, they took it to be copied, assuring the owners of its quick return. My great-grandparents were among the copiers. But they learned that only the copies were given back. The library kept the originals."

Rashidi's jaw tightened. "My great-grandparents didn't agree with that practice. They called it 'ill-gotten treasures.' As punishment, they lost their jobs and their access to the library. They were barred from even setting foot on the grounds."

Tallis shook his head. "Politics. I am sorry, Rashidi."

"A generation later, my grandparents tried to be scribes at the library." Rashidi's voice turned gravelly. "Copying and cataloging its writings would at least put them on the fringes of all that knowledge. But they were denied that chance as well.

"They loved learning. They were Magi in their hearts," Rashidi said. "But, after those rejections, the family line was disgraced. My parents didn't want that fate to continue, so they left Egypt, the only home they knew. They started over in Anatolia to give me a chance to study engineering and architecture among great learners. They reasoned, if not in Alexandria, then in Anatolia and Persia. They wanted me to do what my family was never allowed to do."

"Alexandria will be the chance of a lifetime for you." Akilah clapped his hand on Rashidi's shoulder. "It is a great serendipity that we are now pressed to go there, yes?"

Rashidi collected himself. "An unauthorized study?"

"Rashidi, forget about that," Tallis snapped. "Due west from Petra is a major trade route skirting Idumean territory. We can't go that way. Idumea is the southernmost region of Herod's rule. It's also his father's homeland. Herod's father may have adopted the Jewish faith, but everyone in that land is descended from Edomites, a lineage famous for one thing—war. The governor of Idumea is a member of Herod's family as well. Idumea is a triple threat to us."

Akilah frowned. "Well, that limits our travel options."

Rashidi clenched and unclenched his hands. "What if Herod's men are following us?"

"Herod is too smart to stir up territorial politics. He wouldn't risk sending a contingent to Nabataea," Tallis replied. "He'd send only a scout. Someone who could blend in."

"We must remain vigilant." Should Akilah tell his colleagues that he thought he'd seen one of Herod's royal guards? Best to keep his fears in check until he could confirm them.

"How can we be safe? Or find provisions?" Rashidi's voice cracked.

"The God of the Hebrews showed us a light that led us to the Yeshua child. And one of God's messengers spoke to us in a dream," Akilah said. "If this God is as powerful as the scrolls say He is, He can guide us again. Nothing would be impossible for Him."

Chapter 79

Messages in Riddles

The three hurried back to the caravansary. Their only comfort was Hesed's warm greeting and smile.

"Does one of your staff have time to help us pack for our trip?" Akilah asked.

"Of course. How soon will you need him?"

"In an hour or so."

"I'll send him to your room to receive your instructions."

"Thank you." Akilah palmed a small pouch to Hesed. "Here is extra payment for his service—and his silence."

With an understanding nod, the caravansary owner pocketed the money.

After checking their stored gear and confirming that all the servants were back, the Magi hurried to pack the trunks in their room.

They had just finished when Akilah answered a knock on the door. He stiffened, his spine tingling. It was the old man who'd been spinning tales near the market stall.

"You act surprised to see me again."

"No. Ah, it's a pleasure," Akilah stammered.

"I am Haruz. My son, Hesed, owns this place. I help out, doing this and that."

"I see." Akilah exhaled in relief. "Do you still lead trips across the wilderness too?"

Haruz grimaced. "No, my son says I'm getting too old for that. These days, I stay here and do what I can for those who venture where I can't."

Haruz shifted a bundle he held at his hip and looked past Akilah. "May I enter?"

"Of course. Please."

Haruz crossed the threshold, careful to close and latch the door. He nodded to Tallis and Rashidi, then turned to Akilah. "You didn't need to empty your stomach earlier, did you?"

Akilah's face heated. "No."

"What turned your stomach was Nabataeans."

How did he know?

"Understandable," Haruz said.

"You are in a hurry. So, a word about where you're going."

He and I talked only about the Wilderness of Paran. How could he know our destination?

"Keep heading west by northwest—first through the great and terrible wilderness. When the color of the back side of the mountains changes, head north to the Bitter Lakes. Beyond that is the Nile delta."

Haruz searched the Magi's faces as if to ensure they had absorbed all he said.

"Be wary," he continued. "All the territory between Arabia and the delta is disputed. Egyptians claim the entire peninsula as part of Egypt, but the Nabataeans also consider it their own. Romans want the land too. If they could annex it, they'd control land and sea trade between Egypt, Judea, Saba's coasts, and the countries east of Ayla—ending the Nabataeans' trade monopoly. Augustus tried that twenty years ago and failed. The Romans are due to try again. Avoid them at all costs.

"But"—Haruz met the gaze of each person in the room—"know that the land is really the territory of the One who made all things. He dwells there."

Akilah paused. Was Haruz referring to the Hebrews' God? One of the Books of Moses said He was God Almighty. Akilah still had trouble grasping how One could be powerful enough to create everything in the heavens and on the earth. "The One who made all things. Is that your God's name?"

Haruz's eyes narrowed. "Throughout history, He has revealed Himself with multiple names. But, out of reverence, we do not say His written name aloud."

"I see."

"Many people do not believe in Him or His power. But He has done great things for His people, particularly throughout the peninsula you will traverse."

Haruz dropped his bundle and fixed his eyes on Akilah. "I sense you aren't going *to* a place as much as you are escaping *from* a place. But your reasons for doing so are honorable. I will pray for your safety. Know that Adonai is with you. Of all the gods people call upon, He is the only One Who Was and Is and Is to Come. The One who lives outside of time but controls time and steps into it for the sake of His people. He is directing your lives and your destiny."

Who dared to speak with such authority about spiritual matters? Part of Akilah rankled at anyone or anything other than his well-laid plans shaping his destiny. Another part wanted to trust this God that Haruz spoke so confidently about.

Haruz clapped his hands and beckoned the trio. "Come. You are heading where no beaten roads exist." His tone shifted from crisp to terse. There is much gravel and little soil in the mountains and vast plains. Take extra care of your camels' feet. Keep your animals tied together, three abreast, for protection—except when a pass gets too narrow. And watch for acacia trees.

They tell you stream beds are nearby. When you get to Egypt, find my people. They will help you."

The Magi exchanged puzzled glances.

"Most important." Haruz held up three fingers. "Seek what is concealed so it can be revealed. Guard what your heart has seen and hide it there until the right time. Finally, look less for signs and more for the One who has the power to give you signs."

Riddles? Why speak in riddles in the privacy of a lodging room? A map would be more helpful. Or a guide. And who were Haruz's people? Did the success of their trip hinge on this old man's mutterings?

Before Akilah could sort what Haruz said, he motioned toward their trunks. "Now for your immediate business. Will you take all of them?"

"Yes." Rashidi rushed the word.

"Very well." Haruz glanced at all three Magi. "But you would do well to want more of what you need and less of what you desire."

Another riddle? Arrogant presumption? Or prophetic wisdom? Either way, Haruz seemed dead serious.

He moved to the heaviest trunk and unceremoniously flung open the lid. Before Akilah could stop him, Haruz picked up the bundle at his feet and pulled yards of black fabric out of it. In rapid succession, he tossed black tunics, trousers, hooded robes, and gauzy black face scarves on top of the Magi's embroidered robes. Without regard for their importance, he crammed his additions into the trunk. The black garments extinguished the sun's glints on the robes' metallic threads.

Haruz pointed. "Black is best for traveling through a hot desert. Absorbs body heat. Trade or buy tents of the same when you can. No time now." He slammed the lid shut.

"Um, thank you." Akilah locked the trunk. "Now that our, ahem, clothes are packed, would you be so kind as to take them to our servants? They're by your stables, packing our food and gear."

Haruz bowed and lifted the largest trunk with the ease of a man half his age. As he crossed the room with quick strides, his steps stirred the bottom of his garment. A gust of wind caught the hem, sending white tassels fastened with blue threads into a dance as Haruz disappeared into the corridor.

Rashidi waited until Haruz's receding footsteps faded, then locked the door. "I think that old man is a few pieces short of a full *Latrunculi* board."

Tallis stared at the door as if he could still see Haruz through it. "I told you we should burn some of our clothes."

"If we leave our Magi robes here and Herod's men track us to this place, we could endanger Hesed, Haruz, *and* our caravan," Rashidi argued.

"Enough." Akilah swung his arm toward the door. "The robes go with us for now. As for Haruz, we may not understand everything he told us. But, of all the things he could have said, he chose to say what he did—so we should heed it. We will have time to sort what it means after we leave. For tonight, let us enjoy this evening and be grateful for the hospitality, for it may be our last until we reach our destination."

Chapter 80

Last Supper

That night, Hesed set out a splendid spread. Extra servings of grain and hay for the camels. Roast lamb, spicy lentil stew, cucumbers, olives, melons, and sun-dried flatbread dipped in olive oil for the humans. The savory aromas mingled with the group's laughter. Entwined, they wafted skyward with dance-like grace. The evening's ease and warmth felt like home. No wonder everyone lingered over their food.

As Hesed bent to offer everyone more, Akilah noticed the tassels swaying on the hem of Hesed's tunic were identical to Haruz's. Were they a sign of Haruz's people?

Akilah shifted his attention to the camels on the other side of the courtyard, munching contentedly on hay, relishing second helpings as much as his servants were. He cringed. *They have no idea what they're heading into. But neither do I.* Soon, he'd have to tell the caravan about the threat from Herod. But not tonight. Let tonight remain perfect. Peaceful. Undisturbed.

"Where's Haruz? I thought he'd join us for dinner," Rashidi said.

Akilah shrugged. "Maybe he's checking our gear."

Tallis wiped his mouth. "I'll go look."

"Why? You'll miss the sweets." Rashidi pointed to Hesed approaching with a tray. "Here they come."

Tallis shook his head. "You and sweets."

As Hesed served bright-yellow clumps of a chalky-looking sweet, he bent low over the Wise Men. *"Khirret,"* he whispered. "Made from marsh reed pollen. Adonai protected Moses in the reeds. He will do the same for you. Take one."

Tallis obliged and reached toward the tray Hesed balanced on one hand. The sunny globes slid to one side; but instead of steadying the tray, Hesed caught Tallis's arm in a fierce grip. "Take one. *Please.*"

Akilah pushed himself up from his reclined position at the table, but Tallis stayed his hand. "Stay here," Tallis whispered. "The caravan needs a leader who doesn't compromise his convictions. Tonight you'll ask again whether knowing Yeshua is worth the risk—and the cost."

He waited until Hesed was halfway across the courtyard, then followed at a distance.

In the main building's shadow, beyond earshot and sight of the guests, Tallis whirled in front of Hesed. "Where? When?"

"Before I served seconds. A guard or soldier—seemed like one of Herod's. Father had gone into the city to buy extra teben for your caravan as a gift. The guard must have forced himself upon father to get into our compound. I stayed out of sight. Your room had already been emptied, but the guard searched it. He sounded intent on ... He took ... They were in there." Hesed pointed toward a storage room.

The two crept to the door. Scuffling, wood splintering, and pottery shattering seeped through the cracks. "Tell me what I want to know, or I will kill you and your family," a voice barked. Footsteps scrunched across broken pottery. More scuffling, then a muffled scream.

"That's father." Hesed's wide-eyed fear was palpable.

"Wait." Tallis reached for Hesed's arm but caught only his sleeve as he barged through the door.

Hesed tackled the guard, knocking a bloody pottery shard from his hand. As they rolled on the floor, Tallis poked his head around the corner. Haruz was slumped against a wall, one arm covered in blood. He weakly lifted the other in warning to Tallis, who ducked back into the shadows behind the door.

Hesed was no match for the guard's skills. After a brief struggle, a thud signaled that he, too, was on the floor.

Peering through the spaces between the door's hinges, Tallis saw the soldier's hobnailed shoe connect with Hesed's stomach. He curled into a fetal position, gagging and heaving.

"Where are the Wise Men from the East?" The guard backhand slapped Hesed's face.

He rolled his head side to side.

"I can cut the information from you, piece by piece." The guard reached for his dagger.

Tallis exploded from his hiding place and hurled himself onto the guard's back. Before the guard knew what was happening, Tallis had locked one elbow under his chin and both legs under his ribcage. Maximizing his momentary element of surprise, Tallis tightened his legs and punched the guard's face. The guard gasped for air, spun, and slammed Tallis against the wall. Another spin shoved him into the opposite wall.

The guard managed to unsheathe his dagger, but Tallis knocked it from his hand in one deft move. The guard's hardened body tensed, his muscles coiling like a Caspian cobra. He threw himself on the ground, trying to force Tallis over his head. Pottery shards ripped through Tallis's tunic as both men hit the floor. A crack told Tallis he had broken at least one rib. Stickiness oozed onto his tunic. The guard's segmented iron carapace welted Tallis like a whip's lashes. Despite the searing pain, he hung on until the guard went limp.

The two collapsed on the floor.

Panting, Tallis pushed the motionless body off him. He jerked the guard's belt from his waist and flung it at Hesed. "Cinch this above your father's wound. Tight as you can."

Hesed gulped and nodded.

Tallis pointed to the guard's iron-tipped lance, broken in half. "Your father fought well. Be proud."

Hesed stared, frozen in place.

Ignoring his own wounds, Tallis stood, all business. So much to do in so little time. Activity would dilute Hesed's fear. "Can you make a sleeping draught?"

"Yes ..."

"As strong as you can. Go." Tallis turned to Haruz. "Where can we hide your attacker?"

"Gardening shed." Haruz's pinched voice was barely audible. "No one goes there but me."

Tallis nodded. "I'll put him there."

Haruz struggled to sit upright. "That won't buy you much time. You must leave before first light."

"Agreed. But we also need to put at least two days' distance between us and Ayla."

"I can keep the guard bound and gagged."

"Too risky. Your wound is deliberate, inflicted where it weakens your arm the most. It needs cleaning and stitching. I'll get one of our healers. He won't ask questions."

"So be it," Haruz mumbled.

"Do you have bitumen and sulfur crystals?"

Blood drained from Haruz's face. With a shaky hand, he covered his eyes as if to block a terrible memory.

Tallis grabbed him by the shoulders. "If this guard gets loose, our entire caravan could be killed."

Hesed returned with the draught, towels, and a bowl of water.

"Hesed, pour the draught down the guard's mouth. Then hold it shut." Tallis issued the orders with a terse voice.

"But—"

"Do it." Tallis snatched the towels and water from Hesed.

With difficulty, the innkeeper complied. "Now what?"

"We bind and hide him."

"No. I need to clean my father's wound first."

Tallis didn't argue or wait. He bound the guard himself.

Haruz groaned at his son's touch. "Tallis, I didn't tell him anything. Nothing about your travels or intentions. He doesn't know you were here. You are safe."

"None of us are safe. The guard recognized me from Herod's palace. This is a quest for him, a way to seal his future in the king's service. He won't stop pursuing our caravan—unless you stop him."

Haruz looked away. "I cannot. Adonai values all life."

Hesed paused from cleaning his father's arm. "I'll do it. What do you need?"

Tallis gave him a hot-blooded stare. The innkeeper blanched. "What did I agree to?"

"Make sure the guard stays bound, gagged, and asleep in the shed until our caravan leaves. Then give him extra draught. Surround him with the extra teben your father bought for us today. Place a lamp and a pot in the shed. Leave the lamp there. Light a fire in the *pot*, then add bitumen and sulfur crystals—and get out fast. The fire will create fumes. Do *not* breathe them. When you see gas seep under the door, burn the shed to the ground. If anyone asks, say you left a lamp burning and suffered the consequences of inattention."

"Murder?"

"Herod wants something from us that we cannot give him. If his soldiers find us, much worse will happen to us and countless others. More explanation must wait."

Hesed and Haruz exchanged agonized, conflicted glances.

"Our lives are in your hands," Tallis said. "Whatever happens, we will not forget your kindness."

Chapter 81

What Lies Ahead

The next morning

Two hours before dawn, Akilah scanned the caravansary one last time. The structure that had welcomed and shielded his group now groaned along with Haruz and Hesed's efforts to pull on the heavy iron chains of the caravansary's massive door. Haruz could lend only his unbandaged arm to the effort. Hesed, also limited by his fresh wounds, joined his father in straining at the chains. The door opened with agonizing slowness, seemingly as reluctant to release the caravan as Akilah was to leave.

In all his travels, Akilah had never met a stranger willing to risk his life to help someone else. He ached with unspoken gratitude. He bent over the side of his camel to speak with Haruz, but the older man silenced him with a shake of his head.

Haruz's hand shook as he extended a small papyrus packet to Akilah. His fingers closed around an ornate outline, perhaps that of a key.

He nodded and slid it into the hidden pouch in his sash. The same pouch that had protected Fakhri's Simurgh before the start of their journey.

Akilah's head swam with impossible questions. Would he see Haruz again? How could he honor Haruz? What else would it cost Haruz's family—and the caravan—to protect the knowledge they carried? Akilah couldn't let himself think of that. Too many unknown challenges lay ahead. Perhaps ones beyond imagining. *Would the risk be worth the cost?*

Rashidi leaned toward Akilah. "Are you sure we should do this?"

"Not should. Must. However long it takes. Our course is set." Akilah fixed his gaze on the two Imperishables, the star beacons of the north that never dipped below the horizon. Pointing due west, he motioned the caravan forward. *God of the Hebrews, please guide and protect us.*

The caravan lumbered, somber and silent, beyond the shelter of the caravansary toward the Wilderness of Paran.

To be continued ...

What's in a Name?

A character's name can be a story within a story. That's why I pore over names before settling on them. Every character's name reflects one of their key traits. Here are the book's named characters, pronunciations of their names, and what they mean. Despite my consulting numerous sources for pronunciation, we can't know with certainty how all the names were spoken, so say their names however you want. The characters are listed in alphabetical order, not order of appearance. Can you find similarities in the characters' names and their motivations or behaviors?

Character	Pronunciation	Meaning	Origin	Notes
Akilah	a-KEE-lah OR AK-i-lah	Wise	Arabic	Lead Wise Man His head servant: Hakeem His camel: Dain
Antipas	AN-ti-pus	Against the father; instead of the father	Greek	A son of Herod the Great
Azazel	a-ZAZ-el	Scapegoat	Hebrew	Sassanak's closest colleague In Jewish culture, Azazel was an evil spirit or fallen angel
Babayi	ba-ba-EE	Grandfather	Arabic	How children commonly address their grandfather
Burhan	BUR-han	Religion	Arabic	An Ordeal; he catalogs Magi research and writings His full name, Burhan Al-din, means "proof of religion"
Fakhri	FAHK-ree	Honorary	Arabic	Alludes to his status as a Magus Honorific (like a professor emeritus)
Farzaneh	FAHR-za-NEH	Wise and intelligent	Persian	Akilah's orphaned cousin
Gadiel	GAD-ee-ul	God is my wealth	Arabic	Chief Megistane of the Upper Council and Akilah's estranged father
Hadi	HAH-dee	Leader; guider	Persian	Farzaneh's Persian mastiff, her guard dog
Hakeem	Hah-KEEM	Wise	Arabic	Akilah's head servant
Haruz	HARE-us	Earnest; zealous	Hebrew	Hesed's father, a devoted Jew
Hesed	HAH-sed	Kindness	Hebrew	Caravansary owner in Ayla
Ihsan	ih-SAHN	Perfection or excellence; benevolence; compassion	Persian	Farzaneh's second husband; embraced Judaism late in life

Character	Pronunciation	Meaning	Origin	Notes
Javad	jah-VUD	Righteous	Arabic	Farzaneh's head servant
Kassim	KAS-im	Divided	Arabic	Rashidi's head servant. Kassim's name reflects his divided desires in this book.
Keket	kee-KET	Goddess of darkness	Egyptian	Alludes to doing dark deeds (with or without Nakal's help)
Malachi	MAL-a-kiy	My messenger	Hebrew	Tallis's head servant
Mamani	ma-man-EE	Grandmother	Arabic	How children commonly address their grandmother
Mekonnen	may-KAHN-uhn	Honorable	Ethiopian	Javad's name in the language of his homeland (Cush)
Nakal	na-KAHL	Swindler	Hebrew	A Susita merchant who takes bribes for dishonorable tasks
Omid	OH-MEED	Hope	Persian	One of Farzaneh's servants; he attempted to ford the Jordan
Rashidi	rah-SHEE-dee	Wise; Rightly guide	Egyptian; Arabic	Wise Man. His head servant: Kassim. His camel: Moody
Sadiq	suh-DEEK	Loyal; true	Arabic	Akilah's chief healer on the trip to Jerusalem
Sarbaz	SAR-bahz	Caravan leader	Arabic	A vendor and a mercenary, doing dirty work for others
Sassanak	SASS-a-NAK	(A sibilant name to reflect his character)		Head Magus of the Lower Council
Tahrea	TAR-re-uh	Anger; contention	Hebrew	One of Farzaneh's servants who causes a lot of trouble
Tallis	TA-lis	Wise	Persian	Wise Man. His head servant: Malachi. His camel: Tashi
Varinius	vahr-IN-ee-us	Versatile	Roman	An informant to Antipas

There's more to this book than the book!

Check out the Resources section of my website for downloadable goodies to go with each book:

A book club kit

- Discussion questions and tips for making book club meeting an immersive experience. Includes recipes for food mentioned in *New Star* so you can nosh authentically while chatting about the book.
- Would you like for me to join your book club? Ways to arrange that are in the kit.

Bible study questions

- Want to dig deeper? Visit this page to download a personal or group study around the theme of this book.

Family Extras

Age-appropriate information on different topics

Examples:

- Fun Facts about Camels
- What Instruments Did the Magi Use to Navigate
- What was the Star?
- What was Special about Adiabene in Early Christianity
- Politics of Rome versus Parthia

Enjoy these topics just for fun. Use them as the basis for homeschooling or a school project. Whatever you do, let me know all the creative ways you use this material!

Acknowledgments

The adage "it takes a village" is true for both children and books. This book wouldn't have come to life without the support of a village of wonderful people. They deserve more thanks than I can adequately express here.

I can't say enough good things about my developmental editor, Erin Healy. Her guidance and encouragement made this book blossom.

Linda Fulkerson, owner of Scrivenings Press, caught my vision for this book, championed it, and nurtured it to the finish line.

My Aunt Peggy (Marguerite Davol), an extraordinary author who wrote children's books for Simon & Schuster and Orchard Books, was my first—and is my forever—role model.

Mary Van Peursem, Diana Haman, Emma Bartley, and Woody Roland rock the house as cheerleaders and prayer warriors. I love and appreciate you more than words can say.

Barbara Britton, a widely published author in biblical, historical, and contemporary fiction spaces, has helped me in more ways than I can express.

Fellow biblical and historical fiction authors, the Scrivenings family of authors, and members of ACFW Wisconsin Southeast, have supported, inspired, and uplifted me. I wish I had room to thank all of you personally on this page. You are awesome!

I've been blessed to learn the craft and business of writing from giants in both fields: master storytellers Stephen James and Jerry B. Jenkins, book launch gurus James L. Rubart and Thomas Umstattd Jr.

Most of all, thanks be to God for how He prepared me for biblical fiction writing decades in advance, how He nudged me to write, guided my research, and gave me countless ideas that fit together in a way I never could have engineered on my own. All glory, honor, and praise to Him!

About Lana Christian

Lana Christian is an award-winning author of business and faith-based writing. Her business writing has garnered numerous APEX awards, a patent, a published book, and many millions of dollars in grants for clients. Since 2019, she has been a semifinalist, finalist, and winner in ACFW Genesis and First Impressions contests. In 2021, she received a University of Northwestern Distinguished Faith in Writing award and a Bethany House Aspiring Author award. Lana is passionate about crafting stories that make the Bible come to life and is relentless in her research to make each scene authentic. Her author website features her biweekly devotional, "Encouragement from Living History." Sign up for that and her bimonthly newsletter at www.lanachristian.com/contact.

Sneak peek of Book 2 in "TheMagi's Encounters"

Chapter One: The Good Lie

Somewhere in the wilderness of Paran

Was heading to Egypt the right choice? Akilah rimmed his soup bowl with his thumb. The Kings Highway would have taken his caravan from Jerusalem all the way back to the Euphrates River, but traveling home on any Roman road was out of the question. Stationarii, special Roman imperial troops, manned watchtowers and patrolled the roads, scouting for runaway slaves and other undesirables. Akilah and his colleagues now fell into the latter category. They had disobeyed Herod in not returning to him with news of the child they sought. Surely he had dispatched relays with orders to intercept the Magi and drag them back to Jerusalem in chains.

The caravan might have hazarded sea travel from Ayla if they hadn't crossed paths with one of Herod's scouts and some Nabataeans there. No, heading northwest toward Egypt was their only option. Akilah had to keep his caravan safe.

New Star

He sipped his bowl of watery soup. The day's unusually cool weather had afforded the caravan more hours to press on longer than usual until grumbling stomachs had forced them to stop for what loosely resembled second meal.

He wouldn't be able to cover this much ground every day. Who knew what challenges the wilderness held for them? He had to remain focused on their goal—Heliopolis. It was a wish, a hope, a prayer—at least a month away if all went well. From Heliopolis, they could continue to Alexandria.

Egypt and true safety. Akilah couldn't muster any thoughts beyond that. Egypt was in the opposite direction of home but was truly out of Herod's reach. They just had to get there first.

Akilah's head servant, Hakeem, approached from the opposite side of the campfire. He had shouldered more responsibility than a servant should ever need to, yet he did so without complaint. Akilah had repeatedly struggled to find the right words to express his appreciation to Hakeem. Instead, he said nothing. Silence was more comfortable.

Hakeem bowed before Akilah. That simple act of subservience and respect seemed out of place in this wilderness, but it was a comforting vestige of what had been. A life they might never return to.

"Master, now would be a good time to address everyone."

Akilah stepped closer to the fire and clapped his hands three times, his universal signal for the whole caravan to meet.

"We regret that urgent business took us away from lovely Ayla," he started.

"What 'business' would take us into the wilderness?" One servant's voice dripped with sarcasm.

Akilah grimaced inwardly. Tahrea again. A force to be reckoned with. Privately. "Business that must be kept secret from certain people."

"Why wouldn't you tell us that 'business' until we were too

far from Ayla to turn back on foot?" Another servant's voice crescendoed. "Now we're your captives."

"That's not true."

The servants' unruliness rose like swells in a storm. Logic wouldn't win them over. Something deeper, more visceral, had to touch them. Motioning for silence, Akilah glanced at his fellow Magi for support. He was reasonably sure of Rashidi's thoughts. *Less is more. Keep the servants in their place; they're under contract. They must fulfill their obligation, regardless.* Tallis's face was an expressionless mask.

"You have a right to know why we are not going home yet," Akilah said. "It has to do with why we went to Jerusalem and what happened there."

Everyone's eyes bored into him. "It's a good story," he added. The servants liked stories. Maybe that would pique their interest.

"In Persia, my colleagues and I studied a star that foretold the birth of a child who would be an eternal ruler and the Savior of the world."

Sniggers and guffaws erupted.

"Inconceivable, yes? But Jewish prophecies over hundreds of years pointed to the birth of a unique person. Not like a king born into royalty, but someone we all could relate to."

Silence descended on the camp.

"We traveled from Persia to Jerusalem to find that child. And we did." Akilah's throat tightened. "But some people wanted to harm him. Especially King Herod. He commanded us to report back to him when we found the child. We did not. Herod has a habit of killing people when he thinks they are a threat to his throne."

Akilah shifted in place. "Our disobedience made us targets of his wrath. We couldn't go home the way we came because that's the first place his soldiers would have looked for us."

He paused to gauge the servants' reactions. Their silence thickened like gathering fog.

"You defied a king?" One servant finally spoke—slowly, as if testing his words.

Akilah nodded.

"Is the child safe?"

He exhaled a shaky breath. "I hope so."

"Do you know where the child is now?"

"No."

"Is Herod still hunting you?"

"I have every reason to believe so."

"Why did we leave Petra? Then Ayla?"

Normally Akilah would not have entertained servants questioning him, but nothing about this trip resembled any other in his career. "Herod has family ties to Petra. We thought we were safe in Ayla, but one of Herod's scouts found us." His throat tightened. "With help, we escaped that trouble"

The servants' murmurs rose again, this time rippling with awe and respect. Akilah gestured for quiet. "Herod's men are one threat. Nabataeans are another. In Ayla, we learned a group of them were looking for us. We're not sure why. To turn us over to Herod, punish us for using some of their secret water sources, or both. We didn't know they occupied part of Ayla, plus territory hundreds of miles east of it. That's why we're heading west." He paused again. "You could say that makes us renegades on two accounts."

He looked pointedly at Rashidi. "Renegades" had become Rashidi's favorite descriptor for their situation.

"So ... you lied and stole but for good reasons?" A crooked smile crept across that servant's face. Other servants seemed to like that idea.

"I am committed to getting the caravan to safety."

"Where are we headed?"

"To Egypt."

"Egypt?" Frenzied chatter erupted. The servants' terrified, wide-eyed stares confirmed the limits of their previous travels.

Akilah called for silence. "Egypt will provide true safety for us. It's far from Herod's reach. The Nabataeans can't touch us there, either. And Egypt welcomes people who believe in the prophecies we studied."

"How long?" a servant shouted.

Tahrea again, posing an impossibly difficult question, tinged with the threat of discord.

"As long as needed," Akilah said.

"Then we don't know when or if we'll ever get home." Tahrea pounded the ground.

Akilah pursed his lips. "We will go home. You have my word. This isn't the journey we planned, but its purpose is still unfolding." Hoping to divert the servants' attention, he added, "In Egypt, I promise you will see more glorious things than you could ever imagine."

The servants exploded again with chatter. Akilah silenced them with difficulty.

"Listen well. Our lives—and the lives of that child and his family—depend on your silence. At all costs. One person's loose tongue could endanger the caravan, the child, his family, and worse. On the other hand, your silence and faithful service in getting us to Egypt will determine the success of our journey. You could say we have sacred secrets to keep. Are you with me?"

He took their murmurs as an affirmative.

Some servants seemed to revel in the intrigue. Others seemed unconvinced.

When everyone turned in for the night, Hakeem approached Akilah. "A few servants want to know more about the star and the child," he said. "What the prophecies say and what you believe. Will you tell them?"

New Star

Visit https://www.lanachristian.com/contact/ to get updates on this and all of Lana's books!

More Biblical Fiction from Scrivenings Press

A Certain Man by Linda Dindzans

A Certain Future—Book One

Mara is a young Samaritan beginning to discover her love for Samuel—and his for her. Soon she will be deemed mature enough to marry. Her hopes are dashed when her greedy father brokers a match with the cruel son of the wealthy High Priest of Shechem. When her loathsome betrothed is killed, her beloved Samuel must run for his life. Mara and Samuel struggle to survive and reunite during the treacherous and scandalous times of the Bible under the merciless rule of Rome.

Along the way, they are entangled within the snares of such notable figures as King Herod, Herodias, Pontius Pilate, Caiaphas, and Salome.

The heartrending tales of Mara and Samuel are interwoven with their desperate love story. Before either meets Yeshua the Nazarene face to face. Before He sets the political, religious, and spiritual landscape on fire. And before either Mara or Samuel are immortalized in the gospels.

Get your copy here:

https://scrivenings.link/acertainman

Scrivenings PRESS
Quench your thirst for story.
www.ScriveningsPress.com

Stay up-to-date on your favorite books and authors with our free e-newsletters.

ScriveningsPress.com

Printed in Dunstable, United Kingdom